THE GUISE OF THE QUEEN

A TALE OF HUGUENOT PERSECUTION FROM PARIS TO LA ROCHELLE

JOHN BENTLEY

1

DIFFERENCES IN OPINIONS HAVE COST MANY LIVES: especially true in the field of beliefs. This is dramatically evident in the country at large and the town of La Rochelle in particular. *Protestants assume that the Pharisees are the Catholics who have made Christianity a legalistic dogma, while we Catholics think they are self-righteous and use God's free grace as an excuse for their sinful discrimination and hatred,* the prisoner contemplated.

A gnawing scratching noise, low, but distinct, woke Lanval. He sat bolt upright and squinted in an attempt to focus in the gloom of his cell. His gaze fell on the cause of the sound: a fat brown rat, some ten inches long. The voracious rodent rocked to-and-fro on its haunches, its front claws digging into the fabric of the filthy straw palliasse that served as a bed, its strong slender tail extended behind it for balance. Unaware of Lanval's attention, the omnivorous creature feasted on residual grain and chaff inside the mattress, its furry cheek flaps expanding as it chewed and swallowed.

Now sensing the man's presence, it froze then raised its head in a single sudden movement, deep dark eyes challenging, sharp yellow incisors bared, a soft hissing escaping through its open jaws.

Lanval got slowly to his feet and sent it scurrying away with a violent kick. It leapt through the bars of the grille that imprisoned the man and made off down the tunnel.

His uninvited guest dispatched, and alone again, Lanval Aubert lay down on the bed. They had put an iron shackle, tight, around his left ankle, fixed by a heavy chain to a ring set into the wall. He reached down and moved it slightly up and down, hoping to ease its chaffing against his skin.

'I don't understand why they've chained me up like this...it's not as if I'm a murderer or a rapist...nothing of the kind. I still can't believe how I've ended up thus...still, not much I can do about it.' A maelstrom of disjointed thoughts raced through his head, sometimes in the present, sometimes in the past, but all contributing to his painful confusion and despair.

Curly blond locks either side of a broad forehead, searching blue eyes, a slender nose and even white teeth: he presented a handsome young man of some thirty years, strong of body and spirit, which ne needed to be in this soul-destroying dungeon.

The cave was rough-hewn rock, three walls supporting a domed roof. The sturdy iron-barred front with its hinged door provided no protection from icy draughts, vermin and foul odours that rose from the open sewer running down the middle of the tunnel floor. The darkness, whether day or night, confirmed to Lanval that he was incarcerated underground. Had he required further proof, water dripped incessantly from the roof and down the walls rendering the cave dank and musty.

After sentencing, the sergeant had tied a cloth close over his eyes and he was led out of the courtroom. Two burly court officers took his arms and marched him through the streets, such that he became disorientated. For all he knew, he could have been near the barracks to the north or the *Tour de la Lanterne* to the south of La Rochelle town. He heard a door creak open, then they dragged him down a flight of stone steps. The officers only removed the blindfold as they pushed him roughly into the cave and threw him onto the mattress. He blinked, bewildered and afraid.

"Not so brave now are you, Aubert?"

Lanval did not answer, one officer continued,

"Get undressed!"

"What? What do you..."

A vicious slap to his temple sent him reeling.

"Boots, belt, tunic! They'll fetch a pretty price and you'll not be needing 'em where you're going."

The wretch had no choice but to follow the order. He sat, shivering and naked, at the men's mercy. They both laughed out loud, their guffaws reverberating in the confined space.

"Put that on!" came the instruction, the guard pointing towards a heap in the corner – a head to foot shapeless sackcloth nightshirt.

"That's better, isn't it? A crown of thorns on your head and you could pass for Jesus getting ready for the cross!"

Again, they erupted into cruel laughter.

"Hey, don't forget to chain him."

"No, we don't want him running about his new home.

So, that's the job done and we'll leave you in peace to enjoy your stay, courtesy of His Honour, Judge Boivin." A key turned ominously in the door and they left Lanval's hole in the rock. He pulled on the rough garment, eager to cover his body against the bitter cold.

Thus, began Lanval Aubert's confinement and he soon lost track of time: no sun to herald the morning, no dusk to announce the night. Food, such as it was, came at no regular point in the day; no-one passed through the tunnel except a sullen brute of a man who would push a cup of water and a crust of bread under the grille. He also emptied the wooden pail, that was a toilet, into the rushing stream outside the cell. Lanval soon lost all hope of conversing with him. But, suddenly, he realised exactly where he was.

'The sewer! There's only one in the entire town...now... the stream rises near the Place des Armes and flows into the gutter that's cut into the Rue Saint-Come. Then it becomes the Rue Réaumur and goes underground near the Préfecture, not far from the port. That's where the gaol is so I must be somewhere underneath it. Yes, I've got my bearings now, for what good it will do. Those streets are where the wealthy Huguenots have their fancy residences – how I hate them, with their church services and bibles all in French and priests dressed in plain robes, fornicating with the womenfolk - and all this with the blessing of their God!'

Lanval's contempt for the Huguenots was a feeling shared by the great majority of Catholics in the Kingdom of France at that time.

He sat on the palliasse, leaning back against the rocky wall of his cell, drank a little water that remained in his cup from the previous day, and resumed his thoughts.

. . .

'Our Catholic brothers and sisters in Paris did a good day's work last year when they put three thousand Protestants and their sympathisers to the sword – to protect our holy cause from the protesting minority. Ay! They may be few in number but they are still dangerous and not to be trusted. I don't know how they ever became the ruling class in our town...here, they must exceed us by ten to one...so, did I not have the right to help my fellow believers, even if it has jeopardised my very survival?

Damned rich Huguenots! They can empty their privies straight into the sewer so their waste is swept away, sparing their houses and delicate nostrils from foul smells, while we poor souls do not know such luxury. We have to leave our chamber pots right outside the front door and the night soil men don't always come, so our houses stink...sometimes for days!'

The sound of clinking keys jolted him out of his daydream. The gaoler, bald-headed and swarthy, arrived outside his cell, gave him a toothless grin and proclaimed,

"Here's your supper, papist dog! More than you deserve is how I sees it, but you won't be getting many more of 'em.'

A small pitcher of water and a dry crust, as usual, was his meal and the gaoler resumed,

"You'll soon be fed as the Lord sees fit and *He* won't be as generous as *we* are, that's for sure!"

The brute was leaving when Lanval called out,

"Gaoler! Guard! A minute of your time!"

"What is it? I've got other duties to be seeing to." There was malice and disdain in his voice: La Rochelle hated its Catholic population with a rancour that defied any spirit of tolerance advocated in the Bible.

"Can you tell me...do you know when..."

"Speak up, man! Your lot isn't usually slow to mouth off."

"When will it be?"

"Ah, I get it...when? In your situation, Aubert, every day longer is a reprieve, don't you agree?"

Lanval nodded, bowing his head, unable to look his guard in the face.

"Anyhow, His Honour has more pressing matters to attend to right now, unless you hadn't noticed? You should know that better than most – I'm informed you have the ear of Catherine, herself, and some say even the King! Probably not true, but you can't deny you've stood up in public for their plan to change us all into Papists."

"I couldn't say, but I've seen the way the Huguenots treat us as second class citizens: decent jobs are given to your kind, we're the stuff of hurtful jokes, you encourage your children to not play with ours and – what causes us most to hate you – we're forced to bury our dead in a graveyard without the town walls, as if we're lepers or plague-bearers!" He spoke all this with his head still bowed as if he were addressing the ground beneath him, from which he thought he would receive a more sympathetic audience. He concluded,

"Enough of it all! It's not my place to express such views. My fate is sealed, that's the only certain event I can look forward to."

The dullard concierge, with his clanking bunch of keys fastened to his belt, gazed hard at his prisoner. If Lanval had looked up he would have seen a countenance that was mellowing with his words, as if he was not aware of these iniquities that the Catholics had to face in La Rochelle on a daily basis. But, he did not comment, only thought,

'Not right for a man like me to show kindness, that wouldn't do at all. His Honour would soon see me out of work.' He cleared his throat,

"Dunno anything 'bout that. Anyway, eat and drink, you need to keep your strength up."

With that, he turned and slouched off into the black malodorous tunnel, still jangling his keys, and disappeared.

Alone, Lanval Aubert felt fear for what laid ahead but he did not regret what he had done. He was proud of his Catholic religion whose scriptures he experienced by the clerics reading them out loud in church – he neither read nor wrote. The good King proclaimed the Faith through his messengers, the priests and, as he was the King's subject, he followed the same belief. In this pit of despair, he reflected,

'I only seek a life without conflict. I would not be shackled like a madman in a lunatic asylum if she had not betrayed me. How I loved her then, but detest her now. A plague of frogs upon her house! It would not bother me if these damned Protestants prayed in the next church – even in the next house – to me, were they to grant me that same privilege, but they do not! They revile us and we are forced to pray in a decrepit building beyond the woods, and when they are not about, in secret. We will never be equal in La Rochelle, nor in the whole kingdom, without bloodshed and strife.'

His thoughts were immediately confirmed as the ground above him shook violently, sending particles of rock and sand into the cell, filling the air. He covered his mouth and nose with his hands to avoid breathing in the choking dust, his eyes closed tight. The place then fell still, for a minute or so, but for the terrible ear-splitting din above him to resume. It was thus, relentless, every day and night – as far as he could distinguish one from the other – since his confinement in this devil's cave. The bombardment by the King's forces, from land and sea, was supposed to save them from the despised Huguenot majority. It had begun the previous year, yet, La Rochelle would not yield.

'Lord help me. It was not my intention to commit a crime, but, here I am, condemned. I wish I knew when my end will come: under jagged rock or face to face with the hangman on the gibbet?'

The cave shuddered again.

2

THE CHATEAU OF CHENONCEAU, APRIL 1572

A GHOSTLY FIGURE, DRESSED FROM HEAD TO TOE IN A monk's coarse brown habit, moved silently along the track that hugged the river Cher. The wan light of a vernal moon reflected off the swirls and eddies of the current, surprising an occasional water vole peeking its head out of the reed bed: no sound broke the still of this dark night but the man proceeded with caution as the path widened, heralding the estate of the chateau of Chenonceau, home of Catherine de Médicis. Should he be challenged by a patrolling guard – Catherine had them, as she did spies, everywhere to protect her and report gossip from her court and beyond – his disguise would serve its purpose. He would explain, head bowed, that he had, that day, visited a poor family who bore signs of a plague infection. They had requested his presence to bless the patient and exorcise evil spirits. That, he was confident, would be sufficient to deter the guard from pursuing his enquiry. The mere mention of the word 'plague' filled people with horror, even if the scourge had not surfaced in the region for some time. Nobody must know of his identity nor the reason for his presence on the lady's land in the middle of the night.

To the shrouded figure's relief, he encountered no guard and, shortly, he reached a bend in the river. Ahead stood the imposing bridge of five spans that supported a gallery and apartments, all designed and financed by Catherine, and united the north side of the river to the chateau and its carefully tended gardens. No welcome light showed in the building but the nocturnal traveller knew what to do now because it was not his first visit to the lady of the residence.

Leaving the track, he moved through the dense undergrowth, making as little noise as possible. He soon found the fallen tree trunk he sought, then, hidden behind a hawthorn bush, a small wooden door that yielded to his touch. Inside, a flight of six stone steps ascended to the gallery, then more steps to the apartments. He had to squint in order to make out the corridor ahead, lit only by the faintest moonshine that penetrated louvre-shuttered windows. At the far end, he made out a solitary flickering candle in a wall niche that indicated Catherine's private rooms.

Two soft knocks brought an equally soft 'enter' and he stood before Catherine de Médicis. He pulled back his hood and bowed.

"Good evening, my lady."

"Evening?" she snapped, "it's night, as dark as the world that besets me, so I trust your visions will cast light on these difficult times. You were not followed?"

"I was not, do not fear, and if I might be so impudent as

to remind you that prophecies come not from the heart but from the alignment of the stars and the situation of the planets. I hold no sway over the heavens, I simply interpret their will -"

"Quite, Ruggieri. So, will you take wine with me, even at this hour?"

"With pleasure." Côme Ruggieri, a gaunt-featured soothsayer and astrologer, with close-set eyes and grey straggly hair and beard, made his living from offering generalised prognostics to wealthy clients. He had learned his trade by word of mouth from the old master necromancer, Nostradamus, now retired on the fortune he had amassed. Ruggieri spoke in such a sincere tone that people – kings, queens, dukes or duchesses – readily believed his forecasts, especially in hours of need when they clutched at straws.

Catherine beckoned him to sit at her desk, drawn close to the warmth of the fireplace where dying embers still glowed. Taking the stopper out of a glass decanter she filled two goblets and, in her turn, sat, saying not a word. Instead, she stared hard at the man, a stare that was well practised over much dealing with men, usually of a lesser intellect than her own. She broke the silence,

"Tell me, Ruggieri, how do your stars augur for my horoscope of the year ahead?" Catherine was, by nature, pragmatic and – even if she regarded this presaging lark with some scepticism – she felt sorely in need of whatsoever reassurance for the events of August 21st to come.

The seer withdrew a small pouch from his habit, loosened the string and emptied the contents onto a parchment sheet, marked with a circle of the twelve signs of the zodiac that she had laid out earlier. A number of white raven's bones and three talisman coins fell randomly. He leaned over the chart to better examine their pattern, glanced at Catherine, then lowered his head in silent contemplation.

"Well?"

He maintained his silence until she prompted him a second time.

"Speak, man."

"Ma'am, your star sign is Aries, the ram. Be aware that different elements of your nature are dominant in different seasons. The crossing of the bones and resting place of the coins reveals to me that, from the present to the advent of winter, you may benefit from your intelligence -"

"Yes! Yes! But what do you see for the month of August?"

"It is not regular to anticipate the prospects of any particular month but, pray, a moment. He picked up three bones from the sheet and let them drop onto the others.

"This chart tells me that, in addition to your Arian qualities of intelligence, passion and strength, you will face any new challenge directly and will not tolerate failure."

"Ruggieri, you have brought me good news. Here, take this."

She pressed two gold pieces into his hand and gestured towards the door. Having put the bones and talisman coins back into his pouch, he nodded his thanks and left Catherine's study without further ado. *That was just about the easiest money I'll ever make,* he chuckled.

Alone, she refilled her goblet, stirred the ashes in the fireplace into life with a poker, and drank more wine. Leaning back in the chair, she mused,

'Ruggieri is right! There is, indeed, a challenge to be met and, by God, I will not tolerate failure in its pursuance, just as he said.'

The next morning, she awoke early and summoned her maidservant.

"You rang, ma'am?"

I did, Mathilde. Bring breakfast to my chamber and lay out my clothes. You will accompany me around the gardens."

"Of course, ma'am."

Mathilde finished brushing her lady's hair then twisted and tied the tresses to fit neatly under a velvet bonnet. Placing a shawl around her shoulders, she fastened the gold clasp at the front.

"Thank you. Meet me shortly, outside."

Mathilde nodded and left.

The gardens would be ablaze with vibrant colour in a month or so although, today, buds were only just appearing in the flower beds and on the trees.

"Tended by man, created by woman, do you not agree, Mathilde?"

"I do, ma'am. In bloom, they are a wonder to behold and a testimony to your name. It is not by chance that the central paths form the shape of a cross. Praise the Lord."

"Praise Him," Catherine responded, to then lapse into profound silence as they walked along the paths that traversed the gardens, side by side. The maidservant had known her mistress long enough to ask,

"There are serious matters on your mind, it is not difficult to see. May I be of assistance, in any way?"

"Yes, serious matters, that's true, to put it mildly. You realise I intended the cross of the paths to symbolise the cross on which our Lord was crucified. His pain will ever be ours and I will defend his teaching and wisdom with my last breath."

"Yours and the King's subjects applaud your leadership and, to a man and woman, are of the same Catholic faith."

"That is where you are mistaken, Mathilde. There are those who are not. But, enough. You must not concern yourself with a...how shall I describe it...a problem such as this."

"I meant no offence, ma'am."

"Nor is any taken. Worry not, my dearest servant, but I fear there are unprecedented violent times ahead. I cannot shirk my responsibilities to our fair kingdom and to our common belief." The Queen Mother paused, raising her face heavenward, as if in supplication to her Lord.

Catherine de Médicis was now in her fifty-third year. Small of stature and thin, without delicate features but with the protruding eyes peculiar to the Médicis line, she was by no means a beautiful woman. However, that did not detract from her determination and ambition. Her political and romantic acquaintances recognised that tight lips and often sullen countenance signified a powerful lady not to be underestimated.

In Florence, city of her birth, she was known as 'the little duchess', in France she was referred to as 'that Italian woman.' She was not universally admired.

At the age of fourteen, she married Henry, the future king Henry the Second, but throughout his reign he excluded her from participating in state affairs and, instead, showered favours on his chief mistress, Diane de Poitiers. In the presence of guests at social functions he would sit on her lap and play the guitar, chat about politics or even fondle her breasts. For the first ten years of their marriage, Catherine failed to produce any children and such was her desperation that she turned to the dark arts for assistance. She eventually gave birth to ten offspring, five of whom survived infancy, and it was the fifth child, Charles, now crowned Charles IX upon the death of his father, who would be pivotal to her designs over the coming months.

Catherine clasped and twisted her hands together in a gesture of great distress, feeling powerless to change the situation that confronted her. Turning, ashen-faced, to Mathilde, her features contorted, she beseeched,

"I ask you, what could a woman do, left by the passing of her husband with children on my arms and two families of France who were thinking of grasping my crown – my own Bourbons and the Guises? Am I not compelled to play strange parts in this theatre to deceive first one then the other, to protect my sons who have successively reigned through my wise conduct? I am increasingly surprised that I never did worse."

"Such things are above my comprehension and station, ma'am."

"That is as maybe, but it is you who hear gossip and rumour in Chenonceau and beyond," Catherine said gently to Mathilde.

"My duties commenced long before you arrived at the chateau when I was, first, a scullery maid and, to speak true, my work was not rewarding. I cleaned and scoured the floors, stoves, sinks, pots and dishes. Then, I peeled vegetables, plucked fowl and even scaled fish!" Mathilde mumbled reflectively.

Catherine smiled,

"How your standing has changed, but I wager you would rather still be toiling in the kitchens than tolerating the fantasies of an old woman."

"I regard it as a privilege," her eyes moistened with emotion, "and long may it continue."

"Ay to that, Mathilde. My aim is to place the honour of God before me in all things and to preserve my authority, not for myself, but for the conservation of this kingdom and for the prosperity and well-being of all my citizens." She wrung her hands incessantly. "I am so wretched that I know, for sure, I will live long enough to see so many people die before my time. I realise that God's will must be obeyed, that He owns everything, and that He leads us only for as long as He likes the children He gives us, if that makes sense. Come, let us go to the fountain, it never fails to calm my anguish."

They turned and walked back towards the central feature of the gardens, an exotic sculpture of four angels spouting water high into the air, as if imploring the heavens on Catherine's behalf.

Looking around to ensure she could not be overheard, she beckoned Mathilde to draw close.

"The day after tomorrow you will accompany me on a journey of the greatest importance: we go to Paris where I have arranged an audience with His Majesty the King. He resides presently at the Versailles palace, no doubt carousing and entertaining the strumpets of his court, just as his father did! He invites problems and is astounded when they duly arrive. Charles! Charles!" She exchanged knowing glances with her maid-servant and continued,

"I brought up that feckless youth and, to the best of my ability, I imbued in him good Catholic values. I presided over his council, decided policy and controlled state business and patronage, but not even I could control the whole country, to my chagrin. History may well decree that this Florentine princess could never have been assumed to solve the complex challenges of *la belle France*."

"History is what it is, ma'am." Mathilde's comment was spoken with the moderate diplomacy of a long-standing confidante.

"Give instructions to the stables to prepare my carriage but do not reveal our destination. The less known about my mission the better."

"Of course, ma'am."

————

TWO DAYS LATER AT DAWN

As ordered, the coachman reined the pair of fine purebred horses to a halt in front of the main chateau gate. Catherine and Mathilde, dressed in bonnets and shawls – the mornings were raw at this time of year – climbed inside and settled down for the journey, while an ostler tied a trunk securely to the luggage rack.

"Ride on', Catherine ordered.

By late afternoon, they had made Orléans, spending the night at the house of the mayor, an acquaintance and supporter of the Queen Mother. The following day, they approached the Saint Jacques gate of Paris, the guards stepping aside as soon as they observed the lady in her carriage, allowing entry into the city. Outside the royal Louvres palace, the two travellers were greeted by the king's steward, dressed in a worsted blue tunic tied at the waist with a gold braid cord, his sign of office.

"Welcome to Paris, my lady."

The steward led them through the maze of corridors that constituted the royal palace and ushered her into a sumptuous guest room, Mathilde's accommodation being the adjacent room, the two connected by a communication door. The maid-servant was unpacking the trunk when there came a knock at the door.

"Enter!" Catherine called.

"Ma'am, the King trusts you have had a safe journey and graciously requests your presence this evening for dinner. I am to inform you that he has selected a menu to celebrate your visit."

"Tell the King we accept his kind invitation."

The steward bowed, took two steps back, turned and

left the suite. Catherine raised her arm in a gesture of exasperation.

"Charles never fails to amuse me," she let out, "I know not whether to laugh or cry! I have not met with him for three months and his first thought is of food. Might he not wonder on the purpose of my visit?"

"You will soon discover the answer, ma'am."

In the private royal dining room, Catherine approached her son, made a perfunctory curtsey and kissed his outstretched hand.

"Welcome to Paris, mother. I trust your room is satisfactory?"

"It is, Charles." Her thoughts were sinking from the lofty to the abject as she stared at her offspring.

The king was tall and had inherited the same pinched smile and protruding Médicis eyes. He sported a stiff ruff around his neck, a snug-fitting doublet over black velvet breeches. She viewed him as a figure of ridicule, weak and indecisive, but to achieve her aim she had to humour him – it would be too easy to remonstrate over a list of failures in his reign since her influence on him had decreased. But that, she knew, would be an ill-chosen strategy.

They dined on a delicate consommé followed by guinea fowl stuffed with chanterelle mushrooms, then lamb's sweetbreads accompanied by a tween of fresh vegetables. The palace sommelier served vintage red and white wines with each course and a platter of confiserie concluded their dinner. Mathilde had taken her – much less grand – food in her room.

Throughout the meal, their conversation across the table was purely banal, encompassing the weather and which tapestries to hang in the Great Gallery. This concluded, Charles ushered his mother into the adjoining lounge with two upholstered armchairs either side of a blazing fire. The same sommelier poured two large brandies from a cut-glass decanter and, with a bow, departed. They were now alone for the first time.

"So, are you keeping well, mother? Your complexion is as fair as ever to me."

"It's kind of you to enquire and yes, I'm in rude health, most likely because I don't endure the stench and debauchery of Paris..."

"There are some things that are not even within the gift of a king."

"Quite, but certain other things most certainly are."

"I don't follow...although it's an opportune moment to ask the purpose of your visit."

"Pour me another brandy, Charles, and I'll explain." She drank then took a deep breath. "The cursed Huguenots are uprising once more and if something isn't done, we'll be overrun. We must act, and soon."

Charles sipped his brandy, twirling his black moustache nonchalantly between two fingers. "What has this to do with me, mother?"

Catherine's countenance darkened, lips pinched tight, her knuckles white from clenched fists.

"What! Are your counsellors useless? Do they tell you nothing? My own spies report to me daily and enlighten me about the hold the Huguenots are exerting on our very existence!"

"They are a...a nuisance but -"

"A *nuisance?* You're a fool, as was your father before you. He bequeathed you his lethargic wayward spirit and, once again, it is I who must decide for *you*. The Huguenots are anathema. Let me clarify for the benefit of my royal dullard!" She took another sip of the fiery liqueur. "Our churches are finely decorated to revere God's glory – theirs are plain and unedifying. Our priests enable us to find God – they scorn such clerical power. We believe the Bible should be only in Latin, for our priests to read out for us – they have their Bible in French and available to all and sundry. Should I continue?"

"Please do. I'm hearing things I never knew!"

Catherine was by now inflamed by the passion of her beliefs.

"Our faith proclaims sins can be forgiven through prayer or donating to the Church, but they say sins are forgiven only by God and Jesus. To conclude your education, we must consider their priests. Yes, the wretched Huguenots state they may marry a person on this earth and do not have the power to turn bread and wine into the body and blood of Jesus! How does that sit with our conviction that priests *do* possess that power: they are divine and should marry only their church. Unlike their vagabond preachers, our priesthood wears rich clothing, speaks in Latin and does *not* marry, they are subject only to Church laws. Surely you see which Church is the right one?"

"I do," came the meek response from the King.

"I only hope you do! Something has to be done, if I may repeat myself."

"What do you have in mind? I understand there have been many treaties, none of them lasting."

"To hell with treaties! A waste of time. We must take action."

"I'm listening."

"The twenty-first day of August will see the marriage of their leader, Henry of Navarre, to your sister, Marguerite, here in Paris. We know half the guests will, naturally, be of the Huguenot persuasion and..." She paused to fix him with her stare and ensure he was paying due attention. "...and they will be assembled, all, in the Great Hall of this very palace for four days of banquets and festivities. It's the ideal opportunity to be rid of the most influential heretics in one fell swoop. That done, the remaining thousands around the city will be easy pickings for our troops. Our Catholic brethren and clergy will, once more, be unhindered in their devotion." Her voice had risen to a frightening pitch such that Charles's jaw dropped and he gawped at his mother, marvelling at her audacious proposition.

"Is this possible?"

"It is and we have a supreme moral duty to see it through. We have time to prepare and, don't worry, I will guide you."

After the wedding on August 21st, the fourth, and final, day of celebrations would fall on Saint Bartholomew's Day, August 25th.

3

Catherine convinced her hesitant son, through reasoned argument but, more often, by the maternal domination she exerted over him, that the time to be rid of the Huguenots had arrived. She addressed him, with no small amount of exasperation,

"The Peace of Saint-Germain-en-Laye that you made with Jeanne, their Protestant Queen of Navarre, now two years past, has all but broken down. It was against my better judgment at the time to grant them authority in Cognac, Montauban, La Clarté and...what was the fourth town...ah, La Rochelle. How they enjoy the power of public office, but how they wield their influence, once more, over the religion they preach in their churches."

Charles lowered his gaze, overawed by a mother who had endured a marriage to a king who spurned her for a mistress, disparaged her inability to bear children for so long, and excluded her from matters of state. Her bitter dealings with the French court had taught her to befriend everyone but to trust no-one. Her husband, Henry the Second of France, now departed, could no longer suppress her free spirit and, like a red wax seal on a secret document, her mark could be seen on royal, aristocratic and common concerns. She continued her tirade,

"Visit any of our towns, Charles, and you can smell their hostility towards us even if you can't see it. They spread their beliefs, ridicule our name, and would see us subjugated on impulse. They must not prosper – we owe it to our children as to theirs. But, it will not prevail, it *cannot* prevail!"

She rose from her seat, brushed her gown and began to pace the room, step after measured step.

"I received a report from our Duke of Montpellier in which he describes forty Huguenots who refused to kneel for Communion. Such heresy! Such affront! He ordered his guard to respond with sabre and dagger so they laid down, dead, for the Eucharist! The Catholic way to praise the Lord, is not a negotiable way: it's the *only* way. Word spread throughout the town so, now, the Church's prescriptions are followed, as they should be." Her pacing brought her face to face with her son.

"What do you have to say on the business, my son, now King of France, my liege?"

Charles recognised the frame of mind that determined his mother's utterances – many a time had he either witnessed her vitriol or been the target for its passion. He answered, with circumspection,

"I don't dispute the truth of what you say, for truth it is. I'm cognisant of my duty to defend the Faith and to take all reasonable -"

"*Reasonable!* My dear boy, *reasonable* is a word that achieves defeat rather than victory, subservience not control, cowardice not bravery! *Reasonable* is not a wise way to behave when respect for out Scriptures is undermined by heathen worship. But, pray, continue your response."

"I thank you for your wisdom, and I should express my gratitude to you, as my mother and counsel."

"Indeed you should." Her tone lowered and the atmosphere in the room became less confrontational. She proceeded,

"However, we need to offer the Huguenots, regardless of our opinion, a chance to live alongside us, even if they continue to congregate in churches close to our own...we should appease them, I like to think, for reasons of harmony, as the Good Lord decrees. It's my intention to agree to the marriage of my sister, Marguérite of Valois, to Henry of Navarre, and with the least delay, if peace is to be restored."

Charles reacted sharply,

"But Henry is of the Huguenot faith! His mother is Jeanne d'Albret, a staunch believer if I'm not mistaken."

"You're not and therein lies the path to regaining a truce between out houses, through marriage. I've conversed at length with my sister and she accepts Henry's proposal, regardless that the Pontiff, our Holy Father, condemns the union. Let him condemn it, I say! The date is set, August 21st in our church of Notre Dame followed by four days of feasting and celebrations here, in the Great Hall of our Royal Palace. All the guests on Henry's side are prominent Huguenots from Paris and beyond, all assembling under the same roof. Tell me if that will not be an event Our Lord has preordained for our rightful benefit! The country will see an accommodation between two beliefs previously at war, whereas I have altogether different intentions." She paused, reflecting on Ruggieri's prediction,

'*You will face any new challenge directly, and will not tolerate failure.*' She concluded,

"I will not fail, that's for certain."

Charles nodded in acquiescence, his attention by now completely focused on his mother's intrigue. Through pinched lips, with expression of intense concentration, she expanded,

"The day before the wedding, there's something we must do to broadcast our will, how shall I put it, to create fear in the people of the city who do not subscribe to the Catholic way. The great generals teach us that, from their experience in battle, an enemy whose nerves are rattled is a foe that will show weakened resolve come the fight." She stopped for breath.

"And what might that be, mother?" Her son asked.

"There is a certain individual in Paris, an elder among the Huguenots, who – I have it on good authority – speaks from the pulpits and excites his people, though he is no priest. He urges them to distrust we Catholics and...I can only describe him as a vile Protestant orator of the worst kind! This man is called Gaspard de Coligny."

"I know that man!' Charles exclaimed, his mind racing, "You're surely not misled? He's a friend and adviser!"

"That's as maybe, but..." Her voice trailed away as she sought the best argument to win over Charles to her plot. "... but his popularity grows apace. If you could see how he manipulates you, the monarch, to take advantage of your better nature – I've seen it, if you can't. He's risen to the rank of admiral, and Marshal of France, that you know, but does your court not warn you that promotion and favour conferred on such a man is, at the very least, inadvisable? I'm afraid that he goes around unchallenged but, Charles, that should not surprise me, given the weeks on end when you're absent from your capital, occupied with other affairs at Versailles, not at all dissimilar from your late father. So, we must not, under any circumstances. allow these Baptists, Adventists, Evangelists – they go by a variety of names, although they are one and the same – to blaspheme at will. I've taken it upon myself, as the Queen Mother, to instruct our Duke of Guise to relieve us of Coligny, with the greatest of discretion, if you understand my drift?"

"I do, perfectly, and much as I now find Coligny's fate distasteful, the royal household must not be associated, in any way." Slowly, the gravity of his mother's proposition hit home: the act was murder! "What's become of religion that we used to admire? It's grown into a monster!"

"That can't be denied, my boy, but as long as *we* control the beast, we will side with the righteous."

"You're right, you usually are."

"At last! I feared you would never see reason! Don't worry, we are not common criminals, always remember that."

———

Paris, 19ᵗʰ August 1572

"Listen well!" Guise spoke, in a whisper, even though he was in the safety of his own home. "Coligny leaves his residence every morning as the cock crows and walks down the Rue du Château towards the Eglise Saint Jean. He's a creature of habit, never varies his routine. You, Edouard, he addressed his trusted captain, will be waiting at the corner of that street and the Rue des Boucheries. From that position you'll have a good view of the man and you can retreat, easily, afterwards. Is that clear?"

"Perfectly, monsieur."

Guise turned to the second man, Gaston, and said,

"There's an alleyway off the Rue du Château from where you'll observe him as he approaches. He'll come straight towards your musket."

"Understood, monsieur."

"The action will take place tomorrow. You'll each fire three shots then report, directly, to me, with all haste. Don't stop or speak to a soul."

Both soldiers nodded their head in a salute and left Guise's house, mumbling their orders to themselves to ensure the correct command would be carried out.

———

Paris, 20ᵗʰ August 1572

The next day a thick swirling fog descended on the city, drastically reducing the distance a man could clearly see but, regardless of the conditions, the two assassins had to follow orders from their leader, the respected Duke. He had been in charge of them through many campaigns and, as one of them reflected, if their master, Guise, has instructed that Coligny be killed, it would be wicked not to kill him.

In position and in good time the murderers waited, motionless, for the Admiral's door to open. The cock crowed and, as if in sympathy, the prime bell of the nearby Eglise Saint Jean tolled its death knell. The cock persisted, but still no man appeared. Then, the murky silence of the morning was disturbed by the creaking of hinges and, as predicted, Coligny emerged, closing the door behind him.

A tall imposing man with long face and nose, broad forehead and piercing brown eyes, one would not have assumed him to be a naval commander of warships and armed warriors, rather an artist or court diplomat. A clearing of his throat and some indecipherable muttering helped the men to take aim at their quarry but they waited for him to walk an agreed four paces before discharging their first shots. A sharp squeal through the dense fog indicated they had found their mark. Guise had chosen his most skilled riflemen, who swiftly placed a second lead ball into their muzzle, ramming it in, pouring a coating of gunpowder onto the pan and cocking the hammer, in a seamless movement, born out of years on the battlefield. Their second then third shots fired, and they made their escape without examining the fallen body on the ground before the alarm sounded.

Events occurred quickly: Guise's men reported to him that they had fulfilled their mission, so he promptly dismissed them with his thanks for their participation. However, to his dismay and disappointment, another soldier arrived within the hour to inform him that Admiral Coligny was not dead.

'What! His injuries?"

"Sire, he has lost one finger and his elbow is severely damaged but, yes, he survives. His servants have put him in his bed to recover."

Guise hurried to the Royal Palace without delay, brushing sentries aside as he made for Catherine's quarters.

"Damn!" The queen cursed. "Word will soon get around so we must ensure that neither mine nor the King's name is connected, at all costs."

The Duke bit his lip, saying nothing. Catherine, her countenance as dark as night, racked her brain to decide on her next move. At length, she spoke,

"We will send the Royal Physician, at once, to tend Coligny's wounds...yes, that will reflect well on us..." Again, she fell silent before instructing Guise,

"This unholy business *will* be concluded, Duke Guise, and this time there must be no mistake. It is read in my stars that this month I will *not* tolerate failure. Do you understand me? Do not use soldiers, no-one in a uniform nor having any association with the court."

"Of course, ma'am. It will be done, as you command."

Accordingly, Guise sent a message to the ringleader of a band of Parisian ruffians whose services, especially when settling a score, he had hired in the past. He paid them well so their reliability, as with their discretion, was assured. This high-profile engagement, fraught with danger, would cost him a good few coins but he had no choice – the failure of the first attempt was down to him and only as fool would ignore his lady's authority. To do so could see him reduced to the ranks, or worse.

At midday, six burly cut-throats approached Coligny's dwelling. A broad-shouldered one at the front took three steps back and charged the locked door that promptly yielded. Rushing into the ground floor room, their only opposition was an elderly manservant sitting at a table who was swiftly rendered unconscious by a cudgel blow to the head. Upstairs, Coligny lay in his bed with the doctor applying balm to the man's injured arm.

"Out! Leave now!" They had no truck with the physician who made a rapid exit. Leaning over the bedridden Huguenot, the leading executioner drew his dagger to plunge it into the defenceless admiral whose white nightshirt turned red as his heart pumped its last. Death ensured success. To compound the murder, with the intention of terrifying the man's adherents, another brute approached the bed and, with one fell blow of his sabre, severed head from body. They dragged the corpse to the window and cast it unceremoniously into the street below, for all Paris to witness.

News of the outrage spread around the city like wildfire and, as Catherine had hoped, it had the desired effect of creating apprehension and fear among the Protestant population. If a senior member of their Church could be blatantly and mercilessly slain in his bed, who would be next, they asked each other, amid an atmosphere of burgeoning panic, and the day before what should have been a joyous wedding?

4

PARIS, 20TH AUGUST 1572

THIS SAME DAY, BEFORE DAWN, JOFFROY, A FORMER sailor, met his old friend Sébastien at the Porte au Blé on the right bank of the river Seine, as arranged. Both religious men who regularly attended the Eucharist of their Protestant church, and both unmarried, with no dependant families, they had taken a remarkable decision, to flee Paris. Shaking hands, they took the path that skirted the river flowing downstream. The men were travelling light, wearing a heavy waterproof cape over their tunic and each carrying a small sack, a drawstring fastening its top to keep their few valuables secure. Joffroy spoke,

"It amazes me not more folk like us are leaving the city. Our priest has been telling us, from the pulpit and in private, that we're in danger from the Catholic powers. I know he's right. It's hard to put my finger on it but snide comments and spitting at us in the street, snubbed by people I thought were my friends, notices posted warning us to pray only in our own churches...almost as if we would *infect theirs*. Yes, it's hard, but it's real enough to know we're not safe."

"Ay, I've experienced the same," Sébastien agreed, "and Coligny's murder yesterday is an alert that there's something evil in the air."

After a few minutes they reached the first of several barges and sailing boats moored, end to end.

"Leave the talking to me. With any luck we'll happen on a captain who's known to me from my younger days, one who'll assist our flight," Joffroy told his pal in a confident tone. At the first barge he stepped on board and shouted into an open hatch,

"Hey! Good morning! Anyone down there?"

A stranger ascended the ladder to face the visitor.

"What do you want? I paid our port taxes when we arrived yesterday -"

"Worry not! We seek employment on your boat, if any there be."

"No, got a full complement but try further on down the quay, I've heard that there's a long sailing vessel further on that's short-handed."

"My thanks, monsieur, and *bon voyage*."

"Sounds promising," Sébastien commented as they clambered off the deck and continued to the boat the sailor had indicated.

"Yes, it does, and regardless of how much work we can get, we won't return to Paris in the foreseeable future. Not safe, to put it mildly."

Their luck was in and this captain was one Joffroy had sailed with in the past. Their friendship renewed, work on the boat for the coming three months was offered and accepted.

"Welcome aboard, Joffroy and Sébastien! I've heard talk they are dangerous times in Paris so I'm glad I don't have to venture far from the quayside when I sail my boat here."

At the same time, in the north of the city, Rue Beaubourg, old Gervese held out his hand to help his wife, Salvia, climb up onto the seat of their cart.

"We should have taken more notice of the warnings our lad gave us, months ago," the elderly woman said, resignation in her voice, "who'd have thought it!"

A small chest containing some clothing and their bible was lashed securely and with a sharp crack of the whip their horse took up the strain and began to haul them along the street, out of the city, to stay with Gervese's brother-in-law in Beauvais, a good two days ride away.

"We'll be safe there my dear and, anyway, what choice do we have? Even our neighbour of thirty years belittles our belief, besmirches our Holy Mass, and mocks our Bible."

"You're right, husband, we have no choice, and I fear for those of our faith who we're leaving behind."

"Ay, but it's up to them, if they can't trust their own eyes."

During the twenty-four hours after Coligny's murder, a rising state of apprehension, then helpless panic, gripped the Huguenot population of Paris – but only a few hundred citizens, like Joffroy, Gervese, Sébastien and Salvia, resorted to abandoning their homes and fleeing. Most remained, their naïve minds convinced that, especially at such a happy marital time, none of the rumours of bloodshed would materialize and affect them.

———

Paris, 21st August, 1572

The morning of the wedding between Marguerite of Valois and Henry the Third of Navarre – the former a Catholic, the latter a Huguenot – dawned fine and sunny with not a cloud in the sky to threaten their happiness. Although they hardly knew each other, it was hoped that they would grow to respect the sanctity of their marriage for the benefit of all parties. The steps of the cathedral of Notre-Dame de Paris echoed to the excited voices of common people, of both faiths, crowding to secure a good view of its massive iron-studded oak doors, whence the bride and groom-to-be would soon emerge after a private audience with the celebrant Archbishop of Paris, Pierre de Gondi.

A line of soldiers, dressed in full ceremonial uniform, linked arms to form a cordon to keep the crowds at a respectful distance. The air trembled with the thunderous peal of Notre-Dame's immense bells in the twin towers, complemented by the chimes of all the churches in the city, from Eglise Saint Nicolas in the north to the Abbaye de Saint Victor in the south. Parisians, believers or not, rejoiced at the unification of the two houses of Valois and Navarre, hoping that tolerance and understanding would regain the sanity of Paris and the kingdom.

. . .

Notre-Dame de Paris, consecrated to the Virgin Mary, began its construction begun in 1160 by Bishop Maurice de Sully, stood proudly on the Ile de la Cité in the swirling waters of the mighty river Seine. Its pioneering rib vaulting and flying buttresses made it the finest Gothic church in the land, and not just a place for worship. Few people could read or write in 1572 so it was the symbolism of buildings such as this cathedral that educated them in the thinking of the Church. Grotesque gargoyles stared with ferocious faces, snarling and spewing streams of rainwater from the buttress ends; wicked imps laughed; angry chimera monsters breathed fire at the *strix* - owl-like creatures that ate human flesh. Everything conveyed a message, predominantly engendering fear and wonder at the power of the Lord – that which no leather-bound tome or pompous erudite preacher could ever achieve. The cathedral served as the poor people's book through its sculpture vividly illustrating biblical stories. The tympanum over the central portal, where Henry and Marguerite were about to present themselves for marriage, showed the Last Judgment with sinners being led to hell and good Christian folk taken to heaven. What more potent an idea for the people? These were visual instructions to the illiterate worshippers, symbols of evil and danger that threatened those who did not follow the teachings of the Church.

It was common for ignorant citizens to enter the cathedral, not necessarily with hope for a spiritual conversion but to sit and marvel at the stories told by sunlight shining through the coloured glass in the three rose windows. Scenes from the life of Christ and those who witnessed His time on earth became real. They learned the significance of the angels, apostles and saints, Old and New Testament subjects through blue red white and purple shards. Jesus's Descent into Hell; Adam and Eve; the Resurrection of the Lord – all magically portrayed to the amazement of ordinary man.

At a given signal, three canons, on their trolleys behind the outside of the apse, fired, one after the other, their cannonballs falling harmlessly into the Seine, a sign for all the churches to cease ringing their bells. The excitement among the people rose as a single slow chime resounded from one of the cathedral's towers. Guests, family, friends and sundry nobility wearing their finest costumes, Catherine and Charles included, ceased their conversations, expectantly facing the grand portal. The bell made its final note as the moment everyone was waiting for arrived. The doors slowly opened and a deacon carrying a heavy brass cross led out the wedding participants: Archbishop de Gondi, the bride and the groom. The prelate was adorned in a white linen chasuble tied with a purple cord; his tall official mitre emphasising a narrow, bearded face; his crozier with its carved ivory top in his right hand.

Two young sisters, awestruck and all but transported by the exhilarating events of the morning, nudged and whispered to each other. Like the rest of the crowd, they had been standing patiently for the royal pair to appear.

"Here she is, at last...have you ever seen anyone so elegant, so resplendent?" gasped one girl.

"In truth, I have not, sister. Mind you, we don't have the

chance to observe royalty every day of the week," the other girl reasoned.

"Behold her gown! It's blue velvet from head to toe... and the sleeves...she's so elegant! And those flowers...but I didn't know she's so tiny, a gust of wind and she'd be blown over!"

"Don't be silly," the sister scoffed, "she'll have ladies-in-waiting to make sure that doesn't happen."

"I suppose you're right. When we get home, I'm going to ask mother to braid my hair, like hers."

The other youngster had been watching Henry carefully. She spoke, but with less enthusiasm,

"He's not much taller than her," and she paused, "if you ask me, he's a toff, yes definitely a toff. Look at his quilted doublet and...are those silver buttons fastening it? It's the closest our sort will ever be to any precious metal, and do you think he wears a cap and feathers like that around his palace? The only thing I admire in him is that...er...badge, if that's the word...no, it's a coat-of-arms on his sash thing. Now, *that* impresses me!"

She was correct to praise the sash that identified him as a member of the powerful royal House of Navarre that would, shortly, be united with the Valois line.

The crowd applauded heartily until a raised hand from the Archbishop brought them to order. Marguerite and Henry turned to face the portal and the ceremony began.

An assistant priest emerged from within the cathedral holding a gold bowl from which de Gondi liberally sprinkled the couple with holy water, mumbling a blessing. The required banns had been posted in Notre-Dame and around the city for four weeks, as was the ecclesiastical rule but the Archbishop still asked the crowd, whether they knew of any just cause or impediment why they should not be lawfully wed. No objection was forthcoming so he proceeded, gesturing to Henry to remove the ring from his doublet pocket. Next, he touched Marguerite's thumb, index and middle fingers for the ring to be loosely placed and, in turn, he gave a blessing,

'*In nomine Patris*,' (In the name of the Father)

'*et filiis*,' (and the Son)

'*et Spiritus Sanctus*.' (and the Holy Spirit)

Finally, after the usual rite, he nodded to Henry who encircled her wedding finger with the band, to then announce,

"I marry you, wife." The Archbishop proclaimed,

"You Henry, and you Marguerite are, this day, wed with the Lord's grace."

Wild cheering erupted. The marriage was warmly received, and while they wished the young couple happiness, they prayed for religious peace in Paris and the Kingdom of France.

De Gondi to the fore, the newly-weds entered the cathedral, followed by the lords, ladies, dukes, duchesses, sundry dignitaries and friends who had witnessed the ceremony outside for a nuptial mass within. This marked the end of the involvement of the commoners who duly returned to their homes.

After mass in the cathedral, a meal was served in Henry's private dining room. Initially the atmosphere was tense and less than cordial but copious consumption of wine relaxed the guests and conversation, leading to laughter, flowed. Catherine flitted from Catholic to Huguenot, drawing on her diplomatic talents and fostering a general feeling that religious unity was possible, if not probable, owing to the marriage they had just consecrated.

———

The Royal Palace Great Hall, 22ND August, 1572

The main feasting and celebrations for the royal wedding began with luncheon and would continue into the evening on this and the ensuing three days. Colourful banners and flags bearing the coats-of-arms and emblems of the royal and ducal households of the guests hung from the walls of the Great Hall, alongside lavishly embroidered tapestries.

With Marguerite and Henry in front, the party for the high table filed into the hall through a rear door to take their places before the assembled company who rose and applauded respectfully. Once Henry sat the rest followed. Attired in rich outfits the royal party looked every inch the epitome of the aristocratic class to which they belonged. The raised dais was not there coincidentally: they needed and would be seen, at all times, by the lower ranks in the room. The pure white damask that covered their tables was in stark contrast with the bare wood on which the ordinary guests dined.

. . .

This was an occasion for the royal family to impress their guests - it would never do if the event was inferior in any way to previous banquets – and they did not disappoint.

In the kitchens, thirty-seven chefs prepared the food; fifteen scullions cleared up after them and peeled and chopped vegetables; spit-turners saw to the roasting of pigs, lambs, and oxen; dozens of staff brought out silver platters laden with all manner of delicacy. The fortunate guests tucked into fresh bread, bowls of whipped butter, sugared almonds, hard-boiled eggs smothered in honey and mustard, pork pot pies, fried oranges, meatballs, roast meats, cheeses, all wolfed down with best spiced wine.

Royal guards in their chainmail suits, with a tabard bearing the royal crest over a sword thrust into a leather belt, stood to attention at either end of the high table.

CATHERINE'S PRIVATE APARTMENT, 24TH AUGUST 1572

"Our good Duke of Guise, are all preparations made for tomorrow?"

"They are, ma'am, you can have every confidence in me and my men."

"And, so I do. Should the venture fail the consequences do not bear thinking about, for our families and the Church."

"I understand and have chosen only my best soldiers,

from each of the seven barracks in the city, to avoid idle gossip."

"The Duke is, to be sure, a loyal and shrewd general. What say you, Charles?"

Charles appeared from a shadowy corner, reluctant to become any more embroiled in the dark business than was necessary. Guise gave a polite bow to his monarch, a slight smile on his lips betraying the contempt in which he held a man who was the total opposite to himself.

"Your majesty," Guise mumbled.

"Guise," Charles acknowledged.

"Speak, my son!" the lady bellowed in his ear. "These times that confound us call for a steadfast spirit and a belief in the righteousness of our cause. The days of treaties and mealy-mouthed diplomacy are long since passed. Even as we talk, the Huguenots gorge themselves on our hospitality, oblivious to their fate." She continued,

"Our Catholic faith must prevail over all others and I pray for a successful resolution."

"Your prayers are, of course, appreciated, even if I envisage a result that is not as immediate as we desire," Guise said, softly. The lady replied in a questioning tone,

"I will repeat the plan, one last time but...but enough. Let us first toast the outcome we seek. Charles! Pour wine for us!"

The king, Queen Mother and duke solemnly raised their glasses.

"To the Catholic faith!" Both men dutifully repeated her words. Placing her goblet on the table, she resumed,

"The twenty-fifth is the day of the principal banquet after which the wedding guests will depart the city. Charles and I will attend, as is expected, and the Great Hall of our Royal Palace will be fit to burst, everyone wanting the congratulate the couple's happiness before their life of dedication to the kingdom begins. We will occupy the prominent dais at the far end of the room and – hear this well, Duke – the guests will be seated at tables running the length of the hall, Marguerite's people to the right, in front of her, and Henry's to the left. Upon your appearance, or that of one of your officers, I will at once order the top table guests and friends out of the place to safety. The good direction of the affair is in your hands, Guise. It is Charles's decree that *not one* of those Huguenots sitting on Henry's side shall survive the attack – *not one!*

She turned to Charles, who had remained silent during her address,

"That is your royal command, is it not, Charles?"

"It surely is. Not one!" Adopting a strangely authoritative tone, he instructed, "you may leave us, Guise. See that our intentions are satisfied. Although these words are uttered by me, they have the force of the Lord Almighty, so you may proceed in the assurance that you possess both regal and heavenly strength."

"Sire, I will see it is done." Guise replied, bowing deferentially and left Catherine's apartment.

———

SAINT BARTHOLOMEW'S DAY, THE ROYAL PALACE GREAT HALL, 25TH AUGUST, 1572

Saint Bartholomew's Day saw every seat in the Great Hall occupied. The servants placed less food on the tables than the previous days but jugs of wine in a-plenty: this final occasion, for the bride and groom's merriment was, traditionally, devoted to singing, dancing and drinking. In the middle of the hall, jesters in their motley coats, tight breeches with one leg different in colour from the other, and Fool's hat, its three points each bearing a jingle bell, performed their acts and tricks. A trio of minstrels played lute, fiddle and sackbut followed by processions of youngsters, not dissimilar to the children led to their doom by the Pied Piper of Hamlin. Ladies dressed in their finery, gentlemen upright and handsome, pranced and trotted jigs, carols and rounds in lines and circles, each trying to outdo the other with their swirls and pirouettes. Laughter rang out and the entire assembly was joyous and proud to be in attendance to bid Marguerite and Henry *bon voyage* for their journey ahead.

Catherine sipped fine claret, smiling and nodding at the dancers who passed before the high table. The choice of exotic flower arrangements around the hall was hers, a reflection of her artistic flair. She sighed with a perverse feeling of satisfaction that was disturbed by Charles sitting at her side who wrung his hands and twitched nervously. Kicking her son under the table, she hissed,

"Keep still! Carry on like this and you're give the game away!" Her thoughts drifted. *To tell the truth, I am as uncertain as he is. The stakes are high and my involvement in the plot must not be revealed, at least until we have properly mustered our armies and I can be sure I am supported by loyal soldiers and not mercenaries, although of them there will be a number. Looking down on these poor souls, I question if it be the right action to take, even in the name of the Lord.'* Shaking her head, she emerged from her contemplation and resumed her specious smiling and small talk. *Did I say give the game away? What we've planned is anything but sport! A more deadly undertaking, I cannot envisage.*

Without warning for those in the room the doors to the rear opened and a troop of a dozen heavily armed soldiers entered in silence. The captain waved his sword in the air, a signal to Catherine that the moment had come. She promptly rose and ushered all the guests on the high table to leave through the small door behind them urging,

"Ladies and gentlemen, we are in grave danger so leave, with all haste, I beseech you." Her severe tone and the appearance of the soldiers were sufficient to convince them to exit without further bidding.

Six soldiers advanced to position themselves the length of the row of Catholic tables ordering the bewildered men, women and children to follow the aristocrats to safety. The rest of the troop moved forward and, drawing their swords and daggers, marched resolutely towards the Huguenots who realised, to their horror, that they were about to be attacked. The women let out shrill screams of fear, the men exchanged expressions of impotent surprise and the children burst out crying – "Mother, I want my mother!"

For them all, there was no escape: contained like sheep in a pen, their only recourse was prayers to the Almighty.

The soldiers began, with disciplined methodical efficiency, according to their orders, to slay the Protestants where they sat. Swords cut through flesh, limbs removed from body, blood splattered and flowed as seething as the waters of the Seine. No soul was spared and, after a murderous few short minutes, every Huguenot man, woman and child lay motionless in pools of crimson gore. The hall regained an eerie silence. The soldiers replaced their weapons in their belts and scabbards, and waited for the captain's order to depart. Trained in the way of battle he inspected everybody to observe no movement so as to confirm death then bellowed,

"Men, out!"

Outside the Great Hall news of the slaughter had not yet broken and life was normal. The narrow streets reverberated with the noise from crowds of people and animals moving along between tightly-packed three and four-storey high houses. Merchants at their stalls shouted the quality of their produce; vendors went door to door selling fish, fruit, vegetables, milk, cheese, chickens, garlic and countless other articles. On every corner, beggars sought alms; flocks of pigs, sheep and cows grunted, bleated and mooed in protest as they were driven to market. Year round, the city smelled strongly of unwashed people and chamber pots emptied out of windows. Such banality, for the Huguenots of Paris, would soon change for ever.

Saint Bartholomew was skinned alive by the flaying knives of his enemies. Such would be the fate of the Huguenots of Paris whom Catherine so hated, in fear of an uprising, especially after Coligny's murder. From garrisons around the city poured Guise's best mercenaries alongside regular soldiers, each led by a captain, each to deal with a named street or road that had been identified as housing predominantly Protestant residents. They began their savage mission in a calm macabre manner, showing neither emotion nor mercy. They had orders to enter the house and that they did. Then, overcome by bloodlust bred from the theatres of war, they slew the inhabitants of the ground floor before climbing the stairs to slaughter the children and the bed-ridden. None was spared. Should they be challenged by any passer-by they must cut them down. While Guise admitted that innocent Catholics might be caught up in the business, he reasoned that it would be a small price to pay for the elimination of the greater Huguenot menace.

By sunset, more than a thousand citizens lay dead in their homes and only those who fled had escaped death. Catherine had achieved her goal of restoring Catholic supremacy in her capital. She had by now retreated to the chateau of Chenonceau with Marguerite and Henry to go into hiding. The fervid Guise and King Charles drew up plans involving lords and dukes with their armies in the kingdom to prosecute the war against all Protestants. Mass extermination erupted throughout that year and towns like Auxerre, Nîmes and Beauvais were taken with Montauban a prime target.

5

THE RIVER SEINE, PARIS, 25TH AUGUST 1572

THE RIVER BOAT'S OWNER, ALBINET, HAD TOLD JOFFROY and Sébastien to report to him at his berth on the Seine by midmorning to set sail downstream by noon.

"Ah, here you are, gentlemen," Albinet greeted the two men. "As soon as my hands show up we can be off. They went ashore some hours ago to *taste some good Paris ale*. And why did that not surprise me? But as long as they're fit for work, how they spends their money is none of my business. Anyway, enough of that, pass me your bags and come aboard."

The men obeyed. They were both very unsure of what lay ahead. Albinet, a sensitive soul beneath a rough sailor's exterior, smiled gently and said, almost in a whisper,

"I'm pleased you're joining my small crew, good to have fresh faces. Your sleeping quarters are below the hatch at the prow so settle in and I'll explain your duties."

First Joffroy, then Sébastien, climbed down the ladder into a dark musty cramped space that would be their home for the foreseeable future. There was barely room for the grubby straw-filled mattresses, each with a folded coarse blanket and the expressions of distaste on their faces spoke more than words. They realised in an instant that their decision to abandon the city would not be as pleasant or straightforward as they had thought.

Back on deck, they rejoined Albinet sitting on the bench, one arm resting on the tiller of the boat's rudder, that formed the boat's stern.

"Now, is everything satisfactory?"

The men nodded, deeming a complaint inappropriate and pointless.

"Good." he continued, "and I won't ask the reason why you're leaving Paris, no doubt you have your reasons and you'd tell me but it's usually better to remain ignorant. All I ask is you work hard."

"We will." Sébastien answered for them both.

"I'm sure you will. Joffroy, you know me from past times, when we were younger, stronger, and could sail this boat nigh on between us. But age catches up and though I don't like having to pay crew, needs must." His gaze fell on the quayside and he announced,

"Talk of the devil, here they are!"

Two men approached and stepped onto the moored boat. Their ebony skin shone in the morning sunlight, both bald, but there any resemblance ceased. It was clear from their colour that they were not of French origin, rather an African country from where many men made the long journey in the hope of a better life in the northern lands.

"About time!" Albinet admonished them but not in a

vicious tone. "Prepare to leave – ah, and let me introduce you to these two fellows, Joffroy and Sébastien."

The newcomers held out a hand that the Africans shook, their faces betraying no emotion. One was a giant of a man, taller than a horse, sinewy biceps bulging on arms exposed by a sleeveless leather tunic. The other, a round-shouldered diminutive figure, shorter than any of them, glared at the strangers through wide-open dark eyes. The giant screwed his forehead into furrows and thrust his chin forwards. They both uttered strange guttural noises and made their way along the boat without further ado.

"Pay them no heed, they're good men, the sort you'd want on your side in a brawl, but they don't have many words and, in any case, don't speak our language. How do we communicate, I see you wondering? Well, we use hand signals."

"Really?" Sébastien let out.

"Ay, there's no need to talk. They knows their duties and performs them well. I pays them as soon as the customer pays me and everybody's happy, just how it should be...been with me four or five years now."

"And what are their names?" Joffroy asked, out of natural curiosity.

"Names? D'you know, I've never asked them, it's not seemed important. When I have to give them an instruction, I say *Big Hand* or *Little Hand, do this or that,* and by waving my arms they understand me. Strange, don't you think?"

'I suppose it is," Joffroy agreed, bewildered by such an unusual arrangement.

"Let me explain your work, and we'll be leaving shortly. Little Hand is the look-out. He stands on the prow and spots changes in the current, whirls and eddies, shallow water and dangerous objects like tree trunks floating ahead.

He lets Big Hand know and, well...they're a team, the best on the river. D'you see?"

"Yes, of course," Sébastien answered quickly, wanting to appear an experienced sailor, that he was not.

"Then, there's Big Hand. He sets the sail, hauls it in, lets it out according to the wind and Little Hand's signals. He's a master at it and I firmly believe he senses which way the air's moving before it moves, if you understand me. When he calls to you it means he wants the sail unfurled and hoisted to the top of the mast – it's a two-man job is that sail, especially if it's wet, damned heavy. Of course, before that you'll raise the mast, or lower it if we're getting to a bridge. When Big Hand doesn't want you, when a strong current means we don't need a sail, you'll work in the holds, tying up bales of cloth or corking barrels, depending on the cargo. When we reach a port, you'll unload the deliveries with a hoist. I'm sure you can handle that. Now, there's just time to take a look around the boat, to get your bearings as it were, before we sail."

Albinet's boat had carried goods on the Seine for as long as anyone could remember: he had inherited it from his father who, in turn, had it bequeathed by his father before him. Designed for rivers, flat-bottomed with a shallow draught, its wide beam from stem to stern boasting cavernous holds – it had provided Albinet with a good living. The canvas mainsail was wrapped and tied to the boom waiting to be run up the thick oak mast that rested in its hinged tabernacle on midship.

"Big Hand! Little Hand! Free the front and aft dock-lines! Big Hand, now raise the anchor!" the owner's voice bellowed. Each man lifted his hand to confirm the order was understood and, within minutes, the strong downstream was sweeping them to the centre of the river. Their first destination was Sancerre, two days sailing broken by a brief stop to buy dinner in a riverside tavern.

Joffroy turned to gaze wistfully at his home city now appearing as rooftops and church spires in the distance, but his attention was drawn to the track that followed the river course in their direction.

'Do my eyes deceive me?' he asked himself, 'There's a line of people walking away from Paris...a woman carrying a baby covered in a shawl...a man driving a mule with bulging sacks tied either side...then folk pulling handcarts laden with household chattels...children, wailing, dragged along by the arm...they're all fleeing Paris! Hundreds of ordinary townsfolk and though they're not close I can hear their desperation and moaning...what horror! What's the reason for their flight?'

Joffroy and Sébastien had departed the city before the massacre in the Great Hall had unfolded. They were, for the moment, unaware of the cruel merciless murders inflicted on the joyous guests at the wedding festivity.

They had been sailing for two hours or so when lighter, faster craft began to overtake them. Sébastien shouted to one boat within earshot,

"Hey, fellow! Why are they all coming away from Paris?"

"Have you not heard?" came the answer, "there's blood on the streets, soldiers with swords and muskets, no-one's spared if they be them damned Huguenots..." The small boat soon left them behind.

Sébastien approached his friend and they exchanged glances that needed no explanation.

"You were right, Joffroy, what you feared is now happening." Word had spread like a fire in a hay barn, terror gripped the city.

———

That same day, old Gervese gave the horse a tap with his cane to urge it on. His wife pulled her coat tight, her advanced years rendering her unprepared for a cart ride. She was afraid for her Church but she had faith in her husband's decision to leave.

"Is everything all right, my dear?" he asked with concern in his voice.

"Yes, it is." Salvia lied. Every jolt as the cart hit a rut or stone on the track shook her body; her arthritic joints cried out, transmitting unbearable pain, but she did not complain. What would be the use? Her husband, over many months, had sensed the mood of Paris turning against the Protestants. She had never heard the word *persecution,* but she understood, with the shrewd wisdom of a woman of seventy-six years, that if they were identified as adherents to her beloved faith, their freedom or, indeed, their very lives would be compromised.

By late afternoon, they had made good progress and wisps of grey smoke from chimneys ahead heralded the village they sought to break their journey. They had planned to buy a room and dinner, resuming their travel to Beauvais at dawn the next day. Only the rattle of the iron-rimmed cartwheels and the horse snorting its displeasure at having to haul a loaded cart and two passengers could be heard in the quiet countryside. Then, as if from nowhere, a lone horseman galloped up from behind and reined in his mount alongside the cart.

"Whoa!" he called out, "have you come from Paris?"

"Yes." Gervese answered in a confident tone, although inwardly he was suspicious to have been stopped thus.

"In that case, you'd best get as far as you can away from the city!"

"What do you mean?" the old man asked. Intuition told him the reply would be disturbing.

"Soldiers, they say under Duke Guise, surprised a wedding banquet and slaughtered all the Huguenot guests – men, women, children, young and old. Next, they ran amok through the streets, killing as they went, and even entered the houses of those who were of that Church... hundreds dead...terrible sight...don't know where it will end but I'd stay out of it if I were you. Keep going, because if you stop you'll block the path for the column of people coming up behind you from back there." He waved his arm in the direction of Paris, terrorised by unthinkable hysteria through the bloodshed the Protestant populace was facing.

Gervese was greatly relieved to steer his horse into the courtyard of the inn. A lad appeared and held the horse's bridle while he climbed down from the cart to, in turn, help his wife. They were safe, for the moment.

They ate well that evening and, for the first time in many months, felt secure, a good distance achieved between themselves and the hostile environment of the city they had hoped would be their resting place but that they now accepted would not be so. Leaving a familiar neighbourhood was bothersome at a young age but, in the twilight years, the effect was magnified and hard on the once indomitable spirit, nurtured and protected in the bosom of the Mother Church.

The following day, Gervese and Salvia resumed their journey to her brother's home in Beauvais. Though unannounced, their arrival was met with warmth and sympathy for their plight.

"You're welcome, sister." the brother said softly, embracing her and shaking Gervese's hand. "You will stay with us as long as is necessary. News of the plight of our Huguenot brethren in the capital has been common knowledge here for many months, although we did not know it had descended into murder – damned Catholics! A curse on them!"

——

THE CHATEAU OF CHENONCEAU, AUGUST 26TH 1572

King Charles, the Duke of Guise and their generals assembled in the Royal Palace of Paris to plan their strategies to expel the remaining Huguenots from the city. The bloodletting of the previous day had gained their principle aim of spreading intense fear among the survivors. They identified towns within the kingdom that were known to harbour a Huguenot majority – towns that faced a bleak future with mass genocide becoming a widespread occurrence in the name of religion.

Catherine, her maidservant Mathilde and two guards clambered onto a waiting carriage and were on the road to Chenonceau almost before the savage business in the Great Hall had concluded. Her sister Marguerite, and new husband Henry, followed behind. Even within the sanctuary that was the chateau, the Queen Mother remained vigilant and, as was her nature, trusted nobody except Mathilde. She instructed Marguerite and Henry to remain in their private quarters until the initial commotion in Paris had subsided and it was safe for her sister but, and more urgent, the Protestant Henry to emerge in public.

After dinner, Catherine sat alone in her chamber, reading her bible, a book bound in fine calfskin embossed with gold leaf, when she was interrupted by a gentle tap at the door.

"Enter – ah, Mathilde, what news?" Catherine relied on her maidservant's web of informants in Chenonceau and beyond to notify her of the latest gossip and, this day, of any trustworthy reports. The girl approached her mistress.

"Everything has gone according to plan, my Lady. Even as we were leaving the Great Hall, yesterday, our men in the taverns and women at market were spreading the word, as they were told, of how you ushered as many guests as possible out of the hall to safety, at great personal risk. You are, by now, a heroine in the people's eyes and, for the moment, your name will not be associated with the murders."

"Excellent! Wonderful!" Catherine clapped her hands

with childish glee, "those peasants will believe anything, especially when they are afraid."

"I could not comment, ma'am. I merely carry out your wishes. Now, may I take down your hair? It's past the compline bell and you need your sleep."

Catherine nodded and moved over to sit at the dressing table with its mahogany frame mirror and pots and bottles of scented waters and fragrant powders. Mathilde took out the pins for the auburn sheeny hair to fall in long tresses over her mistress's shoulders that she proceeded to lovingly brush, humming a tune as she did so. Catherine and Mathilde were content and with the task finished the latter bowed and made for the door.

"Goodnight, my Lady."

"Goodnight, Mathilde, and thank you."

The troubled Queen Mother undressed and put on her white linen nightgown.

'How is it going, Guise?' Have I just asked him that question when he's not here, fool that I am? Perk up, Catherine, it's no time for weakness, you must remain strong!'

She went to a cabinet, took out a green glass bottle and filled a pewter goblet to the brim with a brown syrupy liquid. Some while ago she had mentioned to her personal astrologer, Côme Ruggieri, that she found sleeping difficult. The soothsayer, ever one for an easy profit, told her, tugging at his grey beard as if deep in thought,

'The problem arises, ma'am, when the planets are out of alignment, this I have seen on many occasions. Of course, we can do nothing to influence their situation but, on my next

visit, I will bring for you a remedy to assist sleep, the efficacy of which I vouch personally.'

'That will be agreeable, Ruggieri.' She came out of her daydream, sat on the edge of the bed and raised the goblet to her lips. She was no newcomer to strange potions and beverages and, unbeknown even to Mathilde, her cabinet housed an abundance of toxins for her personal consumption and not, as legend may have portrayed her by her Italian origins, as a schemer in the art of poison. The very idea amused her and she again mused,

'What did the soothsayer advise me...to take only one or two sips...sips be damned! Oblivious to his directions she swallowed gulp after gulp until the goblet was empty.

The drink consisted of a blend of laudanum, a herbal mixture infused dried azurescens mushrooms, a conical fungus, the most powerful natural substance of the age. Within moments, a mighty disequilibrium overwhelmed her and she swooned back on the bed, transported to a vantage point high above Diane de Poitier's bedchamber. With bated breath she was spying through peep holes she had bored into the roof and, surely enough, her husband lay with his mistress.

'Henry!' she called, under the influence of the sleeping remedy, 'You perform better with her than the disinterest and ridicule you show to me! And, hark, what does she tell him? She tells you, Henry, that you should spend more time with your wife, that you have a duty to produce heirs! How she controls you and what a slave you are to her!'

. . .

Catherine regained peace but only until her body shook uncontrollably as she was carried away to Henry's demise, thirteen years ago. The infernal liqueur! Ruggieri could not have foreseen its consequence,

'At least you prove yourself to be a real man in the joust! Yet you have the nerve to sport Diane's black and white colours, curse the woman! This day you account well for your name, husband and...and you see off the dukes of Guise and Nemours, but you luck runs out with young Gabriel, Count of Montgomery, when he knocks you half out of the saddle. Why do you insist on riding against him again? Stay down! Surrender and survive! But you don't, you display a bravery I never knew in you...bravery or madness? I watch your every move and, believe me, I do not wish it to end thus: Montgomery's lance shatters in your face and you reel out of the clash, pouring blood, splinters sticking out of your eye and head. They carry you to the chateau of Tournerelles where the doctors remove five fragments but one has pierced your brain. Nonetheless, I stay by your side and you prevail a further ten days until your speech, sight and reason have ceased to exist.

My dear Henry, you cannot know that, from that day on, I took a broken lance as my emblem with the words "Lacrymae hinc, hinc dolor" (From this come my tears and my pain) and I wore black to mourn your memory. Poor Henry!'

Her hallucinations and frenzied outbursts continued into the night, such was the strength of the laudanum mixture. Her final rant, before she was subdued by sleep, was a tirade directed at Diane, the despised mistress, who, in her delirium, she saw enter her chamber and stand at the foot of her bed.

'*You are come late, Diane, my dear! Henry has passed away and I was obliged to refuse his requests to see you for a final time. What! Do you say nothing?*'

After the king's death Catherine gained satisfaction from banishing Poitiers and her friends from Paris and ordering the surrender of her crown jewels. The chateau of Chenonceau was formally endowed in the Queen Mother's name.

She woke the next day only when Mathilde knocked furiously on the door of her chamber. The maidservant observed the dishevelled bed sheets and anguish in her Lady's eyes and, softly, asked,

"What ails you, ma'am?"

"Do we realise what we've done, Mathilde?"

"Too late to turn back," came the sombre reply.

"You are right."

Catherine de Médicis, guilt-consumed by the atrocities that had begun in Paris, wrestled with her conscience: dark days and even darker nights haunted the Italian woman.

6

"Lanval! Lanval! Are you out of bed? Your father will be waiting on you!" His mother called upstairs.

"I'm coming" the boy answered, rubbing sleep from his eyes. He got out of bed, splashed water from the bowl on the dresser onto his face and pulled on his tunic and boots.

"Good morning, mother."

"And if you'd have stayed up there much longer it will be the afternoon!"

Lanval sat down at the table, broke off a hunk of rye bread and filled his beaker with milk.

"You were late coming home last night, weren't you?"

"Was I? I lost track of time, it was such a beautiful evening. We walked and talked – there's one place on the walls above the port where we watch the ocean stretching for miles, it's just wonderful –

"You're a real dreamer, Lanval."

"What's wrong with that? We –

'We?' Mother interrupted, "Ah, you mean Cicile?"

"Of course, it was Cicile."

The woman pursed her lips and hesitated before continuing,

"She's a good girl, and from a respectable family. It's a pity she's –

She paused.

"She's what, mother?" Lanval asked, although he knew what she was thinking. She carried on, but in a measured tone,

"I've known the girl's mother since we were children, we used to play together. The father, the others of the household...all decent folk, but they worship in the Protestant Temple...not like us."

Her son had often heard her make such statements and he chose to not pass comment as he knew he would react in defence of his beloved girl and that, invariably, led to family arguments. He had associated with Cicile for several years, he was a non-sectarian man – her faith in no way coloured his feelings for her, why should it? From his experience, she thought similarly. He believed with passionate sincerity that Church dogma did not change a person. Unlike his parents – both God-fearing regular worshippers at the only Catholic church in the town – he had little time for religion, seeing it as divisive and irrelevant to his life.

"Anyway, eat your breakfast. Father went out at dawn, says it's a good time to call in some outstanding debts, he'll meet you at the quay."

"That's good, he must have some carting to do today. The weather's set fine...I'll do the job then maybe have the afternoon free to see Cicile."

"You certainly see a lot of her, every spare minute, it seems."

Lanval looked up,

"Is it the case that you're too old to remember the days when you and father were courting?"

"Don't be so cheeky!" she responded, giving him a gentle clip round the ear followed by an affectionate ruffling of his curly blond locks. She went over to the range at the far side of the room and stirred a vegetable broth simmering in a cast iron pot.

"Smells good", Lanval complimented her.

"Tonight's supper – that is, if you can tear yourself away from Cicile! Do you know, I think it's high time you settled down and, if she's your choice, so be it."

"Marriage? Don't know about that and, in any case, we're quite happy the way things are."

Mother said nothing, biting her lip to hide her reservations for her offspring's liaison with a Huguenot girl. He finished eating, rose from the table, and gave her a peck on the cheek before leaving the house to meet father.

They lived on Rue de la Glacière that, with Rue des Voiliers and Rue Amos Barbot, housed almost the entire Catholic population of La Rochelle – a close-knit peaceful community. Back in the day, as a young man, father came to the town in search of work that paid better than toiling away on the land. He moved from one job to another, met the woman he married, and with a baby on the way realised that he had to find a source of income to provide house and home for his two dependents, the single room his in-laws had kindly let them live in now being inadequate for their family needs. To his wife's modest dowry he put his own savings and they were able to purchase their simple dwelling.

. . .

Lanval's father was a jocular sturdy man, well-liked by both neighbours and customers. His ruddy complexion seemed to his son to be redder than usual of late but he had not noticed the puffiness others had commented on. His son recalled him explaining how he had established himself.

'I was ambitious, if you will, and never afraid of wanting to better myself, my boy, never. The Good Lord recognises honest endeavour, remember that.'

'I will, father. So, tell me how it was for you,'

They were sitting on a stone bench at the quayside where stevedores loaded and unloaded the barges and boats.

'I had an idea. When someone wanted to take a piece of furniture, for example, from one place to another, they put it on a barrow and, pushing it along the street, the item was likely to fall off and be ruined. It was the same moving a coffin from the deceased's house to the church. Just imagine the distress for the mourners following on behind if it fell off – a barrow was not the best solution!

Then, here at the quayside, piles of goods had to be shifted to warehouses and customers in the town but there didn't seem to be anyone either reliable or trustworthy enough to employ for the job. Pilfering is a real problem – not everybody's an honest soul.'

'But tell me what your idea was.'

'I'm coming to it, be patient.' he smiled, pleased his son was taking an interest in their family story. He continued after a pause,

'I saw there was a demand for a decent carter, a dependable carrier of goods, so I found our little stable,' he pointed to the far end of the quay, *'bought a working horse*

and the side-boarded cart that we have to this day. Mind you, we're now on our third horse. I don't hold with driving them when they're old nags...it's not kind on the animal, is it?'

"It's not.' Lanval answered, enthralled by his father's account.

'Over time, I earned a reputation and built up trade. There's half a dozen boats that I regularly shift their cargoes from the quayside to their warehouses or wherever else they want them delivered to. People in the town know I'm at their service, be they Catholic or Protestant. Well, that's the story of AUBERT FILS (Aubert and Son). When you started work with me I was proud to have the names painted on the side of the cart,'

Aubert senior achieved the status of a middle-class tradesperson and he provided well for his wife and son. It is fair to call him a decent man – not bigoted or dogmatic, he prided himself in listening to the other man's point of view. In the family's Saint Sauveur church he was a sidesman, assisting the priest with the Eucharist and seeing to the collection from the congregation.

Lanval stepped from the gloomy house and blinked, adjusting his eyes to the bright daylight outside. Walking to the end of their street he turned in the direction of the *centre ville*. At this time of day La Rochelle had scarcely woken and, for the first ten minutes, he encountered only the odd stray cat or dog, the silence broken by an occasional cockerel crowing in a back yard.

'It's a beautiful morning. I'm truly blessed to have such kind parents and live in a house like ours.'

As he approached the imposing Hôtel de Ville the atmosphere livened: voices rose and noises ahead heralded the Arcades on Rue Mercier and Rue du Palais. The streets were lined with stone arches. Their construction, two centuries earlier, was with a view to providing merchants with shelter for their stalls from the frequent prevailing rain coming off the sea whilst still displaying their goods for sale. The arches also served as solid foundations for the residences above that afforded the area an appealing character: heavy brown timbers, fitted and secured by large wooden pegs; the infill of wattle and daub, brick, stones, or a mixture of clay and chalk, covered with a decorated layer of plaster painted with an attractive white distemper.

Already, barrow boys pushed their trolleys along the streets paved with stone slabs, clinking and clanking, collecting vegetables, meat, candles, fabric, pots and pans, all manner of merchandise, to take to customers around the town.

These customers were, as yet, absent, but the stallholders still shouted at one another as if rehearsing their sales pitch for later in the day. Talking at a normal level was replaced by an ingrained predisposition for yelling and yawping.

One of the first arches housed a wooden trestle table laid out with blocks and packets of salt. The proprietor, a fat balding man in a crisp white apron, cut slices of salt with a saw from a bigger block. He boasted he was the 'salt sculptor of La Rochelle', to the amusement of the shoppers who passed in front of his arch to watch his craft.

Lanval was reminded of his father telling him about his years as a young man,

'You didn't know I was once a saunier, a salt farmer, did you?'

'I certainly did not', Lanval answered, an expression of surprise on his face.

'To speak truthfully, I was a worker there, over on the Ile de Ré, when I was maybe eighteen or nineteen. It's a strange place, cut off from our town and only possible to reach over a causeway at low tide. It was hard work, for sure, not that I'm against that – I'll put in an honest day for honest pay. The real sauniers raked the salt off the beds where it formed into piles. My job was to fill sacks with the stuff then tie them to pack mules for another man to lead off to the warehouses. Those poor beasts! Out all day in the sun, not properly fed, mangy and bitten by mosquitoes and midges. Couldn't do anything about that though. Now...what was I saying...ah, yes, I worked there at their salt harvest time, June to September, unless storms flooded the beds and ruined a lot of their white stuff. I hated the other workers, at least the foreign ones...' Father paused as if reliving what was evidently a difficult time for him. 'I didn't know where they came from but they were dark, nearly black-skinned and they fought and cussed in a language I didn't understand. They lived on the island with their black harlots – easy women and. I'll wager. they'd never seen the inside of a Christian church! I couldn't put up with them. I've got standards in my life that I keep to, with the help of the Good Lord above.

'I see what you're saying, father. So, you left that work?'

"Ay, I did just one season with them then came back to our town and founded my carting business. Remember, my young man, you must live by your beliefs and principles: the Bible can teach you all you need to know.'

'I'll do my best.' Lanval both admired and respected this man and sincerely hoped he could lead a similarly exemplary existence.

.   .   .

The salt seller bade him good morning to end his reminiscing.

"And you too.' The two men smiled.

"You're up and about early today."

"I have to meet father at the port, there will be deliveries to make."

"Of course, give my regards to the dear man."

"I will, indeed. Good day to you."

With that he continued down the street, nodding at some of the Arcade traders, stopping to speak to others.

As the morning unfolded and the sun rose in the sky, some citizens of La Rochelle were already around, clearly in the hope of securing a bargain. Brown-painted shutters of the dwellings above the arches opened to let in fresh air; women leaned over the window ledges, exchanging banter, laughter or arguments with their neighbours in the adjacent houses or calling to acquaintances in the street below.

The primary characteristic of La Rochelle was its isolation. Situated on the Bay of Biscay to the west, the town was all but cut off from the interior by marshlands to the east. Yet, this very seclusion allowed it to be one of France's most prosperous places: it blossomed into prominence with the expansion of the export of wine and salt – a salt yielded in abundance by the encircling marshes. Seigneurial rivalries and ambitions meant that it enjoyed an unusual degree of municipal autonomy: it rarely paid any royal taxes, to the annoyance of the elite in Paris, notably the Queen Mother, Catherine de Médicis, whose quest for prestige and influence extended to La Rochelle and the region. She resented the Crown's lawful claim to the kingdom being usurped by a Protestant minority.

The economic life of the commune was regulated by its overwhelmingly Huguenot council headed by its mayor, hand in glove with the feared and detested Judge Boivin. The most dynamic elements of the population consisted of merchants, shopkeepers and artisans. Royal authority was nominally represented by a body of legal officers who, in theory, chose the mayor: in reality, the mayor selected his own successor when he was good and ready. The first consideration was that the holder of this esteemed position showed himself to be a devout Protestant. His right-hand man was the judge who ruled on disputes in the law and dispensed justice in his courtroom. Most folk could not remember when Monsieur le Maire and Judge Boivin had not governed their lives. Lanval's father, conversing with his family one evening after supper, drily remarked,

'We'll have two different scoundrels in office as soon as hell freezes over, not a moment before!'

Leaving the Arcades his son headed towards Saint Sauveur church – the only place for Catholic worship. It was his habit to call in to pray, for a brief moment, before his day's work. Inside, he found himself alone. He dipped two fingers into the holy water of the stone font by the door, crossed himself, and sat on a rear pew, bowing his head in silent prayer. A few moments later, soft voices disturbed his contemplation. He looked up to see two priests dressed in long black buttoned cassocks walking side by side down the nave from the altar. They stopped when they reached him,

"Good morning, Lanval," the elder of the two, Evrart, spoke in a gentle benevolent tone.

"Good morning Father Evrart and Father Servet."

Both priests bowed their heads respectfully in unison. Evrart smiled with the expression of a friend.

"The Lord bless you, my son."

"Accept my thanks, father."

The two men of the cloth shared the clerical responsibilities for Saint Sauveur church. Despite the existence of a number of monastic houses, La Rochelle boasted only five parish churches and, until the Huguenot revival, the ecclesiastical hierarchy was weak compared with that of many towns in the kingdom. This weakness helps explain the receptiveness of the Rochelais to the Reformed, Calvanist, Protestant movement – they adopted different names but were, essentially, of the same belief. Clerics, artisans, merchants and royal or municipal officers all adhered to the doctrine and, by Lanval's time, the district was fairly attached to the Huguenot cause – to the growing segregation of the Catholics, providing a virtually impregnable retreat for Reformed Church grandees in times of difficulty.

"Are you on your way to work?" Servet asked.

"I am, there's no rest for the wicked." Lanval joked. The two priests exchanged glances, raised their eyebrows, and left the church.

They're good men for sure, fine Catholic defenders of our faith,' the young man pondered.

Outside, Lanval passed along two short streets to a gate in the town wall. Although huge strong wooden doors hung either side of this gate, they remained always open, there was no need for them to close, no need for defence, no invaders to repel. The Valin quay where they had the Aubert stable ran the length of the shallow basin running off the main port. There, flat-bottomed barges moored to have their goods onloaded. A lad was mucking out the stable as Lanval passed.

"How's the old nag today?" he enquired.

The lad stopped raking.

"Monsieur Aubert...good morning to you...he's fine. He neighed and shook his head even before you arrived – horses are clever, you see. If I had to choose between a man and a horse, the horse would win every time even if the beast don't pay your wages."

"That's true – I *do*! So, get on with your work!"

With a chuckle he obeyed his master.

Lanval found his father emerging from the hold of a barge tied up at the far end of the basin. He climbed a short ladder and stood on the quayside, breathless but with a wide smile on his ruddy face. He was pleased to see his son and there was another reason to be satisfied.

"Ah, here you are, my boy." He held up a pouch closed with a string. "See this? It's been overdue but I've been carrying wares for this captain for years and I know he's a man of his word. I mean...we each prosper by the honesty of the next man. In short, he's paid me what he owes, so we'll have food on the table again!"

Lanval's jaw dropped until he saw the mischievous twinkle in his father's eyes: he was a man who always tried to recognise the humorous side of situations, no matter how serious. He gave a guffaw, put an arm around his son's shoulder, and walked them back to the stable.

. . .

"Get the horse hitched to the cart," he instructed, "There's a boat arriving soon that's sailed from Bordeaux with crates of wine. We have to take them to the wine merchant up by the cathedral – ten or so crates, I think, so it will mean two journeys."

Lanval enjoyed working alongside his father. In fact, he considered it an honour to be the son in 'Aubert Fils'.

A few weeks later, he was eating breakfast at home, anticipating a busy day ahead.

"Is father not yet out of bed?" he asked.

"No. He's not feeling too well this morning. He says a day's rest will see the fever subside. There's barrels of ale to be taken to certain taverns and you'll know which ones."

"Yes, I do. I'll be off then, I think I can manage without him," he joked.

He finished the deliveries by noon and returned home for lunch. He entered the house to find mother sitting at the table sobbing uncontrollably. Father Evrart stood behind her, a bible held open. He was reading verses in a soft voice, head lowered.

"What on earth's happened? Mother, what is it?"

She looked up, eyes red from crying, and blurted,

"I took him a bowl of broth and there he was, quite still and peaceful in his bed. He didn't respond to me, he didn't breathe. I could see that he was dead.

She broke down, wailing, crying, trembling. Father

Evrart placed a hand on her shoulder. Closing his Bible he pronounced a prayer,

'Eternal rest grant to him, O Lord, and let light perpetual shine upon him. May his soul, and all souls of all the faithful departed, through the mercy of God, rest in peace. Amen.'

"Amen," Lanval and his mother repeated automatically. His position in the family business, through this completely unexpected sad event, would change for ever.

7

THE SUN HAD BARELY RISEN ABOVE THE PORT AND houses of La Rochelle and with daybreak there came a sharp cold rain even though it was still the month of August. The townsfolk were accustomed to the vagaries of their coastal weather, they sometimes lived with summer warmth in winter and icy mists when it should have been oppressively hot. Today was such a contrary clime: closed shutters rattled with the wind; the gutters down the middle of the streets overflowed with torrential rainfall. Lanval and his mother felt relieved that the third and final day of wake for Monsieur Aubert had arrived. A candle in the window of their house, the sign of a death within, flickered and petered out – their vigil was at an end. It was the custom of the town for one to view and pay last respects to their friend in the house: Madame Aubert and her son had sat, in turn, beside the open wooden coffin resting on the table to welcome any person who called, and there were many.

"My condolences, madame."

"He was a good man."

"We will miss him."

One visitor after the next spoke in soft reverential tones. The man, well respected in the town and his church, had been washed, according to tradition, by his wife and dressed in his best tunic. He lay at peace with the world. At midday four men of the parish entered.

"It's time, madame."

She nodded a forlorn glance towards them and stepped aside while they nailed down the casket's lid. Then they took a corner each and carried it out of the house.

The weather had much improved, the rain had ceased and sunlight bathed the funeral cortege.

Lanval stood by the horse's head, holding it still by its bridle and the animal snorted as if it knew it would be hauling the cart and his master to his resting place. Its coat and mane were brushed to a silky sheen, his long tail swished and one might have thought it was enjoying the occasion – it was not, even the animal felt the sadness of the day.

The bearers slid the coffin carefully onto the cart and raised the rear board to ensure its safe journey. A line of friends and business acquaintances – there were no more Aubert family members left apart from his wife and son – waited solemnly behind, extending down the street. The lettering 'AUBERT FILS' on the side of the cart proudly proclaimed the father and son partnership, and Lanval had made a decision that the sign would remain unaltered in deference to the man. Evrart, the parish priest, moved alongside Lanval and satisfying himself that Madame Aubert was in place behind the cart, leading the long procession of mourners, nodded that they should set off down Rue de la Glacière.

As they slowly made their way south through the town, the usual activity and clamour of the streets ceased: folk – whether the Catholics of Aubert's district or the Huguenots further on – remained quite still in honour of the carter's memory. Following custom, the children threw flowers down ahead of the horse. Religious differences, for the moment, meant nothing to the Rochelais young.

Some twenty minutes later the Saint Sauveur church was reached. Madame Aubert stared up at the imposing Gothic edifice and, like so many others before her, felt small and insignificant under its skilfully wrought façade. Its familiarity – for the great rose window, like an eye, gazed over the shallow basin in whose quay the Aubert Fils stable was situated – could not in any way diminish the sensation. Despite her sorrow, the poor woman found a moment to reflect on the blessed reconstruction, as seen in the pristine stonework after the terrible fire of 1419 which had destroyed much of the old church. The bishop had sent for the Clerk of the Works who oversaw the building and given his instructions:

'You will ensure that any man or his kinsfolk employed in the restoration is of our Protestant faith. We receive few enough favours these days, so we must look after our own. Is that understood?'

'It is, bishop, completely.'

Feelings of hatred between the two beliefs in La Rochelle had been growing over decades – history devolves at a snail's pace – and no single event marked its beginning.

In 1546, two young Protestant men, were tried and burned at the stake, deemed heretics by a trumped-up Catholic court. After their death, they achieved the status of virtual martyrs, Defenders of the Protestant§ Faith: to this day, they were referred to simply as Les Jean-Pierre brothers. Such occurrences fuelled the acrimony above others.

The stable boy was waiting outside the church. He took hold of the horse's bridle so Lanval could follow the coffin inside, supporting his mother by the arm, for it to take pride of place on a wooden trestle, his feet facing the grand altar, as was the ritual. He gently ushered her to sit on the front pew, he by her side. It was not necessary to turn towards the congregation to appreciate the charged atmosphere of their spiritual home, the only place of worship granted by the Huguenot-dominated town council. It was widely held that the Curia of Rome, representing a despised Pontiff, should have been grateful they were permitted even Saint Sauveur.

Father Servet, resplendent in his elegant long black cassock, a heavy cross on a chain around his neck, moved from corner to corner sprinkling holy water onto the casket while a deacon recited a funeral chant. Increasing the drama of the occasion, a second deacon swung a pierced brass thurible from a cord, the incense burning within exuding a powerful aroma that drifted around and upwards. The men in the gathered mourners trembled, the women wept softly: old Aubert was, indeed, a man who exerted authority in death as in life, and even those who did not know him personally, knew of him.

Evrart, the senior cleric, appeared from behind the altar, phantom-like from the shadows, his crisp white cassock trailing on the floor, silent, formidable, approaching Madame Aubert and placing one hand on her shoulder, the other held out for her to kiss his signet ring. His mumbled blessing was scarcely audible amid the weeping, sighing, moaning.

"The Lord bless you."

"Thank you, father," the distraught woman replied.

Giving her a doleful smile, he turned his back and knelt on an embroidered tuffet in front of the altar. This immense white marble slab dominated the semi-circular apse at the east end of the nave. In church, ordinary citizens, unfamiliar with pomp and ceremony in their daily lives, gazed at the leather-bound bible guarding a triptych, its three hinged painted panels depicting God the Father, Christ and his angels. To either side, they observed two tall ceremonial candles that flickered, casting a half-light onto the artist's sacramental creation.

The priest rose and faced the people. He crossed himself with deliberate solemn movements, removed a small bible from his cassock pocket and began with an ancient prayer, at first in a tone so low that the congregation strained to catch his words.

'I am the Resurrection and the Life...'

He paused to resume, this time in a booming accusatory voice.

'Grant this mercy, O Lord, we beseech Thee, to Thy

servant departed, that we may not receive in punishment the requital of his deeds who in desire, did keep Thy will and as the true faith here united him to the company of the faithful...Amen.'

'Amen' they all repeated.

He opened his bible and started to recite some verse or other, but in Latin, the language of the Scriptures, according to Catholic doctrine, and Lanval's attention drifted, his gaze rising to the ceiling of the church. Although he had attended many services here, he had never before noticed the sheer beauty above him. Six sections from one end to the other, each rib vaulted to a centre boss carved with barely visible religious symbols – maybe the Lord's face or an angel, he couldn't make them out. The panels between the ribs bore vibrant paintings of Biblical scenes, their significance all the more powerful by virtue of their overhead position, as if they were set in Heaven itself.

Running the length of the nave on either side, from north to south, mullioned tracery windows framed stained glass designs letting in glistening light, all colours of the prism. Below the windows, immense piers supported the low roofs over the side aisles: wonders of the imagination.

Lanval pondered,

'I hadn't appreciated such beauty around us...who thought of it all...must have been clever folk, that's for sure...'

The architects, master stonemasons and wood carvers were indeed clever, as Lanval put it: they had visited or knew of the grand cathedrals of the time – Reims, Rouen, Bordeaux, Notre Dame de Paris, and the rest, and incorporated features of these monumental delights into the humble, but no less impressive, creation that was Saint Sauveur. Father Evrart's stentorian prayer snapped him out of his daydream.

'...to the company of the faithful, so may Thy mercy unite him above to the choir of angels, through Jesus Christ our Lord. Amen,'

"Amen."

The cleric closed his bible and placed it on the dead man's coffin. Climbing the wooden steps with ornate iron railings, he drew himself to his full height in the suspended pulpit, carved with intricate detail, and looked out over the congregation who, as one, turned their heads and stared up at their priest. It was no coincidence that the pulpit, the most important place in the church for the delivery of sermons, afforded the cleric a position of dominance, raised above his flock. These faithful innocent souls believed their priests were divine beings who had the power to turn bread and wine into the body and the blood of Jesus, whereas *they* were sinful and their sins could be forgiven only by praying or paying money to the Church which they did whenever they attended.

Evrart cleared his throat, crossing himself and fixing his gaze on the deceased's wife. His eulogy began.

"We are gathered today in our church of Saint Sauveur to pay our final respects and commend the spirit of brother Waleran Aubert to the Lord God above. *'Requiescat in pace'* (May he rest in peace – Lanval habitually translated into the vernacular, a tiring compulsion). This, and all the other prayers and incantations, followed Pope Sixtus V's precise instruction to priests. The people nodded as if they understood Latin invocations believed to have magic powers – they did not, but their conviction and immovable confidence in their clerics guaranteed their lay acquiescence. Evrart resumed.

"I came across dear Waleran when he was establishing his business as a carter and I was a young postulant. He was newly married with a baby imminent and his desire to prosper in order to care for his family was evident to me, just as was his devotion to his second family, the Church. *'Et lux perpetua luceat ei,'* (Let perpetual light shine upon him).

"Amen."

"He would say to me that..."

Once more, Lanval's concentration wavered, too many thoughts raced through his head to take in Evrart's tribute. For the first time since had had entered the church, he turned around and observed the crowded pews. Every head faced the pulpit, eyes and ears straining to see and hear their priest. The mourning son recognised, from among all the other countenances, one in the darkest recesses, one he had not expected to see in this the home of Catholicism in La Rochelle. Even in the shadows of his corner the man was unmistakable, wearing his usual floppy purple hat: Judge Boivin, the justice, principal councillor of the town and most fervent upholder of all that the Huguenots stood for. Above the nodding heads, Boivin reciprocated his gaze. All noises of the service – Evrart's eulogy, people shuffling, coughing, whispering – for him ceased in an instance: all Lanval could identify was Judge Boivin, present for his father's funeral, in a place that he had no right to infiltrate. He knew little of any real consequence about the judge, rarely was there reason to cross paths with him but, now, a maelstrom of vignettes flashed before him – events and places involving Boivin that he felt he, Lanval, knew about, but the recollections were vague, clouded no doubt by the emotion of this solemn occasion. He realised everything to do with Boivin would have happened when he had been with his father, or what father had related to him. In retrospect he saw the name of Boivin had been mentioned numerous times.

'What was it that father said...ah, yes, he held that folk shouldn't fear the sentence Boivin might hand out as much as the spell he might cast...something about the dark arts...'

The justice lived alone in a three-storey half-timbered house on Rue Saint Léonard, appropriately, next to the Palais de Justice, an austere meeting hall that housed the town's council, when his court was not in session. He occupied the first and second floors of this house, renting out the ground floor to an old seamstress.

Boivin was in his late fifties, a short squat corpulent figure who sweated profusely at the least exertion. Strange manic eyes, broken yellow teeth and unshaven, his general appearance did not enamour the beholder. It was difficult to determine the colour of his hair – or even if he was bald – as he was never seen without his clown-like purple hat, an item of clothing, above the others that, in his mind, combined the calm stability of blue and the fierce energy of red. He regarded purple as associated with royalty, power, spirituality and grandeur. As with the hat, you rarely saw him not dressed in a black threadbare gown, the sort academics wore to indicate their intellectual capacity: Boivin's scholastic level was severely limited but compensated by a native guile and opportunism. He walked with a pronounced limp, widely proclaiming it was a battle wound sustained when fighting with the army of Jeanne, Queen of Navarre, against the Catholic rebels. She fled to

La Rochelle and became the *de facto* leader of the Huguenots, controlled the town and conferred the title of Justice upon him in recognition of his bravery and dedication to her cause – or that's the myth he broadcast.

'Beati mortui qui in Domino moriuntur amodo' (Blessed are those who have died in the Lord), Evrart boomed out, restoring Lanval's attention and linguistic prowess.

"Amen."

Lanval glanced momentarily at the priest, only for Boivin to once again dominate his thoughts. *'Why is he here?'* He asked himself the question, and it swiftly escalating from curiosity to an impassioned desire to find the answer.

'Pater noster, qui es in caelis, sanctificetur nomen tui. Adventiat regnum tuum...' (Our Father, who art in Heaven, hallowed be Thy name. Thy kingdom come...)

The congregation all repeated the Lord's Prayer, the only one in Latin thy knew how to pronounce correctly, led by Evrart from the pulpit. He closed the bible on his lectern, climbed slowly down the stairs and positioned himself between the coffin and altar to offer the concluding petition.

'Lord our God, you are the source of life and move and have our being. Keep us in life and death in your love. and by your grace lead us to your kingdom, through your son, Jesus Christ, Our Lord. Amen. *Mors certa, hora incerta'* (Death is certain, its hour is uncertain)

. . .

Father Evrart spoke true. They know not when death will take them. In the year 1562, more than sixty innocent unarmed Huguenots celebrating the Eucharist in their little church of Wassy – men, women, children – all slaughtered at the whim of the Catholic Duc de Guise who took exception to a few stones thrown at his soldiers! Not content with bloody vengeance, he fired the church and, laughing, watched it burn to the ground. You speak true, their hour of death was not predicted.

Throughout the sixteenth century, there were peaks and troughs in sectarian clashes in both their severity and location within the kingdom. But antagonism, prejudice, and gratuitous hatred seethed and fomented not far below the surface of what passed as a peaceful existence, for it to raise its dragon's head and snap at anyone in its path.

The priest gestured to the four pall bearers who approached the coffin, lifting it gently off the trestles and carrying it on their shoulders past the high altar, he in front, to the doorway in the apse and outside to the church's cemetery. Madame Aubert had requested a private burial attended only by Evrart, herself and her son. As was the custom, the congregation waited patiently in their places for the family to return into the church and proceed down the aisle whence they duly followed on, heads bowed.

Outside, the streets glistened as the August sunshine dried off the earlier rainstorm. Two lady church friends supported Madame Aubert, assisting her to the privacy and silence of her home. Lanval remained on the steps of the church, accepting the stream of sympathetic parishioners expressing their condolences, warmly shaking his hand. At last, his duty discharged, he marched off in an assured proud manner and he quickened as he spotted, some way ahead, a familiar figure: Judge Boivin. The justice's presence had provided him with more questions than answers and shortly he caught up with the object of his confusion and tapped him on the shoulder.

Boivin turned to face Lanval, initially surprised but, quickly, with an expression of feigned sincerity ensued as he held out his hand that the young man, reluctantly, shook.

"Lanval, my friend, may I offer my deepest commiserations on this, the most sorrowful of days. Your father and I grew up together, as you know. He was a kind wise man whose counsel I have sought on many an occasion –

"Really?" Lanval cut in, sensing the justice's statement to be less than honest - more than that, he knew it to be a lie, and coming from this man who was upholder of the laws of the town – but he breathed in deeply and gathered himself.

'Who is this creature? The many casual comments father made about him, over the years, now start to paint a picture of a man who, at best, is not to be trusted!' He needed to unpick this enigma.

"I was...surprised to see you in church. Our faith is not yours so it is...unusual –

"My friend –

'He has no right to call me his friend!'

" – I attended through my lifelong relationship with your father and in my capacity as Judge. It's incumbent on me to keep my honed legal eye on everything that happens in our town. People who transgress and appear before my court say I'm like a kestrel hovering above its prey, waiting to swoop," he chuckled. "Let's say that in these times I maintain an interest in what our Catholic brothers are about."

Lanval said nothing in reply but met the judge's steely gaze, refusing to be cowed by the other man's veiled language and reputation.

'There's a falsehood in Boivin and I feel threatened but is this rational or is my assessment clouded by emotional turmoil? No! Father had been warning me all along, in his good-natured way, to beware Boivin the Justice. What did he say...that as well as pronouncing sentences in court he cast spells in private? Did he exert influence over father's business? I know he struggled to obtain trade when he was starting up and, even from his grave, he speaks to me: I resolve to reveal Boivin for the charlatan I suspect him to be.'

"Good day, judge." The two men went on their separate ways. Lanval would respect his father's memory, now in the bosom of Saint Sauveur church; Boivin would ponder his next move in the comfort of his home, relishing the fact that there was currently one less heathen Catholic to despise in his town.

8

LA ROCHELLE, AUGUST 1571

Lanval came down to breakfast to find his mother in her old rocking chair in a corner, a chair that had been handed down through the women of her family and had seen many a babe suckled and rocked to sleep. She started, looking up from a tapestry she was embroidering, surprised to see her son out of bed at such an early hour.

"Good morning, Lanval, could you not sleep?"

It was only a few days since her husband had passed away, but her sense of humour had not deserted her - on the contrary, it assisted her in coping with her grief. Lanval went over and gently kissed her head.

"What do you mean, it's dawn, isn't it?" He gazed at the work spread out over her lap, "That's beautiful, mother, who is it for?"

She was known and admired throughout the town as an accomplished embroideress and, as well as for pleasure, she took on commissions for wealthy patrons who paid well for wall hangings they displayed in their houses to impress their friends. Her late husband placed her under no compulsion to toil over these creations – she devoted endless hours to them – his income kept them well, but she gained satisfaction and pride contributing to the household. She answered,

"Monsieur Allard, the physician. He described a forest scene to me that he wants me to depict, stags, pheasants, and the like." Smoothing out the panel she was working on she pursed her lips, deliberating, then, after a pause, she concluded,

"Even if I say so myself, it's coming along nicely."

"I wouldn't argue with that, mother, I just hope you've asked for a decent amount – your work is so wonderful."

"The figure was mutually agreed but, as you know, I don't do it for the money."

Lanval smiled. He had inherited her qualities: resilience, honesty and an affinity with hard work. Mother resumed her embroidery while he ate breakfast. Neither spoke, it was a time for them to reflect on life without Waleran Aubert.

Breakfast eaten, he rose from the table.

"I'll be off. I have to collect the cross for father's grave then there's a boat due in that wants its cargo of oil and herbs delivered around the town. It will keep me busy all morning then I'm meeting Cicile. It's a fine day so I think we'll take a walk. I'll be back for supper."

"Your father would be proud of you, Lanval, and give my regards to Cicile."

Mother mentioned her son's Huguenot girlfriend almost as an afterthought.

. . .

Outside, the early morning August sunshine warmed the still sleepy streets. A haunting mist hovered above the rooftops as the moisture from a dawn shower on the orange-brown pantiles dissipated. Silence reigned, with no one abroad, La Rochelle basking in its innocence and beauty. Lanval adored this time of day, alone with his thoughts. Shortly, he reached his church, Saint Sauveur, climbed the steps and entered through the main portal. The interior posed a complete contrast to the street he had left: cool, dark, still. He was the only person in that vast, enveloping, consuming House of God. It was his usual routine to spend a few moments in contemplation and prayer before starting his day's work, preferring to sit on the front pew, in front of the altar with its finely painted triptych, when he heard a noise behind him. He turned around and, in a moment, was transported back to his father's funeral service. He could see row upon row of dutiful mourners; he smelt the pungent incense; he felt the shuffling, whispering, sadness of the occasion. *'It's so real yet, of course, it's just my imagination... but wait! Over there in the obscure recess, hiding in the gloom, watching me...yes, it's Judge Boivin!'*

The figure slowly emerged from the shadows to reveal himself. As it approached, Lanval drew a sharp intake of breath – it was Father Servet, the junior priest of their parish. *'Don't be such a fool!'* Lanval thought. *'You'll be locked away in the asylum if you go around saying you possess ungodly powers to see people who aren't there!'*

"Good day, young man, are you on your way to the port?"
There came no immediate answer, Lanval's

concentration was focused elsewhere. Servet repeated his greeting, but louder, and the boy withdrew from his distraction,

"Good morning to you, Father."

Servet stared hard, seeing the discomfort in his expression,

"What ails you?" The priest asked, experienced in his position of confessor, used to accepting revelations from his flock.

"I thought you were...that I saw..."

"Yes? Do continue."

"Judge Boivin."

"Boivin? In my ministry, short as it may be, I'm sure I've attracted criticism and insults – that come with the job, if you will - but none like that! Has he told you that he *likes to keep his honed legal eye on everything that happens in our town?*"

"Why, they were his exact words after the funeral."

"That wretched man has a...a reputation, should I say."

"I'm not surprised that you speak of him in this manner. My father, on many occasions, inferred Boivin is not all he seems and I was, to put it mildly, shocked to see him attend at the church. After all, he's a Huguenot who would not, normally, enter our place of worship. What say you, Father? Is my concern justified?"

Servet clasped his hands together, disconcerted by the question. He could not, for reasons of propriety, give a candid answer.

"Judge Boivin is a man who wields great power, both as the justice and member of his own church. Yes, great power, and we should respect -"

"*Respect*, Father?"

"Yes, and more than this I cannot comment."

Why does he lie? His demeanour is insincere and there has to be a reason – what does he know but is not telling?

The priest resumed,

"Take my advice: do not cross swords with him. Now, please excuse me, I have a sermon to prepare."

"Of course, Father, thank you. I will now visit old Bruno for...for the cross." His voice trembled slightly as he pronounced the word.

Lanval said a final prayer, left the church through a side door and entered the compound that housed various workshops and stores – the wherewithal to reconstruct the church after the terrible fire. He exchanged polite pleasantries with the Clerk of the Works, already in his office poring over the ledger that itemised all materials and expenses for the project.

"Is the woodcarver in his shop?"

"Ay." replied the clerk, returning to his ledger.

"Good morning, Bruno."

"And to you, master Lanval."

The boy's gaze moved over the racks on the walls that held all manner of chisels – to cut, joint and curve – mallets, hand saws, marking gauges and calipers. A workbench ran the length of the shop where carvings in varying degrees of completion stood. On the other side were piles of planks of oak, elm, beech, sycamore and walnut, drying out and filling the air with a pungent scent that overwhelmed the senses.

"I can see you enjoy coming to my workshop. I remember you, as a youngster with your father. I'd put an offcut in the vice and let you saw it in two. You loved it but, excuse me, that's not why you're here."

"It's not, Bruno. Is it finished?"

"It is, indeed." He went over to the bench and lifted up a cross for Lanval to approve. Made of fine elm, it measured about one metre tall – a cemetery regulation, and skilfully carved in traditional blackletter, the inscription read:

Waleran Aubert: né 1492 - mort 1540
Requiesce in pace

"It's magnificent, you've done well. How much do I owe you?"

"Nothing. Accept it as my tribute to a decent man."

"This is most generous of you."

The woodcarver placed the cross on the bench, went over to the tools in their rack, and picked a heavy mallet.

"Take this and bring it back when you're done with it. The end of the cross is shaped to a point so it should go easily into the ground."

"My sincere thanks, Bruno."

He took the cross to the cemetery behind Saint Sauveur. The plot was at once identified by dark freshly-dug earth. Positioning it where the head was, he hit the cross hard with the mallet until it was firmly planted, then he stood back and bowed his head. A noise behind caused him to turn sharply round.

Surely not Boivin again! Of course, it isn't! Lanval, why do you persist in imagining Boivin at every corner? It must stop!

Father Servet approached the graveside,

"Forgive me if I am intruding upon your privacy, but I realised that earlier this morning, I should have offered my services, as your priest, to read a prayer and say a blessing over his resting place."

"By all means, father."

Servet moved behind the cross, took a small bible from his cassock and cleared his throat.

"In Christianity, the star of the astrologers from Babylon came from the east and so, we believers in the resurrection of the dead, place the body facing the east that will afford the deceased sight of the Second Coming of Jesus.

Grant this mercy, O Lord, we beseech Thee, to Thy servant departed, that he may not receive in punishment the requital of his deeds who in desire did keep. Thy will, and as the true faith here reunited him to the company of the faithful, so may Thy mercy unite him above to the choirs of angels. Through Jesus Christ our Lord. Amen."

"Amen to that," Lanval uttered, clearly moved by the occasion.

"Please give your mother my best regards." Servet turned to go back to the church and commented, casually, 'We are running out of space for burials here in this, our only Catholic cemetery. Soon we will be obliged to open new ground without the walls and that is not a desirable state of affairs. Our beloved departed have a right to eternal repose near their homes."

Satisfied he had discharged his filial duty, Lanval left the graveyard to walk down to the Valin quay. He peered through the open top half of the stable door to find his lad body-brushing the horse with a stiff bristled hand brush.

"When you've finished that, bring him and the cart to the port, we've a full day's work ahead."

"Sure thing, 'sieur." And the boy got on with seeing to the horse's hind quarters.

That day, they hoisted twenty kegs of olive oil off one barge, lifted them onto the cart and delivered them to various customers in the town. After that, from another boat, they repeated the procedure but, this time, the cargo was sacks of dried herbs and spices.

"A good day's work, I'd say."

"No doubt of that, 'sieur. Horse pulled well uphill like the cart was empty. Must be the love and care what I show him."

"It is that, my boy, and I'm blessed to have a worker like you. Here, take this."

Lanval placed two coins in the boy's hand.

"'sieur! It's not payday till Friday."

"I know, it's a little extra for you. You can spend it on ale, as I guess you will, as long as you're fit for work tomorrow!"

"Have no fear, 'sieur, and my thanks."

Lanval Aubert had learned the value to body and mind, of hard work and recognition of the good things that their fellow townsfolk did: *'Remember, son, if it weren't for God, we wouldn't be here and, without us, God wouldn't know what to do with his time, would he?'* his father had advised him one day, a perfectly serious expression on his face, an expression he maintained for some while until he could no longer and erupted into loud guffaws. Although Lanval's sadness, after father's death, was still raw, he liked to think he would perpetuate the man's sense of humour, even in hard times.

Lanval Aubert walked the short distance to the Tour Saint Nicolas, a thirty-seven-metre tall pentagonal stone tower built in 1376 to defend the entrance to the old port. In wartime, when invasion was probable, a heavy iron chain was attached and linked to the Chain Tower on the other side: no enemy ship could breach it for fear of its masts being shattered, bringing them crashing down and sinking the vessel.

He and Cicile frequently met by the Saint Nicolas Tower, it was convenient, half-way between his work and her parents' house in the Huguenot quarter to the west of town. She was waiting as he approached. Whenever he felt in a dark mood, his spirit was always brightened on seeing her. She wore a crisp beige tunic, knee-length, with a belt that emphasised her dainty waist. She tied back her long dark hair to reveal a broad forehead and slender nose. Her piercing blue eyes seemed to ask you a question if she looked at you. Gentle smiling lips framed perfect white teeth: in short, Cicile was a young woman of exceptional beauty.

I swear I love her more with each passing day. There cannot be a fairer woman in La Rochelle – nay! In the whole kingdom! She could have any man yet she chose me.

They kissed, briefly, and set off arm in arm along the promenade skirting the old port that was still animated, the last few boats of the day unloading, a fishing smack lowering and furling its sails, the harbour master prowling up and down, intent on spotting any cargo whose taxes were not paid or any sailor whose presence in La Rochelle could not be considered 'desirable' – he felt it his duty to keep all ruffians out of his beloved town. He had a strong working relationship with Judge Boivin and had held his title of Harbour Master for as long as anyone could remember. While he controlled, to a degree, any bad blood entering via the port, he could do very little about the criminal class already ensconced, of whom there were quite a number. There were not many delinquents, brawlers, drunkards or pickpockets he did not know: he had assisted the Sergeant, on many occasions, in apprehending miscreants to march before Boivin the Beak, as people mockingly referred to him. So, it is fair to say, he was well connected with the town's authorities – all subscribers to the Huguenot faith.

Over her free arm she carried a basket with bread, cheese, fruit and a wineskin.

"Let me take that." Lanval offered in his usual gentlemanly manner. At the far end of the port they sat down on a bench beneath the yellow blossom of a mimosa tree. He filled two beakers with wine, passing one to her.

"Thank you kindly, my dear." she murmured, a flirtatious inviting smile on her face. He stared at her.

There's a mystery in those deep blue eyes: her attraction is somewhere inside her gaze...would that, one day, I will understand it.

They remained in silence, though not forced, for some minutes. She spoke first.

"How was the funeral?"

"As good as might be expected, the church was full."

"Shows what a popular man he was."

"He *is* you mean – just because he's dead folk don't start to dislike him -"

"No, of course not, and that's not what I intended to say..."

He refilled their beakers, she took hers and placed her other hand affectionately on his knee.

"And your mother?"

"She's coping. You know her, she's resilient, immersing herself in embroidery to keep her mind off it. And, it goes without saying, I too miss him terribly."

"Lanval, forgive me, I feel for you also, of course I do."

"The church was full – oh, sorry, I've just said that. My thoughts are in a jumble when I think about him." He paused then looked at her directly.

"I'd hoped to see you there."

"I...I couldn't."

"What does *that* say, *I couldn't?*

"I was told it would not be seemly."

"And who told you that?"

"Judge Boivin."

"Boivin! What on earth has he got to do with it?"

"He came to our house, to see father about some business or other, and he announced that we ...Huguenots... should not enter places where Catholics congregated. My parents agreed so I had no choice. I wanted to attend, believe me, but..." Her voice trailed off, aware that Lanval's mood was changing, from his normal placid accommodating self to an angry frustrated man. He gritted his teeth and clenched his hands tight until the knuckles showed white.

Boivin has a finger in every pie! Who does he think he is? I have the anecdotes of his behaviour that father told me about; Father Servet warned me to steer clear of him – if not in as many words; then, to cap it all, he's instructed Cicile to stay away from the funeral. Oh! I nearly forgot that he's said to dabble in the Dark Arts. What sort of man is this?

But, what's done is done, so perhaps I shouldn't blame her...

They ate the food and drank the wine, their conversation now descending into the banal, avoiding the contentious subject of Judge Boivin.

The sun was setting, bathing the port in a soft warm glow. The water shimmied in gentle eddies created by the outgoing tide and it was time for Lanval and Cicile to return to their respective homes. They kissed and whispered loving words but, as they were about to part, and as an afterthought, he asked,

"The day after tomorrow there's a cockfight in the Ville-en-bois, will you come with me, we might win some money and, even if not, it's an exciting event?"

"Yes, I will. Should be good entertainment."

The Ville-en-bois, to the west of the main basin, was a forested area with low wooden houses that were not residential but workshops for boat repairs and general marine chandlery. An ancient powerful guild of merchants, it was said, had granted hunting rights in the forest, in perpetuity, to the citizens of La Rochelle. The entitlement to *'hunt deer, boar, wolves or hare, and carry them off to the home for the succour and delectation of the man's family.'*

Two days later, a hundred or more men, women and children gathered in the Ville-en-bois. This time, they hadn't come to hunt but to watch another sport, a cockfight.

Lanval and Cicile, hand in hand, followed a narrow path first through shrubs and grass, then into the trees of the forest itself where the canopy cut off the mid-afternoon sunshine above. The further they progressed, the darker it grew, not as night but the dusky half-light that descends, a false evening, a sinister menacing obscurity where every slight noise caused you to start, to freeze as if an attack by some ferocious beast was imminent.

Cicile gripped his hand tight.

"You're not scared, are you? You've got me to protect you, so don't worry," he said reassuringly, playfully, "Anyway, it's not far now." There were folk ahead and behind, all heading in the same direction for an entertainment they venerated. Some people – a very few – thought cockfighting was cruel but they were outnumbered by those who saw it as a harmless game, a competition between two birds. What was wrong with that? It was a tradition going back millennia and, in any case, to proscribe it would currently have required a decree from Jeanne, the Huguenot Queen of Navarre and she was not in the slightest interested. She rarely ventured into the town, instead preferring the hedonism of a privileged life in her chateau, a distance away, where her masquerade balls and sumptuous banquets lasted days on end, frequented by an entourage of sycophants. She was reported, more than once, to say that she did not live in her Huguenot stronghold of La Rochelle – she expressed the typically aristocratic view that her supporters there were 'pleasant enough but dull' – out of choice, and she anticipated returning in safety to her true home, Paris.

The couple reached a clearing in the woods where the sport would unfold, claiming a vantage point on a grassy knoll. Lanval surveyed the scene, enjoying the sense of growing excitement. Cicile feigned interest, but was, in truth, indifferent, and would rather have been elsewhere, gossiping with her girlfriends. His gaze was drawn to the cockpit, a ring with a fence of stakes interlaced with twigs and branches, low enough to not obscure views of the action; bereft of grass, the ground within strewn with golden sand. A voice caused him to turn around.

"Hey, Lanval, where's your money going then?"

"Hello Este," he greeted a boy he knew.

"I'm not sure, they both look good to me."

"Come, let's see them close."

Leaving Cicile, they went to the arena where two cages, as yet outside the ring, housed the antagonist roosters, strutting, clucking, heads nodding to and fro, left to right, eyes bulging, beaks pecking.

"I fancy the darker one. See, it's had its chest feathers removed – that will make it faster on the attack," Lanval decided.

"Maybe, but the other one's fed on special corn, or, at least, that's what I've heard."

"...not really much to choose between them."

The bookie for the cockfight, a weasel-faced unkempt man, passed through the spectators, taking money and whispering the odds, not wanting to prejudice the next bet

– it was a number he raised or lowered depending on the apparent value of the punter before him. He might have been a most unpleasant sort but he could judge a man in seconds, a useful ability in his trade. He arrived at Lanval and Este.

"I'll bet on the darker bird," the former stated, handing over a denier coin.

"And it's the other for me," the latter decided.

The intensity of the atmosphere rose as the owners prodded their fowl with poles through the wire of the cage to increase their levels of aggression, the restricted space driving them to a frenzied desire to escape. Then, it was time. Lanval stared at the master of the cockfight stepping into the ring, gesturing to the men who lifted the cages over the fence, waiting for him to signal the start. After a dramatic drawn-out pause,

"Let the battle commence!" He bellowed. The front grills were raised and the two birds shot, feathers flying, into the arena. Gamecocks possess a congenital belligerency towards the other males and know no fear, making them ideally suited to the game. Now, both birds stood, motionless, accompanied by a sudden silence from the crowd. Slowly, they scratched at the sand and began their cockerel waltz, strutting in a half-circle, one wing down, the other raised, each evaluating the resolve and desire for the contest.

The light brown rooster's pointed steel spurs, tied over its natural claws, gleamed, even in the gloom of the forest; the other's spurs were honed into sharp blades and it stood taller. Without warning, and to the rapture of the spectators, the birds threw back their heads, unleashing demonic squawks, screeches that rent the air, squeals to intimidate and terrify before the first lunge. The noise rose and, in response, the light brown dived forward, its beak aimed at the breast of its opponent. Blood flowed immediately. This move was redressed by the taller one's slashing strike of its blade into the enemy's wing.

The men, women and children, as one, turned their human faces into grimaces of warped hysteria, as frenzied as the creatures battling in the cockpit. And so it carried on – blood spraying around, feathers flying, flesh torn and the longer the fight continued, the less they resembled the fine cockerels they had been at the start and the more their strength and appetite for the confrontation waned. But the rules demanded a fight to the death or extreme injury resulting in only one standing to engage. Among the breeders there was a saying, *no retreat, no surrender,* and their birds were conditioned by this aphorism. On this occasion, death was the outcome: the darker fell to the ground and could not stand back up. It simply laid, crumpled, bloodied, pathetic: the ultimate defeat. The audience burst into obscene applause for their favourite or booing and hissing at the loser.

The master signalled that the owners retrieve their cockerels – the one back to its cage, the other pushed without ceremony into a coarse sack. All that remained was for the bookie to pay out the winnings and this he did. Although he had accrued a healthy profit from the match, he handed out the money reluctantly: a miser by trade and nature.

Lanval, Cicile and Este retook the path away from the clearing, along with the rest.

"Did you win?" she asked her man.

"Not a chance! I fancied the darker bird but you never can tell."

"That's true enough, but *I* made a tidy sum!" Este chirped up, smirking.

"Congratulations." Lanval murmured with an air of envy.

"Mind you, Boivin's cunning."

Lanval gripped his friend's arm.

"Did you say Boivin?"

"Why yes. He's the owner of the winner, didn't you know?"

"I certainly did not."

"He breeds them for a hobby, when he's run out of villains to chuck into gaol. Surely, I mentioned the 'special corn' he feeds them? He's said to cast magic spells over it – claptrap, if you ask me. But there are folk who believe it."

A short way further on, a small group of people surrounded a man wearing a floppy purple hat – Judge Boivin – shaking his hand and, from what could be heard, offering words of felicitation. The Justice broke away from his group of acolytes to join Lanval and his company on the path.

"Good afternoon to you all. Have you enjoyed today's sport?"

None replied, wary of the man, his reputation going before him. But Lanval couldn't resist,

"Why do you ask, judge?"

"No particular reason, my friend, I'm simply taking a passing interest in the citizens of my town." Lanval felt his hackles rise.

He said these words, or very similar, at father's funeral and, yet again, he calls me his friend, damn him! Este says he

casts spells over his corn, so I ask myself over what else, or who else?

"- and I'm sorry you lost money, next time you must try to pick out the winner – no place for losers in my town. I wish you *au revoir*." Bowing, only slightly to Cicile, he turned back to his bevy of admirers.

9

LA ROCHELLE, SEPTEMBER 1571

Lanval sat at the top of the flight of steps leading down to the quayside, from where he had an unimpeded view of the afternoon's comings and goings. That morning he had already made two deliveries and now waited for another boat that he would help unload, but that arrival would not be until the next tide, so he had time to contemplate, to gaze down on a place that was his livelihood. Earlier, a captain, who had a longstanding association with Aubert Fils, had given him a wineskin from his cargo, a kind gesture that Lanval graciously accepted – it would have been insulting to have declined the man's generosity. Friendship and trust existed between sailors since time in perpetuity: a unique munificence of spirit that transcended politics and religion.

Easing the cork from the neck of the wineskin, he sniffed its contents, checking it was fit to drink but he need not to have worried: the captain had insisted, on presenting it to him, *'any wine from those vineyards around Bordeaux is the best, trust me, I'm a connoisseur. And that, Lanval thought, despite his disguise as a rough matelot.'* Satisfied, he took a draught, smacked his lips, and then took a second. It was, as the captain had vouched, a very good smooth wine. A noise behind interrupted his enjoyment. Turning around, he saw the familiar figure of a town dignitary everyone knew.

"Good day, Lanval, and it is, indeed, a fine day."

"Monsieur le Maire," Lanval acknowledged the man, nodding.

"You won't earn a crust sitting here drinking, don't you know?"

"I'm waiting for a boat on the tide but, in any case, what's it to do with you?" His sharp tone reflected his dislike for the town's mayor.

"Nothing...none of my business. I was simply expressing a friendly interest, as I do in all the people I serve."

The only person he serves is himself – he's got a nerve!

"...I have a matter to attend to, so I'll leave you to your drinking." The mayor twitched his nose in a petulant gesture and carried on down the steps.

Lanval drank another mouthful, his eyes following the mayor as he reached the foot of the steps and proceeded along the quayside. Some boats were tied up for the night until their merchandise arrived the next day, others were at varying stages of loading and unloading, and each had a man of interest for the mayor, the captain, who was the only member of a crew he deigned to converse with. All the others, he referred to as *'coarse, offensive and malodorous.'* Whenever Lanval heard this opinion voiced out loud, he was compelled to defend these fellows he knew to be decent, hard-working men – uneducated, he conceded, but nonetheless unworthy of the official's slander and he reminded Monsieur le Maire of this every time it occurred. Few folk had the courage to face up to such a pillar of La Rochelle society. Lanval felt no such intimidation.

Young Aubert had not, previously, really observed the mayor's features. He cut a disquieting figure: tall, thin, skeletal. His face housed close-set dark eyes, pinched lips and a narrow, pointed nose. The near grey curly locks reached his shoulders – the butt of hurtful childhood jibes suggesting his sexual orientation might not be what it seemed. His entire sallow countenance exuded an expression of unhappiness and anguish - few, if any, of the townsfolk had seen him smile.

Lanval watched, captivated, as the lanky form glided along the quay from boat to boat. Off each, a captain climbed from the deck to stand, with some ceremony, before the pallid mayor. Whatever words were exchanged Lanval was too far away to hear but he could see money given by the sailors, coins dropped into a fair-sized pouch held open by the mayor who was clearly counting, piece by piece. The correct amount deposited, he nodded then moved on to the next.

Port taxes, Lanval mused, I bet he's a good sum richer by the time he's collected from the last boat. But it goes into the town coffers, for all our benefits.

· · ·

When the mayor got to the far end of the quayside, another man joined him. Lanval could not mistake that floppy purple hat: Judge Boivin. Quickly descending the steps, he moved at a brisk pace towards the two Huguenot men, compelled by a strange desire to observe them at closer quarters, using the shadow of the warehouses to conceal his approach. A stack of wooden barrels gave him a hiding place and, though not close enough to catch their words, he had a perfect view.

What are they up to? He recalled, once again, conversations with his father who would often mention Boivin and the mayor in the same breath, as if they were accomplices in a plot: the next event confirmed this suspicion. The mayor reached inside his pouch, withdrew a series of coins, and dropped them into Boivin's open purse, counting as he went.

What on earth...ah, I understand! That money is the taxes just collected that they're sharing between them! It can't be right, the judge should not be having anything to do with the town's revenue, it's not within his jurisdiction, is it?

The two men shook hands and departed in opposite directions. Lanval ducked down to ensure his presence was not revealed, it was not and when he eventually peered over the barrels, the officials were nowhere to be seen. The afternoon tide approaching, he walked to the empty berth where the expected boat would soon appear.

. . .

"Hey, Lanval, you rascal! How are you?" boomed the burly captain of the boat, slapping him on the back, almost knocking him off his feet.

"Fine, thank you, Jamet. So, what have you got for me today?"

"Flour, sacks of flour from a mill down south and..." - he pulled a parchment sheet from his tunic, "...here's a list of the bakers you're to deliver it to and the number of sacks each one wants. I'd say your town has more bakers than people!"

"Not quite, Jamet, but there are a few, I agree. It's good bread that keeps the wheels turning, if you get my drift. Shut down the bakeries, shut down the citizens, or so they say."

His words would be prophetic in the weeks and months ahead.

"I wouldn't know about that, Lanval, but let's unload your life-giving flour – the light's fading and I have a lady friend to call on." The sailor winked at Lanval.

Walking into the house he found his mother in the rocking chair, embroidering.

"Hello, son, had a good day?"

"Yes, trade's never better."

"Supper will be a while. Would you please draw me a bucket of water?"

"Of course, I will."

In the centre of the courtyard, behind the house, stood their well: a stone-built circular head with a wooden cover over its top and protect it from leaves, vermin and the like.

The Aubert household was fortunate to have access to healthy natural drinking water: it was only from such a source, or from the current of a fast-flowing stream, that potable liquid was assured. Most people drew their water from muddy conduits or ponds or, if they had the wherewithal, they paid a cob to bring the day's supply in three-gallon tubs carried through the streets on a yoke.

He removed the cover, tied one end of a neatly coiled rope to the handle, and lowered the bucket until he felt it go loose, waiting a minute or so then hauling it back up, full of clean cool water that he took into the house, as mother had requested, not forgetting to replace the cover.

"Thank you, Lanval, you're a good boy. I don't know what I'd do without you since -" Her voice trembled and tears began to run down her cheeks. She was still in a fragile state, her son understood. He had to be strong for her but also, out of respect for his late father. No words were necessary. He turned and went back into the courtyard, sitting on the bench father had made. The yard was bathed in the reassuring warmth of the early autumn evening: it was a retreat, a hideaway, a sanctuary he sought to enjoy his thoughts, safe from the scrutiny of the outside world.

Why does consideration of Boivin continue to prey on my mind? Is he one whose actions affect me, directly? Is he a threat to my business or, even worse, my mother? There has to be a reason unless it's simply a deep dislike of a thoroughly repulsive man!

He sipped a beaker of refreshing water, reflectively, needing to make sense of an increasingly mystifying situation.

The few times I've raised his name, in Cicile's company, she's been quick to defend him and I'm loath to press it further for fear of causing antagonism in our relationship.

Father Servet warned me against crossing swords with him and I'm sure Father Evrart will proffer similar advice. How I wish I could ask the old man. As for mother, she shouldn't be further burdened in her mourning. The mayor? No! I've seen he's on the judge's payroll as is, without doubt, the harbour master. How do I expose Boivin for his corruption and alleged devule worship? I must spy on him, first, to gain proper proof.

He was the jolted out of his contemplation by a chorus of chirps: against the wall opposite him was a wooden birdcage with a wire mesh front door. It housed father's beloved canaries, a bird he had fastidiously bred for pleasure. In and around the town animals of all kinds were kept, for a variety of reasons. Cats – for a logic often based on superstition – were seen as agents of Satan and were more likely to receive a kick than a caress. Dogs were, indeed, a man's best friend, performing useful functions like herding, hunting, guarding and vermin control, 'ratters' as they were known. Horses for transportation; oxen for pulling ploughs and for meat; chickens for eggs and food; sheep for wool and mutton. But, birds, especially canaries, became family companions: they trilled songs and were beautiful creatures in their green, yellow, brown plumage, and they provided company for women as they saw to their domestic chores.

Lanval went to the cage, ran a finger over the grill to make a rattling sound that rarely failed to excite the dozen or so birds within. With a rapid flapping of wings, raucous chirping, and feathers flying, they stood erect and alert on their perches, heads bobbing to left and right, up and down, dark intelligent eyes shining. He picked up a pitcher to refill their drinking tray with water and from a wicker basket took some of their preferred mixture of oats and wheat seeds that he scattered across the floor of the cage.

"There you are, happy now? I bet you thought I'd deserted you but I've been very busy today, yes, very busy...things you wouldn't understand, even if I told you." He pursed his lips close to the wire mesh, making a smacking noise similar to a sound one would comfort a fractious babe with. He'd promised his father he'd take good care of the birds if anything happened to him. They frequently served Lanval as confidants whenever he needed to talk through a problem.

So, what do you think I should do about Judge Boivin? One particular bird, a rare black and white female, trilled and warbled, pecking at his finger pushed through the grill. *Do you really?* He gave a guffaw, *then I'll bear that in mind.*

"Hey, Lanval." Mother called from inside the house. "I've saved some cabbage leaves for the birds." She'd heard her late husband swear these leaves gave them shiny feathers and encouraged them to sing.

"Thanks, mother. Damned birds eat better than us," he jested, chopping them into small pieces. "We're saying goodbye to two of them today though."

"What do you mean?"

"I'm giving a young male and female away."

"Giving away?"

"Yes, there's a lad who's always hanging around the port and we got talking. I told him I kept canaries and his jaw dropped as I explained what they're like and how I look after them. He's a real urchin, but pleasant enough, and when he told me how his parents are poor and can barely afford to put food on the table, I was moved. It's not right in a town like ours, one of the richest in the kingdom I'd say, that a waif and his family live under conditions of such hardship. What's more, my birds have produced enough chicks this year that they fight for space in the cage. We benefit, as does the lad, and it's cost us nothing."

"It's an act of kindness, for sure, Lanval. Where does he live?"

"Rue de la Cloche."

"Do you realise that street is in the very heart of the Huguenot district? And you're showing *kindness* to one of theirs?"

"Mother -" Lanval felt his hair stand on end and his fists clench tight on hearing his mother speak with such venom and prejudice in her voice.

Wait, Lanval, he told himself, she's not herself since father passed away. He continued, but in a conciliatory tone,

"Whether the family are Huguenots, Catholics, Jews or Muslims, it matters not to the canaries!"

The woman's sense of humour returned with her son's witticism. She smiled, then laughed, seeing the validity of his comment.

"I'm taking the birds to Rue de la Cloche but I'll be back in time for supper. Is that agreeable to you?"

"Of course, it is." She replied sheepishly.

He went back into the courtyard, opened the front of the cage, and gently grasped the chosen birds, pushing them into a small linen sack, despite their hostile squawking.

The urchin was ecstatic on seeing Lanval at his door, he knew full well what was concealed in the sack. The father shook his hand and expressed his gratitude for the gift.

"See, Monsieur Aubert, I've made my boy a cage, out of wood from a pile of old broken barrels on the quayside." He pointed proudly to the far side of the room. Lanval went up to it and congratulated the man.

"You certainly have a talent – the woodcarver could soon be out of a job with the likes of you! And, I see you've put seed and water ready for the lucky couple."

He placed the birds, carefully, one after the other, onto the floor of the cage. They immediately began to scratch and peck at the seeds, cooing softly.

"There! They'll be fine in their new home. Good luck with their breeding – you'll have to wait till they're good and ready, can't hurry nature. So, I'll bid you good evening, sir. And you, boy, make your father proud of you."

"I will Monsieur Aubert, I will. I'm much obliged."

Walking back to his house, Lanval felt satisfied his visit had brought pleasure to the impoverished family. He cared not a jot about their faith.

His mind turned, once more, to Judge Boivin, who had become an obsession, a mission, a burning desire to discover the truth about him.

Up to now, I have only rumour and gossip to go on. I need more than that. I've watched him receive money from the mayor but I must investigate where he's said to perform devil worship or whatever else he's part of.

He strolled along the street in an absent-minded distraction, preoccupied, eager to find out what lay behind Boivin's mysterious public façade. He failed to acknowledge several passers-by who said hello, his head bowed, deep in thought.

A man holding his office, the Justice of La Rochelle, responsible for dispensing punishments, sentencing wrong-doers and then, a leading advocate of the Huguenot faith, should be a good man, above reproach, free from allegations of corruption. Ah...I have it...Boivin is partial to drink and he's known to frequent the taverns. There will surely be his social acquaintances who will talk abou him, after a few drinks...yes, that's the way.

Accordingly, Lanval visited one inn after another, but without success. As soon as he, albeit casually, mentioned Boivin's name in conversation, he met with a wall of silence –

'I don't know nothing about him, monsieur.
Must be a year or more since I seen him.
Who? No, never heard of him.
Boivin? The judge? A fine man.'

He was on the verge of abandoning hope of hearing anything, when his luck changed. He began a well-rehearsed script with yet another reprobate in a tavern,

"May I join you...your name is..." Lanval felt a shiver run through his body, could this be the man he was searching for?

"Name's Ansel, and what business is it of yours? I don't know you." The man slurred his words, was aggressive and truculent, and had evidently spent most of the day drinking. Unkempt, dressed in threadbare clothes, he was the right type. *Here we go again, nothing ventured...*

"We've not met. My name is Borde," he lied, "I've had a debt repaid today so why shouldn't I share my good fortune with a fellow such as yourself?"

Ansel screwed up his face, pursed his lips, and looked hard at Lanval before speaking,

"You want to buy me ale?"

"Landlord!" Lanval called, "Bring a jug of ale over here, and a tankard for me."

The two strangers began to establish a relationship, as was the plan, with the drunkard soon laughing and sharing his domestic circumstances the more ale he consumed. All was going well but Lanval waited an hour or more before mentioning Boivin – too soon would make the stooge suspicious: he need not have worried.

"A friend of mine had dealings with Judge Boivin."

"Boivin! Confound him!"

"Do you know him?"

"I damn well do! Last year the sergeant caught me pick-pocketing from a rich gent, a Catholic it turned out, and I'd heard the justice was always lenient with them that's transgressed against said Catholics like me – he hates them but loves the Protestants, or that was the story, but what happened? They put me up before him, in his fancy courtroom..." He drank some more and resumed, "and though I'd only taken a silk handkerchief, he asked me my faith, I said Protestant since it was true and I expected it to get me off, as it were, but he went berserk, screaming and shouting like a lunatic! The rest of the room was as dumbfounded as me but he'd been drinking, that was certain, and in the end, he gave me two days in the stocks and one week in the gaol! The stocks I could stand but *that* *gaol* – a hellish place, believe me...shackled to the wall, filthy rats crawling over me, a crust and water – if I was lucky – and, the *gaoler*! A swarthy fellow with no teeth – he'd see you die as soon as spit on you! Do you realise that gaol is actually beneath us, under the sewers...not many folk know that!"

"I'm sure they don't," Lanval was satisfied with the direction of the conversation, such as it was. The ruffian carried on after more ale, "that Boivin's not a nice man at all."

This was Lanval's chance to elicit the important information from Ansel. He was bound to give him answers so he encouraged the sot,

"There's many who call him bad. What think you?"

"Not nice, bad, all the same to me, but he gets up to much more than just playing the monster in a courtroom."

"Tell me, do"

"He's into the *dark arts*, the devil, curses and other such evil doings."

"Is he really?" Lanval tried to sound surprised.

"Ay, and I know where it's done. Would you like to know too?" His voice descended into a baby-like gurgle for some moments, the drink taking over and Lanval feared the secret would remain as such,

"Yes, indeed I do."

The rogue, Ansel, was not so intoxicated that he would miss a chance to make money.

'It'll cost you, Monsieur Borde."

Without hesitation Lanval took a money pouch from his tunic and placed two coins on the table.

"More than that." Ansel's eyes lit up.

There was no alternative but to increase his offer to find out the place so he put down two more.

"That's better. Now, draw close, nobody must hear. Some time ago, I was walking down the road that leads out of town towards Villeneuve-les-Salines, around dusk, minding my own business, when I saw Boivin with a dozen men behind – can't mistake that purple hat. Well, he turned off the road onto a track that goes into thick woods around the Tasdon marshes. I know that area, I used to play there with my mates when I was young, and the only reason to enter that forest is to get to an old derelict barn. It's hidden from view, a secret place where you can't be watched, where you can do the devil knows what there with your band of followers. Understand, Borde?"

"I do. Landlord, again! Here's more ale for you Ansel, but I must leave now. I've business to attend to." *I most certainly do have business, thanks to this tippler.*

Ansel picked up the money from the table and stuffed it into his tunic pocket. The men parted company, each pleased with their meeting, but for different reasons.

That night, lying in his bed, he mulled over the story he'd been given by Ansel. *So, now I have it confirmed that Boivin is involved in some sort of activity he wants kept hidden, but I have to catch him red-handed so I can be sure of the facts before I expose him for the charlatan he is. I've seen him taking money I'm sure does not go to the town, as it should, and that's sin enough. However, when it comes to the dark arts, what do I know? I understand it to be sorcery, control over others with harmful intention and it's at odds with the teaching of the Church. But, more than that, I'm ignorant.*

Driven by a determination to denounce Judge Boivin, Lanval, for several evenings at around dusk, concealed himself at the junction of the road and track, as Ansel had explained, but Boivin did not come. He was ready to give up his plan when, surely, appeared a floppy purple hat with men behind.

At last! Now, we'll see what you're doing, your honour.

As the procession drew closer he ducked down and waited for them to start down the track, now in twos behind their leader. He followed them but at a safe distance. The further they penetrated the woods, the thicker the undergrowth – a sign, he mused, that few people come there – and with dusk fast approaching, the darker it grew. After half an hour of total silence, they reached a clearing where stood, just as Ansel had described, the derelict rickety barn. The twelve men and Boivin entered, the last man closing the heavy door.

Lanval went up to the barn, his body trembling with anticipation. *From the little I know about the dark arts, they should be practised at night and away from public view: they meet that requirement anyway. But what now? There aren't any windows!*

He crept slowly around the building, one foot placed

after the other, frightened to the core lest he made a noise, snapped a twig or rustled the bushes that would reveal his presence. He prayed for divine intervention then, as if the Good Lord had answered, he found a crack between the wooden planks, a faint yellow light showing. Closing one eye, he squinted, straining his ears to hear what was happening inside: he was appalled by the scene that greeted him.

He felt his heart beating hard and feared it was loud enough to attract attention. Calming himself, he focused again on the interior. In the middle he saw a long table; a bench to each side, each with six men, their hoods concealing their identities. They remained quite still and silent. On the table, three tall candles, the type that adorned the altar in a church, flickered, a pale golden light casting eerie shadows that leapt a macabre dance in the dim periphery of the barn. The only other items on the table were a chalice, a quill, and a stout

leather-bound book that, again, would have been more at home in a place of religious worship, but Lanval observed nothing that vaguely resembled sacred symbolism.

At the top of the table, on a podium, was the master's chair – a throne, to be more exact. Boivin's crazed glare fixed on one man after the next. On the short squat fat man's head, a strange white mitre portrayed a bishop of sorts albeit without parishes or parishioners, a sad isolated caricature of a man who would, in his mind, lead others.

Yes, but to what fate? A headdress that bears not the cross of Jesus, rather a circle containing strange marks.

Boivin clapped his hands three times, rose from his throne and, stepped down from the podium into a circle scratched in the earthen floor. Lanval could just make out a pentagon with lines inside. He clapped again, a signal for the men to rock gently to and fro, giving out low moaning noises, their hoods always obscuring their faces. Next, he uttered his first words,

'We need revenge,
On this black day,
To make our troubles go away.
A curse, a pox, a chanted hex,
Any one should do
To make the Catholics go away.'

Lanval was struck by the banal, even primitive, nature of the incantation – perhaps it reflected the most probable lack of wit of the men who made weird sounds in response. Boivin continued,

'Turn misfortune back to those
Who cause our problems and our woes
And heap upon them karmic debt
Lest they all too soon forget.'

Another clap and one man left the table, to return moments later, a thrashing squealing chicken held tight by the neck with one hand, a short dagger in the other. Boivin picked up the chalice and held it, with theatrical ceremony, under the bird's throat that was promptly slashed by the dagger, spurting out blood into the cup. The judge placed it next to the book that he opened. Dipping the quill into the blood he wrote something Lanval could not possibly see from his distance away, to his annoyance. This initial part of the ritual completed, Boivin turned and sat again on his ersatz throne, a demented grin across his face as he surveyed his people, who turned their heads towards him, mumbling unintelligible words,

If that's a language, Lanval concluded, it's one I've never heard and given all the foreign men I've encountered at the port, I know most.

'*Quiet! Boivin screamed. Glory be to Satan and Belial and to the evil spirits.*'

'*As it was in the beginning, is now, and ever shall be, world without end.*' *The men answered.*

'*Satan be with you.*'

'*And with thy spirit.*'

'*Let us pray.*'

Lanval's disgust churned his very soul as he appreciated the judge's liturgy was a parody of a Christian church service. *The sheer outrage! Such blasphemy!* The disciples bowed their heads until their brows rested on the table in supplication. Boivin breathed in deeply, the pause increasing the drama. Then,

'*Urged by our Lord Satan's bidding, and schooled by his infernal ordinance, we make bold to say...*' His voice seemed to trail off momentarily and Lanval strained hard to hear better until the man spoke, but this time at a volume that raised faces, their gaze fixed on their leader. '*Children of my office!*' He howled. '*From high matters I spare the time to preside over this gathering. By the favour of our Lord Satan, I have the power to grant your wishes, should it please me to do so.*'

'*Rid us of the Catholics, we beseech thee.*' The men called out in unison.

'*Waste no moment in unnecessary babbling or you will incur my anger! Now, lift your faces and tell me, once more, your desires.*'

'*Rid us of the Catholics!*' Came the chilling affirmation, a second time.

Lanval moved as quietly as possible away from the barn and regained the track out of the woods. His breathing was laboured, such was the reeling sensation in his head, so deeply was he affected by the scene he had witnessed.

'*I've seen and heard enough! Judge Boivin is, as Ansel so eloquently informed me, a practitioner of the dark arts. I will tell Fathers Servet and Evrart what I know. But, if they are to believe me, they have to observe it, as I have, for themselves. I will seek them out first thing tomorrow morning.*'

10

CHENONCEAU, OCTOBER 1572

THE COLD INHOSPITABLE DAYS OF OCTOBER MATCHED exactly Catherine de Médicis' state of mind: the biting north wind whipped with it the venom that fomented in her heart for the Huguenot population who, despite the best efforts of her king and favourite duke, still represented the majority religion in the kingdom. Since the purge of Saint Bartholomew's Day in Paris she had retreated to her palace at Chenonceau. Neither domestic staff, emissaries, nor councillors had caught sight of her for the past six weeks – except for her maidservant, Mathilde, who remained her most loyal aide and confidante. During these dark days the Queen Mother had, indeed, carried a heavy burden and without Mathilde, and her trusted brown syrupy liquid that helped her to sleep, she would not have endured those tempestuous times that had befallen her lands.

The laudanum she consumed in ever-increasing amounts ensured her slumber, for sure, but did not chase away her jealous nightmares that dwelt on the king's mistress, Diane de Poitiers, even though the despised woman had died some six years previously. It was beyond her comprehension how Diane had held power over her late husband, Henry IV, who acceded to her every whim and monopolised carnal matters, to the Queen Mother's chagrin, frustration and exclusion.

Filling a beaker from a cut-glass decanter, she sat at her dressing table, examining herself in the mirror. She disapproved more each day of the image before her.

Catherine, you have scarcely seen six winters yet, behold this woman I do not recognise. Your features drawn, haggard, lines that intertwine, heavy bags under your protruding eyes that should show jubilation and zest, not sadness and fear. And...these pinched lips that have not smiled in so long a time...

She yanked the pins out of her hair and, angrily, shook her head causing her shiny auburn locks to flow free onto her shoulders, raised the fine glass to her mouth and took a deep draught of her steadfast companion. Why the private supply of liqueur was sometimes brown whilst from other bottles green, she didn't question – either colour served its purpose. Turning her head, she observed herself, the side of her face foremost, and sighed.

The people in Florence call you their 'little duchess' and to those in France you're 'that Italian woman', but it comes to the same thing: I am a lady eschewed and ridiculed by her subjects. How they smirked, laughed, joked at my expense when Henry and his harlot Diane cavorted and romped, even at court, for the whole world to admire – damn her! damn him!

My dearest father, how would you see me now? You,

Lorenzo the Magnificent, Duke of Urbino, ruler of Florence, how would you see your daughter today? They say you were 'as pleased as if it had been a boy' upon my birth: high praise coming from a patron of artists, scholars and poets, a man who recognised beauty when he saw it! Mother, Madeleine de la Tour d'Auvergne, a cousin of Francis, King of France, no less, and a woman of charm and delightful exquisite taste: shall I ever equal you? The Pontiff, Leo, who blessed your marriage to my father called you 'a beautiful and good lady of noble birth and of my kin.' I am, more than words, indebted to you both, yet you were both taken by the Good Lord within one month of my arrival on this earth. Now, I only have legend and hearsay to paint me a picture of you both...nothing more and how it leaves me distraught.

There came a tap at the bedchamber door.

"Enter." Catherine instructed, drinking more laudanum and breathing in deeply. It was Mathilde.

"I've brought more coal, they're cold days, ma'am. We need to keep you healthy and happy, don't want you catching a cold -"

Catherine turned away from the mirror, glaring at her maidservant, her countenance as black as thunder,

"*Happy*! Do you understand just how impossible it is to be *happy*? You have no idea, woman!"

Mathilde said nothing. She carried the scuttle over to the fireplace, then raked the embers, throwing the nuggets on top with a scoop. Standing back, she waited a moment or two for the fire to begin to flicker then,

"Ma'am, you do me an injustice, if I may be so bold as to suggest it, to speak to me thus."

Catherine took another drink, lowered her head and almost blubbered,

"I'm sorry, Mathilde, you're quite correct. Please accept my apologies. You are dearer to me than life itself, for without you, well..." Her voice faded. Mathilde moved to the dressing table, picked up a brush and ran it lovingly through her lady's ringlets. Neither woman spoke for a while.

"My Queen has achieved many things that should make her happy, from my limited knowledge, concerning matters of state and Church."

"Do you think so?" This time there was no rancour in her tone.

"Indeed, I do and, whatever you have done is with the best interests of your people at heart."

"Not for *all* my people though, Mathilde." She leaned back and gazed to the ceiling, before continuing,

"The Huguenots."

"Ah...*them!*"

"Yes. But to cleanse our fair capital of their sort meant we had to instigate severe measures."

"From what I hear, if my women friends are to be believed, there remain few of them, and those who choose to stay keep their heads down, if you take my meaning."

"I do, and you are a most valuable source of information, my dear."

"My lady has not stepped foot out of her room since... since you decided to reside here at Chenonceau rather than your palace in Paris. You decline my offers of walks in the grounds and you used to enjoy them so much."

"All in good time, Mathilde, at the present I cannot face the world, although these four walls are closing in on me. But, all in good time."

Mathilde finished brushing Catherine's hair.

"Does my lady require anything further this evening?"

"Thank you, no."

Alone in her bedchamber, the Queen Mother pulled on her nightdress and lay on the bed, her whole being overcome with feelings of agonising guilt for the part she had played in the slaughter of the Huguenots on Saint Bartholomew's Day. The devoutly Catholic side of her nature justified the action protecting and promoting the supremacy of her faith: a faith she was born into and would in it die. However, at the same time, she regretted the bloodshed of folk she hated solely because their religion was different from hers. Such dissonance in her dreams was unbearable and, to maintain any semblance of sanity and purpose, she pledged to devote her remaining years to upholding the Church of Rome, come what may. A single-minded leadership was essential. This was neither the time nor the place for fragility or indecision. At last, she drifted off to sleep.

Some days later, she felt the need of a consultation with her astrologer, Côme Ruggieri, and sent word with a trusted servant for him to attend the chateau. She asked Mathilde to stoke the fire earlier than usual with instructions she should not be disturbed that evening as she would be 'praying and reading the Scriptures.' Whether Mathilde knew the real reason or not, she had learned the importance of diplomacy in her position and, in particular, when to ask questions or leave things be.

. . .

Ruggieri, dressed in his monk's coarse brown habit, for both disguise and protection against the cold, had made his way to the hidden wooden door and up the stone steps leading to the gallery in the chateau and then to Catherine's private rooms. The single candle flickering at the end of the corridor told him she was awaiting his arrival. He knocked twice on the door and listened for a soft 'come.'

"Good evening, my lady." Ruggieri mumbled, making a theatrical bow. "I trust all is well with your court as with your family."

"You may trust whatever you want but...but it need not concern you, Ruggieri."

"Of course," He answered in a grovelling tone.

"Sit, pray." She indicated a seat by her desk. "Will you partake of sustenance, it's a cold night?"

"With pleasure, ma'am."

She filled two glasses with wine from a decanter – her precious laudanum was too good for common visitors, such as came those days – and sat opposite him. The part of the desk between them had been cleared, ready for the astrologer's affairs.

"It is some time since I last purchased your services, is it not?" she asked, in the dubious tone she reserved for such occasions.

"That is true, but the stars move in an unpredictable fashion. One never knows when one will feel their attraction or appreciate their significance." He drank more wine. "If I recall, the configuration of the heavens and your birth sign presaged an auspicious period to further ones plans."

"That was, indeed, your interpretation and it proved most helpful. Anyway, you're not here tonight to look at the past."

"I'm not, ma'am, so let us begin."

Ruggieri unrolled his parchment sheet displaying the signs of the zodiac. He shook the raven's bones in his pouch then emptied them with a flourish. He let out an almost imperceptible humming sound, pursed his lips, and screwed his eyes in concentration.

"So, what do you see?" She asked and, although by nature inclined to dismiss his response before he had even given it, she was taken along by his dramatic prowess and command of the ceremony.

"You are born under Aries, are you not?"

"I am."

He took three talisman coins from his pocket and casually scattered them over the bones. Once more, he made strange noises before passing his hands to and fro above the desk and beginning,

"This bone points to Aries..." – from twenty or so skeletal pieces, randomly strewn, there was a fair chance of one falling in the direction of that character "...and the planet Mars is dominant in this season. Yes, Mars the god of war and second in importance only to great Jupiter. Mars is the most prominent of the military supreme deities...therefore, I see battles ahead for you ma'am."

"Go on, Ruggieri."

"Now, see, the biggest bone indicates a man born under that arrangement who is of significance to you. I do not have a name but...a soldier...a lord...or a count..."

Catherine sat bolt upright realising who this man could be. She suggested, her voice trembling,

"Is he a duke, perchance?"

"Ma'am, you have it! A duke, for sure, a man who serves you well. Yes, Mars is in Aries! You must trust your instincts, for your energy is fuelled by a fire that keeps on burning yet must not control you. Pay heed to that, ma'am. That is all I can observe."

He's talking about de Guise! It can be no-one else.

She pulled open a drawer in her desk, took out a small linen bag, coins jangling, and gave it to the astrologer.

"Most obliged, my lady."

He silently packed away his paraphernalia, bowed, and left the bedchamber.

From that moment, Catherine determined, emboldened by Ruggieri's estimations, to pursue a pathway that would advance her avowed intent to eliminate the Huguenots, impossible as that may have seemed. Côme had told her what she wanted to hear – the soothsayer knew his craft – and she instructed Mathilde to fetch the Duc de Guise from Paris, as a matter of the greatest urgency and secrecy.

Some days before de Guise's arrival, she received a letter from a certain Father Evrart and his assistant priest, Father Servet who, between them, ministered from the only Catholic church left in the town of La Rochelle. The contents of the letter disturbed her greatly.

At this point, she saw no reason to involve her son, King

Charles, in her agenda. Without too much time spent on reflection, she decided he would be more hindrance than help at this stage: his name and influence would be called upon, in due course, to establish the Catholic family as the absolute religious force in her kingdom.

We've had the Holy Roman Empire since 1525, she mused, over several glasses of laudanum, nearly fifty years yet we still struggle to worship without Huguenot interference. Our own are often misguided, without a proper ecclesiastical purpose – seeking land, money or political power in the name of the Church. We fought the Turks, but to what gain? We forced Huguenots in Germania to convert to our belief. We signed with the Spaniards in their kingdoms of Asturias and Galicia against the common threat by the Calvinists and Lutherans. Yet, we are still not the masters of the only true religion, as God's will dictates: it has to change, it is our destiny.

Then, one cold rainy afternoon, came a knock at Catherine's door.

"My lady, his grace, the Duc de Guise." Mathilde announced.

The duke, an aristocrat of some forty years of age, cut a fine figure: slim but muscular, dark deep-set intelligent eyes, a long slender nose and bearded chin. His light-brown hair, swept back, revealed a broad forehead. Despite his privileged upbringing, the son of Francis, first duke of Guise and princess Anna d'Este, he could converse in the vernacular with a farm labourer as with a landed baron. From the start, he had been smitten by Catherine's sweetness and pledged to support her role in Church affairs but, neither he, nor anyone, could have foreseen his own rise to leader of the Catholic League and his subsequent quarrel with Catherine who he regarded as too conciliatory towards the Protestants. *Poor Catherine, he thought, she howls with the authority and persuasion of a Boadicea but only a whimper lies beneath her bluster* - de Guise, the dispassionate pragmatist, a man with a general's temper and a nose only for victory. He would progress to heroic stature among French Catholics who would be convinced by his brilliant public and military reputation.

The duke bowed and kissed the ring on her outstretched hand.

"Welcome to Chenonceau."

"It is good to meet with you again, ma'am."

" I have sent for you to issue further orders, that is, over and above the admirable work you do in our capital. Will you take wine?"

"Certainly, ma'am."

The Queen Mother nodded to Mathilde who filled two glasses from an ornate jug then discretely left her mistress and the visitor to their business.

"Sit, pray."

Out of deference, he waited for her to instigate the conversation.

"De Guise, you are one of the most powerful men in my kingdom. Your estates and properties have grown, rightly, and we are indebted for your loyal service. Ten years ago, you led an army into Vassy to put down the Huguenot conspiracy against our government and Church. We have signed treaty after treaty only to see their terms breached.

But you have been at the forefront of our forces, dealing with those devil worshipers, damn them!"

De Guise raised his eyebrows, looking directly at her, wondering what was coming next.

"Tell me, good de Guise, what is your assessment of the situation currently in Paris?

He answered promptly,

"After Saint Bartolomew's Day we prosecuted several operations, *pour encourager les autres*: they fled the city in their thousands, the Protestants, that is. Now, a limited number worship in two, no three, 'designated' churches; the rest keep a low profile and are no cause for concern."

"Splendid, duke! You have, in truth, done well and we will reward you accordingly."

"My lady, it is an honour."

"Quite. We – that is, the king and I – have commanded my sister, Marguerite, and her new husband, Henry of Navarre, who will be converting to Catholicism even as we speak. Thus, she is removed from the frame and resides in Asturias as our ambassador to the Spanish court. Her marriage has benefitted us, as planned. But, pour us more wine, do." They both drank, taking in the magnitude of their deeds. She resumed,

"Throughout the kingdom, we either subdue the rebels by force or grant them immunity, a sort of 'freedom of belief' within their homes, an amnesty, don't you know, but one with diminished rights, as it should be."

De Guise nodded.

"However, we see four important towns – Montauban, Auxerre, Nîmes and La Rochelle – that boast active Huguenot populations and who compose the civil administrations. This day, I am bestowing on you our authority to raise troops and, along with our regular soldiers, will 'arrange' those towns, except Nîmes, as you see fit. This latter place is close to the Holy Father's citadel of Avignon. He has the means to address issues there so we need not concern ourselves unduly. You will be answerable only to me. Our Catholic brothers and sisters must govern those places. Huguenots must understand humility!

Now, La Rochelle is of particular interest in that, it has a large Huguenot majority so we are compelled to congregate in one sole church. This very morning, I received a letter from one Father Evrart, the senior priest and his assistant, Father Servet, expressing grave consternation for...now where is it...ah, yes, I have it. Let me read you some pertinent passages,

'We have only Saint Sauveur church wherein to practice our faith...our stalls at market are shunned, for no good reason... Judge Boivin passes severe sentences against us but is lenient towards the Protestants...we are spat on, cursed, ridiculed...a young member of our congregation knows to not have boy or girl friends unless of our church...Boivin and the mayor collect taxes on the due date, without exception, but if you're late your business will be closed down, leaving you and your family to starve...'

"And so, it goes on, duke. So, you see there's a worrying situation unfolding in La Rochelle, a definite pattern of events, especially around this Judge Boivin character whose name repeatedly features in Father Evrart's letter to us but, first, there is Auxerre."

"My lady, I will visit our barracks and ready our loyal troops. Once our weapons and supplies are organised, we will march out of Paris within the week. You have not spoken about the role the king will play in the mission. I assume, therefore, that he will accompany me?"

"He will not. After the pontiff he is, after all, the

temporal figurehead of the kingdom and its government and, as such, his duty remains in his capital city to inspire and reassure his people."

"I understand, perfectly. La Rochelle is to be treated as a town in dire need of our assistance. I've seen off the likes of this Boivin, ma'am, your trust in me is not misplaced."

11

THE TWO NEW RECRUITS, JOFFROY AND HIS FRIEND, Sébastien, sat on the bench next to the captain, Albinet, his arm resting on the river boat's tiller. That day there was only the slightest wind, so it was not worth unfurling and hoisting the sail, but soon after casting off, the Seine's notoriously strong current swept them away from the quay to the middle of the river. Within minutes, the prow scythed into the murky water sending out a bow wave from either side of the vessel.

Albinet looked at the men, let out a guffaw, and asked,

"Why so glum? Can there be a better life than this, under the heavens? Beats any job on land in a dirty old town, if you ask me, so sit back and enjoy it. There's nothing for you to do until tomorrow when we pick up cargo at Saint Germain – cloth, woven stuff, I think. We'll moor up there overnight ready for an early morning start. I know a respectable tavern used by all the watermen, and at a fair price."

Joffroy and Sébastien nodded their approval. Suddenly, their attention was drawn to Little Hand, one of the two Africans on board, waving his arm towards the port side.

"What's he saying?" Sébastien enquired.

"There's a floating tree or sandbank ahead so we have to steer to miss it."

Straining his eyes and scanning the river the newcomer said,

"I don't see anything though."

"He's never wrong. I sometimes think he can smell danger." And he pushed the tiller over, gently altering the boat's course. Just as Little Hand predicted, clumps of reed confirmed a sandbank just below the surface of the water and invisible to most from a distance. The obstacle cleared, Albinet regained the deep central current.

His boat had come down the generations of his family and provided him with a steady income that had increased year on year as trade on the River Seine between Paris and Le Havre, on the Atlantic coast, grew. It was designed for riverine conditions: flat-bottomed, a shallow draft and wide beam; spacious holds and a central sail mast.

They sailed for another ten minutes or so when Little Hand again raised his arm. Coming towards them was a small two-man rowing boat. Albinet stood up to see the object of the hand's warning and he sent the boat over to the port bank. He shouted angrily,

"The likes of them shouldn't be allowed! It's the first rule of sailing – keep to your left, especially away from a ship that's about to break you in two, is that not right, Joffroy?"

"It is, captain." He answered, having worked with him,

although years before. A collision was averted, and harsh insults exchanged as the two vessels passed each other and continued on their way.

Joffroy and Sébastien gleaned snippets of information from the line of folk that had taken the track on the riverbank, making its way from Paris. It was hard to fully understand their messages but it was soon apparent that a dreadful event, with Protestant bloodshed, had occurred in the capital.

"We were right to get out whilst we could," Sébastien concluded.

"Ay...and by the skin of our teeth."

Albinet saw the men's concern,

"My hands got back to me this morning and, although they don't speak French – don't really speak anything – they told me using signs that many hundreds, even thousands, have been cut down by soldiers. Soldiers? Must be the work of the king. Nasty business then."

"You could say that," Joffroy agreed in a cynical tone. Albinet sat back down on the bench and resumed his concentration better to steer the boat. Sébastien nudged his friend,

"To begin, I thought maybe we were panicking but it's a brave or stupid soul who would not flee a bloodbath. We couldn't take the risk."

"Yes, confound high and mighty King Charles and his Catholic courtiers!"

The boat glided smoothly along on the river's powerful flow. The men fell silent, the enormity of the day's events weighing heavily on their minds. Sébastien's gaze bore into the black swirling water forming dark bubbles in its wake; Joffroy scrutinised the line of humanity on the towpath that became less as they moved away from the city. After a mile or so, it ceased completely. Albinet read the man's thoughts,

"You'll not spot anybody now, but I have to say I've not seen so many folk on the path. It must be serious, whatever it is happening in the city."

"It surely is." Sébastien confirmed.

Without the sail, their progress depended on the stream. The boat's complement said nothing, the only sound the lapping of water against the hull. Silence before the storm? An imminent scourge? A pending horror? All manner of conjecture raced through their now troubled senses and they would discover more when they went ashore. Dusk was fast approaching and at that moment the captain announced,

"See those lights in the distance? That's the Saint Germain tavern and I must say I have a right hunger - a thirst too!"

The boat slipped alongside the wooden landing stage, halting with a slight thud at a vacant berth in line with several boats already moored. Big Hand and Little Hand, from their fore and aft positions, jumped from the vessel to thread the mooring lines through the iron rings of the quay's bollards, pulling them tight and, with a well-rehearsed motion, tied them off.

"Done?" Albinet shouted to his men and a wave of their arms confirmed the captain's question. He turned to Joffroy and Sébastien,

"Here we are, Saint Germain."

.   .   .

The town, some ten miles west of Paris, was a good walk from the quay but the tavern by the river was their only destination.

Inside, a roaring fire in one corner warmed the place in that autumnal August. Upon their entering, general welcoming cheers erupted from customers already ensconced, with tankards raised and whistles shrill enough to split an eardrum. Albinet was, evidently, well-known and -respected.

The landlord, a stout bearded fellow, his grubby apron covering his paunch, hailed them loudly above the din of the drinkers. He approached the visitors and gave Albinet a rib-threatening bear hug and broad smile.

"Hey, old man! Good to see you! Is all well with you?"

"Thank you for asking, landlord, indeed it is."

"Pleased to hear it and -" He eyed the guests with an interest bordering on suspicion.

"Let me introduce you to Joffroy and Sébastien, two crew I've taken on."

The landlord stepped forward and extended a hand to them that was shaken, politely.

We've passed the first test then, Joffroy thought. It strikes me like a place where strangers are not regular patrons.

"So, sit, I pray. Your ale is on its way as I speak and I assume you'll dine with us?"

"The only reason we've come – because, if you're still watering down your ale..."

The stout bearded proprietor slammed a fist into Albinet's stomach and gave a raucous howl that descended into a fit of laughter.

"Always the joker, that's you! Away, afore I do you some real damage."

Big Hand and Little Hand had by now joined a table in a corner with eight or nine similarly dark-skinned strongmen: they always profited from the chance to catch up on news from their own kind. Albinet, Joffroy and Sébastien sat at the table the landlord had indicated and they hardly had time to remove their capes when a woman of indeterminate years, but buxom with exposed cleavage, leaned provocatively forward and out down a pitcher of foaming ale followed by three pewter tankards.

"Genteeelmen, as I'm sure you are, welcome." She smiled broadly to reveal an almost toothless grin. Looking directly at Albinet she stood, waiting, until he pushed the obligatory coin into her hand.

"Most generous, kind sir." And, with a jiggle of her ample breasts, she left the men to their drinking.

Joffroy filled the tankards; they each clinked the others' vessels in a toast, and took a satisfying first draught that barely touched their dry throats.

For the first half hour, Albinet was repeatedly slapped on his back and shaken firmly by the hand as one after another acquaintance enquired as to his health and business. *Long time no see* seemed to be the only audible feature of the meetings. Joffroy and Sébastien were introduced to the well-wishers and they soon felt less like intruders into a sailor's coterie.

The serving wench brought three bowls of steaming eel stew and a freshly-baked loaf that Albinet promptly and without ceremony tore into three.

"Enjoy this, men," he invited them, not that any invitation was necessary, they were ravenous, "best eel stew in the kingdom, believe me." They nodded their agreement with every mouthful: apart from belching and spoons clicking on bowls, no other sound could be heard.

Mopping up the last drop of stew in his bowl with a chunk of bread, Sébastien pronounced,

"That was exceptional."

"Yes, exceptional." Albinet repeated, mimicking the man's use of that high-aounding word, and filling the tankards,

"More ale!" He called towards the counter.

As the evening wore on, the atmosphere grew more animated. Ale flowed freely; jokes were made and received from friends and passing cronies, but all united by the fellowship of men who plied their trade on the great rivers of their land; they exchanged news,

How's your wife? Did you repair your boat? Does he still owe you money? Don't take him on, he's a rogue.

Joffroy turned to his companion, noticing a sad countenance,

"Is it the ale? Tastes good to me."

"No, not at all, the ale's fine, best I've tasted in a long while."

"What is it then?"

"I feel like I don't belong to the gathering."

"Don't belong?"

"You, Joffroy, were a sailor once so you slip into conversation easily with them, whereas I'm an outsider."

This admission earned him a hearty slap to the shoulder, an expression of friendship.

"I agree you're new to the game but a few trips and that will change. You'll soon learn."

"Thanks, I hope so."

At that moment a man, young enough to be Albinet's son, sat down at their table. The older man hugged him and beckoned the serving wench to bring another tankard. With obvious pleasure he introduced him,

"This is Benoist. He worked for me...must be ten years ago, is that right?"

"More than that, master, you taught me everything there is to know about sailing on rivers."

Albinet blushed slightly.

"I wouldn't say that but, anyway, Joffroy and Sébastien, meet Benoist." They all shook hands and clinked tankards together.

"How is it you're here in Saint Germain, do you have a boat?"

Benoist interrupted,

"No, it's not like that. I arrived here this afternoon from Paris."

"But the last I heard anything was you going into service in one of the royal palaces...you always were above a lowly sailor's lot."

"And, so I did. I started in the kitchens of King Charles' banqueting halls, moving from one to another, scrubbing floors, washing pans, lighting fires, jobs like that. I worked hard and earned a name for myself. Then I became friends with an aged butler, a real nice chap who's with us no more. One of his duties was serving wine to the guests at banquets. He wasn't the sommelier, the main man, but he had a key to the cellars where the wine was stored. He'd take me down there and going from rack to rack he told me all about where this or that wine came from, its vintage, its nose...I loved it! It was like going to school for me, so much to learn from it. He'd take the selected bottles upstairs, polish them clean then out to table – nearly forgot, he uncorked them as well." His audience smiled. "After a time, he named me his *assistant*. I followed, always one step behind, handing him bottles from the trolley I was in charge of. It was a wonderful job."

"Then why have you left it?" Joffroy asked.

From the second Benoist explained that he'd come from Paris, that same day, both newcomers hung on his every word knowing, instinctively, that the man's account would be of great interest to them. Benoist resumed,

"Today, I was working with the old butler. It was the banquet for the marriage of Princess Marguérite of Valois to Henry of Navarre in the Great Hall of the Royal Palace. I saw it as one of my duties to know the names of the people we served. I was fascinated by royal folk and, do you know, the more I saw of them the more, apart from fancy titles and clothes, I realised they're no different from you and me.

Anyway, it was a joyous celebration – food, wine, men, women, children, jesters, clowns and tumblers. The hall rang out with happiness. On the top table was the newly-married couple, of course, and Queen Catherine and the king himself! So many nobles together. The princess looked radiant; you could say blissfully happy sitting next to her new husband. There was talk that she was a Catholic and he a Huguenot and that it wasn't right – I don't understand what that meant. All the years I lived and worked in Paris, I never knew who went to one church or another...it didn't bother me one jot, nobody cared." He paused and took a slow deep draught of his ale. Glancing round the table, the three men's gaze was fixed on him, each enthralled, needing to know more.

"Of a sudden, everything changed and I won't forget it as long as I live." His hand started to shake, his voice trembling with emotion. "This very morning, I watched a troop of soldiers, swords and daggers drawn, come into the hall then, for what seemed an age, there was a terrifying silence. All the guests sat motionless; how could they have expected this to happen on a day of merriment? I looked down to the high table and, in the blink of an eye, the king, Catherine, Henry and Marguérite rose and got out of the place through a rear door. The leader of the soldiers, I think he was a duke or similar by his elegant uniform, called out an order. *Now!* His men divided into two: some ushered all the Catholic guests sitting on one side to leave and with all haste, the others started an unholy killing of the remaining Huguenots. Women screaming, men howling, children wailing – all put to the slaughter on the spot. Not one left alive, my friend the butler included."

"What you recount is beyond all comprehension but I suppose there are two sides to everything..." Albinet suggested in a sad tone. Benoist screwed up his eyes, the veins on his forehead standing out with anger,

"Master, you speak the truth, there are without doubt two sides – the saved Catholics and the condemned Huguenots! I'd seen enough. I escaped from that bloody mayhem; it would have been me next for all I know. I ran, and ran, in and out of alleys for safety because the city was filled with soldiers, swarming like bees in a hive, rushing into houses and, from the pandemonium, murdering all those inside. They knew which were Huguenot dwellings for sure...I could hear *Protestant swine! Blasphemous pagans!* All as they carried out their work. This carnage went on throughout the city, from what I saw. Must be so many dead. At last I found myself on the quayside where the news hadn't yet arrived. I went from boat to boat and boarded the first one that offered me passage, and that tells you how I'm here tonight."

Albinet gripped Benoist's arm in a reassuring gesture and said softly,

"You will come to my boat, now. Tomorrow at dawn, once we've loaded, we sail. You'll be safe with us."

"Master, I thank you, with all my heart."

They finished their ale and trudged towards the river, each with a feeling of impending catastrophe.

Beauvais, 1572

Like Benoist, Joffroy and Sébastien, old Gervase and his arthritic wife, Salvia, had fled Paris on their horse and cart. They too had been aware of a growing mood of antagonism towards Huguenot people, their priests and their churches, over many months. Gervese's decision had not been taken lightly for, throughout their fifty-year marriage, his wife's medical condition had been plagued by severe joint pain and a bone-shaking journey would prove almost unbearable for her. However, their lives were at risk so it was Beauvais, to the north, with its magnificent Gothic cathedral, that they sought. Salvia's brother welcomed them to his home,

"You will both stay here until...well, until it's safe for you to return to Paris. What you have told me is truly atrocious. But there's one thing you should know."

"What's that, brother?"

"The bishop of Beauvais is of the Catholic faith and he holds the town in a menacing grip. He's not a man anyone would argue with, he's not someone worthy of the title of a holy bishop. The citizens of Beauvais are opposed to us Huguenots. We do not live a pleasant life and they grant us but one run-down church for our worship – the roof leaks when it rains, the mortar in its walls crumbles, the cemetery is all but full." Gervese looked at his wife, and they both shared the same awful realisation: had they gone from one religious misery to another? They were not to have known that Beauvais was led by a corrupt bishop and, they assumed, uncompromising vindictive clergy who carried out his every order.

Salvia burst into tears, sobbing uncontrolledly. Gervese pulled her close in an attempt to comfort her, but to no avail. They saw, in that moment, that they could not stay there, but where to next?

12

The Duke de Guise's meeting with the Queen Mother, Catherine at Chenonceau, had granted him complete authority to lead his troops in the name of King Charles, to 'arrange' – her euphemism – towns she considered the Huguenots had too great an influence over, to the detriment of the Catholic population. In any event, she would distance herself from the duke's operations, anxious to appear innocent in the public perception.

De Guise returned from her office to his imposing detached residence on the Rue Saint Antoine, in a fashionable quarter of Paris. He told his manservant to bring him food and wine in his study with further instructions that he was not to be disturbed for the rest of the day. He needed to give careful consideration to his plans, determined to live up to Catherine's expectations. He had succeeded in creating a predominantly Catholic capital city, according to her wishes, through merciless military action. Ever ambitious and beguiled by her charisma, he paced around his study for an endless time, contemplating and analysing various strategies. Against one wall stood a large table on which he had unrolled and weighted down maps and charts covering the kingdom. Leaning over them he pointed to this or that town, tracing a road, identifying streams at which the horses could be watered, measuring distances: his experience as a soldier had taught him the essential importance of thorough planning.

I have three companies of one hundred men in each at my Paris barracks, he reasoned, all fine swordsmen. In the stables, there is stationed a troop of thirty cavalry, skilled with the axe and flail. Each body of men is ably commanded by two sergeants and a captain who are, and be cognisant of this, de Guise, devout followers of the Catholic faith. The ranks, so long as they are paid, couldn't care less what the enemy believes in. Now, where are we...ah, November...that gives me five maybe six weeks before the weather turns to snow and ice. The last two winters have been bad and I don't expect it to change – or, at least, I must assume that it won't. Snow and ice...unfit for man or beast.

He sat in his armchair in front of a blazing fire and filled a goblet with wine. Staring into the flames, his mind raced with the excitement of the battlefield, his past campaigns and honours. He accepted, though, that his present challenges would unfold in streets, house to house, a world away from the green open meadows where conflicts usually come to pass. His strategy decided, he rose and went over to the table. Checking towns and roads, he clicked his tongue and gave a wry smile.

Catherine will be pleased with me, for sure. I will take Auxerre before Christmas; in the New Year, we will march on Montauban and, to see off my orders, there will be La Rochelle, the hardest of them, by all accounts, but by the summer.

Standing in front of a long mirror hanging on the wall, the slim strong duke, bearded chin, narrow nose and searching eyes, breathed in and pulled back his shoulders, admiring his aristocratic figure. Aware of his powers of leadership from a young age, confidence was embedded into his very spirit, by virtue of a privileged upbringing in a titled household.

He summoned the four captains to his house. They lined up, nervously, in the hall at the foot of a wide oak staircase leading to the private quarters. The manservant knocked on his master's door and put his head inside,

"Sire, your captains have arrived."

"Thank you. Now, position yourself outside in the grounds and ensure there are no gardeners, delivery men or the likes around. My meeting is private."

"Of course, sire."

De Guise waited for ten minutes before appearing at the top of the staircase where he stood, motionless. Attired in a finely embroidered doublet over black hose; gold medallion and chain under a loose purple cape; velvet cap at a jaunty angle; his ceremonial sword in its jewel-encrusted scabbard: he looked every inch a duke.

. . .

He walked up and down the line, as if conducting an inspection, then he spoke,

"The day after next, we embark on our mission, one of several ordered by good King Charles, in the name of our Holy Church. Arrange supplies for a march of three days, canvas blankets, weapons and leather armour. The roads we will follow are not as even as those of our fair city. The men will rest each night from dusk, to prepare them for the fight. Tell them they will be well paid, as ever, under my command."

He turned to the captain at the end of the line,

"We take thirty horses, choose your finest and load the carts with hay sufficient for the march." Then, to them all, "that is all you need know for the moment. Return to your barracks."

The captains saluted, bowed and filed out of the house to break the news to their troops.

That evening the barracks, although sworn to secrecy, were alive with gossip and conjecture – *where are we going to? are you ready? – when do we get paid?* These soldiers were regulars, the retained Paris units and not mercenaries whose reliability and motive were all too often different from theirs. They enjoyed seeing action, they spoiled for a fight, they were accustomed to bloodshed and, in the main, felt loyalty for their master, the king.

'I've heard old Charlie is going away on holiday and he wants protection in case of bandits.'

'Stupid! He's got his bodyguard for that.'

'Ah, yes, I hadn't thought of that.'

Although well-endowed with brawn, they were less so with intelligence.

'Back home for Christmas, and the money will come in handy, that's for sure.'

I reckon we'll be doing the same as that Saint Barthalmy's day business...against...what are they called... against them Huggenerts.'

De Guise spent the coming days poring over maps, deciding the best roads, considering his strategic options, not least of which the degree of opposition he was likely to encounter.

The day before their departure he recalled his captains who, this time, were shown upstairs to his study. As was customary, they were kept waiting. Once inside, the duke, dressed in a plain tunic and, except for his chain and medallion, was indistinguishable from his men. His success as a soldier, in many conflicts, had been achieved thanks in no small part to an astute assessment of his own troops and those of his enemy. He was about to issue his final orders and appreciated his simple clothing, not aristocratic finery, would better engage them.

'Will you take wine?" he asked.

"With pleasure," the men answered, in almost perfect unison.

Having filled five goblets, the manservant left the study.

"Here's to the king and victory!" de Guise proposed.

"The king and victory." came the response.

"Tomorrow we march on Auxerre," the duke announced, his voice steady, "a town where Huguenots prosper, to the displeasure of the king who would see their stronghold crushed. They will not expect our arrival so we have the advantage of surprise." The day after his audience with Catherine, when she had announced her wishes, he had written to Bishop Jacques Amyot:

'Your excellency, Bishop of the Catholic Church of Auxerre, I write to you as the appointed general of His Majesty King Charles.

Be advised that the king has ordered me to march on your town with the intention of restoring those of the Catholic faith to a position of authority over the loathed Huguenots, in both religious and civil affairs.

To this end, inform your priests, prior to our arrival, to ensure their parishioners are safe in their houses on November 20*th*. Furthermore, the north gates must remain open as, nowadays, they usually are. Please attend to this, it is of crucial importance to our action.

All this must be done with the utmost secrecy, lest the Huguenot people are warned. They must suspect nothing.

I await receipt of your seal on parchment to signify your agreement.

De Guise, general of King Charles.'

The bishop read the message, then again, hardly believing his eyes. After so many years of increasing repression by the Huguenots, rendering his people powerless and greatly distressed, here was a missive of salvation, manna from heaven, a light in the darkness. The messenger stood silent all this time, waiting for the reply he had to take back to de Guise.

Bishop Jacques Amyot heated a small block of red wax

over a candle's flame, pushed a brass seal into it then made an impress on a parchment sheet, his acceptance of the king's assistance. He rolled it up, tied it with a length of blue ribbon, then handed it to the courier who left immediately for Paris.

'I will follow the general's orders, and to the letter. Praise be!'

He took a key from his cassock pocket and unlocked a small wooden box on his desk. The remarkable letter was placed within and he locked it away, safe.

De Guise continued his address,

"There are three barracks that we will seize to accommodate our men, one company in each. I am reliably informed that their bishop's army – call it that if you will – consists of no more than two dozen soldiers who will be no match for our own. You will muster, tomorrow, at the Bois de Vincennes, outside the city walls, at dawn. Do you have any questions?" The captains were silent.

"So, to the king!" de Guise shouted, raising a clenched fist and punching the air.

"To the king!" they replied, saluting in a similar defiant manner.

And to Catherine, the duke pondered.

The following day dawned misty and damp, a sign that autumn was upon them, though not disagreeable. Such conditions suited an army on the march. The Parisian soldiers were assembled, as instructed, on the road by the Vincennes woods: three hundred infantry, thirty horsemen, carts loaded with hay, supplies and weapons – a formidable force in the name of the Catholic Church, a battalion to engender fear in the Protestant enemy, a strength to be reckoned with.

Leading the line were the cavalry, three abreast, the riders standing beside their mounts, holding them by the bridle. The horses, the finest in the stable, tossed their heads, letting out strident whinnies that rent the still morning air. The time for which they were bred and trained was nigh.

Next came two infantry squads, each with their two sergeants and one captain standing also in threes. The sergeants wore black caps, the captains white – a means of easy identification in a skirmish. All the soldiers wore a thick brown tunic, waterproof capes and strong leather boots

The supply carts, each hitched to two working horses, groaned under their load. Then the third company of foot soldiers brought up the rear, completing the assemblage, ready with growing impatience for the signal to go.

With a typically dramatic flourish the Duke de Guise emerged from the woods, upright in the saddle, reins held in one hand, the other raised in a salute. Tugging at the bit the beast came to a halt in front of the men. Dressed in a purple velvet cap and cape, he looked every inch a general, exuding authority and pride, head held high. Pressing his heels gently into his mount's flanks, he walked it slowly down the line, an almost imperceptible smile on his lips, a gesture he had learned early on in his career that gave the troops encouragement and belief in their invincibility. He spoke only,

"Ready?" to each captain who affirmed,

"Ready, sire!"

From the front of his soldiers he turned in the saddle and called out,

"Forward!" Upon which the column, at first slowly, began its march on Auxerre.

As a child, tales of ancient warriors and their campaigns, as told to him by his tutors, enthralled him: the Hittites in chariots, cutting down their foes; the fearless Celts; the Scythian warlords, and how they were described –

Always courageous, their quivers like an open grave. They will eat your harvest and bread, they will eat your sons and daughters, your sheep and oxen. Yes, they will eat your grapes and figs. They are almighty, for sure.

But there was one conqueror, above all others, that the duke admired: Alexander, King of Macedon, rightfully bearing the title of *great*. The Lord of Asia, undefeated in battle, the only man to tame the ill-tempered stallion, Bucephalus. It was a beast from the best strain; its black coat shone; the large white star on its brow marked it out from the rest – but, it had a savage spirit, unseating every man who attempted to bestride it. Alexander was the first to achieve this feat, gaining him the status of a demigod.

Notwithstanding his present horse was not Bucephalus, de Guise regarded himself as *the Great* when it came to leading his men in a conflict.

The procession halted each day at dusk. The horses were tethered and watered; the men received their food from the carts then, covered with their canvas blankets, slept soundly by the roadside.

Come late afternoon on the third day, a scout who had gone ahead, galloped back, his mount skidding to a stop in a cloud of dust alongside the duke.

"Sire, Auxerre lies round the next bend, perhaps twenty minutes march. I have ridden through the streets. The people are out taking the evening air, children playing, men coming in and out of the taverns. They suspect nothing, that I could tell."

Just as I had hoped. The bishop has acted according to my instructions

"Is that your carefully considered military assessment?" de Guise asked sarcastically.

"Sire?"

"No matter, you are dismissed." *We sleep here tonight and make our entrance tomorrow.*

At first light, the four captains gathered around a map that the duke had unrolled on the ground, held down with stones.

"Pay attention, men. Follow my orders and we will achieve the victory we seek for His Majesty and for the great and only Catholic Church."

Using a twig, he pointed to the map as he spoke,

"We go into the town, as one, through the north gate... here. Three of you will divide and proceed, with all haste, to take the three barracks on the east, south and west sides... here, here and here. We know that there are but a few soldiers in each. With the element of surprise, it means they will be easily seized – and, from my experience of Huguenots, they will likely be fainthearted. Relieve them of their weapons, then drive them out onto the streets – rough them up, show them who's the master, put the fear of God into them. But, at this stage, no need for bloodshed unless, my comrades, any will raise arms against you in which case, dispatch them! Yes...we will keep lethal force in reserve, no point showing our hand too early. Any questions?" *For Alexander and Bucephalus though, it's not the hardest of actions.*

There were none. Their commandeer had explained the plan perfectly. He continued,

"You, cavalry officer, will pass through the streets and squares, at a gallop. Cast aside anyone in your way. They will not have known the likes of thirty magnificent chargers rampaging past their houses. Begin with the Rue de Paris, here, and when you reach the end, down by the river, turn and do the same again. Choose your streets, split into twos and ride hard. Tell your men to cry one simple message at these citizens: *We are King Charles's Catholic soldiers!*

When you hear the noon bells ring, you will all converge on the main square in front of the cathedral, here.

The captains passed on the orders to their sergeants, though in plain language, so it would be easily understood. The latter moved along the lines of sleeping soldiers, shouting 'Wake up! Come on now!' and prodding the more reluctant men roughly with their wooden staffs. They then rose in short order, aware that today was the reason for their march. Filing past the supply carts, they received and knocked back the measure of brandy, an old tradition prior to a battle.

Sitting proudly in his saddle, head held high, the duke led his force towards the town, the infantry bringing up the rear. Auxerre would soon be under Catholic rule as his king – or more accurately, Catherine – had ordered.

Auxerre, November 1572

By noon, the invasion was achieved and the men assembled in the main square, surrounded by an ever-swelling mass of Catholic citizens, cheering, clapping, calling out their welcomes and thanks. Adherents of the suppressed faith were nowhere to be seen, all shut away in their houses, too terrified to show their faces.

De Guise moved to the next stage of the operation. Inside the immense cathedral of Saint Etienne, he stood in front of the altar facing his hastily convened audience. In the pews to his left sat the Protestant bishop, dressed in a plain black cassock, and his clergy; to his right was Bishop Jacques Amyot, head of Auxerre's Catholic populace, his mitre embroidered with gold thread, his ceremonial blue chasuble on a white linen underrobe. His assistant priests filled two rows behind him. Succumbing to temptation, he cast a jubilant yet hateful glance in the direction of those dejected clerics opposite who feared for their lives.

For one moment, still as stone, the cathedral might have been the scene for a wedding celebration, the bride's family and friends on one side, the groom's on the other.

But, a marriage of convenience if ever I saw one, the duke mused, a union that cannot endure over time. Catherine got her sister to wed a Protestant noble – that won't last. I suppose, today, we are arranging for the faiths to coexist albeit with the Catholics dominant. It all comes down to what Catherine de Médicis wants.'

De Guise solemnly withdrew his sword from its scabbard and held it upright, touching his nose. The chatter that hummed around the cathedral subsided. Sheathing his weapon, he waited until the silence was absolute.

"To all of you present," he began, "I speak with the authority vested in me by His Majesty King Charles, rightful and blessed ruler of this kingdom." His voice resonated, commanding the attention of those to both his left and right, "His judicial supremacy is in the royal prerogative, his spiritual guidance is in the gift of the Holy Father in Rome, Gregory the Thirteenth. The edict signed in Saint Germain, some two years ago, that accorded Huguenot people safety and tolerance in the town of Auxerre is, by sovereign decree, hereby annulled. Their ascendancy has been to the disadvantage and diminishment of the Catholic believers. His wise Majesty will not accept such a situation.

"Our bishop, His Excellency Jacques Amyot, will forthwith appoint a mayor and justice of his sage choice. His Excellency will replace the river master with a person suitable for the office, this person to collect taxes and ensure they are paid directly into his coffers, for the benefit of his congregation, also, for the needs of the town."

Quiet reigned in the vast nave, the only sound an uncomfortable shuffling and shrugging of shoulders from the Huguenot faction. Those on the other side wore pleasant expressions. De Guise paused to allow the import of his proclamation to be appreciated. He resumed,

"His Majesty rules that there will be, from this day

onward, but two churches in the town of Auxerre where Huguenots are permitted to worship. All the other churches are now intended for our Catholic brethren. Our esteemed Jacques Amyot possesses unqualified discretion in this matter.

"Now, hear this final notice: the place known as Auxerre will readily and warmly welcome any and all Catholic persons from the wider kingdom who desire to take up residence. They will dwell in such houses that His Excellency requisitions. Former occupants will seek accommodation wherever."

At this last statement, gasps of disbelief and dismay rose and filled the air. Drawing his sword once more and holding it aloft, he concluded, gazing steadfastly at those to his left,

"Depart! Inform your wretched followers of this good news. In the unlikely event that they have learned reading, notices will be posted. Depart!" A wave of his blade and twenty armed soldiers appeared from the transept, to bundle the petrified Protestant priests outside onto the square. The crowd clamoured, pushed, jostled, impatient to know what had passed within the cathedral They would have to wait a while longer: the exiting clergy, heads lowered, scurried off in all directions - despondent, crestfallen, tight-lipped.

The four captains and de Guise made their way to Bishop Amyot's private chapel behind the choir. The cleric filled six silver goblets with red wine from a communion decanter.

"Please, take wine. It is blessed as, indeed, are we, the Catholic citizens of fair Auxerre. Your Grace, I beg you to convey our eternal indebtedness to His Majesty King Charles. Our town now belongs to its rightful masters."

"I will pass these sentiments anon, for I must return to Paris. One company, two sergeants and, ably commanded by a captain, will remain to enforce the instructions of your mayor, justice and, for certain, Your Excellency. Rest assured, they will not hesitate to unsheathe their weapons should there not be total compliance by the Protestants. The Lord be with you."

"And with you." Amyot responded, a tear of happiness in his eye.

De Guise and his officers drained their goblets and left the bishop to consolidate his clerical and civil dominance of Auxerre.

The soldiers entered Paris triumphanly, led by the duke, in the second week of December 1572, as he had envisaged. He went directly to the royal place.

I will report our success to the king, then to Chenonceau where the Queen Mother will surely have further plans. These are such hateful times between Catholics and Huguenots. How will it all end?

13

In Paris, with the Duke of Guise absent on the Auxerre campaign, his anonymous henchmen and their merciless accomplices delivered a thousand death blows – a persecution of anyone who admitted allegiance to the Protestant religion or was even suspected of the same. Beatings occurred daily; humiliation by insult; market stalls upturned; old women spat on. All this to earn their coin and curry favour with their master.

During this time, Catherine the Queen Mother, kept her distance from the capital, disassociating herself and, when advantageous, denying any knowledge of the atrocities. These appalling outrages were committed by both Catholic and Protestant sides and, in this respect, the one was no better than the other. In public, she was seen as a devoted mother, a wife usurped by her husband's mistress, a sympathetic tolerant woman who wanted only the best for her kingdom whose interests she held dear. Her court provided her with an excellent service in broadcasting this propaganda but, in the privacy of her palace, she behaved in a quite contrary manner, especially where her son, Charles, was concerned. She possessed him entirely and did not care for his opinions, certain as she was that she could change them in an instant. Her perceived altruism could easily turn into self-interest and vanity.

Upon the duke's return to Paris, he first went to his house to be greeted by his manservant who greeted him at the foot of the grand staircase. He knew better than to enquire how any expedition had fared, it was a matter between the duke and his king.

"Welcome home, Sire. I will bring food and wine to your study and hot water for your bath, shortly."

"Thank you. It's good to be back."

It's of no import to keep the king waiting a while longer. He cannot fail to be satisfied with my discharge of his orders, he mused.

Slumped in his comfortable armchair, he ate and drank, pondering his actions over recent weeks. Would that move have been better? Should I have said this? Did we take enough horsemen? His soldier's brain analysed all possibilities with a view to improving his next offensive, ever the tactical supremacist. The manservant knocked on the door,

"Your bath is ready, Sire.

Refreshed, de Guise donned his formal doublet and hose, cape, purple cap and ceremonial sword. He adjusted his gold medallion so it hung precisely on the centre of his chest. It would not do to meet the monarch in anything less than his most splendid attire. His horse-drawn carriage was waiting.

"To the royal palace, my man." They moved off on the short journey across the city that he had made many times before.

Two armed guards stepped out in front of the carriage at the heavy wrought iron main gates.

"Who goes there?" Called out one.

The duke leaned forward,

"De Guise, for the king."

The guard went through the charade of examining the visitor at close quarters, although they were well known to each other and the bodywork bore the proud family crest.

"Proceed!" He instructed the driver.

At the far side of the courtyard, an immense iron-studded wooden door, again flanked by guards, was the usual entrance for strangers, who would find themselves scrutinised several times within, to reach at last the king's offices in the heart of the building.

The general's meeting with the sovereign was a routine affair when it came to the former reporting a successful expedition: neither man entertained failure.

"You have done well, de Guise. Please convey my gratitude to your soldiers. I anticipated your arrival and have ordered my lawyers to prepare deeds, in your name, for a fine country house, with stables and land, on my estate by Chartres. Well-stocked with game, too, good for hunting. Accept this as a token of our appreciation."

"Your Majesty is generous beyond belief. I accept your gift." The men raised a glass in a toast.

"I will take my leave of you, Majesty, for I must away to

Chenonceau and your mother. She will be anxious for news."

"Of course. Pass on our regards. It's a while since we shared time together."

With a bow and right arm swept through the air, he made his exit. The carriage left Paris through the Saint Jacques gate and, after an overnight stay in a friend's home near to Orléans, he arrived at Chenonceau the following day.

"...so, Auxerre is a Catholic town once more." The duke finished his report and Catherine's expression changed from tight-lipped and sullen into a broad smile.

"This is indeed good news and our brethren of Auxerre will celebrate a fine Catholic Christmas this year, led by bishop...bishop..." She momentarily forgot his name.

"Bishop Jacques Amyot, Ma'am." Her smile endured.

"Now, I have a superb vintage brandy." She moved over to the sideboard, uncorked a bottle and poured the light-brown nectar into two cut-glass goblets. The next hour or so was spent on pleasantries, a relief from the severity of the religious wars that surrounded them, the very reason for his visit.

"You will stay tonight, after we have dined?"

"Gladly, Ma'am."

"However, we should now return to grave matters, duke." Her features hardened. "Our struggle knows no endgame," her protruding Médicis eyes fixed on her general, "there remain two places dominated by the Huguenot allegiance that we must cleanse in the New Year, before turning our efforts further afield. Montauban, in the south of our kingdom and, although a good way from here, has been particularly vocal in deriding Catholic teaching. Next, we will address the problems in La Rochelle on the Atlantic coast. All this will be under your able stewardship but, for the present, your men will rest and enjoy the holy Christmas season."

"Amen to that, Ma'am."

"My maidservant, Mathilde, will call you from your room when dinner is served. De Guise departed, his military brain already considering different strategies for his next action.

Catherine poured another stiff brandy and sat in her armchair in front of the fire – she felt the cold at this time of year – satisfied with her general's achievements, but her thoughts swiftly fell on her son, the king, and whether she should relent and allow him to accompany de Guise for his assault on Montauban. Her prime consideration in this respect was the successful protection and furtherance of her Catholic faith. Would Charles' inclusion in de Guise's force help or hinder the cause, she asked herself, torn between her religious responsibilities and maternal desire that her favourite son should be fulfilled as a man and solider?

Her own ambition was born in her Italian beginnings; her bitterness arose from her late husband's mental cruelty and mocking when she did not produce him heirs strong enough to survive birth for the early years of their marriage. This was compounded by his mistress that she loathed, Diane, who had bewitched him, even casting spells, Catherine maintained.

To her subjects she portrayed confidence and happiness

but she was, in reality, desperately sad, constantly asking herself if she was to blame for her cheerless union with Charles and whether she was a good mother. Was she the reason her children so rarely visited? The brandy was most welcome that day as she took stock of her offspring.

My youngest daughter Claude, is, this very year to be wed to the Duke of Lorraine – King Charles of that kingdom. He's of good Catholic stock, I'll give her that. Then, son Henry... strangely, I can't say I know the boy but I don't think he holds me in any great esteem. Well, he's the Grand Duke of Poland now, and they have more than enough problems to keep him occupied without thinking of me. She slowly sipped more brandy and her expression softened, a gentle smile on her lips. *Margaret, my Margot, we planned your escape on the day you married Henry of Navarre...yes, then away to his homelands in Spain. Oh dear...they all take such different paths that I sometimes find myself confused. My boy, Francis, given the dukedom of Anjou, but we hear nothing of note from you. My soldiers slew the Protestants at your wedding banquet but, heavens above, am I cursed, is it divine retribution, is there a mother on earth who has lost four children?*

Little princesses Joan and Victoria, you knew barely one month's life. Then my first, Francis...you had a brief reign but your health, in body and mind, was fragile and you were taken from us too soon.

She rose from her chair and paced her office from one side to the other, deep in contemplation, wracked with anguish and breathed in, revisiting more painful times.

When my two baby princesses departed this life, my royal physician ordered no more children: otherwise, he could not be responsible for any resulting complications. That was enough to drive Henry into Diane's waiting arms.

The thought of his infidelity, back then and even now, created a profound jealousy in her breast and she frowned and screwed her eyes tight.

I think back to my wedding night, thirty-nine years ago, when both my father and Pope Clément hovered around my bedchamber for proof of consummation. Such ignominy! Such shame! Me, a child who had barely seen fifteen winters; a girl, so innocent in the ways of the world that I could not have imagined the path my life would take. With the start of marriage shared with three men, it's no surprise I took so long to conceive!

Was she naïve to not appreciate the mood of her kingdom? Did she place too much store on a message delivered to her by a diplomat and from a land she had long since abandoned?

Why do my people dislike me so? Do I deserve their censure? I recall, years ago, my messenger reported to me on royal affairs after a visit to our ambassador in Venice. It's extraordinary how the Italians perceive me. Now, what were his words...'No step, however unimportant, is taken without her. Scarcely has she time to eat or drink or sleep, so great are her harassing cares. She runs here and there between the armies, doing a man's work, without a thought of sparing herself. Yet she is loved by no one in the land.'

Her frustration was such that she stamped her feet in a petulant action and waved her arms as if there was someone in the room – how she wished there was.

My people admire me, that I know, so why do I escape their love? With the exception of Diane de Poitiers, I have not seen my relationships with women to be an issue – solely with men! If the truth be out, I'm happier fighting the Church than the male species.

She sat down, gazing into the fire, pondering her progeny Charles the king and Henry, Grand Duke of Poland. As they were growing up, Catherine's difficulties in managing them increased. She no longer had the same authority over them. He sons were men and her once controlling hand in their affairs was no more. She reminisced in her armchair, gazing up at the ceiling, eyes wide open.

I appointed my son as Lieutenant General of the realm and, although I admit I petted him, he had a chance to prove himself three years ago when he commanded an army to defeat Huguenot battalions at the Battle of Montconcour after German Protestant mercenaries had defiled our churches – burning the bones of our saintly King Louis i X and the heart of King Francis i.

How her very soul pained her. Was it possible for a woman of intellect, acumen, experience, to still fret? Were her fears and moments of self-doubt justified?

My boy had exacted revenge for the desecration of our beloved relics and how I was proud of him! Yet, Charles was insanely jealous of his elder brother's brilliant success on the battlefield. I tried to bring him to reason and, it's true, I constantly played on his jealousy and fear of Henry who was waiting impatiently to take the throne. After much consideration, my court agreed to Charles joining our army against the Dutch – but, at a distance from the front line. After all, he wasn't a seasoned soldier. I was glad he returned without injury.

The next thought that flashed through her head was one

she felt well-qualified on which to pass an opinion, an affair of the heart.

He fell in love! The boy should have looked around him and learned from the mistakes of others. The girl in question, Marie Touchet, was a warm, simple and honest soul and the one person at court who cared for Charles himself, not his title. She provided him with peace and understanding. I remember him saying that stealing away from the Louvre palace to her house was like going from purgatory to paradise! I empathise with that sentiment, for sure.

She drained the last of the brandy from her glass then stared at the vacant chair on the other side of the fireplace where she saw Charles, as clear as day, spindly legs and hunchback. Her voice became, in a moment, tender and she spoke with convincing charm and warmth, an alluring woman appealing to her boy.

Dear Charles, when we arranged your union with Elizabeth, the Austrian lady now your queen, you frequented both women and both have borne you children! And, you say you love your mistress who is kind to your wife, respects her piety and approves of her habit of spending most of the night in prayer: this is not the decent Catholic way to behave, if you would but hear me.

She paused her thoughts when saw her glass and the bottle were both empty, ringing a bell to summon her maidservant who quickly came.

"Ma'am?" Mathilde asked.

"Fetch me another bottle, my dear. I have heavy matters

to decide and brandy is of great assistance." *I'll resist the laudanum, I can't afford a deranged mind.*

"Of course, Ma'am."

The maidservant returned shortly and refilled her mistress's glass. Catherine took a sip and put it down on the dressing table, sitting at its stool.

"I will tend your hair so you can retire, then, when you so desire."

"Good. I don't know what I'd do without you." Within this austere exterior her repressed tenderness was sometimes displayed, but only before Mathilde who removed the pins and began to brush her hair.

"I see you are troubled and, if I had to hazard a guess, I would say it concerns the duke and King Charles. Put your head up, please, so I can brush properly."

"You are, as ever, correct, Mathilde and you are so close to me, day after day, that you know most things about me – often before I do myself!" Mathilde blushed and continued brushing. "We have successfully taken Auxerre, it is in safe Catholic hands once more, thanks to the good duke's skill as a soldier. Bu, all is not over, far from it. In the New Year, when the weather improves, and the roads are not a mud-bath, our army will march on Montauban, the Huguenot stronghold in the south of our kingdom. Like the other towns, it will fall, but it will be a stern test for my duke and his men. The enemy will not succumb easily."

"From what I understand, you could not have a more competent general than Monsieur de Guise."

"Indeed, I could not, but the situation is complicated."

"Complicated, Ma'am?"

"Yes, Charles."

"The king?"

"Who else, you dimwit!" But her attempt at friendly

jest quickly faded as she carried on, "You will be aware that he is not in the best of health. He appears strong and tall but a weakness overcomes him, at times. His body is supported by his overlong spindly legs and he cannot walk altogether straight. His arms are muscled but his shoulders bowed. Have you not noticed?"

"The king comes here but rarely so I have not had the opportunity to vouch for this, but I'm sure your description is true."

"Yes, he hides it from public view, and have you not wondered why he wears a coat that touches the ground, even in the warmth of summer? To cover his deformities. However -" She took another sip, "...it is not his body alone that ails him, would that it was so. No, he is more emotional than is reasonable, one might say he is mentally unbalanced, on occasions. I have known him burst into sudden fits of uncontrollabe rage and I fear even for my own safety when anger consumes him."

"I did not know that His Majesty suffers thus."

"He has learned to conceal it well. When the children were young, only his sister, Margot, knew how to calm his tantrums but she is now away in Spain and I wish she was here, but I doubt her influence could now control him, so severe are his fits. More brandy, please." Mathilde obeyed, filling the glass to the brim.

"My lady will sleep well tonight."

"I certainly will not! Charles is determined to accompany de Guise against Montauban. I have done my best to dissuade him but to no avail. He is uneasy, aware of his deteriorating condition, and he broods lest he loses a final chance to emulate his brother, Henry, in the theatre of war. I understand such rivalry between siblings but I cannot jeopardise de Guise's campaign."

Mathilde put the brush down on the dressing table then spoke,

"I would not presume to express an opinion, Ma'am, I am a mere servant,"

"You may leave." Catherine instructed the woman, a frosty tone in her voice.

The Queen Mother trusted Mathilde more than anyone in the world, but there were aspects of Charles's nature that were too disturbing to describe and were best kept a close secret. When he had been with Henry's army against the Dutch Protestants, at Montconcour, there were instructions in place to ensure that he would not be allowed near the front line, and with good reason.

Charles's excessive passion for the chase was, in part, an attempt to exorcise murderous fantasies. He preferred to use the knife because he liked blood and insisted on seeing the life spurting from the stag. Catherine cast her thoughts back,

Mere hunting and field sports did not satisfy his bloodlust. He had fiendish bouts in which he amused himself by torturing and dismembering domestic animals. He also liked lashing people until they bled, but in the privacy of his hidden dungeon, under the palace. I knew, he invited like-minded cronies to drink and observe this pastime.

She took a drink, distressed by events she preferred to forget, but could not.

When hunting was impossible, in inclement weather, he would turn blacksmith and beat out weapons in his armoury until he was prostrate with exhaustion. I think he was hammering out his demons, but he never killed them.

If he follows de Guise to Montauban, he will surely

experience the sight of blood and I cannot predict how he might react.

At this same time, Charles became tubercular. He was fever-racked and grew weak, although he made a slow recovery. He was routinely bled by his physicians, causing an infection in his arm where a huge abscess developed. Surprisingly, he came through the crisis sufficiently to resume his duties.

River Seine, Saint Germain, September 1572

"Hey, you two! Wake up, we're away!" Benoist bawled into the sleeping space in the boat's prow. The day began fine, a noisy dawn chorus heralding their departure from Saint Germain quay. Big Hand and Little Hand, as one, threw the mooring ropes onto the deck, jumped aboard and pushed away from the bank with long poles. The air was still but the downstream current swept them smoothly in the direction of Le Havre.

Little Hand was in his customary position on the small foredeck, sometimes standing, straining his eyes for any obstacle ahead. Big Hand sat amidships mending a tear to the edge of the as-yet furled sail with a sailmaker – a strong needle used with thick canvas. Sébastien watched, fascinated by the nimble movement of the man's fat fingers. Joffroy chatted with captain Albinet, as ever at the tiller alongside the boy Benoist, who had joined the boat from the tavern at Saint Germain the previous day. After three hours without any incident of matter, Little Hand raised his arm and cried out something in his foreign language, but a sign that the captain understood.

"Quay ahead." He shouted and, sure enough, just round a bend in the river was a length of moorings – boats tied up, piles of cargo, low warehouses, men moving trolleys, shouts, laughter ringing out.

The hands made fast the boat and the captain gave his instructions, using his remarkable sign language, then turned to the other three men.

"Follow them boys. There's a good number of bales – wool – needs bringing down here on trolleys, if you can find 'em, then loaded into the holds. That should keep you busy for a while." He gave them a friendly grin.

There were, indeed, a *good number*. After an hour or so, Sébastien pulled back his shoulders and, wiping the sweat from his brow, informed Albinet,

"That's the last, captain. Phew!"

"Good. You boys sure don't mind hard work, I'll give you that. See – he leaned over the edge of the boat, "she's sitting much lower in the water and that makes steering her easier."

"I see." Sébastien said, having learned something new about rivercraft.

"And the wind's picking up." He continued, "Look at Big Hand, he's waving to me it's time to hoist the sail...he's never wrong either, so both of you get over there and help him. Don't worry, just do like he shows with his hands, it's simple."

Not long past noon, they cast off and sailed

downstream with the wind behind them to the next quay where they would unload some of the cargo and take on new, the rest to be taken to their destination of Le Havre that they neared two days later. The river widened, mile by mile, and the towpath became a track for horse-drawn carts. The environment they had become accustomed to – occasional cottages and quays – altered. Trees on the riverbank were replaced by rows of buildings bearing signs of the trades they housed: chandler, vintner, provisions, stables, lodgings, ales, blacksmith, baker. Behind these could be seen residences, their chimneys smoking - life in communities.

The nature of the water, as did the terrain, developed from a smooth even predictable flow into a choppy altogether more swirling current, bubbling up into white-crested low waves They had arrived at the start of the estuary of the Seine, Le Havre on its north side, the mighty English Channel ahead. Then, out of nowhere, appeared a boat sailing upstream that came perilously close to their bows.

"Watch out!" Benoist screamed, thinking there was an imminent collision. But not so, it steered parallel to them and a sailor on the offending vessel held out a pole with a piece of parchment attached to its tip. Little Hand reached out and grasped it, upon which the boat veered away on its correct course, left of the river. Albinet unrolled it and read its message.

"Ah, that's fine."

"What's fine, captain?" Sébastien asked.

"It's our way, we river boatmen, of communicating with each other. We recognise this or that boat so we pass over orders from merchants, traders from Paris and beyond. See, this – He held the sheet for Sébastien to read.

'*Captain Albinet – wine barrels – Cabourg to Paris – as soon as possible – Gagne Fils, Cabourg*'

'Old man Gagne, the captain explained, he's been a customer for twenty years. So, we unload the wool at Honfleur port, then on to Cabourg and Gagne's warehouse. Pretty little port is Cabourg, he mused, and I guess the note means we'll have a full boat to take back."

Sébastien looked at Joffroy with a steady gaze – both men saw what the other was thinking. Returning to Paris was the last thing they could entertain. They had fled the capital to save their lives and for the religious freedom to worship in the Protestant way. For all they knew, Catholic zealots followed them in their hoards, such was the mistrust and fear between the faiths.

Joffroy spoke first.

"Captain Albinet, we are indebted to you, taking us on as hands, and we trust you have been satisfied with our work."

"I have no complaints, but why do you ask?"

"We will sail with you to Cabourg where we must part company. Our fate lies ahead, to lands unknown, for certain, but it is forward we must go to –

Albinet interrupted,

"To avoid the Catholics. I had meant to tell you to be careful around these parts and I'm not surprised you've taken this decision. There's so much bad blood...with this or that so-called belief fighting for whatever reason they have. I'm glad I don't have anything to do with it." He paused a moment then, in a reflective tone, went on, "I think Rollo's to blame."

"Rollo?" asked Joffroy, "who's he?"

"Not *is* but *was*. He's been dead these six hundred years."

"What did he do?" Sébastien said, fascinated.

"Well, my father would tell me tales about King Rollo, when I was a small child, and usually when he came home from the tavern...ale loosened his tongue, I think. He was a Viking chieftain in the year nine hundred, or thereabouts, and he sailed over here with his warriors in long-ships. All his men spoke in a strange tongue – a bit like my two hands. He was a giant of a man with a fiery red beard and a battle axe so sharp it could slice a man in half with a single blow, quick as a blink. He was so heavy that no horse would bear him so he entered the skirmish on foot!" The captain had an enthralled audience. "His men were savages but brave, ay, feared nothing nor nobody. Now – and I know this is true because I was born there – his goal was the town of Rouen because once he had that place, he would control all the lands around. He wanted his own kingdom, do you see?" Both men nodded. "For his sins though, Rouen held strong and despite three or more attacks the citizens wouldn't surrender. In the end, the poor people had endured enough and their king, Charles the Simple, paid Rollo with chests of gold to leave them alone. That he did and he was also given many of the lands around us as well as the province we know call Brittany. You see, he had his kingdom, didn't he? What I'm getting around to saying is Rollo was a pagan who worshipped false gods yet Charles converted him to Christianity, baptised him, even had him marry his own daughter, Gisela! That's how it all started, according to my old father, anyway...praying to Jesus, priests, churches...and, ever since, one Christian has always fought with another. So, you see, it's all Rollo's fault."

· · ·

"You have the measure of it, captain, we could all learn lessons. But, we are not seeking to avoid work. No, at Cabourg we will gladly load old Gagne's barrels. You'll need some muscle for that."

"Agreed. We will make Honfleur by dusk." Albinet turned his attention to steering the boat, having enjoyed telling his tale. They skirted the south side of the estuary, leaving Le Havre behind. With their work at the first port completed, Albinet, Joffroy and Sébastien walked through its charming Normandy town to an inn the captain knew where they would eat and drink well. The swarthy hands and Benoist went off in another direction.

"I know where they're going to, and it doesn't serve ale." Albinet commented, a smile on his face, "ladies of the night and all that."

The evening meal was hearty and much-needed – fatty roast pork belly, boiled potatoes and onions, fresh bread, all washed down with fine local beer.

"When we make Cabourg, tomorrow, where do you intend to go?" the captain asked.

"As far away from the Parisian Catholics as possible," Joffroy spat out the words. Their boss took a deep draught of his drink before pronouncing,

"I have a suggestion, if I may be so bold."

"Be as bold as you like, we're strangers to these parts," the other man invited.

"On my travels, of late, I've heard there's one town in particular that's ruled by your own kind."

"Huguenots?"

"Ay, the same. It's said they're wealthy, well-connected

and devils when it comes to defending their churches, if I can put it thus."

"Where's that? Come on, captain, tell," Joffroy urged him, frowning.

"Montauban."

"A place I don't know."

"Nor will you. Montauban lies a week's ride from here, in a different kingdom, or so I understand. Yes, in a different kingdom but, it will be a safe town. You'll need two decent horses and...but we'll leave all that until tomorrow. Drink up, it's my turn to pay!"

The men did as told excited yet fearful for what tomorrow might bring.

14

CHENONCEAU, DECEMBER 1572

With two weeks remaining before the Christmas of 1572, it was time for Catherine to relocate to the Louvre palace to be beside her son, the King, for the seasonal festivities. She anticipated this landmark in the calendar with mixed feelings: while she relished the religious meaning of Christmas and her beloved Catholic Church; she looked on the ribaldry and hypocrisy that was displayed by her son's courtiers and, indeed, his clerical grandees as abhorrent. Her sharp eye identified those close to the King who were driven only by self-interest and others whose motives were sincere. But, for this short period, she carried out her duty as queen dowager and overlooked the excesses of the administrative and governmental coterie that feasted and cavorted in and around the palace.

"Is everything prepared for tomorrow?" she asked her maidservant.

"It is, Ma'am. I have packed your trunk and with

enough gowns to attend a dozen balls and banquets. You will, surely, be the best dressed lady in the King's hall."

"As it should be, Mathilde, I have my reputation to consider."

The next morning, she ate a light breakfast, left her room, and descended the stairs to where her carriage awaited outside the stables. Breathing in the crisp clean air, she smiled at Mathilde and nodded to the footman holding open the landau door. Two steps up and she sat on the green upholstered seat facing her maidservant who was already installed. They each pulled a travel rug over their knees, sat back and prepared to enjoy the journey – even though the ride on tracks hardened by the early-morning frost would be bumpy. Neither woman was in her prime and both had endured far worse ordeals. The footman pushed the door tight shut, dropping the latch to ensure the safety of the passengers, and took a polite step back. The coachman looked over his shoulder and, satisfied all was in order, cracked his whip and called a sharp command,

"Move on, lads, move on!"

He pulled the reins taut to steer the pair of slick strong working horses towards the gate, through the outer palace walls to the track without.

"You strapped the trunk well down, boy? Wouldn't do to lose the lady's belongings, would it?" He asked the lad by his side who nodded and answered in the squeaky voice of a youth of barely thirteen winters, "All done, think I don't know my job?" His impudence earned him a painful elbow in his ribs.

They cut fine figures in their royal blue greatcoats trimmed with gold braid and black felt hats sporting a white ostrich feather. Another crack of the whip and they were soon moving along at a moderate pace, occasionally jolting when they hit a rut or a stone.

Catherine undid the ribbon tying her bonnet down,

"That's better. Now, Mathilde, we're on our way so I think it's time for a drop – to keep out the chill – so, purely medicinal." Reaching inside a leather travel case she took out a bottle and two miniature pewter goblets.

"Hold them while I pour," she ordered, not that Mathilde needed cajoling. They sipped the brandy and looked at each other, neither wanting to speak first. After refilling the goblets, the maidservant said, hesitantly,

"My lady does not seem happy."

"I am not. This year, above all, we should be focused on matters that will determine the Church's future and its very essence, faced with the danger from the Protestant heretics. We have annulled their threat and restored the Holy Father's dominance in many towns of our kingdom, but victory is not yet ours. In the New Year, our Duke de Guise will take Montauban, of that I am confident, but there remains one jewel, a prize that we must seize."

"What is that, Ma'am?"

"La Rochelle, a port to the west that bristles with Huguenots. When that place is, once again, a part of the Mother Church, we will celebrate but," Mathilde interrupted,

"My lady, the duke is a fine general who has served you with loyalty and distinction. You must trust his soldierly ability and, of course, he will have the King at his side."

"Mathilde! My dear Mathilde! How I love thee, as a mother loves her daughter, but our success depends on more than mere trust. The duke is directing his thoughts to the Montauban campaign: he readies his troops, thinks of horses, supplies, weaponry, as a good officer should. However, I feel he underestimates the challenge La Rochelle will pose. It will require careful planning for, from what I understand, it will not surrender like a dog rolling over."

"And the King's part in this?"

Catherine drank more brandy and spluttered her answer,

"The King is what he is. While I intend to shield him from the Montauban struggle, I fear I will be forced to allow him to be at La Rochelle. It may well be his valediction as a warrior monarch, but he will scent blood and react...but you need not know that. I am no soldier, but I have a schemer's brain. I have had to fight all my life, and to take that port means we have to be familiar with the beast, how it breathes and sleeps, who are its rulers, where it worships. All this, and more."

Mathilde leaned back, her grave expression mirroring that of her mistress.

"We will use the opportunity of the season to meet with de Guise. The sooner we begin our preparations, the better and sweeter will be our rightful triumph."

Fortified and warmed by the medicinal brandy, the two women passed the journey chatting, laughing, and gossiping about light-hearted things, from Catherine's plan for a new water feature in the gardens, to Mathilde's account of an affair between the head chef and a scullery maid. By dusk, the carriage pulled up outside the King's chateau, just outside Orléans, where they would spend the night. Paris was reached by mid-afternoon the following day.

At the Louvre palace the lad jumped down from his seat, opened the carriage door and unfolded the two steps for Catherine to alight, Mathilde next. An attendant dressed in purple and royal blue livery stood stiffly to attention, bowed and gestured to a lackey to see to the trunk. He then greeted the visitor,

"Welcome to Paris, Ma'am. Your room awaits if you would care to follow me."

She only raised her hand – exchanging words with a footman would be unthinkable.

"Your trunk will be brought up at once."

Relieved to be out of the cold, Catherine rubbed her hands together in front of the roaring fire.

"No sign of the King." She commented, casually.

"Did you expect him? He is one of the few people on this earth who would keep you waiting."

"You know him, and me, too well."

"Indeed, I do."

Looking round her bedchamber, her gaze fell on a mahogany side table with Italianate carved legs.

"They've put that here in my honour." She quipped. The bottle of brandy on its top held a certain appeal and she promptly poured a glass and watched Mathilde diligently unpack her trunk and hang her robes, one by one, on a wooden rack.

"There, now which will you wear for dinner this evening?"

"The blue, I think, in deference to Charles. It's the royal colour that features on his crest and banners."

"A diplomatic choice, Ma'am."

Dinner was served in a small dining room off one of the halls. Some twelve guests were seated at the table that was covered with a pure white cloth, the entire service being of silver, an elaborate centrepiece bearing candles giving off a gentle light. A bell rang and everyone rose as King Charles and Queen Elizabeth entered. No-one sat until the King and Queen had done so. In a corner, a flaxen-haired girl plucked soft melodies on a harp: the atmosphere was peaceful and welcoming, as Charles had intended for his mother's visit. Her place was, as protocol required, at the King's right side. This facilitated conversation, albeit of a mundane sort. Dinner parties, regardless of their intimate setting, were not the best setting to discuss subjects of a sensitive private nature. The Queen Mother would have her chance, and soon. She grasped her son's arm, put his head close to hers, and whispered,

"Charles, it is of the greatest importance that I speak with you and de Guise. I will reveal all when we are met and not overheard. I assume the duke to be in his Paris home, so summon him here, tomorrow, without fail."

The King pulled away, flustered at the peremptory tone and continued talking to his wife. The evening passed pleasantly with good food, good wine and convivial company.

'There are hard times ahead, if they but knew.' She mused.

. . .

The next day, Charles and the Queen Mother sat in his study, impatiently waiting for the Duke de Guise to arrive. Lateness was a fault in most men, she had concluded many years ago. Then, a servant opened the door and announced,

"His Grace, the Duke of Guise." At which the nobleman entered and stood by the vacant chair until gestured to sit, which he did, but he felt uncomfortable. It was not every day that he was called for by the King and his mother, so he wondered what was in store.

"Gentlemen, you will forgive my presumption in starting proceedings but it was, after all, I who convened them."

Both men now looked uncomfortable.

"Allow me to explain. Our good duke, you are currently preoccupied by your preparations for the imminent excursion to Montauban."

"That is correct, Ma'am, and I am making progress. All will be in place for February."

"We are pleased to hear that."

"I expect it will be your finest hour, de Guise." Charles butted in, a tremor of excitement in his voice. Immediately, de Guise's jaw dropped.

"Has the King not been informed he will not join the troop?" Catherine was silent so, displaying the quickness of mind that had saved him from many a perilous situation, he continued,

"Majesty, we have envisaged a far more important role for your good self. While I am away, the Queen Mother must be protected from whatsoever faction might do her harm. These are dangerous times and I would not consider any other person – even from my own officers – to assume my duty as protector of the royal household. I have every confidence in you.

. . .

Catherine held her breath. Would he go along with their idea or raise objections? After a pause, he replied,

"I am honoured, de Guise. I will ensure Her Majesty's safety in your absence." He turned to his mother, "What, therefore, is the reason for summoning us?"

She looked both men in the eyes and waited until she had gained their full attention,

"We continue to receive alarming reports from the town of La Rochelle. The duke will recall our last meeting when I shared the letter from Father Evrart, the senior Catholic priest there. I was repulsed to hear how our brethren in Christ are forced to worship in only one church, while the powerful Protestants can choose between any of the others. Because they outnumber us there by ten to one, they act against us with impunity, overturn our market stalls, spit and curse our elderly folk who are too frail to put up any resistance. Just as abhorrent is the vile Judge Boivin – who is, presently, known to us only by name – collects taxes, seemingly, on a whim and is involved in evil demonic gatherings. Gentlemen, when our work is done in Montauban, the port of La Rochelle is our next, and possibly final, objective."

Charles raised an eyebrow and was on the verge of intervening: she had her proposition ready,

"I would be indebted, my son, for you to accompany me as we follow our soldiers, as a rear-guard, if you will."

He will be less difficult close to me.

"While you are away, de Guise, we must take measures to assist your eventual success in conquering La Rochelle which, of course, you will. But we cannot slay the dragon unless we can find his cave and his haunts. It is paramount that we know every feature of the place, and I do mean *every* feature, to give us the upper hand when we strike. Mere anecdote is worthless – we must have facts, not stories!"

"Your Majesty shows a remarkable insight into matters military, so, what is your proposal?" *I would normally dismiss suggestions for martial strategies, but Catherine is no normal woman, this I know and, in any case, my work will lie in other places at that time.*

"Spies, de Guise, spies. Seven days after Christmas you will send two men to Chenonceau where they will rest and dine before continuing to the port. The men you select must have a soldier's mentality – they must also be intelligent, sociable, sensitive and, I nearly forgot, they should know reading and writing. Do two such men even exist in your band of thugs?" The duke gave her a broad smile,

"Not an easy question, Ma'am, but rest assured I will choose two of my best."

"I'm sure you will. The mission depends on absolute secrecy and anonymity. They will pose as two men who seek to purchase a small fishing boat. This should afford them the cover to mix with the Rochelais in their taverns, markets and churches. Each night they will write down the day's observations to provide us with a report on which to plan our attack. Do you have any comments?"

Neither man spoke: her pragmatism was unequivocal.

The days before Christmas for Charles and Catherine were taken up by an endless stream of dignitaries, emissaries and bishops who descended on Paris at this time of year to plead their cases for increased royal patronage and consideration from the exchequer – all of whom bored the couple to distraction but could not be avoided. The religious highlight of the season was the Christmas Eve communion service in the Notre-Dame de Paris cathedral. Every Catholic personage and commoner in the city attended, so many that the Eucharist mass began at midday, with a relay of priests before the grand choir dispensing the sacramental bread and wine. The assemblage was so great that its shuffling and whispering drowned the orators from the pulpits. The entire congregation was made up of Roman Catholic zealots for whom being seen was just as important as praising the Lord. Elsewhere in the capital, Protestant churches marked the coming of Christ reservedly, with less pomp and ceremony, fearful, anxious that they should not attract undue attention.

The King, the Queen Mother, Queen Elisabeth and the royal and clerical elite took communion at Vespers. They were attired in respectful outfits commensurate with the religious occasion, nothing elaborate or gaudy – that was kept for the following day, the annual Christmastide banquet and ball in the Great Hall of the Louvre palace. They prayed to be included on the auspicious guest list. Was this attitude an indication of their indifference to the fate of their fellow citizens, the Huguenots, whose blood had flowed through the streets but three months ago? They could not have been ignorant of the massacre, but many had turned a blind eye.

Perversely, the Great Hall – the setting for the Saint Bartholomew's Day slaughter – was bedecked with white, purple and blue festoons, and brightly embroidered wall hangings. On the tables were vulgarly lavish vases spewing winter-flowering pansies, Christmas roses, cherries and irises; pure white damask tablecloths; silver gallon jugs brimming with mead and wine. The room hummed and bristled with women giggling, children hushed, men shaking hands – all anticipating the entrance of the good and great. A gong boomed three times, the signal for the company to be upstanding.

Charles led Elisabeth by the hand, to rapturous applause and cheerful whoops that filled the air while the principal guests took their places on the high table extending from one side of the hall to the other. To Catherine's right, her favourite bishop of Paris, Pierre de Gondi, nodded fawningly; to Elizabeth's left, the Grand Almoner smiled pompously. The rest represented the rich and powerful: the Head of Ceremonies, the Leader of the King's Council, the Chief of the King's Domestics, Duke de Guise, this and that duke and duchess, faceless counts, all honoured on public display.

Charles rose, raised his goblet heavenward, smiled benevolently and cried out,

"A happy Christmas and God bless you all!" At which the rear doors opened for platter after platter to be placed on the tables: boiled fowl, roasted swan and peacock, steaming whole fish and haunches of venison and boar for the guests to slice off portions and put on their plates. These dishes were interspersed with tureens of potatoes, carrots, kale, onions, green beans and cabbage. The final item was freshly-baked bread – plain white, seeded, plaited, long batons and crusty baguettes. Thus, the holy feast began.

· · ·

In the minstrel's gallery, lively jigs, rounds and carols were struck up on lute, flute, violin and tambourine. Dancing started in between eating and drinking, with couples finding room despite the hordes of excited children who tumbled, screeched, chased the jester, sat cross-legged while the clown pulled funny faces and performed sleight-of-hand tricks. The juggler kept five balls in the air at once, to everyone's amazement.

The musicians suddenly stopped playing and all eyes fell on King Charles and his wife who left their seats to enter the dance floor. Adults and children, as one, moved back towards the tables leaving the centre free: those guests who had read their bible would have been reminded of the parting of the Red Sea, in Exodus, for the Israelites to escape to freedom. Charles held his wife's hand level with his shoulder, waiting for the music to strike up again, upon which they faced each other breast to breast and bowed. The King made swooping motions with his arms, like a falcon, she floated effortlessly like a dove. They linked arms and circled clockwise to then separate and repeat the sequence.

The guests watched the royal couple's every move and, at the end, burst into unrestrained cheering.

A fanfare from a horn rang out from the gallery. The army of waiters cleared the tables after the first course to replace it with silver dishes bearing tartes, fritters, fruit, nuts and cheeses.

This was, for sure, a joyous affair. The men sported fancy doublets over colourful hose with soft leather dancing slippers; for the women, the Christmas Day banquet was the opportunity of the year to show off their ball gowns –

velvet dresses with flowing trains; costumes with tied waists and edged with gold thread; outfits with long flared sleeves – all chosen and worn to achieve fashion superiority.

Catherine was asked to take to the floor by de Guise, Charles, and even her bishop, among others. She diplomatically danced with each. Some of them, so fowl-breathed and pockmarked, turned her stomach, but it had to be done, to keep the Catholics on her side.

As time wore on, with increasing amounts of drink consumed, so the behaviour of certain men and women descended into flirtatious impropriety, all quite acceptable for a Christmas ball, but not in Catherine's opinion. She glared at her son who had sat at the lower tables next to Marie Touchet, his mistress. He fed her sugar-coated almonds and tiny cake fancies and whispered sweet nothings in her ear...*you make me so happy, Marie...I'm so proud to be the man sitting beside you...I can be myself with you...* He curled a tress of her hair round his finger to pull her face gently to his and kiss her. No-one payed them any heed. Even the powerful Queen Mother had no authority over her son.

It will end in tears, it usually does. With this belligerent thought she rose and nodded to Mathilde who had sat dutifully on one side throughout the banquet. The two women left the hall quietly and unnoticed.

In the corridor Catherine shook her head and muttered with disgust,

"I suppose it's out of the way for another year."

"Ay, and the King should -" But she stopped short,

realising it was not within her remit, close as she was to her mistress, to proffer an opinion of the monarch. She tightened her lips, expecting a reprimand, but none came. Catherine squeezed her maidservant's hand and looked at her affectionately.

"Mathilde, there is little in the King's behaviour with which I am not familiar. *I always arrive at this point but I will not – cannot – divulge his bloodlust or sadistic leanings. I will protect him for as long as I can. After all, he is my flesh.* Releasing the woman's hand, she regained her senses.

"Inform the stables that we will depart tomorrow, at dawn. Then, pack my trunk. We cannot idle our time away on trifles. We must return to Chenonceau where I will finalise my plans, ready for the arrival of de Guise's chosen men."

"Will Your Majesty bid farewell to the King?"

"Certainly not! He will doubtless be in one bed or another tonight. Were I to be presented to him I would not hold my tongue and, at this delicate moment in our scheme, we can do without unnecessary bad feeling. So, tell the kitchen we will dine in my bedchamber this evening."

"As you will, Ma'am."

On the homeward journey, the rhythm of the carriage, with the occasional jolt, sent her asleep, dreaming of the best instructions to give to her spies.

15

CHENONCEAU, JANUARY 1573

On New Year's Day, 1573, the two soldiers selected by the Duke de Guise knew Chenonceau was not far ahead by wayside cottages, carts, carriages and people walking in either direction. They reined their horses back to a walk, mindful of a possible collision – drawing attention to themselves was the last thing they wanted, their anonymity being of paramount importance. They had departed Paris the previous day incognito and it was essential it remained thus.

De Guise had thought long and hard, given Catherine's requirements of the men entrusted to accomplish her scheme.

Captain Bertrand stood over six feet tall, broad-shouldered and muscled, square-set jaw, and an amiable face with dark candid eyes. He cut a handsome figure astride his black bay stallion. He had fought alongside his general on many campaigns, despite still not being forty years of age, and was the duke's most trusted and capable officer. Issuing orders came as second nature to him - his intelligence and swift mind enabled him to be one step ahead of the enemy. He was brought up in a home surrounded by books, globes and a family that saw learning as the prerequisite for a civilised man. His father was a physician to the wealthy aristocrats of Paris and beyond, who supported herbal remedies and the scientific investigation of human anatomy in preference to, in his medical opinion, unnecessary and all too often injurious blood-letting. He studied in the principal schools of the capital and exercised the tenets of the Hippocratic Oath, in particular the *non-maleficence* promise that it was better to do nothing for the patient than cause more harm.

His companion was Sergeant Monaud. Some years younger than Bertrand, and a fair bit shorter, he was, nonetheless, powerfully built with a shock of ginger hair falling over a round smiling face. His fearsome clenched hands belonged to a colossus, not a mere mortal.

'Steady boy, steady!' he urged as his dapple-grey reared. Like Bertrand, he was astute and had been singled out for promotion in his military career.

They rode into Chenonceau town down the main street to the main square.

"Whoa!" the captain called to his horse. "Which way is the palace?" he asked a man selling vegetables at a stall.

"Straight on, out of the town, then take the left track at the fork. You can't miss it."

"My thanks."

The men walked off, looking forward to respite and a

meal after the day's riding. Dressed in ordinary coarse brown tunics, their saddlebags made of poor quality canvas, they would not have been seen as soldiers. They soon saw the palace of Chenonceau looming, dominated by its ancient keep, the white limestone of the magnificent chateau glowing and tinted by the mellow afternoon sunshine.

They passed slowly along the plane-lined way to the gatehouse, at which two armed guards stepped out, crossed their pikes, to prevent entry, and cried out in unison,

"Halt! Your name and your business!"

"Bertrand and Monaud, for Her Majesty, Catherine."

The guards were evidently expecting them (the lady had received notice from de Guise the day before) and, at the names, raised their pikes.

"Enter!"

Through the gates they went into a small courtyard, with a water fountain in the middle surrounded by flower beds and shrubs. Around the perimeter, elegant shaded cloisters, that would not have looked out of place in a monastery, formed three sides, the stable doors the fourth. A lad approached the visitors and gripped the bridles of the horses, one in each hand, to steady them while the men dismounted.

A servant in fine livery came out of a doorway,

"Gentlemen, follow me. I will show you to your room. You are awaited and, when you are refreshed, I will escort you to Her Majesty's dining room. She trusts your journey has passed without incident."

Their large room contained two beds with smooth counterpanes and crisp white pillows; two armchairs either side of a fireplace; a sideboard and table with chairs. Simple, but welcoming.

Monaud spotted a bottle and glasses.

"This is what we need, my friend. To be honest, I could easily forego food tonight and see off this tasty stuff." He filled the glasses and passed one to Bertrand, who said, immediately,

"It would be a fool who angered Catherine, believe me. I've had the honour of meeting her and she's a fine woman but one who speaks her mind, so best let her do the talking. Understand?" Monaud said nothing.

A couple of hours later, came a knock at the door and the same servant entered to announce,

"It's time for dinner, gentlemen. This way, please."

Catherine's room was not dissimilar from theirs apart from one wall with shelves and hundreds of books and rolled documents and a desk at which the lady was writing. A circular table was set for the meal: a soup tureen, several silver bowls with covers, a wicker bread basket, two bottles of red and white wine and cut-glass goblets. Their host put down her quill and rose from the desk,

"Welcome to Chenonceau. Pray, be seated."

A servant poured out three glasses of wine and stood back. She raised hers towards the men who reciprocated and waited for her to speak.

"Introduce yourselves to me." The captain, rank first, said,

"I am Bertrand, captain, Your Majesty."

"And you?"

"Monaud, sergeant, Ma'am."

"Good. It's not necessary to say who I am, is it?" They were flustered, for an instant, before realising it was a jest. They smiled politely and she continued,

"We will dine, now, our business can come later."

The servant ladled consommé into bowls. A roast meat with vegetables followed, then a platter of sugar confectionery and cake fancies – a restrained menu but, nonetheless, quite adequate for her common guests. Their goblets were regularly replenished. However, the atmosphere was strained given this unconventional setting: two soldiers dining with the mother to the King of France, in her private room, chatting about the weather, the town, families, the food – anything but the actual purpose of their visit. Was the banal nature of the conversation created by her, so when they dealt with the real business, they would by then be ravenous for her instructions? The meal over, she got up, the men followed suit, a little unsure of the protocol when in the company of royalty. She indicated three studded leather wingback armchairs by the fire.

"You will take brandy?"

Both men assented.

"Now, let's get started. I assume the duke has not yet given you any details concerning the...the venture?" Her voice was hesitant. She wondered how much they really knew and if there was a chance they might, already, have let it slip, maybe drunk in a tavern.

"He has not, Ma'am," Bertrand answered.

"On the western seaboard of our kingdom is a port, a pleasant prosperous port. It goes by the name of La Rochelle. Do either of you know this place?"

They shook their heads.

"Nor I, nor the duke, nor the King – that is to say, it is an unknown quantity to us, if you get my drift, and this is something we must remedy. But, of one thing I am certain, the majority of its citizens are of the Huguenot faith...yes, the great majority. As a result, the small number of our fellow Protestants there are governed by oppressive unjust Protestant elders. Do you comprehend, thus far?" She thought – *I'm never sure about a soldier's intellect, even if de Guise has assured me they will be two of his brightest.'*

They nodded, by now spellbound.

"The King's army will shortly advance on La Rochelle to reclaim it and install the only true faith in the churches there that, currently, are monopolised by Huguenots.

Because we are unfamiliar with the town, we are sending you to collect information that will ensure our victory." She paused and took a sip of brandy, then,

"It is essential that we know how to best attack it: what are its defences, its walls, its gates, its port? How many soldiers lodge in their barracks and how well are they armed? Then, which are their main streets, could we ride down them on horseback and which are to be avoided? If we understand their people it will greatly assist our action. Are there more women than men, are they mainly aged? Where are their churches and which are their most important? Finally, the port. Access to La Rochelle from the west, we know, is via its harbour. So, can we find out its depth and how near our warships could safely sail?" She drew breath and smiled on seeing the utter panic on their faces as they strove to process all she had said.

"This, gentlemen, is knowledge and knowledge is power! What do you say?"

Both soldiers sat back in their armchairs, consumed by battle fatigue even before they had drawn a sword –

overwhelmed by the maelstrom of demands the Queen Mother had laid out.

By Jupiter! She doesn't want much, does she! This job's going to keep us busy, to put it mildly, Bertrand mused.

She passed the bottle to the men for them to recharge their goblets. Her gaze unfaltering, she went on,

"I understand that we are asking much of you but your general has expressed his total confidence in your expertise to carry this out." She got up and went over to the sideboard, taking a canvas pouch from the drawer. "Here, for you." She handed it the captain. "It is a generous amount of silver coin. You may keep what you do not spend – consider it a bonus in addition to whatever remuneration the duke pays. You will have to find for your lodging, food and drink and," she paused, "a coin or two may well loosen the tongue of this or that man."

Bertrand nodded his agreement.

"Over there, by the table, is a sack. It contains parchment sheets, quills and inkwells. You will record all that you observe to ensure, on your return, that we have a comprehensive picture of the town. And, I almost forgot, when you get there, seek out Father Servet, at Saint Sauveur church, before you do anything else. At dawn, tomorrow, you will ride to La Rochelle. As a cover, you are two friends wanting to buy a small fishing boat and start a business. Anyone will believe that. Gentlemen, I suggest you retire shortly because you will need a good night's sleep. I wish you Godspeed."

The men drained their goblets and returned to their room.

"She's a hard taskmaster and no mistake," Monaud said casually.

"Hold your tongue, man! Bertrand snapped." Whatever

she says, goes – she speaks for the King, and the King is our monarch – get it?"

"Of course, I was only saying -"

"Well don't! Blow out the candle, tomorrow we have work to do." Indeed, they had more than enough to occupy their dreams.

The sun had barely risen when a boy led their horses to the doorway where Bertrand and Monaud were waiting.

"Good morning, sires."

"And to you." Bertrand replied.

"They're fed, watered and brushed down. All ready for you."

Bertrand pressed a coin into his hand.

"Many thanks, sire."

The sack of writing effects and money pouch stored safely in the saddlebag, they mounted their steeds. A window above them opened and Catherine appeared,

"Good luck, gentlemen," She wished them with a wave.

A tug on the reins and they moved towards the gatehouse where the guards stood, this time their pikes held upright. Once they reached the road, they began a gentle canter in the direction of La Rochelle.

———

La Rochelle, January 1573

They entered the town through the east Porte Gambetta and slowed their horses to a standstill - they whinnied and sweated through the exertion of the ride. Monaud leaned forward and patted his mount's neck affectionately.

"Right, we're here. Remember what the lady said, our task starts now. Keep your eyes and ears open – see everything, say nothing." Bertrand said softly across to his colleague.

"Understood." Came the reply.

Dusk was rapidly falling so they hade made it just in time before darkness would have halted their progress. An old man crossed their path.

"Excuse me, 'sieur." Bertrand hailed him, "which is the way to Saint Sauveur church?"

"Straight on, left down Rue des Fonderies, down to the port. Follow the Maubec Quay and you'll not miss it."

"My thanks to you."

They moved on and, as the old man had described, soon found the church. They dismounted and tethered the animals to a post in front of the steps. Inside there was not a soul. Three candles on the altar and only an occasional light from side chapels spilling onto the nave cut through the gloom. There was an atmosphere of peace and calm that soothed the men and they felt relaxed after the rigours of the journey from Chenonceau. They dipped their fingers into the water of the stone stoup and crossed themselves before walking silently down the nave where they sat on the front pew in deferential reflection. The sound of footsteps broke their meditation and, from a doorway behind the altar, emerged the figure of a priest in a long brown cassock – Father Evrart. Bertrand looked up,

"Good evening, Father."

"Good evening, my son, and to you." He nodded to Monaud. "There is no service tonight, if that is the reason for your presence. We are only permitted one Sunday evening mass, nowadays."

"That is not the reason we are here. Sit beside me and I will explain."

The priest sat down, eying the newcomers who he did not recognise.

"We have come from our home town, a day's ride away to the east. I am Bertrand and this is my companion, Monaud. There is little work there and we have heard many tales of fair La Rochelle – that it is prosperous and welcomes fresh blood, as it were. We seek to buy a small fishing boat and set up our own business. But, we know no-one here and were advised to approach the Catholic church upon our arrival."

"Are you of the Catholic faith?"

"Indeed we are, Father, and most devout."

"I see. Well, you were given correct advice for, how shall I put it, our town is not the safest place for we Catholics at the present time."

Both men feigned surprise.

"Not the safest place?" Monaud decided to join in the conversation.

"No, we are greatly outnumbered and, to use an analogy, many days we lie battered and bleeding by the roadside knowing who our attackers are, yet no Good Samaritan stops to help us. But, forgive my rambling, you have barely set foot here and there will be time for all that anon. Tell me, do you have lodging?"

"I was about to ask, Father, if you could recommend a room for the night. We hope to stay for two weeks and we will make further arrangements tomorrow. Then, we have the horses to be fed, watered and stabled."

"I can help you on both of these. Leave the church,

cross the bridge over the Maubec Canal to the Valin Quay. Look for the 'Aubert Fils' sign over a stable door. With luck, the lad will still be there. Mention you have come from me and he will tend your horses. Now, your lodging, let me think...ah, take the Rue Saint Yon to the right as you leave, and half way up you'll see 'Auberge Tournon'. The landlord is one of my parishioners, a good man, and he has rooms to let. You will eat and drink well, and at a fair price."

"Father, we are indebted to you."

"Don't mention it and, by the way, you will be most welcome to attend mass tomorrow."

"We surely will, Father. Good evening to you."

The stable lad took in the horses, assuring the strangers that they would be well cared for. Bertrand handed over two silver coins for the stabling and a third for him. They then found the inn where a blazing fire and jovial landlord greeted them within.

"Father Evrart, you say? He's a decent priest. Talks a good sermon, don't you know? So, you want lodging? How many nights will you require? You've come far? The inn's owner had an amusing habit of asking a question, whether he enquired about anything or not. The men provided answers and the smiling man said,

"Will you go upstairs? My daughter will show you to your room, if that suits? Marie!' He shouted and a pretty fresh-faced girl scampered to her father's side. "Show these gentlemen upstairs, that's an angel." She giggled and motioned towards the stairs.

Their double room was clean and tidy – crisp white sheets on the beds, a table and chairs. a washstand and basin, a corner fireplace. Bertrand put their saddlebag on the bed and withdrew the writing materials. He arranged the parchment sheets, quills and inkwells on the table and sat down.

"We must make a note, every night, of anything we've seen or heard, no matter how trivial. That's what our lady said, that's the reason we're here."

"Correct." Monaud concurred, "and two men are better than one."

"That's pretty profound for you." Bertrand chuckled.

That evening, they dined well on a ragout of locally-killed venison washed down with copious amounts of ale. Chatting with the inn's friendly customers, their senses were ever on the alert for morsels of information, this comment or that, a joke or an insult, all with a view to formulating a battle plan to invade La Rochelle. After several convivial hours, they went upstairs and slept like babes, looking forward to the days ahead.

At first light, after a breakfast of milk and fresh bread, the men stepped out into the street that was, as yet, deserted. Capes fastened tight to protect against the morning chill, they walked down to the quay and climbed the stone steps onto the town walls that were the first obstacle an army would confront.

"We'll follow the walls and see whether they encircle the town, their parapets, watchtowers and, in particular, where the gates are." Bertrand reminded Monaud.

"Ay," the latter agreed, "and. apart from a hellish cold wind coming in off the sea, we've got clement weather in which to do it." He began saying to himself, as they walked,

'*Quai Maubec – narrow gate – takes a cart – no barrier – unarmed...*' – his aide-memoire. The further they went, the more there was to remember in their heads to be written down later.

Bertrand imitated his sergeant, '*Maubec Canal – footbridge – Valin Quay – Grosse Horloge – major gate, wide*' then, a few minutes on, '*inner port – deep – warehouses – sea towards south.*'

Thus, they strolled, leisurely, because they had time a-plenty, along the walls of the ancient town, between Catherine's kingdom and the mighty Atlantic Ocean, to the west.

They saw, ahead, a structure that, by its size and position, was surely of some strategic function for the port, standing on a rocky promontory that jutted out into the water: a circular tower, as wide and tall as a house without windows. It was made of grey granite blocks and shaped like an old beehive but with its point cut off and replaced by a crenellated turret. A flagpole proudly flew King Charles's banner.

On a stone bench in front of its wooden door sat a bearded old man wearing a battered tricorn hat and threadbare sea officer's frock coat, still bearing a few of its brass buttons. He looked up as they approached,

"Stop! Stop, I command!" He stood, shoulders pulled back in the military way.

They smiled at each other and Monaud chortled, sarcastically,

"Best not get in a fight with him!"

"We are friends." Bertrand declared, "visitors to your beautiful town."

"In that case, you may pass."

Catherine's envoys were faced with their first real opportunity to glean information. They sat at the old timer's side and Monaud said, gently,

"You're a sailor, I see."

"Used to be. Forty years on the high seas, in this and that king's navy. Got pensioned off. Too old...past it, they said, so now I'm the keeper of the Chain Tower."

"A strange name." Bertrand commented, casually.

"Ay, come to think of it, you're right...the Chain Tower"

"Why so?"

"I'll tell you, not many folk ask me that."

Bertrand took a hip flask from his tunic and offered it to the sailor, who gratefully accepted.

"Nice drop of brandy, that. From the top I can see the whole port one way, the ocean to the other. It falls to me to alert the harbour master if I spot enemy shipping although, the main look-out is the Lantern Tower down yonder." Monaud got up and went to the wall, peering in the direction of the port. Square-rigged skiffs, single-mast fishing boats, narrow rowing boats, cogs, barges – decks laden with barrels, crates and sacks.

"There's all manner of craft." He observed, "and they come and go as the like?"

"Heavens, no! Once they've gone past my tower they're in La Rochelle waters and are due taxes."

"Who collects them?"

"Why, Judge Boivin, everybody knows that. But, sorry, you're strangers."

"I see." Monaud glanced knowingly at Bertrand.

"And that boat over there?" He pointed to a caravel tied up at the mouth of the port.

"That's the King's boat – see his colours flying?"

"I do, and I can see cannon on board." He admired the sleek vessel built for speed, with its poop deck, its figurehead at the prow, furled lateen sail and two square ones.

"When that boat weighs anchor, there's trouble for somebody – usually a Catholic intruder."

"Is she always moored there?"

"Ay, unless she sails into action to defend the port."

Monaud continued to scrutinise the scene before him, then asked,

"And that tower opposite?"

"That's the Saint Nicolas Tower. It's got a powder magazine inside it and cells – it's said they used to lock up unfriendly giants and even they weren't strong enough to break out. Probably just a tale. Anyway, as it bothers me, if we need to barricade the port under attack, we row the chain."

"Row the chain? What's that?" Bertrand asked, puzzled.

"Under that canvas cover," he pointed to their left, "is an enormous length of iron chain. If there's ships aiming to get inside the port, we have two men who will hitch the chain to their rowing boat and row across to the Chain Tower on the other side. There, the chain's fixed to a windlass and pulled tight across the entrance. Any ship sailing towards us will have their masts cut down, their sails shredded and their crews headless!" He gave a mischievous grin. "We've not had to row the chain for some time but they keep me on, just in case, if you will."

Bertrand offered the old man another drink that he took and all but emptied the flask.

"It's time we were on our way. Thank you for your time and the fascinating explanations you've given us – most useful."

He might have said 'most useful for planning an attack on your town.' They shook hands and continued along the walls. Monaud rubbed his hands together with pleasure,

"He's the sort we should find – locals with precisely the information the duke wants. Also, they'll never realise what they're really doing nor what we're up to."

They soon reached the Lantern Tower, similar to the one behind them but featuring a tall octagonal spire. Standing at its base, they gazed out over the Aunis coastline before it meets the ocean proper. Bertrand stepped back from the tower, straining his neck to see the unusual upper part.

"I think it's a lighthouse. See those glass windows?"

Monaud laughed, "With a name like Lantern Tower, I wouldn't be that surprised!"

"No, of course," the other man blushed at his mistake, "you're right, but let's call it a day. I'm starving."

"Me too."

Returning towards the town, they stared down onto the quaint bustling port, still busy trading late into the afternoon. Eagle-eyed, they committed to memory anything of possible military significance.

Ensconced in their room at the Auberge Tournon, and glad to be out of the January cold, Monaud warmed himself in front of the fire that the jovial landlord or his daughter had set and lit, while Bertrand laid out a parchment sheet, dipped a quill into the ink, and continued his list with his friend contributing.

"Two heads are better than one for this," the ever-cheerful Monaud pointed out.

"You can't help coming out with the profoundest of statements," the captain joked, "but you're right. Tomorrow we will resume our mission from the Lantern Tower, following the walls northward through what I reckon is pretty dense woodland – just the place to conceal an army. That done, once we know all the gates into the town, we will turn our attention to whatever lies within."

"Sounds like a good plan to me. When you're done writing, I'll see if I can add anything, then food and drink is very tempting. We've earned it."

16

Satisfied with their observations the previous day in the port area, their attention now turned to the town walls from the Lantern Tower northwards.

"Fine day, so let's get started. We should complete our tour by nightfall." Bertrand said to his sergeant with a chirpy tone to his voice.

"Ay, captain, and decent weather means there will be people out and about to question. We're beginning to put together a picture of the place, as Catherine demands."

They walked slowly along the stone slabs and cobbles of the walkway on top of the walls. To their left, they had an unimpeded view of the land any potential attacker would have to negotiate. After a few minutes, they paused.

"It's dense woodland as far as you can see. Imagine it in spring and summer when the trees have their leaves."

Bertrand knew what Monaud was thinking.

"Indeed, an army could hide there with nobody the wiser. Hannibal and his elephants couldn't have sought better cover."

"Hannibal? Who's he then?"

Bertrand smiled,

"Just an ancient general except, today, he would be called de Guise. My father used to tell me stories about him when I was a child." He strained his eyes, "the sea's over there, somewhere." Beech, chestnut and sycamore trees grew side by side with pines just discernible in the distance. Hawthorn and a prolific variety of shrubs thrived.

Bertrand could not drive the amusing image of de Guise atop an elephant out of his mind.

They noted that, every hundred paces or so, the parapet had a gap of one yard with iron railings to impede entry but allowing shooting on or firing arrows at the host below. Next, they came to the first gate through which ran the Avenue Léonce, its name engraved on a wooden sign. It would pose a real obstacle if its heavy doors were closed. They passed eleven or twelve railed gaps, before the second gateway, the Porte Neuve. The road running through it was overgrown with weeds, indicating it was relatively disused.

They looked down on the wide Rue de la Repentie – even at this early hour, a man drove his cart laden with winter fodder into the town, so it was, they knew, of strategic importance.

The wide Porte Dauphine marked the end of the woodland and the northern limit of the town, after several minor entrances, some wide enough for a carriage, others too narrow for a horse. However, this would not deter infantry.

"Let's stop a while," Bertrand said, sitting on a bench and removing the hip flask from his tunic pocket. He took a drink and passed it to Monaud, who accepted it, readily.

"We've walked the west side of La Rochelle and we can give the duke a detailed report – not that we've finished, of course. Will you accompany him to Montauban, captain?"

"I will, and you too."

"Really? I regard it as an honour."

"As you should." He gazed hard at the man, "You have acquitted yourself well in our campaigns and you are one of my most trusted sergeants. If all goes according to plan at Montauban, you could end up a lieutenant. I have discussed it with the duke, and he is in agreement. Better pay, officer status, and you will have earned it. But, back to the business of the day - there's much more to discover. We must be mindful that although gates are a conventional point of entry, the walls could be scaled, and there's the port yet to be examined."

Monaud said nothing but his heart was bursting with pride.

'Me, a lieutenant!' He said to himself. *'Who would have thought it of me, a labourer's son, in a house where we often had no food on the table. I remember when I joined the duke's army as a mere boy...first saw action at Wassy when we put a crowd of Huguenots to the sword. I didn't understand what the religion thing was about but, by the time I fought alongside the captain at the Battle of Saint-Denis, just outside Paris, when our constable, Anne, Duc de Montmorency fell, I was sure I would die for our Catholic Church and the House of Guise, so strong had become my faith.'*

"Hey, Monaud!" The captain slapped him on his shoulder. "Wake up!"

"Sorry, I was day-dreaming."

. . .

"Over there, what do you think they are?" Bertrand pointed to one rectangular-shaped basin, filled with water, after another. He could just make out figures pushing carts between them.

"I don't know, it's strange." Monaud mused.

Fortuitously, an old woman, her shawl drawn over her head against the chill, approached them.

"Excuse me, ma'am, a moment of your time?"

She pulled back the shawl to see who hailed her. The pathway was so narrow that she couldn't avoid them and she stopped, but began to shake, trying to utter words though unable to do so, through visible fear.

"Old woman," Monaud took over the situation, "we wish you no harm. Do not be concerned."

She gathered her senses and calmed enough to ask,

"You Huguenots?"

"I beg your pardon?' He asked, seeing a gentle tone was needed.

"If we are, if we are not, is that important? We simply intended to enquire what that is, over there?" He pointed to the basins.

"Ay, gentleman, it certainly *is* important, nowadays. If you be Catholics, I will help you. If not, I will flee for my life and no mistake."

"Rest assured, ma'am, we are Catholics. Long live the Holy Father and long reign the King!"

Monaud's words had the desired effect.

"You must understand why I don't trust strangers – they could be the judge's men -"

"So, old woman, answer my question: what are those square lakes over there?"

She chortled, "they're not lakes, they're salt pans. This town is wealthy thanks to salt and wine."

"Is that so?" Monaud asked indifferently, "and are those...those pans deep?"

"Some are, some aren't, for all I know."

He took a coin from his pouch and pressed it into her hand.

"We are grateful for your time. Good day to you." The sergeant wished her as she shuffled away.

"Well done, Monaud." The captain almost whispered – giving compliments did not come naturally to him, "You extracted useful information from the old crone."

"It's why we're here. If the rest of the Catholics in La Rochelle are half as frightened as she is, they are at serious risk."

"I agree, and we know that, when planning an attack, this area should be avoided. Our men could walk into the salt pans and drown! Let's move on."

After a short way, the number of people around increased. The salt pans ended, giving way to clusters of cottages and large buildings that Bertrand guessed were warehouses. The sound of children laughing, squealing, playing, rose; dogs barking, horses whinnying – although it was still quite early in the day, this place was alive, a settlement in its own rights outside the main walls. They came to the next entrance and stopped to observe a significant section of the town's defences: the Porte Gambetta, according to the sign.

A sentry box stood either side of a wide road passing through the gate. Its heavy wooden doors were open, and a wagon loaded with barrels trundled through with room to spare.

"There would be no problem getting any of our wagons into the town here and – look there!"

Bertrand drew Monaud's attention to the sentry box. "There's soldiers inside, can you see?"

"Ay, and the road leads eastwards, to Paris, I'd say. So, they would expect a raid to commence through the Porte Gambetta, but a shrewd commander might consider alternatives."

"Monaud," the captain said in a slightly smug tone, "you're right and if it didn't come from me, I'm sure the duke would recognise its merit himself. We'll make an officer of you yet."

For the rest of their scrutiny of the fortifications, down to the port, they saw only infrequent doorways in the walls with narrow paths affording entry into the town's confines. In any case, they could see more salt pans, if further away than the first, so it did not seem, to Bertrand's tactical way of thinking, a suitable point to mount an assault.

The walls gave way to a footbridge over the Marans Canal – wide enough for two barges to sail by with ease. On the other side the ramparts resumed and began a downward slope and surrounded a bastion, an abutment shaped like an arrowhead that was built into a rocky crag. The parapet was two stones higher than the ordinary wall, with two steps, enabling an archer or rifleman a panoramic view over the exposed lower land. An army would be mowed down if they were foolish enough to approach from the south.

"I hope you're making a note of all this?" Bertrand questioned his sergeant.

"Of course, I am," he replied in an indignant tone.

The walls now resumed their previous level and they saw yet another major gate – Porte Saint Nicolas. Monaud leaned forward over the bastion's parapet, straining his neck to view it more clearly.

"In the name of - "

"What's wrong?" Bertrand asked, concerned.

"I've just seen a big burly guard prod an old woman with his staff and laugh at her distress."

"Is she still there?"

"No, she's gone through. I'd like to know what she's done to deserve that. I've a mind to - "

"Monaud, no! What the guard did is unforgivable, but we cannot risk revealing our identities. Two strangers beating up a town guard? Hardly! Not the way for us to remain incognito."

"You're right. I hope that sort of behaviour isn't normal for this place."

The left the walls and descended four steps to find the *intra muros* for the first time that day. To the right, they could see the Valin Quay where the horses were stabled; on the left, a shallow pool with rowing boats and other light boats tied up; ahead, the Saint Nicolas Tower stood proudly guarding the approach to the main port.

"About time we enquired about fishing boats for sale." Bertrand said, tightening his lips and giving his colleague a nod. Although they had an exploratory circuit of the port to achieve before the church beckoned, they were in no hurry and strolled at a leisurely pace.

"Captain."

"What is it?"

"Over there, sitting on that bench, it's the old woman we saw earlier, the one the guard hurt and, see, she's crying. Come, we can't simply ignore her."

She wore a threadbare coat, shoes that let in water, and they saw a pewter dish by her side that, with their approach, she quickly picked up and hid in her pocket. Wiping her tears on her sleeve, she looked up, her face wrinkled and toothless but a twinkle in her deep blue eyes that was instantly endearing. She breathed in deeply and began,

"I wasn't begging, gentlemen. I know the law and I'm not the criminal sort so I wouldn't beg, would I?"

"Dear lady," Bertrand whispered to calm her, 'we saw nothing and if we did, it's of no interest to us."

"You're not the judge's men? For all I know, you could be." Her voice trembled.

"Pray, don't worry, we're not from the judge, whoever he may be."

"But everybody in La Rochelle knows Judge Boivin, so you must be strangers?"

"Indeed. We are here on business, with a view to buying a fishing boat."

"You're at the right place then." She cackled and was promptly overcome by a fit of coughing. Bertrand took his hip flask and handed it to the wretched woman.

"Here, drink this."

"Thank you...thank you kindly." She had a sip and, spluttering, said,

"Can't remember the last time I tasted anything as good as this. We have to survive on charity and my husband is bedridden with a sickness." Her pained expression moved even the two battle-scarred soldiers but they had their mission to accomplish, with no time for sentimentality. Monaud wrested the flask and drank himself. Both men realised that she was a useful source of information.

"Do you know who we might visit regarding a boat?" The captain asked gently. She thought for a moment then,

"I can tell you who *not* to visit – Boivin. He will steer you towards this or that Huguenot crony and they're not to be trusted, believe me." She paused, then, "find Aubert. He's a good man and one who stands up to the judge."

Bertrand took three silver coins from his pouch and pressed them into the woman's hand.

"Accept this, buy food and pay a physician to tend your husband."

"This is for me? You are generous, sire, and no mistake!"

"We're pleased to help a fellow Catholic believer who's down on her luck."

"Ah, I see. Be careful, boys, we are hated, despised, derided and, do you know what we would do, me and my husband, if we were twenty years younger?"

"Tell us, do." Monaud urged her.

"Get out! Leave for somewhere that has a Catholic future. Here, all the best jobs go to the Huguenots and if we step one foot out of line, the judge's bullies will pounce on you and before you know it you're in the dock of his courtroom. You'll have the stocks, a flogging, or worse, to look forward to and you may just as well be hanged for a sheep as a lamb because, the way things are, if they could, they'd string you up for both!"

"Out of interest, my dear, where exactly is his courtroom?"

"A few streets away, down there." She pointed. "Rue de l'Escale next to the Palais de Justice. Justice? That's a joke! Anyway, I'll be away, it doesn't pay to be in one spot for too long...have to keep moving."

"We understand. Good day to you." Bertrand wished her, smiling gently. She roamed off down the quayside and was soon out of sight.

"We're hearing Judge Boivin's name more and more, are we not?" Monaud thought out loud.

"Yes, we are, and it wouldn't surprise me if he holds sway over the military. He's a man we must meet face to face, and I'm sure we will." They sat in silence, as they regularly did, to assimilate whatever they had just heard or seen. Then, Bertrand spoke,

"What was the name the old woman told us?"

"Aubert." The sergeant answered.

"It's the name over the stables where we left our horses. He must be the owner so, one way or another, we will definitely speak with him."

Their afternoon was spent wandering around the port quarter, continuously reminding each other of Catherine's expected outcome of their work: La Rochelle's walls, gates, streets, boats and anything else that caught their fancy. Sitting down and draining the hip flask, Bertrand issued an order,

"Go to the Aubert stables. Ask the lad where his master works today."

"A good idea." Monaud set off as instructed. Fifteen minutes later, he returned,

"No Aubert?" The captain asked.

"No, his lad says he's out of town making deliveries, but he'll be back tomorrow."

· · ·

It was Sunday evening and the bell of Saint Sauveur church chimed for vespers – a slow monotonous drone to remind the Catholic believers that it was the hour for their sole Eucharist convocation of the week. They stood in a long serpentine line around the square in front of the church steps. waiting patiently to enter. Father Servet positioned himself at one side of the massive doors, Evrart at the other. Both wore ceremonial white cassocks, the senior cleric displaying a heavy cross on a chain. Each parishioner was greeted with a handshake and a simple *God bless you* salutation.

When it came to Bertrand and Monaud's turn, Evrart made a point of adding, "Brothers, it is good to welcome you." It was a further thirty minutes before the entire congregation was seated, there not being an empty space in the church.

Monaud raised his gaze to the painted vaulted ceiling and experienced a feeling of insignificance in the presence of his God. He looked at the fine tracery of the windows of the side walls, then at the immense white marble altar, its two candles burning brightly on either side of the open leather-bound bible. Evrart began intoning a prayer of intercession to which the people responded but the sergeant's mind was elsewhere. He could not say how long passed until Bertrand nudged him,

"Hey!" He hissed, "You're missing the service," at which the soldier straightened his back, and watched the cleric climb the wooden steps to the pulpit. Leaning outward in a dominant pose, he waited for perfect silence before starting his homily for their spiritual edification.

. . .

His opening words were delivered slowly and in a low voice, causing the people to strain their ears, their attention fixed on his every word.

"Brothers and sisters, we are living in hard times. We may feel unloved and persecuted, often with due cause, or so it seems. But, did not our Lord, Jesus Christ, undergo such torment? Yes, He did! Yet, He rose above the pain and endured. He chose a state of mind to be an example to us, because He loves us and, in this faith, you will not be alone. In the psalm of David, we hear,

'Even though I walk through the darkest valley, I will fear no evil, for You are with me.'

He paused for a long moment, then,

"David's 'darkest valley' is our home town, where we are born and where we will die. For our sins, there is no relief from the wickedness that makes of us second-class citizens."

Monaud put his hand over his mouth and whispered,

"He doesn't pull his punches, that's for sure."

"No, and he's painting a picture of life for Catholics here." Evrart continued,

"But, my people, we must stand strong and, even though we are a minority and cannot fight back with our fists, we can be resilient and keep the faith. In the Sermon on the Mount, our Lord Jesus told us,

'You have heard that it was said 'An eye for an eye and a tooth for a tooth'. But, I say to you, do not resist the one who is evil. If anyone slaps you on the right cheek, show him the other.'

We are proud Catholics! Our strength and our defiance

come from doing what the Lord told us to do – *that* is our strength that will, one day, prevail. Let us pray."

The congregation all kneeled together as Evrart read out Latin prayers that no-one understood. Only when he said 'Amen' did they know he had finished and sat back down on the pews. He again waited until the murmuring and shuffling has subsided. Then,

"For Jesus's final temptation, He is taken up to a high mountain by Satan and told that if He bows down to the Devil, He will be given all the kingdoms of the world. Yet, He refuses the temptation, choosing to serve God instead. And so, *you* must turn your back on the natural desire to strike out – you must show *forgiveness!*"

On hearing him say 'forgiveness', and immediate whisper went from man to man, woman to woman, growing into audible words of amazement. *'Our priest...telling us to forgive the Huguenots...and with all they are doing to us...'* Evrart had anticipated this reaction.

"Hush!" He ordered. "Hush, I say! Jesus gives us the perfect example of forgiveness for you to observe. While in agony – a thousand times worse than yours - on the cross, He called out *'Father, forgive them for they do not know what they are doing.'* Banging his fist on the pulpit, he challenged them with, "Who among you would compare your unhappiness with the Lord's suffering? None of you! Our day will come but, in the meantime, trust in the Lord, turn the other cheek and forgive the oppressor! Bear no malice in your hearts, for God has pardoned you, not seven times, but seventy-seven!"

He bowed his head, crossed himself, and climbed down. He, Father Servet and two church attendants then stood in front of trestle tables, covered in white cloth, that bore the Communion bread and wine. Raising the Host in the air, a bell sounded, the signal for the worshippers to rise, join the line in the nave, and receive the Eucharist. To each person the priest stated, 'The body of Christ', placing a morsel of bread in his hand and offering a sip of wine from a silver goblet. Each man and woman responded 'Amen,' and made the sign of the cross. By the time the Mass was completed, it was nine o'clock but, with only the one Catholic church in La Rochelle, queueing and waiting for the most precious of all religious rituals was inevitable and supported by the people.

Bertrand and Monaud walked the short distance to the Auberge Tournon and, on entering, gestured to the jovial landlord. Within minutes, his fresh-faced daughter brought a jug of ale and two tankards to their table, giggled and skipped away.

"What did the stable lad say when we first arrived...ah, that Father Evrart 'talks a good sermon' Monaud said pensively. "What do you think, captain?"

Bertrand frowned and took a draught of ale,

"If forgiveness is their best weapon, the Catholics of this town are sorely in need of our intervention."

"I couldn't agree more." The sergeant said, in turn drinking.

17

On leaving the Auberge Tournon, Bertrand and Monaud were greeted by an icy wind that blew through the narrow streets – a wintry blast off the sea for which La Rochelle was renowned. They held their capes tight and lowered their heads to avoid taking its chilling force in their faces. Saint Sauveur church, their first destination that day was, fortunately, nearby and the calm and relatively warm interior was welcome. They dipped their fingers in the holy water of the stoup, crossed themselves, and sat on a pew halfway down the nave, resting in silence for a few moments until a voice broke the peace.

"Good morning, gentlemen." Father Servet appeared from a side aisle and sat beside them.

"And to you," Bertrand replied, relieved that one of the two priests was present at that hour. He wanted to gain a clerical perspective on Judge Boivin, yet without revealing their scheme.

"You are up and about early," the priest began.

"Yes, Father, we have a busy day ahead. We hope to find Monsieur Aubert. We understand he has worked at the port for many years and he's a man who might help us in our search for a fishing boat." Bertrand explained.

"Ah, yes, I remember. He's a well-mannered honest person." Servet stood, waiting for their next words. Monaud obliged.

"It's damned foul weather though, if you'll forgive my language."

"It is so, but we have learned to live with it. You will find, as day breaks properly, it will brighten and the wind will subside."

"That's good to know." Monaud smiled, then the priest continued,

"Tell me, is your visit to our town proving satisfactory?"

"La Rochelle is a most pleasant place," Bertrand stated, preparing himself for his next words to steer the conversation, "and I feel I could well decide to live here permanently, as it were." He paused, then, "Walking the streets, I get an impression that it is, how shall I put it, a community little bothered by crime...although I may be wrong.'

"No, my son, you have it correct. Our citizens respect the rule of law, as they should -" The priest was interrupted.

"Of course, Father, and may I suggest that your magistrate must know his office well."

"The mayor is our magistrate."

Bertrand gazed steadily at Servet, a puzzled expression on his face. The latter carried on,

"The mayor is an employee of Judge Boivin who is the final arbiter of the law, who has his own – how shall I put it – his own band of *assistants*."

"That's a rum way of doing things, is it not?' Monaud asked, "And does the Church not have a voice?"

"It does not, Monsieur Monaud. The Huguenot bishop keeps his distance and it would be a matter of great wonder if we in the Saint Sauveur family were ever consulted."

Bertrand readily understood the priest's diplomatic answer and concluded,

"We will detain you no longer, Father, it's time we braved the weather."

"I wish you a productive day," Servet said, raising his eyebrows knowingly.

Outside, the biting wind of twenty minutes earlier had abated and, although it was a chilly morning, the men headed to the port eagerly anticipating what the day might bring.

Boats and barges were already tied up in various states of unloading and loading. An assortment of languages drifted over the quayside and, when this cosmopolitan marriage did not understand something, it resorted to shouting, sneering, coughing but, somehow, orders were followed and the port was a hive of industry.

As they walked slowly past each boat, they gave a cheerful 'good morning' to this and that matelot, and their eyes scrutinised the line of horses and carts, searching for the name 'Aubert Fils.' Approaching the Saint Nicolas tower at the far end of the port, Bertrand was about to abandon that particular part of their plan, when Monaud seized his arm, bringing him to a halt,

"There! I think it's the Aubert cart." And, so it was. Lanval was sitting on the rudder bench of a wide-beamed single-mast barge on the water, next to another man Bertrand took to be the captain. They were solemnly counting coins from one purse to another.

"Not the best time to interrupt them." Monaud observed.

"You're right. We'll hold back a while."

Three strapping youths were passing barrels from the cart on the quayside into the hold. The horse gave an occasional whinny but stood quite still, accustomed to the procedure.

"Hard work?" Monaud asked one of the youths, to initiate a conversation.

"Certainly not, sire – not nearly as heavy as the crates of gold ingots we carted yesterday!"

His mates let out guffaws, seeing the amazed expression of the strangers.

"Pay him no heed, sire," said one, "his mother says he was born under the Zodiac sign of madness! They're full of wine so, heavy enough. Can I help you?" This lad seemed to be the senior of the three.

"Is that gentleman Monsieur Aubert?" Bertrand pointed aft.

"Ay, he's the boss."

"Thank you." And Bertrand slowly walked the length of the barge followed by his companion.

"Excuse me, Monsieur Aubert." Lanval looked up on hearing his name.

"That's me."

"We would like a word with you but -"

"If you can wait, I have business here to attend to but I'll be with you shortly."

"Most grateful, I'm sure." Bertrand stepped back respectfully, as did Monaud, so as to not intrude on a private matter. They sat on a stone seat and gazed on the port and harbour before them.

· · ·

"It's a very narrow distance between the two towers. What do you think, Bertrand?"

"It is so. Stretch a chain or two across the water and it's more or less blockaded. With cannons atop the walls they'd surely have the upper hand over any invading army. Now, don't forget our story." He whispered to his friend, "we want to buy a smallish boat to set up a fishing venture and become La Rochelle residents."

"Of course. Dangle the bait in front of people and they usually take it," Monaud said behind his hand. They did not have too long to wait. The boss climbed from the barge to join them. Shaking their hands, he greeted them with a smile.

"Now, gentlemen. What can I do for you this fine day? I won't be able to be of service to you this week, before you start, I'm fully booked up with deliveries."

"That's not why we're here, monsieur. Father Evrart has told us to find you concerning the purchase of a fishing boat. He said you were a respected member of his congregation whose advice could be trusted."

"Are you Catholics?" Lanval asked bluntly. "In these times, it's a reasonable question."

"We are." Bertrand answered.

"A fishing boat, you say? Let me think...there's one man who comes to mind, a Monsieur Prothet. I've known him since I was a child, he's a good man who catches and sells fish for a living. Sadly, his brother passed away last month and he, too, was a fisherman. His boat is moored at the far end of the port – he won't need it anymore." Lanval's words were said half in jest, half as a statement of fact. He continued, "I know that Prothet is charged with disposing of the boat on behalf of the brother's family."

"It would seem to be our lucky day. We will speak with

him." Monaud, as usual, said as his contribution to the proceedings.

"Not today, he's fishing down the coast and won't be back until tomorrow." Lanval informed them.

"That's not a problem," Bertrand answered, "we have some days of our visit remaining. While your boys are unloading those barrels, why don't you allow us to buy you ale – there's surely a tavern nearby, and maybe you can tell us about your fair town?"

"An offer too good to refuse, so I accept – follow me." Lanval led the way towards, in his words, *'the best ale this side of Paris.'*

"It's kind of you to spare your time, monsieur." Bertrand spoke in a soft friendly tone.

"Call me Lanval, please, and I'm only too pleased to assist a fellow member of the faith. So, what would you like to know?"

"We come from a town where we are at liberty to worship where we choose, but Father Evrart suggested that isn't the case here."

Lanval took a draught of ale and paused, concerned, because he suspected that informants were all around. He gestured to the men to draw close.

"In La Rochelle, we Catholics have only Saint Sauveur church, and we may celebrate Mass there only once a week." Bertrand feigned surprise.

"But, what of the other churches, there must be many?"

"Indeed, there are but, they are open to Huguenots alone. It's the law."

"Then the law is wrong!" Monaud interjected.

"Friend!" Lanval hissed, "not so loud, we must not be

overheard. How to change it when we are so outnumbered, by ten to one? We have neither civic nor religious rights and Judge Boivin ensures it remains thus."

"Ah, Judge Boivin is a name we come across at every turn." Bertrand mused solemnly, leading Lanval towards the real purpose of their encounter. The carter resumed.

"The Huguenot bishop resides on a large estate a good distance from here and rarely visits, entrusting the governance of his priests to the justice – Boivin, who also sits in the courtroom, as and when an 'offence' is committed. If you are to fully appreciate the degree of our persecution – a word I use without apology – you should attend his court. Tomorrow would be an ideal day as I know three Catholic brothers are charged and will appear before him."

"Lanval, that's an excellent suggestion. More ale, landlord!"

Outside, Lanval took his leave and walked back to the port. The day was by now crisp and pleasant, weather that reflected the satisfaction Bertrand and Monaud felt after their meeting with a man whose opinion could be trusted.

"What's our plan now, captain?" Monaud asked.

"We'll go our separate ways then we'll meet back at Auberge Tournon to exchange notes. It's market day so I'd like you to go there and, especially, to see what the people are like – a market is always the place to start. I intend to discover what I can about the barracks."

"Understood, captain." Monaud set off, pleased to be independent of his superior, if only for a short time.

. . .

The Arcades, stone arches running the length of Rue Mercier, were the heart of market trading, each housing sellers of a wide range of goods that reflected the economic influence of La Rochelle. Monaud, dressed in his tunic, boots and cape, blended effortlessly into the crowded street. He began his tour, ostensibly inspecting merchandise on sale, but observing, eagle-eyed, everything around him, as Bertrand had instructed.

Shuttered windows and balconies above the arches indicated residences, Monaud decided, and some were two or three stories high and, so, a concentration of inhabitants. He idly picked up the edge of a roll of patterned fabric on one stall, as if to test its quality.

"Best silk, 'sieur, all the way from China...do you a good price depending on what length 'sieur buys...present for the wife, is it?" The stallholder, a man in a dandyish blue doublet, hailed the sergeant, who shook his head and moved on.

At one display - joints of beef and pork, long fat sausages, pink cured hams, salt beef and pâtés – the butcher was doing a brisk trade. Monaud watched an evidently wealthy lady pointing to this and that item for the butcher to hand it to a girl bearing a wicker basket over her arm. *Plenty of rich folk here then,* he decided. He carried on along the street and was taken by surprise when people to his right and left parted to allow the unimpeded passage of two burly men wearing black hats, both with a heavy cudgel in their hand, glaring menacingly at anyone in their path. He quickly moved to one side and. as soon as the ruffians had gone by, the street filled up again. *I'll take one guess who they report to,'* he thought.

. . .

All of the arches were occupied by one trader or another and, he noted, all sporting clean white aprons. Whatever they sold – vegetables, fruit, candles, salt, wine, cloth – was tastefully laid out, not in the random piles and haphazard scattering he was accustomed to seeing back home in his poor quarter of Paris.

He reached the last arch after which lowly houses lined Rue Mercier, distinctly underprivileged compared with those he had just passed. The stalls in the fine Arcade bays gave way to lines of trestle tables piled high with bric-a-brac and assorted second hand sundries. Behind them - the stallholders, he assumed – were, here, an old man with a straggly grey beard and threadbare tunic and, there, a young woman with dishevelled hair and a grizzling babe in her arms.

He next spotted a figure he recognised talking with that same old man – Father Servet. *There's a man who is in the know,* he thought, approaching him.

"Good afternoon, Father."

"And to you...um..."

"Monaud, in your church the other day."

"Of course, how are you and have you had success with a boat?"

"Lanval Aubert has told us of one that we will inspect tomorrow."

"That is good news. But, what brings you here to the market?"

"Just curious, Father. After all, if we are to live here, it's best to see what we can spend our money on."

"I suppose it is." Servet agreed, a note of doubt in his voice, "And there's a good selection of goods.'

"That's true enough, except where the arches end, and a quite different set of sellers begins, if you see what I mean...why is that?"

The priest placed an arm on Monaud's shoulder and guided him away from the tables.

"It doesn't pay to be overheard, my son, believe me." Lanval had used the exact words in the tavern. *Must be spies all around the place,* Monaud decided. The priest continued, satisfied they could speak.

"Well, if you want to know, all the arches are owned by Huguenot worshippers – regardless of their wealth – they simply have to be believers in that faith. Whereas -" He paused and lowered his head as if ashamed – "These wooden tables are the property of good Catholic men and women, subject, of course, to their licences being renewed by the judge."

"You mean Judge Boivin?"

"There's no other justice in the town."

"I see. They would seem to be a world apart, the arches and the tables..."

"You have the right of it." They walked on in silence. Then, Monaud spoke up.

"Earlier, I saw two men in black hats bearing cudgels."

"I hope you didn't try to engage them in conversation?"

"Indeed, I did not. I saw better."

"You certainly did! They are two of his law and order patrols, as he likes to describe them. To my mind, they are nought but thugs who will lash out as quick as blink. But, forgive me, a man of the cloth should not condemn people thus."

"Speak as you find, Father. I do."

The men parted and Monaud headed back towards the tavern, satisfied he had witnessed enough of the market.

. . .

Bertrand had a half-hour walk, during which he stopped two people to ask for directions, before he approached the barracks.

I'm now on the Rue Dauphine so the Porte Dauphine that we saw the other day must be close. It would make perfect sense to establish your major garrison between a wide road and the north access to the town, his military brain concluded.

Entry into the barracks was through an imposing stone wall with a crenelated top. In its centre, two heavy iron-studded wooden gates were shut and guarded either side by men armed with swords sitting in their sentry boxes. The wall extended left and right for a considerable distance so it could easily provide accommodation for several hundred troops. Bertrand was sure of his assessment even before he had furthered his ploy and spoken directly to any of the men inside. It was not possible to gain access so he sat on a bench nearby and waited. He was relying on the enlisted man's propensity for drink at the end of the day's training or whatever other duties they got up to. In this, his suspicion was impeccable. The doors swung open and a platoon of a dozen or more soldiers exited together, laughing and jostling each other, eager to start their evening's drinking in the town.

Bertrand needed to think and act in seconds, and this he did. As they passed noisily in front of his seat, he bided his time until the last man was level with him when he sharply extended a leg, tripping and sending his victim sprawling in a heap to the ground. The captain immediately helped the fellow to his feet, apologised profusely and patted his tunic vigorously to dust him down.

"I am *so* sorry, I didn't mean to...how careless of me... pray, sit a moment to recover yourself."

"It's nought. Been through worse," was the curt response.

"I'm sure you have, but sit, do, and take a sip of this." He produced the hip flask from his tunic, removed the stopper and pressed it into the soldier's hand as he all but tugged him onto the seat. The very scent of alcohol did the trick.

"Maybe I will then." He began to drink, followed by a loud spluttering.

"Good stuff, eh? I get it special from a dark-skinned matelot I know."

"It...sure is," came the laboured reply, and Bertrand progressed his ruse without delay.

"I don't suppose you're allowed strong drink inside the barracks?"

"No. Strictly against regulations."

"Just how it should be for a well-disciplined army, don't you agree?"

"I do, yet I feel our officers are too strict."

"I'll wager there's a good few of them in there?"

The man answered, seeing nothing untoward in the question.

"Ay, must be twenty or more."

"Really? Then there must be so many ordinary privates like you?"

"Dunno exactly...could be three hundred..."

"Here, drink some more – to make up for my clumsiness."

The instruction was obeyed – the brandy was, as planned, loosening his tongue.

"It would take a particular sort of man to command such a number."

"We've got one general – a fine man – but even he answers to Judge Boivin."

"That's unusual.'

"Not in this town, my friend!"

"Three hundred troops...so, do you keep enough weapons...cannons, bows, swords...inside?"

"Ay, you should see the size of the arsenal and, I might add, there are stables with the best grooms in the kingdom. Horses are ridden out through the Porte Dauphine every morning for exercise." He took a final swig and handed the flask back to Bertrand. Standing, he concluded meeting, to his way of thinking, a stranger taking a healthy interest in his life behind the massive stone walls, and set off to catch up with his pals.

That couldn't have gone any better! He thought. *How useful those disclosures will be for our Duke de Guise in Paris!* He realised, amazed that it had been so easy.

Back at the Auberge Tournon, Bertrand and Monaud drank ale at a table in a shadowy alcove where they could talk in private. They each gave the other a detailed account of their findings.

"I'll write them up after supper." The captain whispered.

"It's been a most rewarding day's work." Monaud decided smugly. "Tomorrow we'll attend the courtroom to watch Judge Boivin in action."

18

LA ROCHELLE, JANUARY 1573

AT FIRST LIGHT, THE FRESH-FACED LANDLORD'S daughter knocked sharply on the bedroom door.

"Rise and shine, gentlemen." She called, "father says your breakfast is served, when you're ready." She gave her customary giggle and went back downstairs.

"He looks after us well, doesn't he?" Monaud said, splashing cold water from a bowl onto his face.

"He does, indeed, and it's no coincidence he's a Catholic like us," Bertrand replied detachedly.

Their table in the empty tavern awaited them with still-warm bread, a basket of fruit and pitcher of milk.

"Ah, good morning to you, sires. Did you sleep well?"

"We did, thank you."

"What do you have planned for today?" The landlord asked, sitting down beside them.

"We're going to watch J -" Monaud was stopped short as Bertrand kicked his shin under the table and continued his friend's words,

"We're going to watch how things are done in your courtroom."

"Then you will see our judge, Boivin. A little advice, do not draw attention to yourselves, not a good idea. I suppose that viewing our court in session will open your eyes and, who can say, it could be you, me, anybody in the dock."

"Is that so?" Monaud asked, hoping to coax information from him.

"Yes, it is. But, I do not seek to prejudice you." He became silent in thought then, "Boivin has been the justice here for over twenty years and I well remember his bishop – I say *his* bishop – coming to this very tavern. Unusual, to say the least, and I forget his purpose, apart from testing my fine ale, but I got into conversation with him and he asked me whether I knew Latin – can you believe that? A simple innkeeper familiar with the language of kings and pontiffs! What a joke! So, he proceeded to explain the Boivin family motto because, he said, not many people would understand it, only a privileged few. Well, it's '*Conscientia et fama*'. I wasn't at all sure why he was telling me this. Why me, unless he needed to get it off his mind? Anyway, he said that '*Conscientia*' can mean 'knowledge' or 'complicity in something' and '*fama*' is either 'good reputation' or 'ill repute'. Do you get the picture? It was Boivin's own bishop expressing a lack of confidence in his own justice. I'll say no more. Enjoy your day."

They ate a hearty breakfast, taking in the thinly-veiled account from the landlord and suspecting, beforehand, the nature of the man they would soon scrutinize.

Outside, they followed the Rue Saint Yon to their Saint Sauveur church where they took a left turn for the Palais de

Justice. There was nobody about so early, the eerie silence surrounded them, creating an unsettling apprehension.

"Damned quiet," Monaud half-whispered.

"Ay, but it pays to get there in good time. The other day a man told me the sessions are very popular and we want a decent seat, don't we?"

"We do that! I don't intend missing a thing."

Shortly, they came to the Palais de Justice, a two-storey structure with ordinary looking doors and scarcely bigger than a house. Only the king's ragged banner hanging limply from a flagpole and *Palais de Justice* carved into the stone in small letters announced it was an important building. But, the squat windowless edifice to the left, the courtroom, was the object of their visit. Half a dozen men and women were already in a line that Bertrand and Monaud joined in front of the entrance.

"Hey, look at that, above the doorway," Monaud said in a quiet voice. Bertrand raised his gaze to a wooden heraldic shield boasting the name Boivin and, at its top, the motto *'Conscientia et fama'*, just as the jovial landlord had described.

They had not been in the line for long when, looking over his shoulder, Monaud now saw a score of people. The man in front of him turned around,

"They won't open the doors until the Terce bell rings."

Monaud nodded, aware of the warning to not attract attention. *'Best to say nothing,'* he thought, *'but it's a good while yet for that bell. Still, can't be helped.'*

. . .

Bertrand's mind dwelt on his late father who had been a magistrate in the 'arrondissement' of Paris where they lived and who had spent long hours explaining legal organisation to his son, hoping he would follow in his footsteps. He chose a military career instead but never forgot his father's accounts. Yet, he wondered if Boivin would, in any way, conduct *his* court according to traditional judicial practices.

'*In the army,* he contemplated, '*we have our own rules and authority, we deal with transgressions in-house. What offences will we see today? Father told me that, even in modern times, there are punishments – or 'ordeals' – by combat, fire, bread or water. But, this is La Rochelle, not Paris, where they at least concede to a common customary law, even if it's an aggregation of Roman, Frankish and feudal legislation, royal decree and canonical precedent. From what I've found out, this place is more civilised. Why, then, keep hundreds of soldiers in the barracks? If Boivin doles out sentences as my father said, the population must live in fear of the regime. For theft, it could be amputation of the hand; spies might have their eyes gouged out; poachers could lose an ear. Then, there's the stocks, a flogging or fines – mind you, how you collect a fine from penniless wretches, I don't know. I like to think my parent showed compassion, listened attentively to the pleas of the accused and encouraged witnesses, be they lay or priests, to come forward and to empower his decision to be fair, within the laws he was sworn to uphold. However, I suspect that human behaviour, justice and neutrality may be tested today.*'

By the time the long-awaited Terce bell chimed, the queue easily numbered three score of townsfolk, each man or woman intending to secure a seat to watch the proceedings.

Some were present out of macabre curiosity, others were family and friends of the indicted, the latter group praying for a compassionate outcome. The sturdy doors opened and there was pushing and jostling to gain entry but two burly attendants allowed only one person in at a time. Inside, a third directed them to a wooden staircase. The captain and his man followed the six townsfolk from outside and ascended the stairs to the public gallery. Without giving it a second glance, Monaud tugged his companion towards the front bench affording a direct view of matters below.

"Best seats in the house," the sergeant observed.

The gallery consisted of three benches that ran around three sides of the courtroom and a balustrade with a hardwood top rail buffed to a shine from years of elbows and hands resting on it with people straining, leaning forward to catch the interrogation of those below.

It seemed only a few minutes until the benches to the left and right were all occupied with old and young men, girls and women, children and babes-in-arms. Yet, it was not a clamour that they caused, merely a subdued humming noise that reflected the tension and apprehension the ordinary folk felt. For them, the day would end in either celebration or lamentation, one extreme emotion or another, nothing in-between. The finality of an innocent or guilty verdict weighed heavily on the poor spectators as much as on the accused.

Bertrand peered over the rail and surveyed the scene. The first – and most pivotal – item he saw was the dais, one foot high, which supported the judge's seat – a throne by any other name, or even a carver chair at the head of a dining table, turned legs and a back of three vertical spindles topped with decorative finials that framed a smaller version of the shield above the entrance. Boivin's motto and name, carved and coloured blue, silver and gold, stared at all present.

'*Nobody can fail to be impressed by this.*' Bertrand mused. '*The occupier of this chair is a powerful man.*'

On the dais, in front of the chair, a solid table bore, neatly arranged, a pile of parchment sheets, a glass inkwell, a bundle of quills and a gavel.

'*Boivin likes tidiness and order.*' Was Bertrand's opinion.

Both men concentrated, assimilating every detail to go into the report to their general. The way ordinary people reacted, the manner the judge and his cronies behaved – all to provide a crucial insight that would facilitate the successful assault on the town.

Two smaller chairs, arranged either side of the dais, suggested the presence of dignitaries or guests. '*But who? Must be acolytes that he trusts.*' Was Monaud's silent appraisal. He looked at the wall and nudged Bertrand, indicating with a nod an enormous painting of a cleric in a scarlet gold-braided robe, his hands clasping a chalice to his breast in a devout posture.

"Their Huguenot bishop," the sergeant hissed, but softly, out of the corner of his mouth. Bertrand nodded.

Incongruous stained-glass windows in the side walls depicting saints and angels, that the men could not identify, filtered the pale morning light into intense blue, red and green hues that penetrated the otherwise gloomy courtroom. The effect was dramatic.

On another low podium, a three-sided dock awaited the defendant to stand in full view of all present. On either side of a small table sat the clerks, quills at the ready.

The only other items of furniture in the hall were benches for accusers, witnesses and officials that were soon occupied and the level of anticipation and excitement rose. It was the judge's established ploy to keep his audience in suspense and play on their emotions and prejudices to carry them along and agree with his eventual pronouncement.

Bertrand did not expect to recognise anyone around them or down below except two figures, in clerical attire sitting on the bench immediately in front of the main lectern: Fathers Servet and Evrart. *'Of course,* he thought, *who else would lead the defence of Catholic suspects than their own parish priests.'*

The public gallery was growing impatient – adults muttering, children restless. Then, the two priests were joined by a dozen or more men and women, in ordinary tunics. *'The witnesses, I'll wager.'* Bertrand, again, assessed them correctly although they were by no means impartial regarding the upcoming offences. Bribes or personal vendettas ensured their testimony would paint a damning picture of the accused. It was believed, among the Catholic population, that the majority Protestant Church was often complicit in instances of witnesses making palpably false statements, without challenge, though it was impossible to prove.

. . .

Just as it felt the courtroom would be enveloped in unruly clamour, a door to the rear opened and silence fell in the room. Judge Boivin emerged and took his place on the dais. Next came a man wearing a ceremonial chain – the mayor, leader of the powerful town council, and a woman who, rarely seen out and about, was recognised as his wife. They sat on two chairs to the left. To the right were two other priests, representatives of the prelate whose portrait hung imperiously above them.

This was the first time Bertrand and Monaud had seen the judge or mayor: they studied them intently, knowing their subsequent report was eagerly expected by the Duke de Guise. Muttering again started among the irritable participants in the hearings, thirsty for the proceedings to get underway.

"What do you think of him? Remember, his name means 'wine drinker." Monaud whispered.

"Can't say I like him, but we'll hear him out." Came Bertrand's fair-minded answer. His gaze fell on the short squat figure, around sixty years of age, with an odd floppy purple hat that hung over a sweaty forehead. Unshaven, he revealed yellowing broken teeth as he smiled pompously at those before him. His eyes, in Bertrand's estimation, shone with a degree of rage – though he couldn't explain why he felt thus.

Monaud's perception of the mayor was equally unflattering. *'A tall skeletal man with lank long grey hair, close-set dark eyes and pinched lips in a sad anguished face – a man not to be trusted.'* He concluded.

. . .

Boivin rose, only his head and torso visible above his table, picked up the gavel and brought it down hard, three times, to call the room to order. Crossing himself, he announced,

"All cases heard today are declared before God. Remember this well." He resumed his seat and gestured to a burly court bailiff who gripped the arm of a woman sitting on the front bench and tugged her to the dock, to then stand one step behind, folding his arms across his chest in an intimidating fashion.

"What is your name, woman?" Boivin growled.

"Aalis, Madame Aalis." she replied, trembling.

"Clerk, read out the charge."

The clerk got up and bellowed, as if to raise the roof,

"Drunk and disorderly, Your Honour, six days since, in Rue Massiou!"

"So, do you plead guilty or not guilty to the offence?" Boivin asked, screwing his eyes as he addressed her, in a menacing tone.

"Sire, it wasn't like it sounds -"

"Enough for now!" He commanded. Turning to those in front of him, he asked, "Who will vouch for this woman's transgression – you see, she's already admitted it!"

"I will, Judge!" A man called out, raising his arm.

"Speak then, and make sure we all hear it clearly, no mumbling...can't abide mumblers."

The witness stood,

"I was walking along Rue Massiou, and as I passed the tavern there, that woman fell out of the door – all but bowled me over she did! Well, I'm not used to -"

"Yes, yes, we gather your drift, and do you know her...do you have issues with her or her family, perhaps?"

'It's not fair questioning, he's leading the witness.' Monaud observed. 'No, but it doesn't surprise me.' Bertrand whispered back.

'No...not personally...but I've heard she drinks until she can't stand."

"Who else accuses her?" Boivin invited, resuming a well-rehearsed script, tapping his fingers on the table.

"Me!" an old lady crowed, "I saw her in that street, sobbing and moaning. Nobody acts like that 'less they be under the spell of demon drink, do they?"

"Quite." The judge agreed, "Who defends her?"

Father Evrart stood up at once,

"I do, Judge. I wasn't there, but she is one of my parish and attends Mass, without fail. Her husband left her and her new-born child passed away from a fever. It's no great surprise she was weeping and, even if she had drunk a little too much ale, who can blame her, given her sad circumstances? Also, I dispute she 'nearly bowled' that man over since he's a giant up against her."

"Um..." The judge paused, then, "Mind you, we would expect her priest to say that, wouldn't we?" Turning to the dock, he asked, abruptly,

"What is your defence Madame...um...Madame Aalis?"

"What Father Evrart says is true and...yes...it would have been my son's first birthday if he had survived." Tears ran down her cheeks, "I had met friends in the tavern and, on leaving, I stumbled, that's the truth, Your Honour. I admit I was crying, but it had all got too much for me."

The judge leaned over to the mayor and the two nodded and conversed for a short time. The public gallery started to jeer, boo, stamp their feet, urging Boivin to declare against the woman.

. . .

With three strikes of his gavel, he brought the court to an expectant silence,

"Madame Aalis, we find you guilty of the offence of being drunk and disorderly in a public place. You will be taken from your house at the Terce bell and put in the stocks until Vespers, for three days. We trust you will learn that your behaviour was unacceptable and contrary to the law of La Rochelle."

The poor woman burst into uncontrolled crying as the bailiff pulled her out of the dock and saw her out of the room to mocking applause.

Monaud moved close to his captain,

"Nine hours a day, for three days? It's monstrous! And, for what? Any reasonable man would understand her special circumstances." He whispered.

"Ay, but her special circumstances are worshipping in a Catholic church." Bertrand said quietly, knowing he was stating the obvious. "And, look, there!" he continued, nodding at the judge's table, "He's taking wine, as if this was a pleasant social occasion!"

A girl had placed a decanter and goblet in front of him. He drank, then ordered,

"Next!"

The official ushered a young man from the benches to the dock. He could not have been more than twenty years old and appeared terrified, as well he should.

"Name?" Boivin shouted, taking another sip of wine.

"Domard, sire,"

"Bailiff, his crime?"

"Poaching, Your Honour, eel poaching on the bishop's estate."

The young man lowered his gaze, fearing what would come next.

"Who accuses Domard?"

"I do, monsieur." A thick-set youth wearing a purple hat stood up. *'He's one of Boivin's bullies, see his hat.'* Monaud spoke lowly. The judge continued,

"Let us hear your testimony, then. Come on! We haven't got all day." Boivin muttered in an indifferent tone.

"I own up to taking one eel, but only *one*. See, there's no work for Catholics like me, and I've a family to feed. I didn't think the good bishop would miss just *one* from his pool."

"That's sufficient. Witness, tell us what you saw." Boivin snarled.

"He had a sack that was wiggling about and I swear there must have been at least six eels in it...yes, six."

"Thank you for that." Boivin turned to Father Evrart, inviting him to speak on behalf of Domard.

"You Honour," he began, "your bishop is a generous Christian and a credit to the leadership of your Church." He had learned to give opinions that were contrary to his true belief, for the benefit of those who had a far lesser voice. *May the Lord forgive my falsehoods. It is not my disposition, but the reality of our oppression dictates my sorrowful actions,* he prayed, each and every time he had to play out this charade. His powerful submission continued, "He would, surely, show clemency for Monsieur Domard's situation. And, although the confidential nature of confession prevents me from revealing any personal exchanges, this man in the dock has displayed contrition and implores your mercy."

The judge – watched fixedly by Bertrand and Monaud

– leaned over to the mayor, then to the priests sitting to his right before pronouncing,

"Monsieur Domard, having heard the declarations, we find you guilty of poaching, an abominable crime, for which we must set an example. As is our way, we are a lenient court and you should be grateful you're not hanging from the gibbet!" A burst of acclamation rose. "You will be tied to the whipping post to receive thirty lashes. Step down."

"Boivin hears what he wants to hear. How can he not question that man's word...in his pay, I don't wonder. It's no justice the likes of which I've ever seen. It's nothing short of a mockery." Monaud said through gritted teeth to his companion, the anger in his voice increasing.

"Not so loud, Monaud, we can't give ourselves away."

"The third case, bailiff, announce the charge." Boivin ordered, nonchalantly, sipping more drink.

"Your Honour, this woman was seen begging."

"Your name?"

"Guinand."

"Is the offence admitted, Madame Guinand? – you will save the court valuable time if it is."

"I will not lie to you, sire. My husband is dying from a sickness and I have to have a physician attend him...we have no income...and it was only in a street where I knew wealthy people passed...wouldn't take from the poor like us..."

This time, the judge did not confer with anybody but came directly to his sentence,

"You are fined two silver coins, to be paid within one

week. Consider yourself fortunate you will still have both hands – it could be worse...um...far worse."

The pitiful old woman wept. She had no means to settle such a fine and when she was, subsequently, hauled before him for non-payment, she would be thrown into the dungeon, chained and forgotten, at best. What hope for her, and her kind? She accepted this would be her fate and, sadly, all the Catholics of La Rochelle lived under such tyranny. In a desperate plea for compassion, she implored Boivin to forgive her behaviour, if he had it in him. The courtroom became quiet as the justice refilled his goblet. Smacking his lips, he responded,

"Madame Guinand, by your own admission you are a beggar and, as the upholder of the laws of our fair town, it is incumbent on me to perform my legal duty. I put it to you, we would be all the worse if I did not so do! The penalty stands, but may I suggest that, if madam will entertain honest toil, despite her advancing years, she presents herself at the tannery where they are always short of...um...skilled workers."

At this, raucous sneering cries rose to the rafters accompanied by stamping from the gallery. The tannery, secluded in woodland to the west of the town, was a cavernous warehouse-like building. No matter how dense the woods surrounding it, the nauseous putrid stench that it discharged was overwhelming. Animal hides arrived dried and dirty with soil and gore. Any flesh or fat was removed for it then to be soaked in urine to release any hair. Finally, the skin was scraped and dung was pounded into it: all to produce fine leather – gauntlets for knights, splendid boots for the king's horsemen, demand was high.

. . .

Only the night soil collector, shovelling the contents of privy vaults, was considered a lower employment than working in the tannery. The judge's proposition was calculated to cause maximum offence. Bertrand and Monaud had seen enough.

"Come on, let's get out of here." the captain ordered his sergeant.

"I don't need asking twice." Came the swift reply.

Outside, they headed for the stables on the Valin Quay. The lad was busy brushing down a horse as they entered.

"Have our horses prepared by first light, tomorrow. We are leaving La Rochelle." Bertrand instructed.

"Consider it done, sire."

Back in the Auberge Tournon, they savoured their ale near the roaring fire.

"There's a lot to take in." Monaud said, pensively.

"Ay, you're right, but we've seen sufficient to make our report to the Duke de Guise and, of course, to Catherine, the Queen Mother."

"After that, we'll be on our way to Montauban – and I'll have my lieutenant's stripes, if all goes well."

"So you will, Monaud, so you will."

19

A MATTER OF HOURS BEFORE THE SAINT Bartholomew's Day massacre in Paris, old Gervese and his arthritic wife, Salvia, had fled the capital fearing for their lives and embarking on an arduous journey with their horse and cart to Beauvais. It was thought that this town was dominated by people of their own religious persuasion, Huguenots and, therefore, a safe haven. The couple were taking up a kind offer of accommodation from her brother, Michel.

Reining the horse to a standstill outside the house, a lad, as if from nowhere, appeared and grasped the bridle, announcing,

"Good day sire, madam. Leave it to me, I'll see he's fed and watered for the night."

"You come at the right moment, boy, as if you knew of our arrival," Gervese spoke softly.

"Ay, it's a small place, that's for sure...not good to hold secrets..." The youngster answered, knowingly.

"Help me to unload our chest, then."

The noise they made brought the brother to the door.

"Salvia, Gervese, welcome to Beauvais." To the boy, he instructed, "bring the chest indoors, and here's something for your help with the stabling." He pressed a coin into his hand that he accepted with a broad grin and proceeded to lead the horse and cart away down the street.

Their host filled three tankards from a barrel on supports in a corner of his living room, brought them to the table, and raised his in a toast. His visitors reciprocated.

"How was your journey?" Michel asked.

"Not too good for Salvia. Her bones aren't as strong as they used to be – very painful, isn't that right, dear?"

"Afraid it is, but I don't complain. There are greater ills around." She stated, wide-eyed, her gaze drifting over their heads."

"There are, indeed, Salvia," Michel agreed.

"You know why we've left Paris, don't you?" Gervese asked, looking his brother-in-law straight in the face.

"From what I hear, the Huguenots are being run out of the city, for want of a better expression." He replied.

"They are, and the future there doesn't bear thinking, which is why -"

Michel interrupted him, "– why you're here, and I quite understand that. However – he drank some ale – I must warn you, from the start, that we who uphold the Huguenot doctrine have been badly treated of late, and it shows no signs of improving."

Gervese's jaw dropped, his wife shook her head in disbelief. Surely, they had not uprooted, sold their house, left their friends and neighbours, and all for nothing?

Michel refilled the tankards and continued, a sadness present in his voice,

"We've not had anything like a massacre, that's true, but we endure a slow, insidious erosion of our rights. The town council is made up, in the main, of Catholics. Any suggestions we put forward go, first, to the magistrate and – you can guess – he's a prominent Catholic man who protects the interests of his own kind. Whenever he makes a decision, it's not the council who hear it first but his priests. They inform their congregations and so the corruption goes on. We are in the minority for all town matters. Anything you've heard to the contrary vouches for the effectiveness of their propaganda. The world outside Beauvais is duped!"

Salvia looked down and started to weep, quietly and, despite her husband's comforting embrace, it was some minutes before she stopped.

"Now, now my dear, do not shed tears. It simply *can't* be as unjust here as in Paris." Then, he explained to Michel,

"We let our house go – for a bargain price – which is why we call upon your kindness to give us shelter until we find one to buy in your town."

"For as long as it takes, Gervese...after all, you are family." He paused, his lips pinched, "But you will find vendors are reluctant to sell, believe me, once they know which faith you follow and, they *will know!*"

Salvia stared at her husband, the anguish in her countenance asking him whether they had made a catastrophic error of judgment. The aching in her joints, at that moment, grew through her distress and she wrung her hands to ease the pain in her heart.

. . .

The next morning, after breakfast, Michel invited them to stroll around their newly-adopted town.

"Don't worry, Salvia, we'll keep to level streets – no hills for you."

"Thank you, brother, you're a kind man." She told him, gently, as he helped her to put on her cape.

The three of them stepped out into the crisp morning air.

"Keep close to me." Michel advised his guests, "and we'll be safe."

"Safe?" Gervese nearly choked and had to summon his self-control to prevent an explosion of anger.

"You'll soon see." Michel led them slowly down the street.

After a few minutes, he broke the silence,

"On that door, to your right, what do you think it is?"

Gervese stared at the door and, without stopping, answered,

"I'd say there are...are rotten fruits splattered over it."

"You're right. Rancid tomatoes and apples hurled against an innocent man's house. Why? Because he's a Huguenot! I know him well."

No-one spoke. They turned into another street that was, as yet, deserted. Michel leaned over to Salvia,

"Down there, on that doorstep, look."

She recoiled, almost falling into his arms, horrified and revolted. Someone had spread faeces ready for the unsuspecting householder to tread in.

"I'll show you one more example of what we face, day by day. Come, further down the street."

They arrived at a house in the shadow of the town's principal Huguenot church. Nailed high up on the door, for the world to observe, was a dark bird, its wings extended as if in flight.

"What does that mean?" Gervese asked, hardly able to believe his eyes.

"In the folklore of the town," Michel started, "from centuries ago, for all I know, it was thought that a blackbird fixed to a man's property would bring a curse on him and his family, regardless of his alleged offence or impropriety. And, before you ask, most of those people, would be thrown into cellars, as a punishment. Today, it's not so different, sad to say, and if we have erred from the straight and narrow... the town dungeons are full, of Huguenots."

The husband and wife were amazed to hear this.

"But, here we are, our church. Let's go in and pray, for we are in dire need of divine intervention as and when it might come."

After this first experience of Beauvais, Salvia's despair and sorrow became so profound that it continued to accelerate her physical infirmity. Within just a few weeks, she had developed a raging fever accompanied by convulsions. The doctor's best remedies – for they had the wherewithal to pay for his services – proved ineffective and, with Gervese at her bedside, she passed away. His heart was broken and, unable to endure his sadness, he waded into the river Oise for its current to sweep him downstream. His body was never to be found. The old couple had escaped Paris, like thousands of their contemporaries, in search of a new life in their golden years, free of religious tensions. They had found that the grass was far from greener on the other side.

Montauban, 1573

The same day the elderly husband and wife had climbed onto their cart and rode to the disaster that was Beauvais, Sébastien and Joffroy worked their passage on a barge, sailing on the Seine from Paris westward through Saint Germain, Le Havre and, finally, to the small Channel port of Cabourg. The barge's captain asked why they were parting company with him because he was quite satisfied with their efforts since he'd first hired them. Sébastien answered, with regret,

"To steer clear of Catholic hordes who would cut us down as quick as a blink of the eye: folk like us don't have a right to worship as we see fit...we're seen as blasphemers, nothing less."

After a short pause, captain Albinet made a suggestion,

"There's one town I've heard talk of, one governed by your own kind, Huguenots. It's said they're wealthy, well-connected and fanatical when it comes to defending their churches. Now, I don't get involved in anything to do with that bible business...stuff and nonsense if you ask me...but I'd vouch you'll be safe there. Only one drawback, it's a week's ride from here."

Undeterred, they bought two decent horses from the town's stables, together with saddles and bridles, and set off for Montauban, their spirits high, having slept well and considered Albinet's encouraging words. Waving a cheery farewell to the sailor, who had come to wish them a safe journey,

"God speed, gentlemen! Don't pull up for too long – bandits know no religious confines, so have your daggers at the ready!" This was not exactly what the two men had wanted to hear but, it was as it was: their fate, their final chance lay in an unknown faraway place. Their faith would see them reach their destination and, before kicking the horses into motion, they shared a silent moment of prayer, before,

"We'll remember that, Albinet! Give our regards to Big Hand and Little Hand and buy them ale next time you're in the tavern." Joffroy threw a coin in the man's direction, smiling broadly. He had come to enjoy the company of those dark-skinned hands, whose language he couldn't fathom, and felt a twinge of sadness to be leaving them.

Fortunately, such ruffians as there were left them alone and they made good progress south, from one overnight auberge to another, until on their sixth day of travelling the town of Montauban was in sight.

"From the information we've picked up – and it's a miracle how a man's tongue is loosened after a few drinks – we shouldn't have a problem finding a house to rent, since we're Huguenots." Joffroy said to his friend.

"Agreed, but we'll first find the Temple des Carmes where our fellow believers worship -

a priest always has the best local knowledge." Joffroy concurred, spurring on his horse.

They crossed the Vieux Pont over the river Tarn and passed through a town gate that was unmanned, the wall to either side in a crumbling state. Walking their horses, slowly, the beauty of Montauban was striking. Everywhere, buildings constructed from red bricks giving out a pink glow, the likes of which they had never seen.

Daylight fading, the town's inhabitants were still out and about: couples linking arms, boys pushing barrows, children playing and screaming with a happiness that only youngsters exude.

Sébastien and Joffroy exchanged glances. Montauban seemed, at first sight, exactly the contented easy-going place they sought to spend the rest of their days, and this they felt after but an hour.

They found stables for their horses and continued through the town on foot, having obtained directions to the Temple des Carmes, their anticipated church. A bastide, fortified against invaders, the central arcaded square had walkways beneath imposing townhouses, bricks combined with stucco, balustrades and statue pedestals. The visual strength of the red bricks assailed the senses, yet, left the spectator with a unique impression of warmth and calm. Its reputation for the reddish buildings was surpassed only by its pre-eminence as a Huguenot stronghold, the very reason that Joffroy and Sébastien intended to make it their home.

As they approached the Temple, noises from within indicated a service in progress. Two unusual iron doors, framed by fluted classical stone columns supporting an ornate frieze, were firmly shut. But, as Sébastien pushed, it gave and creaked open. It was hard to see inside, at first, because people standing to the rear blocked their view. They stood since every pew, from the altar at the front to the rear, was occupied. Joffroy spotted a vacant area by one of the side chapels and tugged at his friend's arm,

"Over here, come."

Although Montauban boasted several more Protestant temples, this one was, unquestionably, the seat of power from where all important proclamations – religious or otherwise – emanated.

Off either side of the nave were four arched chapels for the veneration of the saints. The altar sat under an apse whose vaulted ceiling ran the entire length of the building. It had no transept, a feature that served to emphasise the rectangular nature of its design. Its walls, plain and without paintings or carvings, possessed a naïve charm that distinguished it from Catholic counterparts.

"It's certainly popular." Joffroy commented with his typical talent for understatement.

"It is. I think we'll be safe in Montauban." Sébastien replied, his gaze encompassing the church.

The respectful whispering that drifted from the congregation gradually ceased as, one after another, they saw a priest, in a plain black cassock, climb the steps of a raised pulpit on the right of the altar. This priest, the first cleric the two visitors had yet seen, drew a cross in the air for silence to prevail and, accordingly, the people now settled, eagerly awaiting his sermon. This preacher and his cohort would, from now on, be their spiritual mentors, whose interpretation of the Holy Word would guide them through what remained of their lives.

.   .   .

The person in the pulpit gathered himself before starting his address. He was a learned man, a well-read scholar, but single-minded and militant in his adherence to the Huguenot doctrine. His views had galvanised the town of Montauban where the opposing Catholic voice should have counted for little, being outnumbered by thousands. He was the undisputed religious and secular law of his populace, a pragmatic personality, well-connected with sympathetic noble houses, especially that of Queen Jeanne of Navarre who had fled Paris after the massacres there and relocated to the Protestant bishop of La Rochelle's chateau.

He opened his bible, breathed in deeply, then,

"Brothers and sisters, may the Good Lord bless and keep you." He crossed himself and the captive audience copied him.

'As for the cowardly, the faithless, the detestable, as for murderers, the sexually immoral, sorcerers, idolaters, and all liars, their portion will be in the lake that burns with fire and sulphur, which is the second death.' "So are the words of Revelations." His face contorted into a passionate expression,

"Never has the message of the scriptures been more relevant to us in our beloved Montauban...to you, you and you!" His finger pointed directly at his flock, accusing, menacing, deliberate. He resumed,

"Never!" His voice boomed out, filling the vaulted ceiling,

"We are secure in our belief, are we not?"

"Ay, father! Ay!" The congregation called back.

"But, we must not become complacent because there exist evil forces who would see us divided and, perish the very thought, expelled from our rightful home. Within our denomination, within our households, there is no room for cowards, faithless, liars, or sorcerers – our Bible tells us so!" And he crashed a fist down onto the edge of the lectern.

Sébastien leaned over to Joffroy,

"He's one who doesn't pull his punches."

"No, and I wouldn't like to get on his wrong side." Joffroy agreed.

The priest, again, waited for calm, then continued,

"Be prepared! Be strong in your belief! But, should calamity come to you, my brethren, it will be because you have deserved it. It is God's way of separating His human wheat from the chaff, and the chaff are the sinners!" Beads of sweat formed on his forehead that he brushed away with his sleeve, giving the congregation below him a moment to be, predictably, frightened by his warning. He had learned over many years that, if he instilled fear into his listeners, he was half-way to gaining total control over them. His gaze lowered, first to the farthest left corner then across to his right and his people felt he looked at them directly in their face. How they adored this man! Turning over the pages of the bible, he resumed,

"In Corinthians, we read, *'Be on your guard, stand firm in the faith; be courageous; be strong.'* And, so it is! But, God is tired of waiting for people to become *devout* Huguenots. Do not incur His wrath! We will offer up to Heaven one truly Christian prayer of love and pleading. He will see to the rest."

The congregation knelt, as one, and repeated after him the prayer he recited.

· · ·

One hour later, the service over, everyone walked, silently, out of the Temple – some impressed by the message the priest had imparted, most simply scared by premonitions of a catastrophe that could befall them at any moment.

"If ever we wanted to live in a Huguenot place, we've found one here!" Joffroy said, behind his hand.

"For once in your life, my friend, you're right!" And Sébastien clapped the other man's shoulder warmly, then decided, "We'd better find accommodation for the night."

They soon came to an inn with rooms and, that night, they ate and drank well. After a journey from one side of the kingdom to the other, they slept like babes.

In her chateau at Chenonceau, Catherine had, that day, received her Duke de Guise. After dinner, they retired to her private rooms to take brandy.

"It's good to meet with you again." She said, raising her glass.

"Your health, ma'am." He reciprocated.

"So, to business. What news of Bertrand and Monaud, it's time they returned from La Rochelle?" The stare from her dark blue eyes left him in no doubt that this woman, who he respected for her convictions if not always for the methods she employed to achieve them, was in an unsentimental frame of mind. As a career soldier, he had known battles won and lost depending on the disciplined astute capability of the general as much as on the loyalty and bravery of the troops.

"They are expected any day now and will come to my

house immediately. I will let them rest a while then they will accompany me back to the chateau for an audience with yourself, ma'am." He took a sip of brandy, his gaze fixed on the Queen Mother to gauge her mood. He knew only too well she could laugh one moment but scream the next. *Strange creatures these highly-strung noblewomen,* he thought. Today, she seemed calm.

"That is excellent, for we cannot even think about La Rochelle until we learn more about it from your men, what say you, duke?"

"That is correct, my lady, a successful campaign will always result from meticulous planning, and we both share this view."

"Quite." Her tone was markedly abrupt. "But I – I mean *we,* the King and I – cannot wait for ever. La Rochelle is one jewel I would dearly love to see embedded in our royal crown. So many towns in the kingdom are now subject to Catholic administration. Since Christmas, we have taken Orléans, Lyon, Troyes, Meaux, Autun and Beauvais – the list goes on, but -"

"- forgive my interruption, ma'am, but there remains the small matter of Montauban. I'm sure my lady will not have overlooked our present objective." At that moment, he realised he should not have spoken with the slightest degree of sarcasm. Fortunately, she did not react adversely.

"Of course not. May I assume your army is prepared?"

"Ready to depart, upon my return to Paris. We will overwhelm Montauban, they will not suspect our invasion and by the time they do, we will have men at the doors to their churches, taverns, offices and whorehouses!"

"I'm pleased you have not lost your sense of humour, duke."

He smiled. They understood each other well,

"Tomorrow, I depart for the capital and will return shortly with Bertrand and Monaud. I'm certain we will learn much about the...the jewel in the crown."

"I'm certain we will." Her eyes twinkled, even at the thought of bloody conflict.

20

"Good morning, Monsieur Aubert."

Lanval turned around from loading his cart at the quayside, hearing his name, to see a man he did not immediately recognise,

"And to you," He answered, out of politeness.

"You don't remember me, do you?" The stranger asked.

Lanval thought for a moment, then,

"Of course, you're the boy's father I gave the canaries to. How are they doing?"

"That's the reason I'm here. I'd hoped to find you. I've got a problem, of sorts."

"I'm sorry to hear that, but how can I help you?"

"It's my lad and those birds. He dotes on them, you wouldn't believe how much he's changed. Since his mother passed away...well, he took it very badly, as you can imagine and..." The man stopped, his eyes welling up with tears. "Last year, the pair you gave him had two chicks but, I can't say why, they died. It wasn't his fault, monsieur, he fed and cleaned them out proper but they just died in the cage."

"That happens." Lanval said gently.

"Ay. I wonder, do you have another pair I could buy from you? I've got the money here." He reached inside his tunic and withdrew a pouch.

"Put that away. I understand and, yes, I've got two more that are looking for a good home."

"Is that so? The boy will be overjoyed."

"Consider it a gift." Lanval replied. "Come by my house this evening."

"Can't thank you enough, Monsieur Lanval." The man turned, wiping his moist eyes on his sleeve, and left the quay.

Lanval resumed piling barrels on his cart but was interrupted again by a voice, but not a fraction as mild as the one before.

"Aubert!" The harbour master approached and Lanval knew he wouldn't want to pass the time of day with him, but he owed no taxes so has wasn't unduly concerned.

What do you want?" The carter asked with a note of suspicion in his voice.

"Do you have business with the man you were talking with?"

"And what's that got to do with you?" Lanval knew that attack was the best form of defence with this man,

"We don't like to see your sort mixing with -"

"Mixing? What are you saying?" Lanval screwed his eyes and stepped towards the other man, menacingly.

"Yes, you Catholics are only bad news for us."

"Ah, I understand now!"

"Then, see to your own affairs and leave us alone, otherwise..."

"Otherwise, nothing! Clear off!" Came the

commanding response and he gave the man a shove to support his order.

What's it coming to in this town? I'm of the Catholic faith and they treat us as if we're second class citizens. It's getting worse, by the day, and they outnumber us – we aren't many more than ten to their thousand!

Fathers Servet and Evrart left their Saint Sauveur church after prayers and strolled leisurely towards the Arcades in the Rue Mercier. It was market day and the priests regarded their showing an interest in the commercial situation of their parishioners to be as important as the spiritual side of life in La Rochelle. Passing by the Huguenot arches, they nodded and smiled in a lacklustre manner at the traders in their smart aprons arranging their merchandise, preparing for the day's business. Few, if any, words were exchanged, the hostility and mistrust between the town's religious persuasions were intensifying by the moment.

As the two men got half way along the Rue Mercier, where the Protestant trade ended, the pleasant aroma of candles, cheese, fish, leather and hog roast from behind them dissipated and was replaced by the smell of acrid smoke ahead.

A distressing unexpected scene unfolded: in the middle of the street, impossible to ignore, a bonfire blazed, spewing sparks and flames into the morning air. On either side stood women, weeping and consoling each other; men punched the air with anger, voices raised, their paltry goods strewn on the ground.

"What's happened?" Father Servet asked the first group they came to.

"Soldiers! Damn soldiers!" One man screamed.

"Compose yourself, brother, what do you mean *soldiers*?"

"We'd just finished laying out our stalls when a gang of armed men – I recognised them, they'd come from the barracks – rushed down the road, pushed us aside and cleared our tables. They piled them up and set fire to them, every single table!" He pointed to the flaming heap. "What you see there, Father, is a funeral pyre! Ay, our livelihoods gone up in smoke. There's nothing left for us in this godforsaken place. Do you think they're telling us something, Father Servet?" There was no mistaking the sarcasm in his voice.

"This is, truly, shocking. We will raise it with the judge, and directly. It is a blaze born from prejudice, is it not, Father Evrart?"

Evrart had moved away and was doing his best to comfort some distraught women.

"Come, Father." Servet interrupted them, "We must discover the cause of this outrage. Let us pay a visit to the mayor, first."

The tall thin skeletal man sitting behind a desk, laden with dusty rolls of parchment and quills in varying degrees of usefulness, many blunt, looked up surprised to receive two clerics.

"Fathers, to what do I owe this honour?" He asked,

"You present yourselves at my office infrequently nowadays..."

And it's to our detriment that we've not done it a lot sooner, Servet mused.

"...and how can I help you today?" The mayor asked in a dismissive tone.

"Mayor, you will, no doubt, be aware of the heinous act perpetrated at the market this morning." Evrart began, as the senior of the two priests.

"Indeed, I am not." The functionary sneered.

"Our Catholic stalls are smashed and burned like so much refuse and we hear, from reliable witnesses, that soldiers were responsible." Father Evrart tried to sound accusatory but, in his heart, he knew he would not gain satisfaction, the odds being stacked against them.

"May I offer you wine, gentlemen?"

"You may not!" Servet clenched his fists wishing he was not, at that moment, a man of the cloth who could not resort to violent retaliation.

What's the verse..."The Son of Man is going to come with his angels in the glory of his Father, and then he will repay each person according to what he has done?" This mayor and his crooked breed had better watch out come the day of judgement!

He continued,

"We are not here for social reasons! Did you authorise this attack?"

"Me?' The mayor tossed his head back and guffawed. "Who do you take me for, I have nothing to do with the market, nor the soldiers, come to that. I am a humble representative of the people. It is Judge Boivin to whom you should address your enquiries. Will that be all?"

The priests saw the futility of prolonging their meeting and left.

"He knows." Servet spoke through tight lips.

"He does, for sure." Evrart agreed. "We'll find Boivin to hear what he has to say."

The courthouse and the judge's office were but a few streets away. Evrart knocked on the door and they entered without waiting for an invitation.

Boivin, a short fat man in his usual purple hat, smiled to reveal yellow broken teeth and asked fawningly,

"So...proponents of the faith – even if it is the wrong faith – you are unexpected. What do you want?" He spoke with a brazen hateful tone to his words.

"Why did you authorise our peoples' stalls to be burned to ashes?"

"Ah, that. These things happen, don't you know?"

"For what reason?" Evrart snapped.

"Your people are in arrears with their market rents, were you not aware? I could not renew their licences, it would have been against the law. And, besides, the traders from the arches need to expand their business."

The priests could not find a response, so acute was their anger in the face of such blatant discrimination.

Some days later, Boivin presided in his court where a woman was accused of adultery with the petitioner's husband who was of limited intelligence and, therefore, unable to appreciate what he did was wrong if not for the accuser's contemptible influence.

The woman in the dock was known to Lanval's mother through their church. One evening, over supper, she had explained her friend's plight to her son.

"I cannot believe that woman, Gisa, has the temerity to blame my friend, Aldessa. It's appalling and, surely, the judge will dismiss her. She has nobody to speak for her, so will you be her character witness?"

Lanval listened to his mother carefully and with respect. If he accepted her request, it would not be the first time he had defended a member of his Church in court.

"Tell me about her, then, but you know how every authority in the town – from the council to the harbour master – is hell-bent on finishing us off."

Mother gathered her thoughts then began her explanation,

"Aldessa's a good woman, even if she is, strictly speaking, answerable for the charge. It's widely known that the accuser, Gisa, is a loose woman who will lie with any man for a coin. She neglects her house and children, preferring to drink to excess in the taverns. It was left for her poor husband to care for the family and it's no surprise that he confided in my friend, Aldessa. They became friends and nature took its course. Neither is culpable – it's Gisa who should be accounting for her behaviour." Mother stopped and wiped a tear from her eye.

"I'll see what I can do, but I can't predict the outcome." Lanval said, moved by her story and, as ever, one to champion the underdog.

. . .

The public gallery of the courthouse was full, mainly with Huguenot folk. Boivin brought down his gavel to indicate the court was in session.

"Clerk!" He boomed, "Read out the offence."

"Your Honour, the Catholic woman, Aldessa Lebrun, is reported to have committed adultery, contrary to the scriptures which are well known to yourself -"

"Yes, yes, enough of all that!" He poured a goblet of wine, then asked,

"How do you plead...um...Madame Lebrun?"

"Guilty, but -"

"Guilty, good! Then my verdict is easy."

"Your Honour, one moment." Lanval stood, and approached the judge's table. Leaning close so as not to be overheard, he spoke, softly,

"Judge Boivin, I found it most enlightening to observe your strange rituals in the barn, the one concealed in the Villeneuve-les-Salines woods."

Boivin's face turned to a grim ashen-grey hue, in an instant, as Lanval continued, drawing even closer,

"Collecting the chicken's blood in your chalice then offering up prayers...what was it...ah, I remember,

By the favour of our Lord Satan...glory be to the evil spirits...we need to make the Catholics go away...schooled by the Devil's infernal ordinance...

"Yes, Your Honour!" And he spat the words into the justice's face, "I have witnessed you practising the Dark Arts yet, until today, I have not broadcast your wickedness. However, will this courtroom, packed and always delighted to hear this or that tittle-tattle, have it exposed what their esteemed judge gets up to in his leisure time? What will they think? Then, there's your bishop, a fine man who would be left with no option but to..."

Boivin was sweating profusely, his goblet shaking as he raised it to his lips,

"What do you want, Lanval, speak!" He hissed.

"Dismiss the charge. Tell the court whatever you will, but let her go." He sat down. The public fell silent, anticipating the verdict. Crashing his gavel down on his desk, he announced,

"Certain facts have been brought to my attention and I am grateful to Monsieur Aubert in this respect." He looked across to the trembling woman in the dock,

"You are free to leave. The accuser, called Gisa, is instructed never again to bear false witness, this notice to be posted around the town. Court is closed!" He beckoned Lanval to come near. "Don't think you've heard the last of this, Aubert. You and your kind can expect severe retribution."

As people filed out of the building, their hatred for Catholics was tangible, enflamed by the judge's ruling, and their outrage was expressed to their own priests, in no uncertain terms. Over the coming weeks, resentment mounted: church by church, street by street, neighbour by neighbour, to such a pitch that Catholic citizens were contemplating plans to leave the town where they were born and that they loved.

Lanval walked into his house after a day delivering goods from the quay to addresses around La Rochelle and, although many comments were not directed at him personally, they derided the wider Catholic populace, branding them as everything from beggars to murderers.

His mother and another lady were at the table, their embroidery laid out before them. He recognised the visitor at once,

"Hello, Madame Lebrun, how are you?"

"Master Lanval, I'm fine, and thanks to your invaluable intervention in court I can carry on and put my mistake behind me."

"Amen to that." Mother added. "Supper is not ready yet, son."

"That's all right, I'm going to meet Cicile, it's a while since I saw her." He nodded, politely, to Madame Lebrun and left the women to their embroidery.

He met Cicile at their customary place, the Saint Nicolas Tower. Sitting on a bench, even with her back to him, she was unmistakable with her long shiny dark hair tied with a ribbon. He approached, stealthily, then jumped in front of her, as a surprise. Instead of laughing at his little prank, she glared, her eyes screwed and lips, normally framing her even white teeth with a smile, were tight closed.

"Why did you do that? You frightened me." She growled. Something was amiss.

"Sorry, I didn't mean to...it was just in fun."

"Ay, and fun I can do without!" Her tone indicated deep trouble.

"What's the matter?" He asked, taking her hand only for it to be sharply removed.

"We can't continue to see each other." She said the words unable to look him in the face. Immediately, his thoughts returned to his father's funeral that she did not attend because Boivin had told her it would not be *seemly*.

So, the man's poison is now infecting even innocent

young women. I know you've always defended him, Lanval said to himself. Love her as he did, he recognised in an instant that it would be futile to try to persuade her to change her decision,

"It's Boivin, again, isn't it?" He knew the answer.

"Yes, he's threatened my parents with eviction since the house is somehow Huguenot church property. Then, he will see my father's wine stall in the Arcades is boycotted by all and sundry. We will have nothing to live on and mother's not in good health."

"That's enough, Cicile. I'd expected it given the way every Huguenot is behaving towards us. Give my regards to Judge Boivin." Without even a farewell kiss, he turned and walked back towards his house, distraught and resigned to the calamity that had befallen their town.

Later, that same month, a horseman rode through the Porte Gambetta. Having obtained directions, he soon found the Saint Sauveur church. Tethering his horse to a post he entered, seeking Father Evrart. There was nobody about, apart from two old women sitting, heads bowed in prayer, who he approached and asked, softly,

"Ladies, permit my intrusion." The ladies looked up. "Is Father Evrart here?"

"I think he's in his office, it's the door to the left of the altar." One woman answered helpfully.

"I'll disturb you no longer. Thank you."

"Enter!" Evrart called as the horseman knocked on his door. He expected his fellow priest and was taken aback when a stranger appeared. From his attire – tunic, boots and cape – he could have been any passer-by until he pulled back the cape to reveal a red sash, worn from his left shoulder to the right of his belt. Red was the Pope's colour, always associated with significant events, and Evrart was alarmed. To receive a visitor who, subject to scrutiny of his credentials, appeared to have come from Rome was, he mused, if not impossible, certainly out of the ordinary. The man stood, stiffly, without speaking until the priest invited him to sit.

"Who are you and what brings you here, my son?" Evrart asked, his thoughts racing.

"I come from the Holy Father, Gregory, Vicar of Christ of the Roman Catholic Church. This morning, I had an audience with your bishop who, in turn, has directed me to you, his parish priest."

What on earth! He's come from the Pontiff! This is a matter of great and solemn consequence, Evrart pondered, *the legate...the personal representative from the Vatican City! From what I know, our leader does not welcome intervention nor seek advice yet, without doubt, he guides us in the good service of the Church...*

"Sit, pray. Will you take refreshment?"

"Gladly, Father."

Evrart filled two small cups with brandy, passing one to his guest and sitting behind his desk. The emissary reached inside his tunic and withdrew a rolled parchment document and ceremoniously handed it over. He sipped his drink as Evrart undid the string and began, silently, to read its contents,

In the name of Gregory, Pontiff
Diocesis, Rupellensis et Santonensis
(To the Catholic diocese of La Rochelle and Saintes)
et Episcopus Servas Servorum Dei
(and the bishops, my servants of God)

Our Church has faced challenges since the days of our
beloved Lord, Jesus Christ, but none more grave than today...
these are exceptional times...through our belief in the
righteousness of the Catholic faith we will...justice is on our
side...through our prayers...never has the threat to our
freedom to worship in our own churches, in our own manner,
been greater than in the Kingdom of France. The wicked
Protestant armies invade...we cannot resist through force, so
we must beseech the Lord, by our esteemed priests, who
should advise their congregations to live in safety and take no
risks...do not offend your neighbours...be silent when...

Evrart read these final words, took a deep breath and sighed,

It is as I feared. Our leader in Christ is advocating
surrender, cowardice by any other name! How do I express
this message to my poor people – acquiescence to the enemy,
or resistance whereby we will exit the day with pride and
religious honour?

At the bottom of the parchment, was the Papal seal in red
wax, and,

Datum augustus 1573
Georgius
Rome

...no doubting the letter was genuine, its source the Vatican City.

21

PARIS, AUGUST 1573

DUKE DE GUISE RECEIVED HIS SPIES, BERTRAND AND Monaud, at his Paris house on their return from La Rochelle. He shook their hands warmly and a wide smile indicated his pleasure to see them, even before they had recounted their visit.

"Well met! I assume that your expedition has borne fruit?"

Bertrand slapped the saddle bag draped over his arm,

"All in here, Your Grace, as requested by my Lady," he answered, reciprocating his officer's smile.

"Excellent, and there will be time to examine your work but, first, we will sup ale in the tavern. I know how to treat my men and I'm sure you have a thirst."

"Don't need asking twice!" Monaud guffawed.

The ale flowed freely, and paid for by the duke. He knew, from experience, the value of creating a bond with his troops.

"Fill it up, landlord!" He called out, indicating the

empty flagon on their table. "I propose a toast, gentlemen, to the King and the Queen Mother!" Three tankards were raised and the words heartily repeated. The duke's expression then grew serious, as if an admonishment was coming,

What now? Monaud thought, putting down his vessel.

"Monaud, our esteemed sergeant, your service to the king's army is recognised, so it pleases me to promote you to the rank of lieutenant, as of now. What do you say to that, Lieutenant Monaud?"

His captain had mentioned this as a possibility but its execution took him aback,

"Your Grace...um...I accept. It is, for certain, an honour and I won't let you down."

"I'm sure you will not, Lieutenant. I will require every decent soldier I can muster over the coming weeks. Tomorrow, our destination is Chenonceau, then back here to Paris from where our Montauban offensive begins. In your absence, I have made all the necessary preparations."

The mere mention of military action fired their spirits: they were professional soldiers and served their paymaster, whoever he might be – lazing in the barracks became odious to fighting men.

The next morning, their progress on three freshly-fed and - watered horses was swift and the smoking chimneys of Chenonceau town soon appeared on the horizon. At the avenue leading to the chateau gates, they reined their mounts to a slow trot.

"The King has arrived before us." De Guise announced, pointing to the royal banner fluttering from the flagpole. Monaud shook his head and proclaimed, amused,

"Who'd have thought it! Me, rising to the grade of lieutenant, a commissioned officer, then sharing the same air as the monarch? Who'd have thought it?"

Bertrand tugged at the bridle to bring his horse alongside his lieutenant's and, cuffing his ears, replied,

"You've earned it and this is where your responsibilities as an officer start." Monaud gulped, overawed by events.

"Will she be expecting us?" He asked. De Guise chuckled,

"Ay, she will, news reaches her before it's happened…"

Monaud gave a puzzled frown, so the duke explained,

"It means she is extremely well-informed, very little escapes her notice."

CHENONCEAU

The guards at the entrance to the chateau raised their pikes to the vertical and waved them through. In the courtyard, three grooms held the horses' reins while the men dismounted. Bertrand removed the saddle bag containing the precious documents as a footman approached,

"Welcome - gentlemen. Follow me. Their Highnesses await you."

They were led not to Catherine's apartments, that de Guise knew, but to a room within the heart of the chateau. The footman tapped on the door, pushed it open and gestured to the men to enter. Inside, Catherine and Charles were standing by the fireplace, the maidservant, Mathilde, by their side. Two large mullioned windows bestowed light, creating a pleasant airy ambience. On one wall stood a sideboard with an array of bottles and glasses, the only other items of furniture being a round table with a dark mahogany top and five chairs. Catherine stepped forward, offering her hand to be kissed by each man, in turn. The king nodded but did not move from the fireplace.

I wonder what mood she's in? De Guise thought, knowing she was a temperamental woman, *just as well we're not staying over here.*

"It's good to receive you in Chenonceau. Please, be seated." The five chairs were positioned one equidistant from the other and there was nothing to indicate seniority, so no man risked sitting on the King or Queen Mother's seat by mistake. Mathilde placed a fine cut-glass goblet in front of each guest then proceeded to fill them from a decanter with Catherine's best brandy.

"That will be all, Mathilde. You may leave us."

"Ma'am." The maidservant replaced the decanter on the sideboard and left the room as instructed.

They sipped their drink in silence, waiting for the king to address them. He leaned forward, deformed shoulders visible, then,

"Our Duke de Guise, Captain Bertrand and Lieutenant Monaud, we have anticipated your visit eagerly and trust you bring us an appraisal of La Rochelle, a campaign I am minded to accompany and -"

Catherine interrupted her son, anxious lest he said the wrong thing that would embarrass her, as was his wont,

"Majesty," she said, deferentially, "there is the matter of Montauban before that. De Guise, is everything in order?"

"It is, ma'am, and we will depart Paris the day after tomorrow."

"Excellent and, of course, we wish you God speed and may His blessing see you victorious in a place that will benefit greatly from a Catholic administration." The duke nodded and she raised her glass to the men, ceremoniously, fixing them with a steely gaze from her protruding eyes. Many a guest had wilted from its intensity and she revelled in its power. Monaud casually ran his finger over the table top.

"I see you appreciate true craftsmanship, Lieutenant. This table is a gift from my sister, Marguerite, who resides in the Spanish province of Asturias." In truth, Catherine had herself commissioned the piece with a specification that it be 'of the best quality wood and round' and, 'of a size for a dozen men to conduct their business yet not constricted', by her sister's carpenters. As a child in Italy, her country of birth, she had been fascinated by the fables of King Arthur and his famous Round Table constructed precisely in such a shape so no one knight would feel superior or inferior to another or to himself. Arthur believed that the wisdom of his knights would be best shared in a spirit of equality and comradeship. She admired the principles of chivalry as followed by those knights and her own son, Charles, had been a source of disappointment to her in this aspiration. She continued, there being no doubt who was in command, despite the round table,

"Before you set off for our certain success in Montauban, what has your men's excursion to La Rochelle revealed? We must be ever mindful of the advantages afforded to a well-prepared general."

De Guise looked at Bertrand who opened his saddle bag

and withdrew ten parchment sheets written in his own hand.

"Lay them out so we may understand their significance." She ordered, sharply, and he did as she requested.

"Now, Captain Bertrand, please talk about the town, as you found it."

He took a deep breath and, with all eyes upon him, began,

"The only Catholic church is Saint Sauveur," he pointed to its location on a sketch map he had drawn. "Its priests, Fathers Evrart and Servet, both devout men, will co-operate fully, of that I'm sure. They have the ear of the congregation.

"The land to the east is composed of marshes and salt pans and, so, unsuitable for a marching army except along the main road that passes through the Porte Gambetta. More about that in good time." He indicated the next sheet.

"The entire town, apart from the port, is protected by a wall of granite blocks with parapets, the height of four men. There is a clear view of the ground below. To the north the land is heavily wooded and would conceal the advance of our soldiers."

Catherine listened, tight-lipped, taking in every detail. The captain turned another sheet to face his audience,

"The port is both a stronghold and point of entry. On one side of the water is the Chain Tower...the chain, when drawn across will wreck any boat attempting to sail in...I've never seen the likes of such a contraption...but, once breached, the harbour within is of a good depth."

Then, de Guise spoke for the first time – his captain was doing such an effective job he had seen no reason to interrupt – to provide some naval information,

"Our warship, *Robuste*, lies in Le Havre and she can sail with short notice."

The King, eager to make an impression and convince his mother and the duke that he was fit to join the cause, asked,

"What is the strength of the armed force of the town?"

"Well-asked, Highness, an important consideration." It was difficult to decide, from Bertrand's voice, whether he spoke in a complimentary or sarcastic, patronising tone,

"The barracks are a fortified building to the north side but within the walls...next to the Porte Dauphine...heavy wooden doors...guarded...well-disciplined men...three hundred strong..."

Charles gave out,

"I see," as if he did.

Catherine made a gesture whereupon her son went to the sideboard, brought back the decanter and refilled the empty glasses.

Not every day of the week, I'm served brandy by the king in person, Monaud chuckled to himself.

The lady took a sip and smiled at de Guise,

"Your men have performed their duties admirably."

"Indeed, ma'am."

She pursed her lips, deep in thought, then continued,

"I believe I know the answer but, captain, tell us who rules La Rochelle."

"Judge Boivin, Your Majesty," came the reply.

"Boivin, you say, and it is a name with which I am familiar. He is slow to pay the taxes he owes us and it would not surprise me to hear that the town is in arrears this very day."

"Yes," the captain agreed. "He controls the mayor, the

harbour master, the sergeant and even the priests of his Huguenot persuasion. The town council is at his beck and call and they, in turn, ensure that their people are privileged, be it with housing, trade, the law, and the Catholic few are overlooked. No doubt, I've made an accurate portrayal of the place."

"I'm sure you have, Bertrand, and what role do the clergy perform?"

"Their Protestant bishop is rarely to be seen around the town. He seldom conducts services and has a laissez-faire attitude that grants Boivin complete autonomy."

"A reason, in itself, for us to remove him." She said, her frown and tone expressing a hatred for the justice, "And our own bishop?"

"He is isolated in his residence several leagues away. He is, how shall I put it, a *persona non grata* and, as such, has a minimal influence on affairs."

"Is that all?"

"Not quite, ma'am. There's a certain man named Lanval Aubert, a carter, who is respected and decent. He knows everyone in the town and will prove a fine leader of our new Catholic council."

She sat back in her chair, staring at Bertrand, then at Monaud, and finally at the duke.

Is she not satisfied with us; heaven forbid? The latter pondered.

"The King and I are impressed by the manner in which you have achieved the mission and we will draw up a detailed battle plan while you are away in Montauban. Pray, leave us the sheets for our further study. Mathilde!"

She called. The door opened and the maidservant entered to escort the men to the courtyard for their return to Paris.

They rode out of the gatehouse, along the track to Chenonceau town, then the road to the capital.

"It went well." Bertrand observed.

"You have the right, my man." De Guise leaned over and slapped him on the back, "I've rarely seen her in a better mood."

———

Paris, August 1573

De Guise's army lined up on the road leading out of Paris - fifty cavalry followed by sixty horse-drawn carts carrying ninety infantrymen. Four wagons with supplies. tents and weapons brought up the rear. The day dawned fine and the men were in high spirits. Many of them had fought alongside the duke before and trusted his leadership and courage. Furthermore, he had promised them a handsome bounty for this campaign.

None other than Pierre de Gondi, the Bishop of Paris, drew up in his carriage. Adorned in his full regalia – white linen chasuble tied with a purple cord, his tall mitre of office emphasising a narrow, bearded face. He exchanged some private words with de Guise before standing, his ivory-tipped crozier held by his side,

"Men!" He cried out loud, "However rigorous the task that awaits you, may you fulfil your duty with bravery.

Should death overtake you in the field, grant that you die in a state of grace, your sins forgiven. May you persevere under trial because, having stood the test, you will receive the crown of life that the Lord has promised to those who love Him." He crossed the air and sat down, then his carriage turned and he went back to his cathedral, Notre Dame de Paris.

"I've heard that from him a dozen times." Bertrand remarked to lieutenant Monaud. "Don't know if it makes any difference though. Mind you, we've survived, this far."

———

MONTAUBAN, AUGUST 1573

On this occasion, the duke's army had no need of divine assistance. After a march of four uneventful days they halted, at dawn, with Montauban in sight. He called his captains to him to issue his final orders before attacking the town.

"The cavalry will enter the north gate. You will scream, yell, make as much noise as you can and that will bring them out of their houses. Gallop the length of the main street, turn, then repeat it. They will be terrified seeing your brave men on their chargers and they will scuttle back inside. It's our usual way and it always works. Then, have the horses line the market place. Any resistance, cut the people down, be ruthless." He looked at another group of officers,

"You must lead your infantrymen over the river Tarn by

the Vieux Pont that is never guarded. Inside the place, fan out and take the town hall, the goal, the cathedral, the courthouse." For each order he pointed at a map unrolled on the ground, then,

"To secure Montauban, we need their Huguenot bishop's surrender. His house sits behind the Temple des Carmes, here. Bring him to me in the market place, for all to see. Any questions?" None were asked.

Fifty riders galloped into Montauban, swords drawn, astride their fearsome mounts that strained at the bit, snorting, exhaling white breath from their nostrils into the crisp morning air. They raced, three abreast, down the street. Most residents still slept but shutters quickly opened and, faced with this unexpected horror, remained indoors, as de Guise had predicted.

Two men, however, were overcome by curiosity and ventured out. Sébastien and Joffroy had fled Paris to escape Catholic persecution and had taken up residence in this community after a long journey over land and sea. The horses surged forward, neighing wildly, iron shoes clanging on the stone cobbles. Too late! Sébastien and Joffroy were trampled underfoot. As with old Gervese and his wife, who had hoped for a better life in Beauvais, without finding it, these two friends perished: for them, too, their grass was not greener on the other side of their river. Would they have fared better remaining and defending their religion? Should an innocent elderly couple have felt so oppressed that they deserted their home?

. . .

Two soldiers had entered the Huguenot bishop's house to find him still in his nightshirt, eating breakfast. They seized and dragged him outside, not allowing him the dignity of even his cassock. In the market place, de Guise's troops whooped and jeered seeing the arrogant bishop reduced to a figure of ridicule. By this time, the Catholic folk had heard it was safe to assemble and join the soldiers in their derision of a cleric who, for so long, had preached hatred for their own beliefs. The town secured, Duke de Guise led his army, triumphant, back to the capital, leaving a small force to convince the authority and its populace of the error of their way in worshipping in their Huguenot churches. The exiled Catholic bishop then resumed spiritual command.

———

LA ROCHELLE, SEPTEMBER 1573

The captains of three barges, lifelong friends, met in the port tavern frequented by their kind. The landlord placed tankards and a pitcher of ale on the table and left them to their business.

"Has he been to you?" One sailor asked. *He* referred to the harbour master.

"Ay."

"Me, too. I've plied my trade in and out of La Rochelle for twenty years and I've not known any such instruction. In fact, until today, I was ignorant about the Chain Tower. I assumed it was just some old lighthouse."

They debated and speculated on the reason they had been given one day's notice to sail their boats out of the port or, otherwise, have them impounded, their subsequent departure blocked by the defensive chain that would be drawn across the entrance.

"I have customers elsewhere." One man spoke up. "So, I'm leaving on the tide. There's something amiss, believe me." He drained his tankard. The other two agreed.

Judge Boivin had summoned his mayor early one morning to his office behind the courtroom. He beckoned him enter,

"Come in, quick, and close the door! You weren't seen, were you?"

"Seen?"

"Ay, seen! Are you cloth-eared? Sit down!"

The mayor had known the justice in foul moods but none as objectionable as this. He did as ordered, racking his brain to fathom the reason.

Boivin filled two beakers from a bottle, his hand shaking – he had, evidently, consumed a fair amount already. He emptied his vessel almost before the mayor had begun his own and refilled it, struggling to avoid splashing wine over the table.

Sweat ran in rivulets from under his purple hat that he wiped away with the sleeve of his threadbare gown. His yellow broken teeth bit into his lips, such was his hateful humour. He rose, mumbling, uttering profanities as he paced the room, drinking as he went. After a while, he seemed to calm and sat down in front of the bewildered mayor.

"Bad times, awful times ahead, don't you know? And soon, very soon!" His voice was slurred. "But, allow me to explain because, of course, you could not possibly be in possession of the dreadful facts and, monsieur mayor, I will be in sore need of your services...we will soon discover those townsfolk we can trust and those we can't."

The mayor tossed his grey locks back to reveal his sallow complexion, contorted and exasperated. He could contain himself no longer so, taking a gulp of his wine, he blurted,

"Judge Boivin, you know you can depend on me – whatever you require of me – but, pray, what is it that troubles you so?"

Boivin wiped his brow again, took wine and said, pensively,

"Today, at first light, I was still in my bed, and there's a banging on my door – enough to wake the dead. I couldn't believe my eyes to see the bishop, *our* bishop standing there with a bodyguard either side. He's not had cause to bother me for three, nay, four years, so I realised it was no social visit. He sat there, where you are, and with heavy heart informed me that La Rochelle will, ere long, be attacked by King Charles's army so we must take all necessary steps to protect the town. By that, he meant we have to barricade the gates to prevent anyone entering or leaving until the danger has passed and Charles retreats. To use his very words, he bestows upon me his *full authority* to achieve this goal. It could be any day so, there's not a moment to lose.

22

A SWIRLING AUTUMNAL MIST SWEPT OVER THE PORT and entered the town of La Rochelle whose streets and houses transformed its chill into a gentle dew. The salty tang of the sea air pervaded the atmosphere. It clung to the doors and shutters, still firmly closed and battened down, and shone on the stone cobbles encircling the Lantern Tower, down the Rue Saint Jean, through the Cours des Dames and seemed to hover prophetically around the courthouse.

Judge Boivin had convened an urgent meeting with his mayor, harbour master and general of the barracks. His bishop's words of the previous day haunted him, the chilling thought of hostile invaders who could assume the privileges and powers he had worked for so long to make his own, had created a state of frightened stupor in his mind.

The mayor was already privy to the situation, as was the harbour master but not so the general. The justice wanted to address them together, and in detail, ensuring there was no misunderstanding about the severity of the problem. They sat, nervously, around the table in his office behind the courtroom, saying nothing while the judge moved from one to the other, filling their goblets from a decanter of claret – most unusual for him to offer even half-decent wine to his visitors. More often than not, it was a rough *vin ordinaire*. It must be a serious matter, the general decided.

Today, the judge was living up to his name of 'Boivin' – 'he who drinks wine.' The townsfolk appreciated the significance of the epithet equalling his characteristic love for the fruit of the vine. But the Huguenot majority chose to avoid making negative comments, being satisfied with his single-minded protection of their interests: they did not, necessarily, like him, but better the devil they knew.

Despite his having consumed drink prior to his underlings' arrival, there was nothing hazy about his instructions,

"We face the gravest challenge to our faith and lives here in La Rochelle that I have ever known. King Charles intends to attack us with armies raised from his kingdom and beyond and – mark this, gentlemen – it could be at any moment, without warning, so we must be prepared." His men drank from their goblets, their countenances stern and focused on Boivin's ominous words. He continued,

"Harbour master, by Vespers today, the chain will be drawn across the port. Inform the old retainer in the Chain Tower, I forget his name, that the time has at last come for him to earn his money. Visit any boats tied up and warn them to sail out while they still have the chance. Understood?" The harbour master, whose most challenging duty since his tenure of the position had started was usually to check deliveries of fabrics and olive oil, gulped and nodded.

Boivin next addressed the general,

"You will post two soldiers at every gate in the walls, their watch to be changed every twelve hours. Should they fall asleep or fail you in any way, they will be punished without mercy, to set an example for the rest. Ensure every gate is shut with the bar in place and the wicket doorway bolted. No citizen is to leave the town, no visitors will be admitted. But, General, and forgive my presumption. You are a most respected officer and I apologise for telling grandmother how to suck eggs, as it were." However, he proceeded to do just that, "Bring all our cannons from the arsenal and mount them on the parapets – we'll see how they like that!"

"It will be done, Judge," the man replied.

The general of La Rochelle barracks, a tall muscular soldier with broad shoulders, piercing blue eyes and square-jawed, was a passionate adherent to the Huguenot faith. He had risen through the ranks of Jeanne d'Albret's army – she, the Queen Regnant of Navarre to Henry, future King of France. Jeanne was one of Catherine's main detractors, often referring to her as 'the Florentine grocer's daughter.' In this general, Jeanne had a military leader who was prepared to lay down his life for her. When she resided in La Rochelle, secure from the detested Catholics, she assumed control of the fortifications, finances and discipline among the civilian population. Shortly before leaving the town, fearing plots and treachery, she appointed Boivin as the judge, upon his father's death.

"She was a fine, bold, handsome woman," was Boivin's usual portrayal of Jeanne, a lady he revered. She was, unquestionably 'bold': the previous year, she met Catherine, at Chenonceau, where the promiscuity of the young women and the corrupt, vicious atmosphere offended her puritanical nature. It was a story Boivin told and embellished – "She knew the Catholic court there was bad, but found it even worse than she'd feared. She said to me that you could only escape it with special intervention from God. She may well have had the right of it."

Next, the justice turned to the mayor who waited with trepidation.

"Monsieur Mayor, you know our people better than most." He nodded. "So, your responsibility will be to inform them, through notices and criers, that we are taking every precaution to protect their well-being and that they can place every confidence in the town authorities. Do you understand? We are imposing a curfew at Compline, so watch out for any Catholic dwellers, in particular, who do not observe it and report them to me, in person." He paused a moment, then added, "And also...if you even hear that this or that person has been talking in public...against us, if you see what I mean, I need to know."

"Certainly, Judge." *If he means what he says, it will be the first time I've known him show concern for anybody other than himself,* the mayor pondered. Boivin went to his writing desk, picked up a parchment sheet and placed it in front of them.

"Mayor, your first duty will be to take this proclamation from the bishop" – *it's from Boivin,* the mayor contemplated – "to every priest in the town, its contents to be announced to their congregations, of whatever persuasion, as a matter of urgency." It read:

I, the Most Reverend Bishop of La Rochelle
hereby authorise BOIVIN, Judge and Justice of the diocese
to exercise his rights and powers to defend this town against
all and any assailants
le 4 septembre 1573

He added,

"And make sure Fathers Servet and Evrart see it, and
clearly, in Saint Sauveur church. It will be of great interest
to them and their people. That done, nail it to the board
outside this office for all passers-by to read – those who
can."

Orders issued, the three men drained their goblets and left
Boivin. The harbour master went directly to the port.
Making his way along the quayside, he gave the captains,
who had not yet heard of the situation, a final warning.

"Best be out with the tide, boys – command from
above!"

The sailors obeyed without arguing. They were traders
who made their living from cargo and they got out just in
time.

As he approached the Chain Tower, he saw the old keeper,
bearded and, as ever, wearing his seaman's coat, leaning
over the wall, a fishing line held securely.

"Caught anything?" The harbour master asked
cordially. The old man turned and answered with a nod
towards a wooden pail with a fish thrashing around.

"Nice sea bass, but don't go asking me for tax – don't pay no tax to the judge if you're the tower keeper."

"Calm, my friend, that's not the reason I'm here."

"Is that so?" At that moment, the line tugged his hand, "Here's another!" He pulled in the cord, a silver-blue fish hooked that he freed with a skilful twist of his wrist and dropped it to join his companion in the pail.

"My good lady will be well pleased with those two beauties for supper..."

"I'm sure she will," the harbour master commented, but his gaze fell on the chain covered by a canvas sheet at the foot of the granite tower.

"Now, listen well. I have this hour met with the judge and have instructions for you. The chain -"

"Do you mean -"

"Ay, you're to row the chain by Vespers because we fear an attack from the king's navy, and at any moment."

"Well, I'll be...never did I think I'd have to do this again at my age. But I'll see it's done. Orders is orders." And, so it was. The old man sent for his two assistants who attached the chain to his rowing boat, hauling it across the port entrance to the Saint Nicolas Tower on the far side. They fixed it to a windlass and, with great effort, turned it until the chain was a taut barrier at a height that would take down a ship's mast or, equally, remove a man's head from his body. The keeper oversaw the event with pride as he waved for the town's caravel to weigh anchor and drift to a central position, portside of the chain, its crew readying the cannon on its poop deck.

The general ordered his troops to fall in on the barrack parade ground, behind their sergeants and captains. He climbed onto a raised platform and began, in a loud confident tone,

"Men! You are retained in our barracks, from one month to the next, with little to test your skills apart from exercises on the training ground or brawling with the locals after too much ale in the hostelries!" His troops burst out laughing and cheering their commander. He was, indeed popular but, also, well-respected. A gesture with his hand obtained instant silence,

"The time has come for you to prove your worth to me as soldiers. I have been reliably informed that La Rochelle will come under attack, shortly, so we must man the defences. You will get your platoon orders from your captains today, and I know you will not be lacking!" An enthusiastic cry of 'Ay!' rose and the soldiers were dismissed.

The next morning, cannons on their wooden cradles were wheeled out of the arsenal to be hoisted up to the town walls and positioned through the parapets – fifty facing any assault by the enemy either below them or off in the distance. Flintlock muskets, with powder and shot, were issued to every man patrolling in support of the cannoneers.

All the gates were closed and barred, their wicket doorways securely bolted, each with two men bearing sharply honed swords in readiness, at this stage, to prevent anyone leaving, in accordance with their orders. The general and his captains inspected their soldiers, from the Saint Nicolas Tower bastion to the Avenue Jean Guilon, none was missed.

. . .

Even before the priests had had the opportunity to read out the proclamation to their congregations, word was about and nascent panic and frightened uncertainty spread: rumours went from house to house, tavern to tavern, trader to trader. In living memory, nobody had known the town under threat of invasion. Who would want to attack them? Why would they have enemies? They'd done nothing wrong. Such was the reaction of the populace, selfish although understandable. They felt a natural desire to protect their families and livelihoods so the military had their full support.

Father Evrart, with his assistant Servet by his side, had received the mayor in their room behind the altar. He stood in silence while the clerics pored over the parchment sheet, their faces contorting as they assimilated its ominous contents.

"Finished?" The gloating functionary asked.

"Y...yes, thank you." And Evrart at once resented his making an expression of thanks for such bad news.

"Good. Now, be certain your people are aware of the town's impending catastrophe. By all accounts, it's your Catholic king who's to blame, but that's only to be expected." He snatched back the sheet. rolled it up and departed, clicking his tongue as he went. Alone, Evrart and Servet exchanged concerned glances.

"I'd heard that La Rochelle is practically the last town in the kingdom where Huguenots still dominate, so I'm not surprised if Charles has, at last, turned his attention to us." Evrart said in a resigned voice.

"Nor I," Servet agreed, "but I can't see Boivin surrendering without a fight and what does that mean for us, imprisoned here with no escape? He'll be free to act as he likes."

"That, he will – and by how many are we outnumbered?"

Servet returned with a pragmatic comment,

"Our most difficult task, though, is mass tomorrow evening. How do we announce this to our brethren without increasing the fear they will undoubtedly be feeling by now?" Their countenances were gloomy as they knelt before the altar in prayer.

The time for Sunday Eucharist came. Saint Sauveur church was packed; every pew was taken; men and women stood in the nave; the doors were open for the crowd on the steps outside to catch the service. The atmosphere within was charged with subdued expectant conversations, people anxious to hear, for certain, from the mouth of their priest, what they had heard informally.

Lanval and his mother had arrived early to ensure a good unimpeded view of proceedings. The theme of the last sermon – showing forgiveness to the oppressor, yet remaining resilient – rang hollow given the threat that now faced them. From his business at the port and dealings with folk in the streets, Lanval understood their growing belief that something more than the measures in that sermon would now be needed.

Evrart, wearing his usual white cassock, appeared. He knelt, briefly, at the altar, then went straight to the pulpit. The church fell silent.

"Brothers and sisters, I wish to inform you of a notice delivered to me, jointly, from the Huguenot bishop and Judge Boivin. I will not detain you when I have discharged this duty because we are likely to be attacked by King Charles' army, and soon. A curfew at Compline is imposed. Accordingly, we will not be celebrating the Eucharist." At this, voices rose as they realised the gravity of the priest's words.

"Curfew," one man asked his companion, "what's one of those?"

"It means you have to be indoors, I think." Came the vague reply.

"Ay, that's exactly what it is." Another man said, overhearing them.

Evrart continued, almost as if he'd heard the men talk,

"All citizens of the town are compelled to be at home by this time. Anyone one found out on the streets will be arrested and this is your only warning." The priest's face was etched with sadness. He went on,

"Even as I speak, we are locked within the walls, and there are soldiers at the gates. Cannons are primed, musketeers armed. We do not know when the attack will be, but it is my responsibility to tell you that, come it will! At home, take out your bibles, read the scriptures – if you can – and pray! Do not underestimate the power of prayer for God to protect the righteous."

I hope he's not just harking back to his last sermon...fat lot of good that did to inspire us, Lanval mused. But Evrart had come to the end,

"May the Lord bless and be with you. Amen." After these brief valedictory words, he climbed down from the pulpit and turned his back on his congregation, leaving them confused and afeard.

"Come, mother." Lanval urged. "Let's go home." He had heard what he already knew.

Judge Boivin sat, alone, at his desk, glass in hand, pondering the progress he had made in the light of his bishop's visit. He was satisfied,

The harbour master will see to the chain across the port; the general will man the defences; the mayor has his instructions to notify the priests. Good King Charles and, no doubt, that Italian woman, Catherine, can throw at us whatever they will but they'll not find us pushovers! No, they'll not enter my town without a fight but...we'll have that diehard band of Catholics in our midst...the king will not want to harm them. It's all a mess, we should have seen to them years ago before it got to this. Come the attack, they'll relish the chance of freedom and they surely won't help my Huguenot brothers – no, the Catholics must receive particular treatment before then, from the Judge's own.

It was almost dusk. Boivin removed his purple hat that would easily identify him, pulled his cape over his black robe and set off down the street towards the port, then on to the Saint Nicolas bastion. As he approached the gate, a guard, alert as the general had demanded, drew his sword and barred the judge's way.

"Halt! Halt, or I'll put you down! Who are you?"

"I'm Judge Boivin, let me pass."

The guard thrust his face forward, his nose almost touching Boivin's, suspicious and following orders that no-one was allowed to leave the town. Then satisfied with the man's identity, he unbolted the wicket doorway and let him leave without further ado.

Fifteen minutes later he turned off the road to take the path that entered the dense woods around the Tasdon marches. Feeling confident he could no longer be seen, he reached inside his robe, pulled out his purple hat and placed it on his head. He regarded it as a symbolic expression of his authority, as if his personality alone was inadequate and he needed it as a vain statement of his importance.

Daylight had all but faded, rendering his progress hazardous – more than once he tripped over a fallen branch or walked into a prickly hawthorn bush, each time greeting it with an obscenity that rang out without anyone present to hear.

At last, the path widened into a clearing with the old derelict barn ahead. Inside, he felt his way along the wall in the pitch blackness to a sideboard where he knew he would find a flint, stone and wick. After several unsuccessful attempts, the spark from striking the flint lit the wick and, in turn the three candles on the main table. He found a bottle and goblet that he put down in front of the master's chair and proceeded to pour a good measure of brandy that he drank and sat in the chair, able to relax and prepare himself for the ceremony ahead. He thought,

The general, the mayor and the harbour master all have their orders and, no doubt, they will be carried out. But, it's not enough. The real germ in our society, the very reason we're having to get ready for an invasion, for an assault on our faith, is the Catholic rabble! Deal with them and we

might have a stronger hand when it comes to negotiating with Charles and Catherine. Yes, and that's where my men, my own trusted men, will be of no small service.

His deliberations were disturbed when the heavy wooden door creaked open. He removed his hat and replaced it with his white mitre to welcome his followers. One after another they silently entered the barn and sat down on the benches on either side of the table. Twenty-four anonymous figures, hoods concealing their faces waited, patiently, until the judge rose, clapped his hands three times and stepped down from the podium into a circle scratched on the ground, taking care to not tread on the mysterious lines within. Another clap and the men swayed gently, groaning. This was the routine celebration of the cult's rites – just as Lanval had witnessed months before.

Boivin took a drink from his goblet, wiped his sweating brow with his sleeve and intoned the opening prayer,

> *We need revenge,*
> *On this black day,*
> *To make our troubles go away.*
> *A curse, a pox, a chanted hex,*
> *To make the Catholics go away!*

"Ay! Ay!' Came the response.

A thrashing chicken was brought to the table where Boivin slit its throat with a knife and bled it into a chalice. And thus, with weird rituals, the convention unfolded until, at its end, the judge asked the assemblage,

"What is it you implore to Belial and Satan? Lift your faces and tell me!"

"Rid us of Catholics, we beseech thee!"

"So it shall be. I command you all, man by man, before you depart this dark evening, as follows - if Catholics are out after curfew, if they appear to be doing a good trade at market or spread malicious rumours in the taverns, if they do not move aside and let you pass in the street, if you spot their children up at the parapets where it is forbidden or if you see a man kiss his woman in public...yes! Any of this, be told, is prohibited! You, in my name, have permission to seize them. The gaol is presently empty and the gaoler welcomes new guests, the stocks are also unoccupied.

"Finally, let it never be far from your minds, how the king's hordes massacred our brethren in Paris nor how they terrorise our kin throughout the land!"

"Ay! Ay, Judge! Ay!" Again, they answered their leader.

Boivin revelled in his position as lord of the sect but, was he driven by religious doctrine or evil delectation? He raised his hand for quiet,

"You." He pointed to the man to his right, "You will... visit...Fathers Evrart and Servet, the Catholic priests. We cannot have them preaching resistance or incitement. And you," He turned to his left, "Will observe Lanval Aubert, the carter, because if any one Catholic swine can influence the people to rebel against our authority, it's Lanval Aubert."

23

Lanval had left his house early to discuss the present trouble with his priests. Passing through the Place d'Armes, his attention was drawn to the public water pump where a man exchanged words with a woman who began to cry, the sound resonating around the empty square. Although he did not recognise her, he felt obliged to assist, if he could. The man berating the distressed woman towered above her – a brute holding a wineskin in one hand and a cudgel in the other. His words were slurred,

"Have you not heard – it's the law!"

She had not heard. Taking a drink, he explained,

"You pray at Saint Sauveur church, don't you?"

"Yes, I do."

"Then you're only allowed to draw half a pail any day and I can see yours is already half-full. If you're a Catholic, that's your ration – half a pail – it's Judge Boivin's rule, so be off with you!"

The woman's tears increased,

"But that's not enough! I have two babes at home...I have to make a stew and they must drink."

"Not my problem, lady, take it up with His Honour if you like." He prodded her with his cudgel with no sign of compassion on his face. Lanval stepped in between them,

"Enough! What kind of man are you to threaten her like this?"

"As I said, it's not up to me, but who may you be?" He asked, surprised.

"Lanval Aubert." Came the reply.

"Ah, I know that name." And the brute turned on his heels and, unsteadily, left them. Lanval took the woman's pail and filled it to the brim.

"Come, allow me to carry it to your house."

"Monsieur Aubert, you're very kind." She spoke, relieved he had been passing.

He's definitely one of Boivin's men, he thought, escorting the poor woman away.

He next went to the Valin Quay where his horse was stabled. His lad was sweeping out and, seeing his master approach, he paused his work, leaning with one elbow on his brush.

"Morning." Lanval said cheerfully.

"Morning, Monsieur Lanval. You've just missed him."

"Missed him? Who?"

"Dunno, never seen him before but he seemed to know you. He was asking whether you'd still be carting, given the *present situation,* as he put it. I told him you were but then, and strange of him, he wanted to know if you would deliver to the Catholic part of town. Told him you'd deliver to anybody. Did I -"

Lanval interrupted the lad,

"You told him the truth, don't worry." *Boivin's man,* he

thought, '*but if he thinks he can scare me off carrying, my chosen trade, he's got another thought coming!*

The lad pursed his lips, as if confused, then resumed,

"Yesterday, my mother came out with a peculiar tale that I couldn't fathom out."

"Tell me, boy," Lanval told him, but gently.

"She went into the baker's shop, near the courthouse, and she wanted to buy two loaves."

"Yes, and what's peculiar about that?" Lanval asked, puzzled.

"The baker refused her – broke off part of a loaf saying that was as much as he could sell her and that -"

Lanval cut in,

"It was what Judge Boivin had ordered."

"That's right! But how do you know, 'sieur?"

"It's a sign of things to come, I fear." Came the sombre reply.

The carter knocked on Father Evrart's office door in Saint Sauveur church.

"Come."

Within, the only natural light entered through a small high window. It was usually a dark room and, today, the atmosphere felt yet darker.

"Good morning, Lanval. Sit, please." The cleric's worried countenance spoke more than words. He made a start,

"It's not even Terce and I've already had six parishioners see me here, and each day there are more, with similar tales."

"A matter of bread and water." Lanval anticipated Evrart's elaboration.

"Indeed, and this is but the beginning. Without staple food and drink, our people will perish, even before King Charles can rescue us...and that assumes he will. He's been known to break his pledge in the past and the King's coming is an excuse for Boivin to show his warped desire for dominance and his hatred for our faith. That man and his band of thugs, taking control of the town? I dare not even think."

"Are you advocating forgiveness, Father?" Lanval quipped to lighten the mood but, at the same time, harking back to the priest's last sermon.

"I take your point – it's well made – although I will never abandon my belief in the Lord's final pardon in Heaven."

"Nor would I expect you to." Lanval paused, "but considering the overwhelming strength of the Huguenots, our brethren may need both Charles *and* the Lord to achieve salvation.

"You talk more like a preacher every time I hear you, Lanval!" Evrart joked, giving him a gentle slap on the arm.

Days passed without any sign of the Catholic army although this, by no means, encouraged the population *intra muros* – the level of apprehension remained high, fuelled by repeated acts of resentment towards the town's minority – acts that generally went unheralded but that were committed to cause offence or even injury. However, life went on and the market initially enjoyed a brisk trade for merchants fortunate enough to hold a stall in the Arcades - all Huguenots.

Boivin's thugs were readily identified by the cudgels they brandished and few people challenged their authority.

They swaggered through the streets in pairs, pushing aside anyone in their way, calling out gratuitous insults to the element of their town who were, in their eyes, to blame for the deplorable state of affairs.

The traders under the ancient arches knew the Judge's men who returned familiar winks and smirks. At the end of the Rue Saint Yon stood the shabby Catholic tables selling miscellaneous objects that hardly drew the attention of the passers-by.

"Watch me. I'll show you how to make the Judge proud of us." One sturdy roughneck said quietly to his associate. Slowly, casually, he approached a table where a woman had a barrel on two wooden cradles from which she sold wine, filling people's wineskin or jug to take home. It was a modest concern, but gave her the wherewithal to live and care for her bedridden mother. Her wine was not of a good quality that appealed to well-heeled connoisseurs but those of her own station enjoyed it.

"Good morning, mistress. How's business?" He asked her.

"Not good, times are hard you know and I'm cheaper than most. Would 'sieur like to try a drop before making his purchase?"

"I will, I'm partial to a nice wine."

Hoping to make her first money of the day, she held a small beaker under the barrel's tap and handed it to him, forcing a smile. He took a sip then spluttered, spitting it in the woman's direction.

"Are you joking? I can't say I'm partial to *vinegar!*" And he used his cudgel to dislodge the cradle, whereupon the barrel rolled off the table to smash on the stone cobbles, its red liquid flowing around their feet.

"Oops! That was careless of me, wasn't it? My apologies." Leaving the dismayed woman speechless, he turned to the other man,

"Our master will be pleased with that, won't he?" They moved on to the next Catholic stallholder they could terrorise. Within a short time, many felt so harassed by their unjust treatment that they abandoned their pitches which increased the monopoly by Huguenot dealings.

Elsewhere, a soldier had been patrolling the streets since dusk with nothing in particular to catch his eye. He was bored.

Every day's the same, nobody misbehaving, not even an occasional brawl, nothing. He pulled his cloak tight over his shoulders, the cold of winter was setting in. When he reached the Rue Massion, he was about to turn into the barracks for a warming tot of brandy when the Compline bell began to toll.

Ah, curfew, he thought. The street was silent but, in the darkness ahead, a figure stood at his doorway, just entering his house. The soldier at once ran forward and grabbed the small elderly man by the arm, unsheathing his sword with his free hand. The final chime of Compline sounded, so this was a much welcome event to break the tedium of his shift. The man turned to face his assailant, trembling.

"What's your name, then?" The soldier demanded.

"Arédius."

"Well, Arédius, I'm arresting you!"

"M – me? What for, I've done nothing wrong?"

"You certainly have, my friend." He paused and took a closer look at Arédius's face,

"I recognise you – seen you coming out of Saint Sauveur church, haven't I?"

"Yes, and that's no crime."

"It's no crime, I'll grant you that, but it tells me you're a damned Catholic and...um...it's not exactly the most popular label to wear round your neck right now, take it from me. But, to the point, you're out after curfew."

"No, I'm not, I'm going into my house, can't you see?"

Raising his sword, as if to strike a blow, the soldier explained, not that it was incumbent on him to so do,

"If you're not indoors *before* the last chime of Compline, you're breaking the curfew, simple as that. I don't make the rules, just enforce them. Come on, to the barracks!" And he prodded his prisoner forward with the tip of his sword.

The wretched man was flung into a cell, the iron gate locked behind him. He barely rested for an hour on the filthy straw mattress before he was roused by a booming voice,

"Up! Get up!" A burly sergeant commanded.

"What will happen to me?"

"The pillory, my boy, until Vespers." With that, he unlocked the cell and ushered Arédius out into the yard where day had not yet dawned.

"Have a nice time!" The sergeant jeered. Two other soldiers appeared, each seizing an arm to drag Arédius roughly into the street. Before long, they arrived at the Palais de Justice and its adjacent courthouse. The pale rising sun cast weak shadows over the rooftops of the surrounding houses and there was no sign of human life except for a candle flickering in the window of Boivin's office. Did the man ever sleep? Alerted by voices, he put on his purple hat and went outside to observe the proceedings, in his judicial capacity. The prisoner was made to sit on a wooden bench, placing his head and hands in the recesses of the lower board of the pillory. The upper one was then lowered, to render the man immobile and locked.

"Your name?" Boivin asked, screwing his eyes.

"Arédius, monsieur."

"And Catholic?"

"Yes," was the answer, delivered in a defiant tone, but this attitude would not last as the punishment became clear.

"His crime?" Boivin enquired, his brusque questions an indication of the contempt he felt for Arédius.

"Breaking curfew, Judge."

"Is that so? If you were a decent law-abiding citizen, you wouldn't have offended. Don't you respect the law that exists to protect you? The streets aren't safe after dark, especially if you're a Catholic, is that not so, men?" He turned to them and they, in turn, smiled and chuckled in unison,

"Not safe." Arédius was left alone, to endure the public humiliation that was an integral part of retribution in the pillory: he would be well known to people and this would increase his shame.

One hour before, the sun had risen and the square was coming to life. Two armed soldiers took up their positions at the four corners, sharing wineskins, laughing and swearing at anyone within hearing. Children chased each other; women stood gossiping; men argued and pointed to make a point – all normal activities but belying the charged atmosphere whenever people congregated, one mistrusting the other.

Word had soon spread that there was a Catholic in the pillory and a crowd was forming to participate in this traditional entertainment. Excitement mounted when a man led an ass pulling a low cart. He threw back the canvas covering his delivery, unhitched the animal and took it away. Piled up on the cart was an array of rotting fruit, tomatoes, decomposing vegetables giving up a fetid odour.

"Let the sport begin!" Boivin called out. "Children first, mind!" A lad of nine or ten years selected a large putrid tomato from the cart and approached Arédius in the pillory who closed his eyes and mouth tight as the boy stood in front of him – at such a distance that he could hardly miss the target – raised his arm and flung the red ball with all his strength, yelling with happiness when it burst over the man's face. Applause rang out.

Next, a girl – young but heavily built – picked out a melon, so decayed it all but fell through her fingers, and hurled it at the trapped Arédius whose pain and shame would be complete by Vespers, but not before the soldiers had demonstrated their eagle-eye skill. Not, for them, missiles from the cart. It was approaching midday when the town's rat catcher made his ceremonial entrance, a sack slung over his shoulder. He waited for the Judge to toss a coin to him then emptied its contents: a heap of a dozen or more warm fat rats, freshly dispatched. One by one, the soldiers moved from their positions, picked up their chosen rodent and threw it with all their might at Arédius's forehead, so hard that it burst open, its blood and entrails running down his face. Even men in the crowd, who had witnessed many pillories, gasped at the repulsive sight before them. In turn, the soldiers clapped and hailed their comrades. Judge Boivin surveyed the scene with pride.

· · ·

All this time, the three men tied to the whipping posts looked on, terrified, as the Sext bell neared - the hour for their lashings to begin.

The Auberge Tournon was, from the start of the town's isolation, doing a brisk trade – the jovial landlord worshipped at Saint Sauveur church, as did his customers who, in addition to consuming his fine ale, could swap stories, share tragedies, ridicule the town's authorities and, all in relative safety. Sadly, they were naïve and their innocence would betray them.

The landlord was so engrossed in conversation with a drinker that he started when an unexpected customer appeared at the counter.

"Good evening, mine host." The visitor was Judge Boivin's minion, the Mayor.

"Good evening to you, Monsieur Maire. It is, indeed, most unusual to see you here, in our humble tavern but, may I say, you are very welcome."

The mayor stared at the proprietor with tightly pursed lips and furrowed brow – the mistrust between the two men was unmistakable.

"I'll bring your ale to you." He gestured to a vacant table. *What brings him here, I wonder? Never did like him, even when we were lads playing together and it's not changed just because we're old.*

The Mayor sipped his drink, his gaze shifting from one table to another, his ears straining to catch the conversations drifting from an assemblage he knew to be Catholic and who had not paid particular heed to his arrival. The landlord recognised, as soon as he placed the tankard on the table, that his brothers were at risk, but how could he warn them to hold their tongue? Too late, he feared. It did not take long for the Mayor to hear the incriminating idle chatter he sought. He had come to the Auberge Tournon with Boivin's orders clear in his mind...*anyone speaking against us in public.*

Three men nearby, under the influence of ale, argued over what they could do to resist 'those damned Huguenots'. Their debate was raucous...'the only good Huguenot's a dead one!'

Yes, it was certainly too late, the Mayor knew the streets where these drunkards – unfortunate betrayers of their cause – lived. *They're simpletons! Deserve all they get!* He concluded.

He would stay a while longer and was soon rewarded. A man exchanged heated words with his wife, and within earshot.

"Say what you like, husband, but I don't trust that Judge Boivin. Do you think he cares about the likes of us? No, he does not! He writes the law, and to his own end.'

"What you say is correct, wife."

There were few people in La Rochelle that the dignitary did not know – through church, market or tavern. He placed a coin next to his empty tankard, rose, and left the inn unnoticed by the unsuspecting Catholics.

. . .

The next day, a sergeant and soldiers issued with names and addresses knocked on doors and dragged out three men whose names the Mayor had passed on to the general. Despite their protestations of no wrongdoing, they were taken to the square in front of the Palais de Justice and tied to the whipping posts, their tunics pulled down to expose their torsos to the bitter September weather.

There's no letting up, is there? Boivin thought, wicked pleasure flowing through his body as he approached them and solemnly pronounced,

"You have spread rumour and lies that are injurious to our Bishop and his Church. This we cannot allow and, at Sext, you will each receive thirty lashes. By this time there will be plenty of your brethren around to witness this just sentence - it is, after all, market day." He stood by the whipping posts, sneering into the faces of the bewildered incredulous victims before returning to his office, accompanied by the sergeant.

"Pay a visit to the Auberge Tournon and inform the landlord that, should we discover further treachery, his establishment will be closed, indefinitely."

"Leave it with me, 'sieur."

By the end of September there was still no sign of the King's army and the longer this uncertainty continued, the greater was the level of foreboding within the town, for which the Catholics were repeatedly blamed and berated.

Lanval and his mother sat by their fire after supper. She was, like her late husband, a person of not many words but whose counsel her son valued. She saw the worry etched on his face and began,

"King Charles hasn't yet seen fit to rescue us, has he? I

do hope you don't have plans of your own. It wouldn't be advisable."

"Mother, if only life was simple, but it's not. Remember how father progressed from the salt marshes to build up the Aubert business here, and in spite of the bias of the Huguenots? That didn't happen overnight so perhaps we shouldn't expect Charles to make an immediate appearance."

"You're right, son. But our plight worsens. The ladies of my circle relate terrible stories and they and their families are growing desperate."

"I too see it every day. I'm finding little or no carting work and I'm sure Boivin has put the word around that I should be boycotted. However, we can bear that, for we have money, unlike most. While the floggings and stocks are bad enough, there are the lesser actions our *masters* take that wear us down."

"I probably know, but tell me."

Lanval stared into the flames, his head spinning, wondering where to start. So,

"The other day, a soldier arrested two ladies begging near the market. I'll relate it just how it happened...

"Hey, you women! No use hiding your bowls – you're begging and don't you know it's against the law?" One asked her in a menacing tone. Neither woman replied; they could not deny the act - they had been caught red-handed.

"You." He pointed. "You're a Huguenot, if I'm not mistaken. I've seen you in our church. Stand up and be gone! And consider yourself lucky I'm in a good mood!" She did not need asking twice. Then, his gaze fell on the second mendicant,

"An incorrigible Catholic – I know you as well." And he snatched her bowl – "as evidence" – and marched her, without ceremony, to the steps of Saint Sauveur church. Half an hour later a lad ran up to them bringing a parchment sheet with a cord threaded through it.

"Put that round your neck and don't dare move from here until the None bell tolls or you'll be in even worse bother!" On the sign was written:

I have sinned - I am a wretched beggar - Pray for me

That's terrible." Mother spoke, anguish in her voice.

"It is. Now, the kids like to go up onto the parapets, to talk to the soldiers, the way children do...

"Show us how you load your cannon, mister." The youngster requested, fascinated by the weapon on its trolley pointing out through the gap between the battlement of the town wall.

"Are you a little Catholic lad?"

"Why yes, but what's it to do with you?" He jested with the impudence of youth.

The soldier stepped forward and gave the boy a mighty clout to his head, all but rendering him unconscious but he escaped home, stumbling and whimpering. The harsh blow was unnecessary and quite out of proportion to the jest. The huge malodorous soldier cried after the lad,

"No place for your sort up here! Skedaddle!"

. . .

"Admittedly I wasn't present but it was told me by a man I trust." Lanval got up to put another log on the fire. "That's better. You see, mother, all the small acts of nastiness and slight cruelty, one after another, day after day, build up into a madness I never dreamt I'd witness in a town where Catholics, Protestants, Benedictines, Jews, people of all beliefs, lived side by side for years but, no more. Can you believe a Huguenot mother gave an apple to her own child to persuade him to turn his back on one of ours...to exclude him from their games? Bribery but, using a little child...can you believe it?"

Mother shook her head in despair. Her son retreated into his thoughts for a while before resuming,

"All this pales though, compared to something else I heard today."

"What on earth will you say next?" She wrung her hands and waited, in suspense.

"Some of the bakers are not selling us bread so our women must go to the mill to buy flour and bake their own. The miller sells it by the sack to Huguenots but, and this is the rub, our womenfolk are allowed only *one cupful* - neither use nor ornament to knead into dough. An insult!"

Mother sat upright,

"Lanval, now you mention this, I was embroidering with a lady friend the other day and she described how, at the market, she and her cousin were sold only the poorest vegetables that were barely fit for eating."

"Doesn't surprise me at all. The harbour master patrols the quayside forbidding anyone from our church to cast a fishing line. You see what's going on, under our noses, don't you? Judge Boivin and his gang are starving us, weakening us, reducing us to such a state that when the King finally attacks, his bishop will be forced to inform His Majesty that if he doesn't cease the raid, our demise will be due to him, if you follow, by effectively denying us food."

"It's the Devil's work and that's for sure." Mother spoke the words slowly, expressing the fear and hatred she felt for their oppressors.

24

LA ROCHELLE, OCTOBER 1573

"Phew! They're a good weight." The lad huffed as, together, they loaded the last barrel onto the cart.

"You're right. My father used to say that a barrel with liquid in it was twice as heavy as, say, a barrel of rice. He wasn't far off the mark, either. Do you know, there are – or should say, there were - more and more boats coming here from Venice and, I reckon, they survive on damned rice! Anyway, get back to the stable now, there are plenty of jobs for you to do."

"See you later, 'sieur."

Lanval jumped up onto the cart, tugged at the reins, and they slowly trundled along the quay. The occasional sailor or merchant nodded as they passed but, compared with the days before the port was closed, they were few in number.

He had two deliveries this morning. The first took him through the narrow streets, past the Palais de Justice and into Rue Bazoges for the house he sought.

"Whoa, we're here." He spoke to his horse like a friend.

The imposing three-storey building was in the wealthiest quarter of town, backing onto the Arcades where any Huguenots of note resided.

He knocked on the door bearing the owner's carved name – Rostand. A huge man with a fiery-red beard and broad shoulders and a fine leather belt around his waist greeted him,

"Good morning, Aubert. How are you this splendid day?"

It was, undeniably, a glorious day if he was referring to the weather, but Lanval didn't experience any such pleasant emotion when he had to frequent this part of La Rochelle. He replied, coolly,

"I'm well, thank you, Monsieur Rostand. Got your ale and wine."

"Ah, that's good, we're getting low – not that I'm responsible for that on my own, if you see."

"Of course not, monsieur. So, do you want it in the yard?"

"Ay, and I'll lend you a hand." He pushed open the stout door to the yard and they carried two barrels of ale and one of wine through and placed them gently onto the cradles Rostand had prepared in a shady corner.

He could have lifted them on his own, the brute! Lanval thought, surveying the scene. Against one wall logs were piled as high as a man. Two bonny young girls played chase, squealing and giggling with their game. Taking pride of place in the middle there was a well with a wooden cover, a pail and coiled rope beside it. From a door inside the house wafted the fragrant smell of something good in the hearth and a ruddy-faced woman of ample girth appeared, wiping her hands on her apron.

"Lanval, we've not seen you for a while." She said,

softly. He felt an immediate compulsion to decry her fashionable house, delightful healthy children, water well and food for the table, but he resisted the urge. After all, he knew, he was only doing his job and it was not for him to like or approve of the folk he delivered to. *I wonder what help he's giving to Boivin?* The thought went through his mind.

"Lanval." She spoke louder and he regained his focus,

"Sorry, madam, yes it's a while. I trust you're well."

"We are, in spite of the dreadful worrying times that have befallen us. I really don't know how it will all end."

He nodded, his lips tight and furrowed brow expressing resentment, which she had not noticed.

"Enough of that. What will you drink, there's now ale or wine?"

"I'll take wine with you, madam."

"Husband!" She screamed as if he was in another house. "Pour wine for our guest." Rostand obeyed.

"Sit, pray." She invited, sitting at the table opposite him. "Good health." She toasted and he sipped his wine but his mind drifted as he inspected the room. The fire roared merrily, in front of it lay an over-fed fat dog. Suspended from a rod, a stewing pot was the reason for the wonderful smell that had met him. On a finely-carved oak sideboard, cut-glass goblets and decorated plates and cups were displayed. *Impressive,* he observed. In a far corner his gaze fell onto a prie-dieu and embroidered kneeler, a bible open on its sloping shelf. *All the trappings of a prominent Huguenot family.* He drank more wine, oblivious to whatever Rostand and his wife were saying to him, his mind distracted. He found himself overwhelmed by a sense of rage that these people led such a pleasant privileged life. He emptied his goblet.

"I must be away, monsieur."

"So soon? But I haven't yet paid you." He opened a drawer of the sideboard for a leather pouch, his money bag. Counting, he placed several coins in Lanval's hand.

"There, and there's extra for you. See, I appreciate decent service."

Is he mocking me? Talking as if I was his servant? He took the coins and dropped them into the pocket of his tunic.

"Much obliged, Monsieur Rostand, Madame Rostand." With that, he turned and left them, but his head was troubled as he drove the cart through the streets to a home in Rue des Voiliers in the heart of the Catholic area. The residence was a lowly cottage with only a ground floor. Its roof was a patchwork covering of thatch and tiles; its small windows were unglazed, with cloths hung up instead. He knocked, unannounced, on the door – he knew this house through their church and had heard the tenant had fallen on hard times of late. At length, the door opened.

"Why hello, Lanval, we were not expecting visitors." The man in the doorway was tall and slim, in his thirties, with deep blue eyes that fixed on you, endearingly, when he spoke.

Lanval began,

"I have something for you" and he pointed to the cart which still had one barrel. "I thought, Marcel, you could find a good use for it."

Marcel frowned and then, seeing Lanval's joke,

"For me?"

"Ay, it was going begging in the warehouse so I seized it before anyone else did." In truth, he had himself paid a fair price to the warehouseman.

"Come, help me lift it off." The two men carried it into

the house. In the gloom, Lanval strained his eyes and made out two, three, maybe four beds, a table and benches in the centre. In the grate a smoking fire spluttered. Then, muffled sounds came from the beds and he could just see three young children jumping up and down. In another, their mother slept. Marcel filled two beakers with ale from the barrel.

"Here, Lanval, and thank you."

"You're welcome, my friend. So, how are you doing?"

"We get along as best we can. But, you see, my wife has been ill with a fever for some time...I pray it will pass. We keep the children indoors – it's safer – outside, they're bullied and spat on...awful state of affairs. But, again, many thanks for the ale. I've been giving water, the little we're allowed, to the young ones and my wife and, if there's any left over, I cook a stew but that's only when we can get hold of vegetables. Failing that, there's a butcher in the Arcades who takes pity on me and will give me a bag of meat bones that I boil with mushrooms and acorns that I forage in the woods – it makes a decent enough broth. But if that butcher is found out, a Huguenot helping a Catholic, he'd be in real trouble. Yes, broth..." He seemed distracted for a moment, then, "better than nothing, I suppose."

"Yes.: Lanval had to agree, sadly, "I suppose it is."

With that, he got back onto the cart and drove it back to the stables.

Over supper that evening, Lanval described the day's events to his mother.

"First, I made a delivery of ale and wine to the Rostand house in Rue Bazoges."

"Ah, them."

"Do you know them?" He asked.

"I know they're well thought of in their church because they drop coins into the offertory bowl and make sure everyone in the congregation knows it – or, at least, that's what I'm told."

"I know what you mean, mother. What's shocked me - and, heavens above, I should know, we all should – is the contrast, the inequality between Huguenot and Catholic families whose happiness and well-being is determined by their faith." His knuckles turned white as he clenched his fists.

"There, there, Lanval." And she placed a comforting hand on his arm, "What you say is true but there's little we can do about it. It's the way life is here."

"That's where you're wrong, mother! Through my business I have the ear of men who run the warehouses, traders in the Arcades, butchers, millers, and even those I don't know, personally, will be easily bought. I've got an idea, how I can help families like Marcel's, to deliver basic foodstuffs to them." Mother stared at her son, then spoke, "But you don't know who you can trust and who you can't. Then, there's Judge Boivin to contend with."

"Boivin! A pox on him! He doesn't frighten me and, besides, it's not illegal - not yet. It's something father would have approved of."

Mother nodded.

Lanval's plan, without doubt, helped many disadvantaged families, but it was a drop in the ocean: he couldn't help them all and Boivin put pressure on anyone who colluded with him to cease. As the weeks went by, and with King Charles's army nowhere to be seen, food grew scarce and

La Rochelle's population, regardless of religion, were hungry,

Catholic floggings and the pillory continued apace. The soldiers, patrolling the streets and guarding the parapets, were bored through military inaction and the drink they consumed, even on duty, fuelled random violent assaults. Boivin's men joined in the brutality.

Lanval saw no end to his faith's oppression and his charitable acts raised him to a position a great esteem among his Catholic brethren and, equally, he was hated by Boivin and his kind.

One day, he had a visit at his home from a man and his wife, in sore need of advice. He recounted this visit to Father Evrart,

"So, Lanval, what did this couple seek from you?" The cleric asked across his desk.

"They explained their situation to me, and with deep passion, the husband said,

'Monsieur Lanval, as you can see, my wife is with child and is due in about six weeks.'

"I'm sure your happy event will pass well." - I told him, uncertain of the direction of the conversation.

'It will not, monsieur, if it happens within our walls. It's a bleak place for a babe to be born, and you'll know this, I'm sure. But my wife's parents live in Fontenay, twenty leagues north of here, and we have a donkey.'

"It would be like Joseph taking Mary into Bethlehem for Jesus's birth," I imagined, darkly. The young man continued with genuine anguish in his voice,

'We don't know who to turn to but, if anybody can help us, it's you, monsieur.'

"Straight away, I had an idea. It was obvious. When I was just a child, father often took me 'on adventures' into the woods. We'd pick mushrooms, set rabbit traps, build dens out of branches and ferns. It was real fun and I remember him showing me a little wooden doorway set into the town walls. It was barely big enough for a lad to squeeze through and all overgrown with bushes. Father said it was a 'secret passage' and he was the only man to know it even existed. He never told me why it was there, only that it led to the 'world outside' – father used some strange expressions. But, don't you see, Father, I could take them to the gate for them to make their escape and nobody would be any the wiser. Any Catholic shown the way to freedom has to be worth any risk."

Father Evrart was now eager to hear more. Lanval carried on,

"I told the man I could be of assistance, and his face lit up – you should have seen it. His wife wiped a tear from her face and I explained that, if they were caught, it would be the end for us all so they shouldn't tell anyone. I demanded that they promised me this.

'Of course, we promise, we'll do anything to get out.' She told me, and I didn't doubt her for a moment. Next, I got onto the detail of the plot. I instructed them to meet me the following night, at about one hour after Compline, by the old seminary – no luggage, just the two of them and the donkey. Did they understand? Why, the man shook my hand with a grip that I feared would wrench it from my arm!

'We understand, Monsieur Lanval and our deepest thanks to you. We'll be there tomorrow.'

Father Evrart's jaw dropped, an expression of surprise and admiration on his wrinkled face. He asked,

"How did it proceed?"

"By now, they will be safe in Fontenay! This town was deserted and once we were in the woods it was straightforward, even if they only just squeezed through and the donkey needed a good shove! I'm the only living person who knows of the gate's existence. It's a way of helping our brethren and fighting Boivin's tyranny, don't you agree?"

"I do, Lanval, but you appreciate the risk you're taking?"

"I do, Father, but I'm prepared to take it. And, what's more, at that time of night the soldiers are asleep, drunk at their posts."

The two men considered La Rochelle's plight for some time and agreed that harsh treatment and lack of sufficient food and water would soon drive many more Catholics to try to escape before their lives became yet worse. Evrart took a drink of his wine, sat back in his chair and, rubbing his palms together – a mannerism Lanval had often seen him perform – said, slowly,

"I'll let you into something only Servet and I know. A number of our people have, over the last few weeks, approached me, privately, begging me to help them flee but, until your revelation, I could give them no satisfactory answer. You've changed that now and, in future, I'll send them to you – with absolute secrecy and discretion."

"And I'll do my best for them." He said, crossing himself.

. . .

Over the coming weeks, in collusion with Father Evrart, Lanval escorted a good number of his Church's faithful into the woods to the hidden gate and freedom. Boivin, the mayor and the general were all, initially, unsuspecting of his civil disobedience, but they knew from rumours that the Catholic numbers were somehow decreasing.

One afternoon, after stabling his horse, he decided to visit the Auberge Tournon for a much- needed tankard of ale. In Rue Saint Yon, just before the tavern, he saw Cicile approaching.

I've not seen her for such a long time and I've missed her.

"Hello, Lanval." Her shiny dark hair, perfect white teeth and deep blue eyes overwhelmed him, his mind returning to the days when they were happy together.

"Hello." He replied, sheepishly. Plucking up courage, he asked her, tentatively,

"I'm about to have a drink, would you care to join me? The landlord's ale is still the best for miles around."

She smiled, seductively,

"I will - for old times' sake."

In the tavern they chatted, freely, about all manner of subjects – their families, their friends, things they did and their conversation turned, eventually, to the plight of the populace – the Catholics in particular. He felt extremely pleased to see her again and he had consumed no small amount of ale – though insufficient to render him drunk – so his tongue was loosened,

"...I've heard your Church friends are having a difficult time." He spoke with a tone of sympathy.

"Yes, they are...it's so unfair that..."

Lanval then spoke, sensing the bond between them was not altogether lost, innocently,

"...to leave the town...in the woods...a secret...yes, by the old seminary...nobody knows about it...a very tiny gate..." This was, in essence, his talk with her.

"At last, Cicle told him she had to leave. She leaned over the table and kissed his cheek.

"I've enjoyed our meeting, we must repeat it, soon." She said softly.

Lanval returned her kiss,

"Yes, we must." He replied, smiling broadly, as she rose and left, gazing around the tavern as she went.

He stayed for more ale, gossiping with the clientele, most of whom he knew, before wending his way home, most satisfied with his day. Meeting Cicile had raised his spirits and he was quite unaware he had spoken to her unwisely.

Two days later, early in the morning as dawn was breaking, there came a hard knocking on his door. Mother opened it, to be roughly pushed aside as three soldiers, swords drawn, burst into the house.

"Where is he?" One demanded, menacingly.

"Lanval? He's still in his bed."

"Then fetch him, woman, and make haste!"

Mother did as she was instructed. Shaking her son to rouse him, she urged,

"Lanval! Get up – there are some soldiers downstairs who are asking after you."

"What?" He reacted. He pulled on his tunic and went

down to investigate the problem but he wasn't at all prepared for what happened next. Two soldiers seized each arm and the third, a sergeant, asked,

"Aubert? Lanval Aubert?"

"Yes, you know it."

"We're arresting you on the charge of breaking the curfew and assisting the citizens to escape from this town, contrary to the law."

"But -"

"Bring him out! Come along peacefully or you'll only make things worse and, from what I know of it, you're best advised to not go down that path."

In the street, Lanval was blindfolded and could but guess where they were going. He knew they had entered a building then down some steps. The blindfold was finally removed before he was shoved violently into a cell, landing in a heap on a straw mattress.

"Enjoy your stay with us", a mocking voice rang out.

He squinted to adjust his eyes in the darkness and look around his gaol, a cave rough-hewn into rock, with a domed roof and iron bars to the front. A swarthy bald gaoler appeared outside and demanded,

"Take 'em off – tunic, boots belt, "Now!" He waited until Lanval was naked,

"Now, pass me your clothes and put this on." He took the clothes from his prisoner and pushed a sackcloth nightshirt through the bars,

"You'll be more comfortable in that." The gaoler joked, smiling a toothless grin. "I'll bring your supper soon." And he went off, mumbling some sarcastic comment that Lanval, shivering on the mattress, did not catch.

. . .

Lying in this dark dank place, his head was in a whirl. He pulled the nightshirt tightly to his body in an attempt to keep out the cold, but to little avail. The only noise to accompany his imprisonment was the rushing water of an open sewer running down the middle of the tunnel outside the bars; the sole sign of life was that of an inquisitive rat that gnawed at his mattress until scurrying away after a kick and a curse from him.

His mother and Evrart had both warned him of the risk he ran in helping his brethren to safety. Suddenly, his solitude was disturbed by the jangling of keys that heralded the arrival, again, of the compassionless gaoler. He placed a beaker of water between the bars followed by a crust of hard bread. It was his amusement to ridicule his detainees – he chuckled, then spoke,

"Here you are, Aubert, supper! It's prepared in our very own kitchens, by our very own chef." He turned, again mumbling something, and left Lanval alone, mightily distressed with his contemplations. Questions of how, why, and who raced through his head when, in a sudden intuitive moment, he saw the reality of his situation and why he was there.

Cicile! Cicile! It's coming back to me now. We were sitting in the tavern drinking and chatting about this and that inconsequential subject. I must have drunk too much ale and I can just recall mentioning the gate in the woods...ah! 'Judge Boivin told me it would not be seemly if I came to your father's funeral'...yes, those were her words but I paid them little heed at the time. How could she do such a hateful thing to me, she wasn't a girl with malice in her bones, but how I misjudged her! Her mind must have been turned when that slimy serpent, Boivin, bared his fangs and impregnated her with his poisonous bigotry…

…I should have appreciated what a powerful influence he has over his Huguenot people, strong enough to persuade even Cicile to betray me. To think how I loved her, and all for nothing except my wretched demise.

For the first time in his life, he shed tears, feeling helpless and abandoned. The following day, his sleep was broken when the rock that surrounded him shuddered, bringing down a fine dust. He propped himself up on one elbow, trying frantically to make sense of his surreal early morning awakening. Then, along with this trembling came a strange unearthly booming reverberation.

Cannon fire? It can't be…!

25

MATHILDE TAPPED GENTLY ON THE DOOR TO HER mistress's study.

"Enter," came from within. The maidservant held the door open and announced,

"Majesty, the Chaplain to His Holiness."

Catherine looked up from her desk and gave a slight smile,

"Monsignor.' She greeted him, "Pray, come in."

The priest, dressed in a long black robe, approached the Queen Mother, standing in silence, his head bowed.

"That will be all, Mathilde." The door closed for a private audience convened by Catherine.

"Sit, monsignor. I was notified that you were visiting Chenonceau, and it is right and proper that we meet, before your duties in the capital recall you."

"Certainly, Majesty."

She fixed him with her captivating gaze before inviting him to partake of a purely restorative brandy that he readily accepted. His curiosity was growing about the reason for his summons. She liked to keep her visitors in suspense and poured the brandy into two goblets, slowly and precisely to prolong the tension. She passed him his drink and raised hers to him as a polite gesture. According to protocol, he waited for her to speak first.

"So, tell me, monsignor, how fare our citizens in Paris – I take it that the authorities have quelled those troublesome disturbances of a few months back?"

"The city is now peaceful, Majesty, thanks to the King's timely intervention when the confounded Huguenots dared to usurp our rightful Catholic faith." She clenched her teeth as she thought, *'It was my intervention, not Charles's! If I left it to him, nothing would ever change.'* Breathing out. she replied, "That is most pleasing, and as it should be."

"Indeed, it is. Your subjects do not realise how fortunate they are to have the King and your esteemed self as defenders of our belief."

She did not answer. The priest was, after all, paying her lip service, but with no greater or lesser hypocrisy than any other of his station. In that moment, she struggled to remember why she had sent for him – but how could she forget, after her emotional conversation with Mathilde the other evening?

She'd come to my bedchamber to untie my hair and, as she worked, I saw her reflection in the dressing mirror: tears were running down her cheeks. 'What ails you, Mathilde?' I asked. Never before had I seen her weep and I bid her sit beside me on the bed. I poured brandy to calm her down. 'Now, tell me why you are so sad.' She thanked me for the drink, wiped her eyes and started, 'Majesty, I have received a social visit from a lady friend – we were in service to the same duchess in our younger days - and our chatter turned to the events of Saint Bartholomew's Day, in the capital, last year. She recounted terrible stories from those who survived. You, my lady, had left the banqueting hall so -' In confess that I urged her to make haste with her tale, and in a harsh tone I said, 'Get on with it, woman!' The severity of my tone caused her to whimper afresh. 'Excuse me, my lady, but my friend described a man she knew who had his right arm hacked off above the elbow. He can't find work to sustain his young family and the pain from his wound is constant. Then there was another person whose eyes were gouged out by a soldier's dagger – he'll never see his baby daughter grow up. And a mother, she told me, who saw her little son die before her from a trooper's flaying sword. Well, I knew not what to say, so horrendous were her tales of that fateful day. Even if all the victims were the Huguenots we despise, we -' 'Enough, Mathilde, stop! What your friend told you is, I'm sure, true but such acts are justified in the eyes of the Lord when the cause is worthy and in His name. Leave me now, for I am tired.'

The monsignor cleared his throat,

"As I was saying, Majesty, all seems to be well, for the moment."

Catherine was jolted out of her daydream,

"Yes...but let us pray, let us bow our heads in thanks to the Good Lord." The priest considered her a devout woman. Then, her intimidating gaze turned again on him and she, again, impressed the cleric,

"These are testing times for the King, so, do you have any pertinent passages from the Bible which could focus his mind, as it were? He is in residence here and will join us shortly. He is about to undertake a mission of great importance to us all."

He took a sip of his drink, thinking, then began,

"The Good Book offers us guidance on every page, Majesty, as you know, an embarrassment of riches, as they say...maybe,

'Lead us not into temptation, but deliver us from evil'

'Hatred stirs up strife, but love covers all offences' are two apt quotations although, in the end, only the King can choose."

"Wise and holy words, monsignor, and any advice is appreciated." *I'm best advised to think for myself rather than place stock on this man's vague religious guidance.* She had been troubled for many months by anecdotes such as those Mathilde provided and from her wider network of spies, all of which enabled her to counsel her son. However, doubt was colouring her judgment when it came to the impending campaign against La Rochelle. Why did this excursion, modest compared to some battles they had waged, seem unsure, she wondered?

"Thank you, monsignor, we will detain you no longer." The cleric bowed, turned and left the study. In the corridor he all but collided with Charles who was hurrying towards him.

"Your Majesty, do forgive me, I was not -"

"Of no matter. I'm late to see my mother." He burst into the room, out of breath – partly through his haste, partly with the excitement he felt for the campaign he was, at last, allowed to join.

"What's kept you, Charles? We have a meeting that is, undoubtedly, more important than whatever you've been getting up to. Come, to the chapel." The King followed his mother dutifully, well-accustomed to her admonishments.

. . .

Duke de Guise, accompanied by his Captain Bertrand and Lieutenant Monaud, had arrived at Chenonceau, rested after their successful operation to seize Montauban. She received them, with Charles at her side, somewhat paradoxically given the nature of their visit, in her chapel, a small building in the far corner of the chateau's grounds. After all, she reasoned, the war she waged was, without question, a holy war. After a moment of silent reflection, Charles addressed his general,

"De Guise, we are pleased that all seems to have gone well in Montauban."

"Perfectly, sire, and with minimal casualties."

Charles nodded his approval,

"That is welcome news. So, Orléans, Troyes, Lyon, Autun, Meaux, Beauvais and now Montauban, all under out control. What plan have you devised for La Rochelle, the jewel we seek to complete the decoration on the royal crown?"

Bertrand and Monaud listened attentively to proceedings, pride etched on their faces as the Duke unrolled his map on a small table, placing weights on its corners.

"Continue, de Guise. We know your men have availed themselves of the delights of our fair Paris."

That is so, Majesty, and they are now champing at the bit for their next challenge."

"Get to it!" Catherine interrupted, impatiently, so he picked up a cane pointer and began,

"The ride from Paris will require five days. We will pull twenty heavy wagons, each laden with two cannons on trolleys. We will take troop carriers for our infantry who will number one hundred men armed with muskets and swords. Three supply carts for ammunition and provisions will bring up the rear of the company."

Charles looked approvingly to Catherine.

"Now, to the map, if you will." Everyone huddled around the table in anticipation. "We have my men, Bertrand and Monaud," he waved his hand towards them, "to thank for our intelligence. The main gate is the Porte Gambetta, here," and his cane touched the place on the map. "The Porte Dauphine, to the north, is the access to their barracks. Porte du Bastion, to the south, gets us into the port area and, finally, Porte de Mer, on the west side, leads us to the Préfecture and the gaol. All eastern gates must be approached with caution since there are treacherous salt marshes around." The initial explanation of his strategy over, he stood up straight, waiting for questions. There were none apart from the obvious,

"What about the port itself though?" Charles smirked.

De Guise looked at the monarch directly, minded to express his contempt for a man he regarded as feckless but, resisted,

"Majesty, the port will be taken through its entrance from the sea. Our warship, *Robuste*, waits in Le Havre. I sent notice last month for her to be readied and I have every confidence in Admiral Jean-Baptiste, a capable sailor and officer. I have received word that he has a full complement, so no need for the press gang. He will sail, given the order and, with a favourable wind he will make La Rochelle after three days. The appearance of *Robuste* will put the fear of God into the Rochelais heathens, even before she's fired a shot – she fair bristles with cannons!"

He stepped away from the table, satisfied with his

presentation and the nods from Catherine and Charles confirmed the same on their part. The King exchanged words with this mother then gave the order,

"You have done well, de Guise."

Done well? I'd rather be praised by any one of my foot soldiers than him! the Duke mused, bitterly.

"Thank you, Majesty."

"We will march from Paris in three days. Send the command to Admiral Jean-Baptiste." The King smiled, his spirits rising as he pictured himself as a general alongside de Guise, Bertrand and Monaud.

"We will return to Paris, Your Majesties, to make our final preparations." With that, he rolled up the map, bowed and left the chapel accompanied by his two men.

Catherine dismissed her son, telling him she wanted to pray, alone, for the success of their offensive. She then took a bottle of laudanum from the sideboard and consumed it, in no small amount. Try as may, after her intimate conversation with Mathilde, she could not chase the images of men with only one arm, bloodied and screaming in agony or of the others stumbling, blinded, through the streets.

The same terror will be afflicted on the people of La Rochelle, that is inevitable, and all to prevent a few hundred miserable Huguenots from continuing to worship their own version of the Bible! Or is it for the greater benefit of Catholics throughout the kingdom?

Her thinking, as with her resolve, was in turmoil. There could be no place for a whimpering queen and her insignificant son leading an assault in the name of their subjects. Then, how to regain her courage and determination? She sent for her soothsayer, Côme Ruggieri, to attend her, and without delay.

. . .

Even before the Lauds bell had sounded, under cover of darkness, the gaunt-featured man approached the chateau, his long grey straggly hair covered by the hood of the monk's habit he always wore as a disguise when calling on Catherine. He tapped on her door and she ushered him in, a finger to her lips indicating silence until they were safe, the door locked. She pointed to the chair in front of her desk and he sat down without further ceremony. She began,

"Ruggieri, thank you for coming at short notice, but there are matters beyond my control and I think it timely to employ your indisputable talents."

He smiled, politely, but thought, *it's unknown for her to talk of me in a complimentary manner – this must be serious!*

She continued,

"Although I have my own charts showing the stars, the planets and the rest, I would ask for your interpretation of them, presently, and how they might influence and assist our plans."

"Of course, Majesty." He reached inside his robe for a parchment sheet displaying the signs on the Zodiac that he unrolled and placed on the desk between them. Next, he withdrew a pouch that, by the noise, contained coins and began the babble of his trade only for Catherine to interrupt,

"Yes, yes, don't dwell on that nonsense! Tell me what you see concerning my ...my future plans."

Chastened, he cupped the three talisman coins in his hands, shook and let them fall onto the chart. Staring at them for a time, he tugged at his beard and explained,

"Your Majesty is soon to embark on an expedition of a military nature, is that not correct?" He had, weeks before, heard this from rumours around Chenonceau. "And, you will be accompanied by a member of your family." It was not hard for him to assume this. He moved, next, to the Zodiac signs and he slowly pronounced, "Scorpio, in this quarter, shows me destruction, aggression and...now, Leo suggests a desire to control others." He took a drink then touched the third coin and said, softly, "Here, Pisces determines you are sensitive and compassionate."

"Thank you, Ruggieri. Your work is well done. Here." She handed him a small purse. "You may leave us now."

Over many consultations, the soothsayer had experienced her unpredictable moods and had come to accept them. She called the tune and paid the money, so why should he protest?

She drank more of her favourite tipple before staggering to her bed and sleeping deeply: the soothsayer had told her two different paths ahead that only served to increase her anguish. The next morning, she couldn't say from where the dream had emerged, but it had a profound effect on her perspective of the coming attack on La Rochelle. Could she live with her conscience if one more man lost an arm or another his sight? *I could not!* She concluded as she brushed her hair at the dresser. *Yet, I truly believe the Catholic faith is the only and best way for my people. If so, how do I demonstrate the aggression Ruggieri saw whilst, at the same time, becoming compassionate?* She knew, the closer their expedition came, that it was a problem for her alone to solve, and there was doubt that even *she* had the guile to achieve such a state of personality conflict. *Am I too deeply submerged in this infernal business to ever escape its clutches?* She sent for Mathilde to inform her she would be required for the journey – she rarely ventured far without the company of her loyal maidservant.

"In three days, you will accompany me and the King in our carriage when we depart for La Rochelle, alongside His Majesty's army."

Mathilde raised her eyebrows but said nothing. Her mistress was renowned for blurting something out to elicit a reaction.

"See that out trunks are seen to and the stables informed. We shall be away for two weeks, at least."

"I will attend to it, ma'am." Then she said, casually, and to Catherine's amazement,

"My lady will need to be merciless and resolute faced with the godless enemy within that town."

Is she advising me as Ruggieri did? The voices in my head appear to urge us on to wreak havoc on the populace of La Rochelle. But who speaks to the contrary, apart from myself? I cannot be seen as a weak queen – that Italian woman is surely made of sterner stuff. What a dilemma! What turmoil! She agonised.

———

La Rochelle, November 1573

At dawn, Duke de Guise, riding at the head of the convoy, raised an arm to bring them all to a halt outside the chateau of Chenonceau. The barrier of the gatehouse was lifted for the covered carriage pulled by a pair of Spanish dapple-grey horses with arched necks, refined head and elegant gait – Catherine's favourites – to pass. The carriage bore the Queen Mother, Charles and Mathilde but there was nothing to draw an enemy to conclude that there sat nobility within. Only de Guise and his generals knew, for it was safer to keep them hidden, at least until they were on their way.

The procession moved on, soon leaving the chateau behind. The crisp autumn morning provided ideal conditions for the journey. Hoar frost blanketed the fields on either side of the road; wisps of its white iciness rose upwards as the ground gradually warmed. They passed no-one – few people used this way the further they distanced from Chenonceau.

As dusk descended, each day, de Guise halted the army for the night. He had been advised where streams flowed so the horses could be watered. They ate from fresh hay piled up on the back of a supply cart. The men lined up by the all-important food wagon to be given bread, fruit or salt beef and a good tot of rum. They bedded down under their carts, capes pulled tight, each gaining warmth from the body pressed next to him. The Queen, Charles and Mathilde were afforded the luxury of their own tents.

On the fifth day, they had made the progress the Duke had calculated and, sure enough, a good way ahead, but unmistakable, the skyline changed from trees to rooftops, chimneys and their smoke. He waved his arm, signalling the generals to ride to the front.

"See! La Rochelle – the jewel in the crown!" The

generals did not appreciate the significance of his description. "We make our base camp right here. The men may eat and be prepared for our first attack. I've sent a rider ahead and when he returns and confirms that *Robuste* is in position in the bay, we begin! Couple the horses to the gun trolleys and have the ammunition cart pull up."

At last! I never did take a liking to Huguenot folk and now I've got the chance to show it, for my King and country, naturally.

It was still early morning in the town, with most people asleep in their beds. Guards patrolled the parapets this day, as they had done for weeks since the warning of an imminent attack was given. But the simple truth was that they were bored: if they did cast their gaze outside the town, it was cursory – they saw nothing so they suspected nothing.

The harbour master was taking his normal constitutional stroll around the port and he gave a polite good morning greeting to a fisherman winding in his line.

"Caught anything?"

"Not a chance. I reckon the fish are so frightened they've deserted us." Was the lugubrious reply. Following the quay he came to the Chain Tower where the bearded old sailor in his threadbare frock coat and battered tricorn hat sat, surveying his end of the port.

"Hello. Just checking the chain is as it should be," the harbour master informed him.

"Hey! Do you think I don't know my job? I've served on more ships than you've drunk tankards of ale."

"Nothing personal, old man, only doing my job too, but I can see the chain's all right." That said, he returned to his cabin.

The tall skeletal figure of the Mayor, his beadle carrying his civic brass mace before him, paraded up and down Rue Saint Yon, for all the world to admire, where the Arcade stalls were, strangely, lacking their usual array of goods. There were fewer people out shopping. He stopped by one stall,

"Trade's not good today," the Mayor observed.

"It's not," the fishmonger answered. "I think folk are too scared to come out and, even if they did, I've not got enough fish to sell – my supply from the port's stopped."

"I see, but with luck it will improve." There was little conviction in his voice though. He moved along the street to the Catholic stalls and spoke, through pinched lips, to a trader of bric-a-brac,

"Now then, my good man, you owe us money."

"I beg your pardon?" Came the disbelieving reply.

"I have checked my records, and very carefully I might add, and I see you haven't paid last week's rent."

"That's not so, Mayor, my wife took it to your place six days ago."

"Can you prove it? My clerk has marked the ledger, clearly, 'not paid' on your account."

"Why -"

Without further ado, the Mayor reached over the table and helped himself to a coin out of the trader's bowl.

"That's all sorted. I will change the ledger to 'paid' upon my return. My thanks, monsieur." He pocketed the coin and walked on.

That's my ale for tonight covered, he chuckled.

Judge Boivin, purple hat and shabby gown, sat in the chair outside his office, pompously greeting people in the square and from where he had a prime view of the pillory. He considered it his duty, having sentenced some wretched Catholic or another to the punishment, to ensure it was properly administered by his assistant, a malodorous drunk who worked for the Justice to pay for days on end in the taverns of the town.

This morning, a woman – not much more than a girl – was clamped between the two boards of the stocks, hands either side of her face, waiting for her decreed six hours of torture to begin.

"What's she done, Judge?" A passing man asked.

"Begging, as usual, will they ever learn? They're all up to it, damned Catholics!"

"I suppose they are. Anyway, if there's rotten tomatoes in yon pail," he pointed to the wooden bucket, "I'd keep an eye on it. Some folk are so hungry they'll be dipping into it and taking them home for supper!"

"Really?" The Judge replied indifferently.

The rider reined his horse to a halt in front of de Guise, dismounted and saluted.

"What news?" The Duke asked, anticipation in his voice.

"*Robuste* is at anchor, sire. I found her man, as arranged, hiding among the trees by the Bout Blanc rocky outcrop. He said he hadn't been waiting long and I gave him the parchment scroll bearing your seal. He jumped into his little rowing boat and was away to his ship. He will tell the Admiral to begin his bombardment of the port at the Sext bell, as you instructed."

"You've done well," and he beckoned over his generals to give them their final orders.

"Gentlemen, our moment has arrived. We have planned it for many months and it will be a resounding victory, in the name of King Charles, Defender of our Catholic faith, that follows on from, but eclipses, our subjugation of heathen towns in the kingdom." Pausing, he stared hard at his generals, one by one, demanding obedience by his eyes and voice, then he continued,

"Harness the horses to the cannon trolleys and haul them into position at their calculated firing distance. Space them out to aim at the length of the town walls – along the east, from the barracks to the Saint Nicolas bastion, taking care to find firm ground in the salt marshes...don't want you sinking, do we?" His men smiled. They had every confidence in their leader.

"Drive the ammunition carts behind the guns to make sure they've got a good supply of cannonballs and powder – running out would be something of a problem, be warned!" Again, they smiled.

"Do you have any questions?" Silence. "Right, *bon courage, mes hommes.*"

Each gun had its commander and sergeant, the 'aimer', who determined elevation. A 'sponge man' cleaned the bore between shots for the 'loader' to put in the powder and ball. They worked on their weapons as one, teams forged out of armed struggles from the bleak Belgian border to the warm blue Mediterranean Sea.

The 'rammer' would push the ball in tight and the man with a peculiar honour – that of lighting the vent hole, but only on the express order of 'fire!' from the commander – would stand ready with his slowmatch to perform the final procedure.

"What angle do you have, sergeant?" The commander asked, routinely.

"Forty-five degrees, sir. Best range to clear the parapets, I bet. Soon see."

Every man knew the success of his role was dependent on his fellow – one would never let the other down. Within half an hour, the guns were primed, waiting, ready for action. Out of nowhere, the Sext bell rang across the town – the signal to fire the first diabolical cannonade that rained down onto the unsuspecting townsfolk. De Guise selected his 'aimers' for their consummate skill in judging trajectories by setting the cannon on its trolley at the requisite angle: he was not disappointed this day. Every ball cleared the top of the walls, to the applause of the infantrymen, watching from behind. Their moment of glory would come when the gates opened. The Duke rode up and down the line of guns,

"Good shot! Well done! Make them all like that!" He bellowed encouragement for his troops.

Lanval's cell shook again and again and he swore the ground beneath him lifted, all but throwing him off his mattress. *Or is it my fear playing tricks on me?* He brushed away the dust that fell down on his face. He seized and rattled the iron bars that penned him in, angry but helpless. He would, with all his might, have wrenched them apart, but they were not about to give on his account. Frustrated in the extreme, he screamed,

"Gaoler! Where are you? What's going on?" Nobody answered his call and, he decided,

It has to be the King's army, at last!

Like everyone else in La Rochelle, the soldiers on the parapets were taken by surprise and frantically loaded their guns to get some shots away but, as de Guise had been told, their bore was smaller than his and the enemy response fell short of his line.

The Duke had also carried out a masterful move that would protect the vulnerable Catholic citizens. The day before the attack, he dispatched a trusted foot soldier to enter the town from the quayside where, he knew, the walls ended, and all under cover of darkness.

"Go directly to Saint Sauveur church, here." He pointed to its location on a map. "Find either Father Evrart or Servet and alert them to our assault. Tell them that they must, with all haste, warn their congregation to take shelter in their cellars. Understood?"

"Understood, sire," his man confirmed.

The cannonballs tore through the roofs of the houses, killing outright or badly injuring the mainly Huguenot residents, their tables, chairs, beds, sideboards all smashed, their cries of pain and terror enough to melt the hardest heart. However, this was a religious war, with no place for sentimentality. In the streets and squares people ran, madly, in all directions. This way or that? Right or left? Get down! Hide! Chaos prevailed. But so ferocious was the onslaught that bodies began to pile up, lying where they fell.

The Mayor, his chain of office wrapping around his throat, bounded across the Place d'Armes but, within touching distance of his house, he was struck full on the head by a heavy ball, felling him in an instant. Blood gushed from his shattered skull, but nobody stopped to care for him in his final moments.

By the time the Sext bell tolled, Admiral Jean-Baptiste had sailed *Robuste* up to the chain barring the port and dropped anchor. Her fore and mainsails were furled and she sat well in the water – a fine Spanish-built warship befitting of the king's fleet. Its broadside faced the inner port beyond the chain, a barrier that did not bother Jean-Baptiste because all his shots would be fired over it. The hands had pulled up the covers from the gun ports and ten heavy cannons were aimed at the quayside warehouses. Above them, on the main deck, another ten lighter guns mounted on swivels would blast grape shot at any target within range on the quay, also, at any boats still moored. Its crew was well paid, loyal and eager for action. Their time had come.

"Ready, bosun?" Admiral Jean-Baptiste called from his vantage point on the forecastle. The red-bearded rotund officer shouted back,

"Ay, ready, Admiral!"

"Main cannons – fire!" And with that order began *Robuste's* pounding of La Rochelle's port. The opening salvo wreaked havoc on the warehouses and a good number of men perished under falling masonry and roof timbers. While the guns were reloaded, the Admiral bawled his next command,

"Light guns, fire!"

Two barges were holed and soon sank. Carts, horses and their owners were peppered with destructive grape shot. Some men fled in panic, others died there and then and the stuff of life flowed – the injuries a horror to behold. The harbour master was brought down as he scurried along the quayside seeking safety, his body falling into the cold dark water below.

The initial attack lasted for some thirty minutes, then ceased, an important feature of de Guise's clever psychological tactics.

"Hit them hard! Take them by surprise, then stop all guns!"

"Why is that?" He was occasionally asked by apprentice sailors and Jean-Baptiste would explain,

"Give them time to draw breath, nothing more. They will be in shock and disarray and, mark this, they're not sure when it will be over but, in their heads, they hope that it will. They're now afraid and there's nothing better in battle than an ashen-faced enemy!" The Duke relished a good fight and he knew he was the best around.

Boivin's men on the parapets returned fire but, as de Guise had calculated, his force was beyond their range: they felt vulnerable and prime targets such that talk of retreating to the security of their barracks soon spread. After the second onslaught, even fiercer than the first, they were given just that order, to leave their posts, at least until Boivin and his general came up with a better plan.

The Judge had, wisely, left his seat in the square, abandoning the poor soul in the pillory, and rushing inside his office, crawling his way under the table, fearing for his life. He needed no telling, from the first cannonballs falling, that the King's army was responsible and he realised that *he* would feature high on his list of targets.

The cannonades continued in this pattern until the Vespers bell signalled the gathering dusk and de Guise's men ceased firing, hungry and thirsty but satisfied with their first day's work. The Duke entered the King's tent to update him on the situation. Two chairs, a small table and a mattress had been brought along for his comfort. Catherine and Mathilde shared a second tent for reasons of propriety.

"You will share brandy with us, I assume," she asked, her lips pinched more tightly than ever had been seen before. He nodded his assent and she filled three goblets, passing one to the Duke then to Charles who began the business.

"De Guise, you will appreciate that I have remained behind our cannons, as was agreed when preparing this campaign."

"As it should be, Majesty." *I saw him wincing beside his mother, even from a distance!*

"So, your report to us?"

"We know that, between the walls and the start of the port, there is a gap, wide enough for a man. I sent in one of my soldiers to assess the situation *intra muros*. He found Father Servet who advises us that our Catholic brethren are, largely, sheltered, but there are many Huguenot fatalities and wounded citizens and soldiers on the parapets. Fear and sickness engulf the place as does thirst and hunger. Graveyard plots are running out and we hear that some congregations are burying their dead four or five deep, one on top of the other. Our siege progresses well. Most pleasing, I'd say, Majesty." Catherine raised an eyebrow and breathed in deeply.

"Continue, pray." The king spoke,

"It will not be possible to breach the gates with our cannons."

"What? But -"

De Guise interrupted the monarch, his knowledge of warfare and tactics far superior to the king's,

"We cannot lower the elevation of the cannons such that they fire at the gates below the horizontal and be wasted. Even worse, the barrel might be thrust off the trolley with dire consequences for the crews. Therefore, I propose to you that, from first light tomorrow, we continue to fire into them until they give in...and that shouldn't be too long away. We either starve them or kill them."

Catherine was sure she saw him smack his lips as he spoke, a gesture that offended her increasing antipathy towards gratuitous remarks such as his.

"You speak well, de Guise." Charles concluded, "We approve of your plan and wish you goodnight."

26

THE QUEEN MOTHER RETURNED TO HER TENT WHERE Mathilde was waiting.

"Sit down, ma'am, so I can undo your hair."

Although she had her back to her maidservant, Mathilde felt, instinctively, that all was not right.

"Tell Mathilde, she may help you," the woman spoke, and Catherine did, indeed, want to tell Mathilde, her trusted confidant over the decades. She hung her head, trying to gather her thoughts before giving an explanation – this matter was quite different to discussing the chateau gardens or the latest scandal in Paris.

"Since the first cannons fired, I have not been able to rid my mind of the atrocities we inflicted on the Huguenots on Saint Bartholomew's Day. That man with the lifeblood ebbing from his severed arm...then, the man rendered sightless from our soldier's dagger...and, worst of all, that poor little innocent boy hacked down before his mother's eyes...Mathilde! Within *this* town, its people so close we can hear their screams and unanswered pleas to the Good Lord above, how many will suffer and perish, just as they did in Paris? I ask you, how many?"

Mathilde was taken aback by her mistress's distress for she was more accustomed to a fiery rhetoric decrying any enemy in her path. As happened rarely, protocol forbidding it, she took Catherine's hand and spoke,

"Majesty, the Duke, the King, and the whole country see that what we are doing is necessary – unfortunate, I grant, but necessary. Do you not think that -"

The tormented Italian woman turned her head sharply, her nose almost touching her maid's. Then,

"Do *not* tell me what I should or should not think! The Catholic faith can be traced back in my family to the ninth century when Charlemagne was emperor and Leo our Holy Father!"

Mathilde recoiled, letting the hair brush drop to the ground, so startled was she by the woman's altogether vindictive assault on her.

"But," said Catherine, regaining her composure, "I see a way forward. I cannot accept that I must live with this guilt for any more eyes, arms or mother's sons lost – with misguided religion as the justification. Let others carry that dead albatross around their shoulders, if they will."

Poor Mathilde's jaw dropped: such sentiments were rare and she knew to hold her tongue.

"I must speak with the King, at once!" In her nightdress, not stopping to put on her shawl, she walked the few paces to Charles's tent and, without ceremony, burst in.

"Charles! Charles! Wake up!" She shook him by the arm.

"What on earth is it, mother?" He moaned, half-asleep.

"We must offer the Huguenots an early chance to surrender."

"Surrender? What are you talking about?" He asked, sitting up on the edge of his mattress, "we will be seen as weak, without the stomach to finish the campaign – we will be a laughing stock."

"That's where you are wrong, my feckless son. The kingdom will regard you as a merciful king because compassion is not just an awareness of another person's suffering, it moves beyond a simple desire to alleviate suffering. It is everywhere in the Good Book and my advisers tell me it is true.

"Really?" Charles asked his mother in a doubtful tone.

"Why, yes. We will send for their bishop and present him with *our* terms that, although he won't like them, he will have no choice but to agree, unless he is to become the man responsible for the annihilation of the Protestants of La Rochelle." She paused, her face flushed with the thrill of her plan, then she explained, "We will put our demands in writing. Come to the table, you have a fine hand so we will put it to good use. Bring the candle."

Within a hour they had produced the document the Huguenot bishop would sign to save the lives of his people.

§ I, Bishop of La Rochelle and Saintes, agree to the demands laid out below. I give them my solemn oath, upon which the siege of the town will be lifted and hostilities will cease

§ All soldiers within the town will return to barracks until further notice, their weapons to be deposited and secured in the Arsenal

§ Four churches, currently frequented by Huguenots, will

become Catholic houses of worship, their superintendent priests to be appointed by Father EVRART, namely the Temple Protestant

Église Évangélique
Église Adventiste
Église Baptiste

§ LANVAL AUBERT is, henceforth, called Judge. He will confer titles of Mayor and Harbour Master in due course

§ Every adherent to the Huguenot faith is to pay, annually, a tax as determined by Monsieur Aubert. Furthermore, they will desist from decrying Catholic citizens, on pain of prison

SIGNED by the Bishop
DATED November 1573

The next morning, before dawn, King Charles sent for de Guise to inform him of the surrender he intended to obtain. Catherine remained in the background, she had decided from the start that her son must be seen to be its author and inspiration. It was laid out on the table and de Guise was invited to scrutinize it. This he did, and with every line, he screwed up his eyes, his lips pinched tight, an angry red hue colouring his countenance. He mused,

Have we come this far to leave the job half-done? Does this nincompoop, this mealy-mouthed apologist, believe the Huguenot hordes will comply?

The King spoke to break an awkward silence,

"I sense, de Guise, that it does not meet with your approval? No matter, it's a fait accompli. So, summon their Bishop and order your men to hold their fire – at once!"

The Duke glared first at Catherine then at the monarch,

"As you see fit, Majesty." The contempt in his voice was unmistakable.

Just as Catherine had predicted, the Huguenot Bishop acceded to the terms of surrender. The gates were unbarred and pushed open for the King's troops to march, triumphantly, into La Rochelle, led by two flag bearers, one waving the King's colours, the other those of the Kingdom of France. There was no resistance.

The King, Catherine and Mathilde followed on in their carriage and were driven directly to Saint Sauveur church where they met Fathers Evrart and Servet.

"Praise the Lord!" The senior cleric fell to his knees before the altar, "For He has delivered us from evil and forgiven us our sins."

"Praise the Lord, indeed," Charles repeated, then he turned to Servet. "Our Duke de Guise is, this very instant, ordering the gaoler, by royal command, to free Monsieur Aubert from the cells. We wish to meet him.

"Wonderful news, Majesty," Servet blurted, his voice overcome by emotion.

"...and so, Judge Lanval Aubert, this fair town of La Rochelle is ours once more and we have every confidence in your restoring it to its former prosperity and happiness, all in the name of our Mother Church." Charles had, even late in his reign, discovered a kingly spirit that he – and Catherine – feared to not exist. He breathed in deeply, quite surprised by his newly-found authority, and he carried on,

"We will return to Paris but we leave a company of thirty strong men who will assist you in your duties, as you see fit. You are, in all but name, their general. We must not overlook Boivin. I have considered his position at length and a good stay in the cells would be appropriate. Personally, I would suggest that the pillory is too good a sentence. However, as Judge, the final punishment for that detestable leech, is entirely at your discretion."

Lanval bowed and, beaming, replied,

"Your Majesties, La Rochelle knows no way to express its thanks."

The King nodded, Catherine forced a slight smile.

The army loaded its weapons and paraphernalia onto their carts, horses were saddled and they retook the road to the capital. On the journey, Charles slept. Catherine leaned over to Mathilde, sipping her brandy, and whispered,

"I'm sure, once the dust has settled, there will be challenges anew for de Guise and the King. Our Catholic faith will be protected for as long as I am that Italian woman, the Queen Mother." She, in turn, slipped into a peaceful slumber. Her dreams were, for the moment, benign.

Within a short time of the Huguenot surrender, Fathers Evrart and Servet appointed four priests of their acquaintance and trust from parishes outside La Rochelle to officiate and develop restored Catholic worship in the four churches assigned to them by King Charles. Their fledgling congregations quickly grew with the followers who, under the repression of their belief, had been too afraid to attend Mass but could now celebrate the Eucharist in freedom and joyfully. Many Huguenot townsfolk, disillusioned with their own leaders, with every good reason, felt let down, converted to Catholicism and were welcomed by Evrart, Servet and their assistant priests.

However, to begin – when the King gave them back control of their town – there was but one church where the first Mass of the reborn regime could take place, Saint Sauveur. And, a happy occasion it was! Praise was raised to the Lord; the sermons stirred the people to a frenzy of religious celebration; applause rang out after each verse Evrart read out. This merry clamour knew no bounds when the priest announced,

"Men, women, children, fellows in Christ, be it heard in every corner of our town that Lanval Aubert is your Judge, by royal decree!"

Lanval's recently conferred title marked a new dawn for the judicial arrangements in La Rochelle. To devote all his energy to the office he had sold the carting business, for next to nothing, to his stable lad. His many contacts from that trade would prove invaluable in establishing a new, fairer system whereby a jury alongside the judge, with a majority vote, would determine a miscreant's sentence based on witnesses regardless of his religion. But, he exercised his right to pronounce, in an executive capacity, on one important pending case. Boivin languished in the same cell that Lanval had occupied only weeks before, guarded by the same malodorous gaoler.

"Here you are, Monsieur Boivin, your supper is served." He pushed a beaker of water, of dubious purity, and a crust of dry bread through the bars.

In the Auberge Tournan, Lanval was feted, hailed as the symbol of hope. The jovial landlord called out,

"Boys, the ale is on me tonight! So, let me be the first person in this fine hostelry to propose a toast, to Judge Lanval Aubert, a hard but fair-minded man!"

The former carter held his tankard high, waving it in reply towards every part of the inn.

"Thank you...thank you, my friends." And he drank with them, sharing their optimism. Later that evening, an elderly gentleman, who had been a childhood pal of his late father, approached his table,

May I join you, Lanval?"

"Of course. Pray, sit down."

"I don't know if it's the free ale or your popularity that sees this place full!" The men laughed.

"Your father would have been very proud of you. He was an upstanding but humble man with qualities he's passed on to you that will serve you well as the Justice."

"God willing." Lanval's response was made with a hint of hesitation. His civic duty, he was sure, would be discharged with the utmost integrity and, naturally, it would take time for him to feel confident. The old man then asked,

"And what of the loathsome Boivin? We're well rid of him. I know his family and they're all wrongdoers, of one sort or another and Boivin turned a blind eye to it all. A real bad lot."

"I've heard similar accounts and he's going to be my first hearing – it's ironic a former judge standing before the present one. The last thing the King said to me leaving was that the pillory and flogging were too good for him and, at best, he deserved gaol."

I've disagreed with Charles on many occasions – not in person, but you get my drift – but not here. Where is he now?"

"The King?"

"Boivin, idiot!" Both men roared and drained their tankards.

"More ale, if you will!" Lanval called out and the jovial landlord obliged.

"He's in the cells," Lanval resumed, "and the time's come for him to pay for his demeanours."

"What do you have in mind for him?"

Lanval took a draught of ale the explained, in a serious tone,

"Apart from his followers – who are sworn to secrecy – I'm the only man in La Rochelle to have observed him performing the Dark Arts. Yes, I heard him talk in tongues, saw him dance in circles, even slit a chicken's throat, with my own eyes! Him and his disciples convene in an old barn, away from the town. Now, I will have notices posted and the priests announce from their pulpits that, seven days hence, any interested citizens, and there will be many, are invited to join a special procession, led by the former Justice Boivin, beginning outside the courthouse. Although *I* know the destination, he will still be leading. It will, by this time, have spread around that he's a practitioner of the Dark Arts but that he denounces at and decants. You see, this part of our retribution will be his humiliation, his shame in public."

"I do see. It's a reasonable start and will be seen by the people as such. Where will he lead us?"

"To his barn in the woods," came the furtive reply.

On the announced day, a crowd had formed early in the square and a sense of mischievous excitement grew,

"Where is he? Have you seen him? Is he here yet?"

Seeing Lanval emerge from the court office, they fell silent and the moment they'd been waiting for arrived. Two stocky soldiers, cudgel in hand, dragged Boivin into view. A gasp rent the morning air. He was dressed in a tattered tunic and flimsy boots and Lanval had granted him his request, grudgingly, to wear his floppy purple hat. His hands were shackled and he was, in truth, a pitiful sight to behold but one that could not fail to elicit cries of laughter, slapping, jeering, spitting: his despised chickens were, at last, coking home to roost as the people vented their hatred for a man who had treated them so badly.

"Lead the way, Boivin!" Judge Aubert instructed imperiously. Ashamed and belittled, Boivin shuffled out of the square down the street to the Saint Nicolas Bastion gate and out of town towards the Tasdon marshes. The soldiers prodded him with their cudgels, urging him, "get a move on, we haven't got all day!" The crowd behind had no idea where they were heading but they were, nonetheless, exuberant, wondering what they might see as they turned into the woods.

It took a good half hour of stumbling over fallen branches and being scratched and pricked on brambles to arrive at the clearing with its old barn. They fanned out to have a better view for Lanval to jump up onto a tree stump, raising his arm for quiet.

"Folk of La Rochelle, in the barn behind me, this wretched man, Boivin, would meet with his equally wretched friends and raise praises to *their* Lord, Satan! The devil to you and me! Yes, they worshipped him, but no more. He has yet to appear before me in court to answer other charges and you are all welcome to watch from the public gallery."

Boivin stood, head bowed, floppy purple hat covering his brow, silent. Lanval carried on,

"However, this man has decided the best way to express his sorrow and guilt is to burn his den of iniquity to the ground!"

Cheers rose as a soldier handed Boivin a glowing hemp cord. Surrounding the barn was an apron of brush, twigs and bracken that Lanval's men had put in place the previous day. Boivin blew gently on the cord until a flame appeared that he pushed underneath the kindling and it at once began to burn and spread until, within minutes, the whole barn was enveloped in an inferno the likes of which Dante would approved! The walls succumbed followed by the timbers of the roof for the former barn to become reduced to red-hot ashes. Nothing remained to ever suggest the Dark Arts had once thrived.

Giving one last cheer, everyone turned and trudged behind a fearful dejected pitiful Boivin, back to the town.

Some days later, when Boivin was due to appear before Judge Aubert in the courtroom, the public gallery was, not surprisingly, heaving with, it seemed, half the populace craning their necks to better observe the proceeding below.

An armed soldier dragged Boivin in and pushed him roughly into the dock - still he wore his floppy purple hat. Then, the Judge entered and stepped up to his desk that now bore a shiny brass mace across its front. He brought down his gavel sharply, three times, and began his address.

"Can the man in the dock reveal his name to the court."

"Boivin, Gustave Boivin." Booing started so the gavel was struck again.

"Silence in my court! Monsieur Boivin, under normal circumstances I would ask for witnesses to speak for or against you. However, the two wrongdoings with which you are charged are witnessed by *me*, Judge Lanval Aubert, and it is, therefore, my word that will prove that you, sir, in these extraordinary times, are guilty beyond any doubt."

Cries of "Ay! Ay! Hang him!" filled the room.

"For the first charge, I have observed you, on several occasions, receive coin - port taxes - from our now deceased Mayor, on the quayside. This was coin that should have been given directly to the Bishop for the benefit of us all and instead ended up in your money pouch to be spent nightly in the taverns. You can have no defence for this charge.

The second charge is altogether more heinous. Since my elevation to the status of Justice, I have examined the court ledger recording hearings, their dates and sentences pronounced by your good self. I am indebted to you, Boivin, for maintaining the ledger in such meticulously good order." Boivin looked up for the first time and raised an eyebrow.

"However, it is a record that states, categorically, that

sentences meted out to *Catholic* citizens have been consistently more severe than those, when it occurred, for your *Huguenot* friends. You are found guilty, therefore, of perversion of justice and, again, you can have no defence.

Once more, the room was filled with baying cries from the gallery, townsfolk who wanted his blood! The sad man in the dock stared defiantly at his decriers, smirking at one, snarling at another.

The Judge brought matters to a conclusion as he moved to the sentence.

"Gustave Boivin, you are hereby found guilty of the misappropriation of public funds – theft, by any other name. Equally, you are responsible for extreme, unforgivable bias towards Catholic men and women who found themselves in the very dock where stand today."

He paused, sipping wine – that was one of Boivin's traditions he intended to retain – then, in a solemn voice, said,

"As the Judge of La Rochelle, I could send you to the pillory, have you lashed or commit you to rot in the cells. Be it known, all these are in my gift but it is my view that the punishment you deserve over these is banishment, in perpetuity, from our fair town, never again to darken our doors. By Sext, tomorrow, you must leave this place you made you home and upon which you brought so much misery." Boivin said not one word.

Applause erupted as the soldier manhandled him, in disgrace, from the courtroom.

EPILOGUE

Catherine de Médicis

HER APPEASEMENT OF THE HUGUENOTS, AS SEEN IN the siege of La Rochelle, appalled many leading Roman Catholics who formed a League to protect their religion that took control of much of northern France. She had advised her son, King Henry the Eighth, to compromise his beliefs. He did not, being assassinated in 1589.

Catherine died in the same year. That Italian woman's name was revered and reviled equally by her Church, family and subjects.

———

King Charles the Ninth

After La Rochelle, his physical and mental condition weakened drastically. He blamed, alternately, himself and his mother, Catherine, who called him her 'lunatic son'. He died in 1574 but left behind a book on the topic of hunting.

_____

DUKE DE GUISE

He became a leading member of the Catholic League. King Henry the Third created him Lieutenant-General but the honour bred resentment, perversely, in the king who had him murdered in 1588. A respected historian wrote of him – "He does good wholeheartedly...when deeds fail him he resorts to words...he is courteous, humane, generous...in a word, he is king by affection just as Henry the Third is king by law".

_____

LANVAL AUBERT

He sold the carting business to his stable lad for a song, remaining Judge of La Rochelle until his death in 1613. He introduced a six-person jury to deliver a fair verdict, removing from the procedure any biased opinion of the Church or powerful grandees of the town. With vigour, he petitioned his Bishop and four Catholic churches, in addition to Saint Sauveur, were duly consecrated according to the terms of the Huguenot surrender.

———

GUSTAVE BOIVIN

Boivin went to live with his only surviving family member, an elderly sister, in a town many leagues away from La Rochelle in the land of Normandy. That town was dominated by a passionate Catholic authority. The former Justice experienced, at first hand, the egregious persecution of a religious minority. He died from wounds inflicted on him from a drunkard who took offence when he thought Boivin was speaking disrespectfully about the Holy Father.

THE END

Dear reader,

We hope you enjoyed reading *The Guise of the Queen*. Please take a moment to leave a review, even if it's a short one. Your opinion is important to us.

Discover more books by John Bentley at https://www.nextchapter.pub/authors/john-bentley

Want to know when one of our books is free or discounted? Join the newsletter at http://eepurl.com/bqqB3H

Best regards,

John Bentley and the Next Chapter Team

Lightning Source UK Ltd.
Milton Keynes UK
UKHW021851161220
375343UK00008B/480